STANDARD CANDLES

STANDARD CANDLES

JACK McDEVITT

Tachyon Publications
San Francisco, California

STANDARD CANDLES

"Black to Move" first published in *Isaac Asimov's Science Fiction Magazine,* September 1982. "Cryptic" first published in *Isaac Asimov's Science Fiction Magazine,* April 1983. "The Jersey Rifle" first published in *Chess Life,* January 1983. "Translations from the Colosian" first published in *Isaac Asimov's Science Fiction Magazine,* September 1984. "Promises to Keep" first published in *Isaac Asimov's Science Fiction Magazine,* December 1984. "Tidal Effects" first published in *Universe 15* (Doubleday), 1985. "To Hell with the Stars" first published in *Isaac Asimov's Science Fiction Magazine,* December 1987. "The Fort Moxie Branch" first published in *Full Spectrum* (Bantam), 1988. "Tyger" first published in *Isaac Asimov's Science Fiction Magazine,* May 1991. "Gus" first published in *Sacred Visions* (Tor), 1991. "Auld Lang *Boom*" first published in *Isaac Asimov's Science Fiction Magazine,* October 1992. "Standard Candles" first published in *The Magazine of Fantasy & Science Fiction,* January 1994. "Ellie" first published in *Isaac Asimov's Science Fiction Magazine,* May 1995. "Cruising Through Deuteronomy" first published in *Fantasy & Science Fiction,* June 1995. "Dutchman" first published in *Isaac Asimov's Science Fiction Magazine,* February 1987. A slightly shorter version of "Time Travelers Never Die" was first published in *Isaac Asimov's Science Fiction Magazine,* April 1996.

Introduction copyright © 1996 by Charles Sheffield.

Cover illustration by Michael Dashow

All rights reserved, including the right to reproduce this book, or portions thereof, in any form.

A Tachyon Publication
1459 18th Street #139
San Francisco, CA 94107

Edited by Jacob Weisman

ISBN: 0-9648320-4-6

Printed in the United States of America

TABLE OF CONTENTS

Introduction by Charles Sheffield

For Sheila Williams

Who is inspirational even when
the comet doesn't come.

INSIDE JACK McDEVITT
BY CHARLES SHEFFIELD

While reading the stories in this collection, I had an opportunity to discuss several of them with another Jack McDevitt admirer (it's hardly giving away secrets, is it, to say that I am one also? Why else would I be writing this introduction?) She commented on the narrative technique used in one of the stories. I had been quite unaware of it. In fact, although I had read the story only days before, I had to go back again to realize that she was right.

I could attribute this to my own stupidity, but to do so would be unfair to Jack McDevitt. His stories can be critically dissected, and as time goes on I feel sure that they will be, more and more. Such analysis, however, is quite unnecessary. McDevitt is a natural storyteller and the way he chooses to tell his tales, no matter the method, feels right. In fact, his narrative approach seems simple. There are few tricks, no experimental gimmicks, and no selight of hand. He stays out of the way, and just allows the story to tell itself. All that takes to work are good ideas—and a technique in which art conceals art.

Now having said that, I am going to do what I claim it is unnecessary for the reader to do. I am going to use these stories to take a closer look at Jack McDevitt himself. A collection of short stories, far more than a novel, is likely to reveal an author's own interest and obsessions. We learn a lot about a writer when the same topic occurs several times. What do we find repeated here?

Various things. Sometimes it is a factual subject that happens to interest McDevitt. So, for example, it is clear that he is a chess player, and that he thinks about many of life's situations in terms of chess. "The Jersey Rifle" is, in my opinion, the best chess short story ever written—and I am familiar with Lord Dunsany's "The Three Sailors' Gambit," which is often granted that honor. "The Jersey Rifle" is a humorous tall tale that Mark Twain would have relished and I suspect would have been pleased to have written, but it is also steeped in the history, personalities, and strategies of chess. "Black to Move" draws from the world of chess in a much more sinister way. McDevitt has many themes, and he speaks with many voices.

Sometimes it is difficult to tell how much those voices speak for him, and how much for others. "The Fort Moxie Branch" has a theme guaranteed to appeal to any writer, or would-be writer, who has felt under-appreciated. "To Hell with the Stars" is the ultimate science fiction reader's vindication. In "Tidal Effects," we are exposed to the battle for priorities that occurs in everyone's life, between family and career, knowledge and humanity, self-interest and duty. If those last few sentences seem unnecessarily obscure, I invite you to move forward and read the stories—and then return to this introduction, admitting that I was right.

The most fascinating aspect of this book, however, is the light it shines on McDevitt's involvement with the past, and his rare ability to take a Janus-like view of past and future. He has read, and remembered, a great deal of history. No matter how wildly science-fictional his story's premise, the past is never abandoned. Human actions and attitudes form a continuum. The key to our future lies at least partly in what went before. We may be far off in space, as in "Translations from the Colosian" or "Dutchman," but the powerful roots of Greece and Rome still anchor and guide the action. Gibbon is still a factor, even when the theme is SETI.

This comfortable grasp of history has two effects, both beneficial. First, it adds a sense of solidity and realism to the most unlikely premises. The principals in "Time Travelers Never Die" don't just go to vague times and places in the past—they encounter Socrates, and Michelangelo, and Cesare Borgia and Pliny the Elder, in real historical settings. Second, we never have the feeling, common in much of science fiction, that the writer, ignorant of history, is telling one more time an ancient tale.

I could go on, and talk of McDevitt's ability to create real people. I could tell how his characters (including computer personalities such as "Gus") interact, suffer, succeed, and sometimes fail. I could discuss the breadth of his imagination, or his benevolence and sympathy toward everything human. But why should I? You are going to learn all that for yourself, when you read this collection.

Sit back, then, and let McDevitt carry you far off on a dizzying journey, beyond, in Thomas Gray's words, "the flaming bounds of place and time." Not all your stopping-points are going to be pleasant—"Tyger" and "Standard Candles" are grim stories, though the latter carries at the end a hint of hope. The emotional trip gets rough in places. However, you can relax during even the bumpiest parts of the ride. You are in safe hands. There is no way in the world that Jack McDevitt will let you down.

STANDARD CANDLES

The observatory was warm in the mist. Light spilled out of the administrative windows on the second floor, and played against the moving trees at the edge of the parking lot.

Carlisle was driving too fast, kicking up gravel, alternately flooring and releasing the pedal. He was impatient with the long uphill climb. The wipers sloshed back and forth, and the branches shut off the sky.

There would be a short staff tonight, because of the overcast. But he didn't care about viewing conditions: the Andromeda galaxy could have been blazing overhead, flooding the mountains with light, and he would not have been more excited.

His printouts had worked their way out of his inside jacket pocket. He pushed them back down, affectionately. The numbers were gorgeous, and they flowed through him, and warmed him. My God, how he loved blue stars.

The road went up and up, and at last he bounced out of the forest and rolled into the parking lot. He jerked to a stop beside Boddiker's van and was out of the car, not caring about the cold drizzle, not stopping to lock up. He climbed the three concrete stairs at the front of the building, caught his breath, and went inside.

Toni Linden was standing by the coffee machine. He waved the printout at her and said "I've got it—" and kept going.

Lowenthal was not in his office, so Carlisle went hunting for him and found him down in the lower level control room arguing with Boddiker. Boddiker's thin features were in their negative mode, and the little red spot that always showed up on his crinkled skull when he got excited was glowing. His voice was high and he was jabbing his index finger at the Director. Carlisle didn't know what it was about, and didn't care. He did not back out of the room as a respectful young postdoc should have, didn't even wait for them to recognize him, but simply excused himself and shouldered into the conversation. "I think we've got a new standard candle," he said.

* * *

Judy had also been part of that night. He'd known her only three weeks, but he had already fallen victim to every familiar romantic symptom: his voice betrayed him in her presence, she completely dominated his thoughts, and the knowledge that she was seeing other men drove him wild. He had even come to accept the improbable notion that a higher power had designed events to bring them together. All he needed to do was to find a way to hold on to her.

Even now, fifteen years later, she could jack up his pulse. He'd been right: Judy Bollinger had been worth any effort. Unfortunately, he had only recently come to understand what that really meant.

She had blue eyes that he could never quite see the bottom of. A trim jogger's body. And a smile that was once again troubling his nights. Carlisle, returning to the observatory for the last time, considered the varieties of that resonant gaze.

In their early days, she had worn her auburn hair short. Judy was about average size, but because Carlisle was tall she had to reach for him, and she had a trick of standing on her toes, stretching toward him and holding her mouth up to be kissed, funneling everything she had into her lips.

On that night of nights, when he had so much to celebrate, he had hesitated to call her. It was, after all, late on a weekday evening, and he was still treating her carefully, anxious to do nothing that might damage the relationship. Don't be overeager. Patience counts, whether one is measuring the distances between stars, or pursuing a beautiful woman.

But it was an opportunity to impress her.

He had used the phone in the conference center.

"Hugh?" She sounded pleased to hear his voice, and his spirits soared.

"I'm at Kitchener," he said. "Things are happening." His tone had undoubtedly been self-important.

But she chose not to notice. "What is it?"

"Judy, I've had a major breakthrough. I've found a standard candle."

"Are you sure?" She had sounded delighted, as if she knew what a standard candle was.

"I thought we might celebrate."

"I'm on my way. Wait for me."

And she was gone before he could explain he was thinking about Saturday.

* * *

He parked in the slot marked DIRECTOR, got his empty cartons out of the trunk, and paused before letting himself into the building. The mountaintop was still. He had stood out here that night, watching her lights come up the access road. (The road was dark now, cold and untraveled, save for the contractors who came in the daylight to remove everything that was of value.) Her white two-door Ford came out of the trees right *there*, and she'd parked over by the reserved spaces, under the security lights at the supply entrance.

The security lights were out now. For good.

The Foundation had started closing down Kitchener's operations two years ago. Much of the action had gone to the southern hemisphere, where there was less light and pollution and a richer field for investigation. Carlisle supported the action, had even dissuaded Lowenthal from campaigning against the vote.

But it had cost him. Many of his old acquaintances, some whom he'd counted as friends, no longer talked to him. Furthermore, he would be going back to the classroom. His dreams of greatness were probably over.

He unlocked the door, let himself in, and turned the lights on. The well in which the eighty-inch Cassegrain reflector had rested was shadowy and cold.

"How far can you see with it?" she had asked. She was wearing a yellow sweater thrown over her shoulders. Odd that, after so long, he would remember the details.

It was a naive question. "To the edge of the universe," he'd answered. That was not quite true, of course. They could see as far as the Red Limit, which was the farthest point from which light has had time to reach Earth since the creation.

He had supervised the removal of the telescope only the week before. It was on its way to Kitt Peak, where it would become a backup.

Judy had stood beside him, in this doorway, barely rising to his shoulder. But her physical presence had been overpowering.

She taught history at Franklin High School, which was now a shopping center. She knew damned little science, and less cosmology, but she seemed perpetually interested in what Carlisle was doing. Her father was a policeman, and she was a product of public schools and state universities, not blessed with life's advantages as *he* had been. She talked about wanting to write the definitive history of the McCarthy era. Everything hadn't come out yet, she'd said. His links with Hoover. Deals with Nixon. During all the years he knew her, she was gathering materials, and planning the book. Sometimes she read extracts to him. Carlisle, who had always found the social sciences boring, got caught up in the narrative. He was often appalled that government officials could have acted with such perfidy, and she told him more than once that she loved him because he had retained the ability to be outraged. "Don't ever lose it," she warned.

They were watching Boddiker, who was in the observer's cage. "He's our cluster specialist. What they're doing now is hoping the sky will clear. It won't. But if it does, they'll take pictures toward the galactic interior, so they can compare optical results with X-rays. Over there is the imaging center." Babble, babble. He winced now to think of it, but it all seemed to charm her, and she'd squeezed his hand when she thought no one was looking.

Lowenthal was gone a long time. Carlisle wasn't worried: he knew he was right; he had checked his results carefully. So he suggested they go celebrate.

"Isn't that bad luck? Before you get confirmation?"

"Maybe. But in the meantime, I get an evening with *you*. Worth whatever comes of it."

They took both cars and went down the mountain to Spike's. Spike's was a quiet bar back in the trees off Observatory Road, about a mile from the foot of the mountain. It was favored by the staff at Kitchener and the science department at UEI because management catered to them, hosted their frequent celebrations and parties, and made it a point to treat them like VIP's.

That evening had been their first time there together. They'd found a corner table and ordered drinks and sat in the glow of a small candle in a glass dish. Soft music flowed across the room. Carlisle had realized how little he knew about her, and how fascinated he was by even the trivia of her life. What had she been like in high school? What were her interests? What sort of home life did she come from? *How did she really feel about him?*

It was the happiest night of his life. He was with *her*, a cosmological golden age was approaching, and he was looking forward to his career as a giant. By the end of the century he expected to rank with Hubble and Sandage and Penrose. This was a period utterly unique in the history of the world. A small group of men and women, for the first time properly armed with instrumentation and theory, was trying to make sense of the universe, how big it was, how old, whether the expansion was as precisely balanced as it appeared, and why that should be so. How galaxies formed. Whether strings existed. *Why* there was symmetry. It was a glorious time, and Carlisle was already part of it.

And he intended to make that journey with this magnificent creature at his side.

She had looked at him with undisguised pleasure. *Now,* he understood how easily she was reading him.

I like being with you, her eyes said. But she asked, "What's a standard candle?"

The wax candle burned cheerily on the table top. "If you took twenty of these out of a box, each one would probably put out more or less the same amount of light. So if we saw one on a rooftop, we could figure out how far away it is by measuring how dim the light has become. *That's* a standard candle. It's a light source that always radiates at the same level of intensity. We call it absolute luminosity. Whenever you see it, you can get a decent range estimate." He stopped and sipped his drink. "Cepheid variables are standard candles. You can always figure out how far they are. But they aren't bright enough. We can only see them on local rooftops. What we need is something that's visible in the next town. Or across the country."

"The blue stars," she said, almost breathless, as if she'd been running.

"Yes. The brightest blue stars in a galaxy always have essentially the *same* absolute magnitude. So we now have an intergalactic yardstick."

"I thought you could already measure distances with red shifts."

"A little bit," he said. "The redder the shift, the further the object. But the method's inexact." He looked at her across the rim of his glass. "They're subject to too many interpretations."

The candle glowed in her eyes. "Congratulations, Hugh."

Later, toward the end of the evening, he called the observatory. "Your numbers seem to work," Lowenthal told him. Carlisle could still see the telephone, a big old-fashioned rotary wall model; could hear the soft tinkle of a piano solo; could smell warm wax on the still air. Judy sat angled in his direction, watching, her eyes locked on him, waiting for a sign.

"Thanks," he said into the phone.

He looked at her. Thumbs up.

Carlisle had always been something of a Puritan. But that night a different set of universal laws were in place. He bought a round of drinks for a group of strangers at the next table, puzzled them by toasting "candles everywhere," embraced Judy, and threw a twenty-dollar tip onto the table.

They drove to her apartment, Carlisle leading the way. (No sly suggestions about leaving one car in the lot; he would never have been so obvious.) But it hadn't mattered. At her doorway, she had slipped into his arms, and he became intensely aware of the pressure of her left breast. The other was also engaged with him, but Carlisle had found that the sensation was more intimate, more intense, when he concentrated on one at a time.

She had moved against him, subtly, and invited him in, so to speak. And it was over for Carlisle. He remembered her lips, the line of her jaw, her breathing, the sound of the wind in the trees.

She did not draw away. Not then, nor for many years.

Next day, during the late afternoon, Lowenthal called and asked him to come out to Kitchener. The Director's voice was somber, and Carlisle knew there was trouble. Nevertheless, he hadn't pressed; he was adrift in a euphoric state and nothing could shake him. He put the call out of his mind and completed his classes for the day. Then, after a deliberately casual meal, he had driven back up the mountain.

"You *do* seem to be correct," Lowenthal assured him. By then, he had been director at Kitchener more than ten years. He was lean and polished, self-effacing and eminently well-mannered, a rare breed among the pushy egos who dominated the field. "The blue stars work. Unfortunately, we're late. Sandage and Tammann got there first. It's even been published. Damned thing's been on my desk for three days. I saw it this morning."

Carlisle recalled staring out across the mountaintop. And he remembered what Lowenthal had said next, would *always* remember it: "Don't worry. It's bad luck. But you'll be back. You're too good not to be back."

"How can you sit there and tell me that the universe has no edge?"
He loved those early evenings, when her mysteries were still new to him, deeper and darker than the spaces between the galaxies. And far more enticing.

They became Friday-night regulars at Spike's, and went to the movies and shows on Saturday. Carlisle floated through his days with a warm sense of well-being, anxious only to get to the weekend.

She invited him to Franklin to address her U.S. history classes on how scientific progress since the turn of the century had influenced the course of events. Since Carlisle wasn't entirely clear on the course of events, he needed help from her. But they pulled it off together, talking about atom bombs and computers and gas engines and the glee with which many of the churches had embraced the Big Bang.

They had met at the Kane Planetarium, where Carlisle had been a part-time lecturer. She'd been at their Star of Bethlehem program, had sat off to his right with a man who'd looked like a football player. After the show, she'd asked a couple of questions, and then drifted away with her companion. He saw her several times after that. She was alone or with girlfriends in subsequent visits, and they had always exchanged a few remarks on the presentation. It took a while before he got up the nerve to invite her to dinner.

On the evening after the history class, he had taken another major step forward. She'd been happy with his performance, and he saw a window of opportunity. "Maybe Everett was right," he said, mysteriously.

She frowned between pieces of beef. "Who's Everett?"

"An astronomer. He suggested there might be a universe for every possibility. A place where every wave function is realized. If an event is possible, somewhere it happens."

That got her attention. "That's science fiction," she said. But he could see that the notion appealed to her.

"It's only an idea." He looked at her, and then blurted the thought that had crossed his mind, even though he knew it was not prudent. That it might scare her off. "If there's anything to it, somewhere out there, you and I are wearing each other's rings."

It was an electric thrust. An uncharacteristically daring move.

She held him in suspense momentarily. And squeezed his hand.

Somewhere out there, you and I are wearing each other's rings.

She said *yes* a few months later, and they went to a little Unitarian church on a Massachusetts hilltop, where the only religious symbol was a stylized carbon atom. Judy's family, who were Catholic, were visibly displeased, and suspected the arrangement had something to do with Carlisle. But it was Judy's idea. Carlisle didn't care, had no strong religious views one way or another, and would have married her in a Fiji Island ceremony if she had asked.

His bride had been so taken by the notion of an infinite number of Judys and Hughs living subtly different lives beyond the stars, *beyond our stars,* she had said, that she wrote the idea into the ceremony: *It may be that there are places where your eyes are gray, or where no one here would recognize my name. But wherever we live, if we have met, I love you. The wave function can break in no other direction.*

They exchanged rings engraved with ∞, the mathematical symbol for infinity.

And if Allan Sandage and Gustav Tammann had beaten him to the blue stars, it didn't matter.

One of the great questions of the era was whether the universe was expanding in a uniform manner in all directions. Or whether the superclusters were so massive that they skewed expansion and created an imbalance. Preliminary results suggested that the Milky Way had been drawn off its natural course, and was falling into the Virgo Supercluster. Was that actually happening? If so, how fast was it moving? Could they devise a method to measure the Virgo effect? Carlisle took charge of the Kitchener team and they began assembling data. He virtually *moved* into the observatory. Lowenthal encouraged him and made it clear that Carlisle could expect future high-profile assignments. "It's just a matter of time before you make your mark," he said. "I want to be sure you're in a position to take full advantage of the opportunities." And when Carlisle thanked him, the old man grinned. "Establish your reputation," he said. "When you've done that, you can thank me in public."

The issue proved inordinately difficult to settle. It remains unanswered.

He used the cartons to push the door open. There wasn't much left in his office.

He hadn't taken down his pictures. Carlisle standing beside Brent Tully at the Kona Conference, Carlisle shaking hands with John Schwarz at CalTech, Carlisle eating lunch with Allan Sandage in New York. An aerial photo of Kitchener beneath a full moon. A color enhancement of the Horsehead Nebula. A stylized rendering of an H-R diagram.

And of course his favorite picture of Judy, posed against an ominous sky at Cape Hatteras. He had taken it down at the time of the breakup, and then put it back a few months later.

He found old notebooks in the bottom of the lower right-hand desk drawer. They were spiral-bound, yellowed, tattered. Dated from before the arrival of his PC. He slipped off the fat rubber bands, sat on the edge of the desk, and thumbed through them.

They made painful reading: his comments and observations were pedestrian. With the advantage of hindsight, he could see his limitations quite clearly. Hugh Carlisle's prime talent seemed to be recognizing the obvious.

He flipped through his Rolodex. He had never purged the thing, and there were names of people who had long since retired or died. And names he couldn't remember. He dropped it into one of his boxes.

During the early years of their marriage, they'd gone to a lot of live theater. In fact, they had seen *George Washington Slept Here* on their second date. Later, Judy would insist that it was his reaction to that romantic comedy that had piqued her interest in him.

But their working hours never blended. After he became permanently attached to the observatory staff, he worked primarily at night. He'd get home as Judy was getting ready to leave for school. But they tried to make time for coffee. "What's going on up on the mountain?" she would ask.

"We're counting globular clusters again, but what we'd really like to know—"

"Yes?"

"—Is why the universe is so homogeneous."

"How do you mean?"

"Why is it so balanced? How does it happen that microwaves arrive from opposite sides of the sky, from places that could never, in the entire history of the cosmos, have had any contact with each other, or any influence over each other, *and the microwaves are identical?*"

She loved these vaguely mad notions. "I don't follow. What else *could* the universe look like? Are you suggesting all the stars should be in the southern sky? And nothing in the north?"

It was hard to explain. A lot of it was hard to explain. And it didn't help that, within his own limitations, he didn't quite grasp the finer points that Zeldovich and Steinhardt were making.

He was often too busy, or too tired, to try to lay it out for her. Occasionally, he wondered whether he shouldn't have married a fellow professional. Like Harrigan. Or Cholka. An image of the energetic Russian rose before his eyes. Now *there* was someone he could really have *talked* to.

Judy enjoyed the intimacy of evenings out, together among strangers, as she liked to put it. He tried to comply, even though the weight of his own responsibilities increased after he became department chairman, and then assistant to the Director at Kitchener. Nevertheless, he did not complain, and in fact hid his feelings rather well.

He wasn't sure where things had begun to go wrong.

Judy understood what drove him, knew he needed to put his name to a discovery, to find a Carlisle Effect, or formulate Carlisle's Theorem. She also understood that it was a compulsion not fostered exclusively by vanity, but by a genuine desire to make a *contribution*, to be at the focal point when they broke through into one of nature's secrets.

But she did *not* understand that he saw his time running out. It wasn't that he was getting chronologically old, but he knew that talent, genius, if it is present, manifests itself early. He had begun to fear that he was only a mediocrity, someone to hold the reins for Achilles. When he tried to explain, she assured him that everything would be okay. *You're having a brilliant career.* And, *Whatever happens, I love you.*

In time, the emphasis changed. *You're a Type A personality, Hugh. Type A's get ulcers. Die young. You need to take some time off.*

Eventually, she began to spend time with her friends, and they trooped off occasionally for evenings on the town. She always invited him. "If you can make it," she would say. Or, "If you think you might enjoy this—"

And there was Wade Popper, the superstring theorist. Popper made no effort to disguise his interest in Judy. They began meeting out on the jog path. And having lunches together. *Only friends,* her demeanor assured him. But Popper's intentions were transparent.

She had read his discomfort and discontinued the tête-à-tête. The incident left a dead spot, a neutral zone between them, an area that he was never after able to penetrate.

"What does inflation mean?"

The subject had come up at about the time of Lowenthal's retirement. The Kitchener team was working full time trying to determine how much dark matter would be required to make inflation theory work. The answer: *a lot.* Maybe ninety percent of all the matter in the universe would have to be dark. And Judy had asked about it during one of his rare evenings at home. "It means that the universe, in its early expansion, exceeded the speed of light—"

"But that's impossible, right?"

"Not necessarily."

Her eyes flashed. "Sometimes I think you guys just make up the rules as you go along."

"Sometimes we do." It was a little exasperating, like teaching Cosmology 101. She knew just enough to get everything confused. "The trick is to construct an explanation, sometimes *any* explanation, that fits the observations."

He looked out through his window, down at the treetops, and tried to listen to his own words. What had they sounded like to her?

He lifted the last of his books into a box, sealed it, and put it aside. He took his CD player down off the shelf. The filing cabinet yielded folders filled with papers he hadn't looked at in years.

Gradually, her questions had become less frequent. Conditions at the high school were deteriorating, and she became absorbed in her own problems. But in '86 she was voted Teacher of the Year, and they celebrated with a party at the Radisson.

Carlisle enjoyed parties. The people at Kitchener and in the science department threw them regularly. Threw them, in fact, with such energy that they were barred from the local Holiday Inn.

A substantial crowd showed up for this one. Most of Carlisle's colleagues came. And a small army of Judy's friends. More than he knew she had. There were even a couple of reporters, and a delegation of her students. And although Carlisle was pleased to see his wife get the attention, it hurt to realize that the press had never come for him.

Judy glowed that night. She kept him on her arm, and introduced him to everyone who came within their orbit. She glowed, like in the old days. My husband the cosmologist. And he realized that night that his marriage had undergone some fundamental chemical change.

The evening was still bright and clear in his memory. She had drifted through the celebration, dancing with everyone, laughing, maybe drinking a little too much. Some of the men, some of *his* friends and some of hers, looked at her with such undisguised abandon that he was shocked. Carlisle was not ordinarily a possessive man, and he felt no reason to doubt her, but the sight of all that male interest elicited a twinge even now.

Across the years, her eyes cut him like distant stars.

His old electric razor (which he'd thought lost) was tucked away in the top of a closet. He'd always made a point of looking bright and polished before starting home in the morning. It still worked.

Lowenthal had been wrong. Carlisle never did come back, never again approached a breakthrough. He was a methodical investigator, persistent and precise. He did not make mistakes, but that is a *clerical* virtue. The hard reality was that he lacked the vision of a Zwicky or a Wheeler. He was good on the follow-up effort, performing the detailed analysis to determine whether someone else's brilliance coincided with the way nature really worked. While the long hunt for the value of the Hubble Constant went on, and the debates over cosmic bubbles and macrostructure heated up, Carlisle was always a step behind.

In the spring of 1987, Judy's father died and she received a surprisingly large inheritance. They used some of the money to buy a time-share at Cape Hatteras. The house was big, with broad decks, and ocean views on both sides. It had a fireplace and a jacuzzi, and it was a damned good place to work. One does not need a telescope to do cosmology, he was fond of telling the postdocs. It is essentially an exercise of the imagination. And nowhere else did he feel so free, so *unleashed,* as in the big rug-covered living room, with the fire at his back, and the stars floating on the Atlantic.

Judy preferred to prowl the shops and beaches. One day, she returned with a surprise. "I wanted you to meet Griff," she said. He was average-looking, beginning to gray, a few years older than Carlisle. Dumpy. "He owns the Golden Coin." An antique shop, it turned out.

Carlisle shook the man's hand, and made the appropriate small talk. Good to meet you. Must be considerable business for antiques in a place like this. (Judy had bought a finely worked tray, which she said dated from the 1920s.) He was congenial enough, but slow-witted.

"Griff says there's a concert tonight. By *Prelude.*"

"Who the hell is *Prelude?*" He kept his tone light. Jaunty. He knew she didn't expect recognition from him. It was part of the game they played with each other.

"A string quartet," she said. "Hugh, why don't we go? It would be very nice. It's outdoors."

He would not usually be averse to a string quartet, but he hated to lose one of his few evenings on the Outer Banks. "Sure," he said bleakly. (It occurred to him now, dropping his paperweight and his desk lamp into the packing box, that he would like very much to recapture that night, recapture *her,* and have it all to do again.)

She had responded as he knew she would, allowed her eyes to close momentarily, had turned to Griff. "I'd better pass."

"Nonsense." Carlisle was aggressively generous. "No reason for you to stay home. Maybe Griff would like to go—"

Fool that I am.

Not that Judy would have been tempted to cheat. But he knew he had sent the wrong message.

* * *

He sealed the boxes and carried them one by one down the stairs and out to his car. The wind was picking up and, despite the clear skies, rain was in the air. Lightning flickered to the west. He counted off the seconds until he heard the rumble. Seven miles.

Something about Hatteras had always stirred Carlisle's ambitions. And his discontent. "I need to get away from here," he told her, two years after Griff and his antique shop had passed into oblivion. He was pushed back into a leather armchair, watching sheets of rain pour into the Atlantic. "No, not *here*, but from Kitchener. UEI. It's time to go, to move on."

She was standing near the windows, looking out. Judy *loved* terrible weather. She came alive when the wind blew and the sky rolled, as if the electricity flowed into her. Arms folded, she had been weaving gently to the rhythms of the storm. But he saw her shoulders tighten. "Why?" she asked. "Lowenthal will be retiring soon. You'll be in line for his job."

"I don't *want* his job. Judy, I've been here too long already. I'm getting the wrong kind of reputation. If I'm ever going to break out, I have to do it now."

"You have a *good* reputation." She meant it. And he *did*. He could expect to get the directorship, and possibly even the astronomy chair at the University.

"That's not what I want."

"What *do* you want?" Her voice was soft, but he felt the undercurrent.

"Judy, I'm part of the cleanup crew. Somebody somewhere has a good idea. The superclusters are really pancakes, and they're stacked in layers. Hugh, check it out. The voids between the galaxies are really vast bubbles, and the galaxies are out on the rims. Hugh, what about that? There are people like me in every major observatory in the world. Martin at Palomar. Babcock at McDonald. Leronda at Mauna Kea. Dureyvich at Zelenchukskaya. Flunkies. People who get to bring the coffee while things happen."

She looked at him, and the air thickened. "I'm sorry you feel that way."

How many times had he tried to explain it to her? "Judy, I might be able to connect with Schramm at Fermi. They're looking for somebody. I met him last year and I think I made a good impression."

Her eyes clouded. "When would you want to go?"

"The job's open now."

"Hugh, I can't just pick up in the middle of November and walk *out*. I could leave at the end of the year."

The rain slid down the windows. After a while she rose and came over and sat across from him, on the sofa. There had been a time when she would have tried sex, to ease the moment, put the decision off until they had both had time to think. Prevent anyone's position from hardening. But they knew each other too well now.

In the end, she encouraged him to try for what he wanted. He had, but the appointment went elsewhere.

The evening finally came when she asked him to sit down, when her gaze dropped to the carpet and her voice turned especially gentle.

He took it well. Don't make a scene. Don't embarrass yourself. He understood quite suddenly, quite painfully, that he did not want to lose her, and that to react badly was to throw away whatever chance he might have. He was wrong, of course. But the moment passed, fled, was long gone before he realized his mistake.

He dropped the last box into his trunk, banged it shut, and went back inside to turn off the lights.

The universe was *filled* with light: whole squadrons of suns nearby, creamy galactic swirls floating beyond the Local Group, flickering pinpoints deep in the abyss. From the time Hubble discovered, in 1923, that there were other galaxies beyond the Milky Way, that there appeared to be no end to them, astronomers had argued over distances and measurements.

Something more than Carlisle's blue stars was needed. Something on a qualitatively different scale.

And while he and a host of others thought it over, Sandage and Tammann proposed the Type I supernova. It was visible at enormous range, and it had a reasonably consistent absolute luminosity. The downside was that you had to find one. But it was a method with promise.

Now that someone else had thought of it, it seemed obvious. Carlisle sighed.

He stared at the empty well that had housed the Cassegrain, and could almost feel her standing beside him.

Her departure was followed quickly by divorce papers. She assured him she would harbor no bitterness, and she did indeed look unhappy. But she rejected his last-minute attempt to salvage the marriage. He was stunned. Carlisle had believed that, when the moment came, she would draw back.

He reacted by throwing himself into a new project. Teams from several research centers were making a coordinated effort to map a sixty-degree wedge of the universe, out to about three hundred million light-years. That target area would later be extended, but Carlisle set up and personally led the Kitchener group.

During that period, while he categorized galaxies, and recorded their positions, he waited for her to come back. The long days passed, and he gradually adjusted to his new existence. She was, after all, not the only woman in the world.

Meanwhile, the various teams involved in the mapping project were counting more galaxies than theory allowed. By a factor of two or three. On a cold February night in 1990 he had poured himself some hot chocolate, and sat down with his assistants. They'd gone over all the models, and could not explain their results.

Why?

Construct an explanation, any explanation, that fits the observations.

Easy to say.

He threw the switches, and the building went dark.

There must have been a time when he should have seen what was happening, when he could still have acted before they were flung apart like bodies with reversed gravities. God help him, but even now, with the benefit of all this hindsight, he did not know what he could have done differently.

He stepped out into the moonlight, closed the door behind him, and locked it. The metal felt hard and cold.

The wind blew across the mountaintop.

Carlisle started down the steps when he noticed that a black car had pulled in behind his. He stared, trying to see who was in it. A couple of kids, maybe. Planning to park.

The driver's door was open. The interior light blinked on, and Judy stood before him.

She was radiant. Lovely. But visibly reluctant.

"Hello, Hugh."

She came around to the front of his car and stopped.

Hope rose in Carlisle's breast. And resentment. And a flood of other emotions. "Judy," he said, "what are you doing here? How did you know I'd be here?"

She smiled. "Last day before they shut it down. Where else would Hugh Carlisle be?"

He stared at her. "I'd given up on you."

"As well you should." She glanced at the observatory. "It hurts to see it like this. That surprises you, doesn't it?"

"Yes," he said. "I thought you'd come to resent it."

"It was part of *you*. Part of us." She shrugged. "I'm sorry to see it go."

"I'm glad you came."

"Thanks. So am I. But don't get the wrong idea. I just wanted to be here. At the end."

His voice had grown thick. He thought about the infinity symbol on his ring. (He'd stopped wearing it about three years before she left, because he'd gained weight and it no longer fit.)

"Spike's has closed down too. But I'd like to buy you a drink. Somewhere."

She pursed her lips. And smiled again. "I'd like that."

Somewhere every possibility occurs. He might indeed be one of an interminable number of Hugh Carlisles. And most of them were standing alone in this parking lot.

But Carlisle, *this* Carlisle, was in the right universe.

The stars were warm and bright and went on forever.

TIDAL EFFECTS

"I never walk on the beach anymore." The physicist, Gambini, stood near the window, looking out across the illuminated lawns of the Seaside Condo. Rain sparkled in the flood lamps. The Atlantic was hidden by a screen of poplars; but the two men could hear its sullen roar. "During that summer," he continued, "while we waited for the launch, and expected so much, I went out every evening. I was too excited to work."

Harmon rotated his wine between thumb and forefinger, but said nothing.

Headlights flickered across Gambini's rigid features. "I grew up in a small town in Ohio, and I was in high school before I ever saw an ocean. But I can still remember the first time. I've loved the Atlantic ever since." He gazed thoughtfully through the rain-streaked window. "Even now."

Harmon drained his glass and surveyed the room. It was oppressive: heavy, drab furniture; bulging bookcases; neutral, steely colors everywhere. A computer terminal beside a recliner trailed several feet of printout. "I know you're surprised to see me," he said apologetically. "But I had to come."

Gambini moved away from the drapes, back into the yellow light of an ugly seashell table lamp. A shapeless gray sweater hung from his thin shoulders. "I knew that eventually you would," he said.

Harmon held out his glass. Gambini filled it, and his own. They were drinking port, a vintage bottle that the physicist had been saving for a special occasion. "It must be a magnificent time for you," Harmon said, "now that the data has begun to come in. There seems so little that you and your colleagues have not touched. Perhaps, in the end, only the Creation itself will prove elusive."

"Ah." Gambini brightened. "We have some ideas about *that.*"

"I'm not surprised you think so." Harmon understood, if Gambini did not, that science had its limits.

"But sometimes," continued Gambini as if he had not heard, "the price is high."

"You are thinking of the beach again?" He watched the physicist circle the coffee table and settle stiffly into a wingback chair. "You did what you could," he said.

A gust of wind blew the rain hissing against the windows. Outside, an automobile engine roared into life. The air smelled of salt and ozone. "How much do you know about Skynet?" Gambini asked.

Harmon shrugged. "Only what I read in the papers."

The lines around Gambini's mouth tightened. "Odd. If it were not for Skynet, you would not be here; there would be no need for this meeting." He laid a peculiar emphasis on the last word. "Skynet," he continued, adopting a professorial tone, "is an array, twenty-two infrared receptors in Earth orbit. Capable of seeing damn near anything. They were putting it in place last summer. And I was waiting here, as Ryan was at Princeton, and Hakluyt at Greenbelt, and others . . ." He set his glass down. It was empty. "We knew that, after it became operational, the world would not be the same."

"No doubt," said Harmon. But he had no idea why this should be so.

Gambini inquired, tolerantly, whether his guest had ever heard of Fred Hoyle.

Harmon's perplexity was apparent. "I don't believe I have," he said impatiently.

Gambini crossed the room and took a thick volume from an upper shelf. "Hoyle," he said, "is a cosmologist who dedicated the later stages of his career defending outworn theories on the nature of the universe: what it is, where it came from, where it's going. Trivial matters, really, when contrasted with the question that really absorbed him, that absorbs all of us and knits us together."

"And what," asked Harmon, wondering where all this was leading, "might that be?"

"Simply stated," said Gambini, "it is this: What is *our* relationship with the cosmos? Are we unique? Are we one of many? Has the universe, in some manner, been designed for *us*? It is a question with the profoundest philosophical implications. It is the great enigma. Shapley never knew. Nor did Lowell. Nor Einstein. They grew old with no hope, and went to their graves with no semblance of an answer."

Harmon shifted his weight. He was beginning to feel uncomfortable.

Gambini understood that he must seem disconnected. A garrulous old man with no grasp of his visitor's pain. He should stop, squeeze Harmon's arm, thank him for coming by, accept the man's gratitude. But he plowed on: "Then we got Skynet. They assembled it during late summer, and we knew, by Christmas, we would use it to see other solar systems. *We would be able to see extrasolar worlds, out to a distance of more than a hundred light-years.* We would be able to perform spectroscopic analyses of their atmospheres. My God, Harmon, we could look for oxygen, the infallible mark of life!"

Harmon nodded.

"I neither ate nor slept during those final weeks. They'd already begun testing the system, and success appeared very likely. I gave up trying to read or work."

Harmon examined the Hoyle volume. It was *Galaxies, Nuclei, and Quasars.* "And you," he said, raising his eyes to Gambini's, "walked the beaches."

"Yes. But only at sunset. When the air was cool."

Harmon leaned forward.

"Each evening there was a group of swimmers. Boys. They were young, thirteen perhaps, no more than that. There were three of them usually, sometimes four, and they were always out beyond the breaker line. One in particular. . . ."

"Yes," said Harmon, "he was like that." His voice sounded strange.

Gambini seemed not to have heard. "He was taller than the others. Awkward. With light sandy hair." He got up, slowly, and pushed his fists into the pockets of the gray sweater. "The current can be treacherous, and every night they went farther into the sea. I warned them. They weren't local kids. Locals would have known better."

"We were," said Harmon, "from Alexandria."

"I told them it was dangerous." Gambini hesitated. "But that meant nothing to them, of course. They laughed and retreated farther beyond the breakers. The tall one, he was almost as tall as I: the night before he died, he stood as close to me as you are now, sunburned, preoccupied, with all his life before him. He was inspecting tidal pools, for stranded guppies, I suppose. He saw me, and smiled self-consciously as though he'd been caught doing something foolish." Gambini's eyes clouded. He fell silent.

"Did he say anything to you?"

"No. We faced each other for a moment. Then he was gone, up the beach with his friends, snapping towels at each other."

For a long time there was only the sound of the sea, and of water dripping into foliage. Harmon's chair creaked. When Gambini spoke again, he was barely audible. "It happened, as I knew it would. Hakluyt had called me that morning to discuss the latest test results, and I forgot about the boys. It was cold and damp, after an all-day rain." He glanced accusingly at his visitor. "I was preoccupied. And they should never have been there. But they were.

"The first indication I had that something was wrong came when a fat middle-aged man ran past me. He hurried along the shoreline to join two of the boys, who were standing hip-deep, anxiously watching the sea; beyond them, desperately far out, a head floated over the top of a swell, and arms thrashed.

"One of the boys turned toward me and screamed (though I could not hear him over the roar of the ocean). I looked for help and saw only an elderly woman with two dogs.

"I broke into a run, and was already breathing hard before I even got into the water. The boy sank: he was down a long time while I struggled toward him. He came up, coughing and choking. I got through the breakers into calmer water and began to swim. The water was cold, and the drag toward the open sea was strong.

"I was moving quickly. I'm not a bad swimmer, and the current was pushing me toward him. But the distance between us didn't seem to lessen. The boy struggled, went down, found new strength.

"I realized quite suddenly that my own life was in danger. I knew I could reach him, and I also knew that we would probably not get back. It was odd; the possibility of my own drowning raised only a single emotion: the stiletto sensation that it was too soon. *By a few weeks, or a few months, it was too soon!*

"And I hated the child!"

Harmon's mouth tightened, but he said nothing.

"He fought stubbornly for his life. Time after time, the sea rolled over him, but he would not stay down. The tide dragged me in all directions, and I lost headway in a swirl of currents. I got desperately tired. And I could see that his struggles were growing weaker. He saw me coming and tried to wave, but he could not lift his arm out of the water. Each time, after he had been pushed beneath the sea, he broke the surface looking for me." Gambini's voice had been rising; but now he stopped to refill his glass. His hand trembled. "At last he must have seen my despair, because I read the sudden swift terror in his face as he realized, I think for the first time, what was going to happen . . ."

"So you turned back," Harmon said uncertainly. "No one can blame you for that. No one could expect more."

Gambini threw the full glass of port against a wall. "Who are *you*," he demanded, "to make that judgment? I left him to *drown!*"

"No!" Harmon said desperately. "You tried! You did what you could—"

Gambini's eyes were cold. "I did not abandon him," he said, "because I was afraid. I did it because I was curious. I sold his life for some tracings on a few hundred pieces of paper."

(On the veranda below his apartment, people were talking. Someone laughed.)

"I should not have come," said Harmon.

"Is that all you can say?" snapped Gambini. "You're his father."

Harmon rose. His face was calm, but there was something of the drowning boy in his eyes. "What do you want me to tell you, Gambini?" he demanded. "That you too should have drowned? That nothing less would have been decent?"

Gambini slid his fingers under his bifocals and rubbed his eyes. "Why are you here? After all this time?"

"I don't know." Harmon exhaled. "I thought they were safe. Out here, away from Alexandria, I didn't think anything could happen. We were always grateful that you tried. I wrote you a letter."

"I know. It's in my desk."

Harmon softened. "Under the circumstances, I guess it was painful."

Gambini stared a long time at his visitor. "Were you supposed to be taking care of him?"

Harmon nodded.

"You are right to feel guilty," he rasped. "Your son and I, we were both your victims." Gambini's smile trembled on thin lips. "Do you know what we found when we looked beyond the solar system? No, don't turn away. This concerns your boy. We examined several thousand stars, Harmon. About a quarter have been planets. Most are Jovian: nothing more, really, than enormous sacks of cold hydrogen. It was, of course, the terrestrial worlds in which we were especially interested: those Earthlike planets orbiting stable suns at temperate distances." A nerve near Gambini's jugular had begun to throb. "I assume I need not tell you that we found no oxygen. Oh, there were traces here and there. But everywhere we looked, among the terrestrial worlds, we saw carbon dioxide. In vast quantities. Do you understand what I'm saying, Harmon?"

Harmon's eyes blazed, but he did not reply.

"No biological processes. Anywhere. We'd always assumed that something had gone wrong on Venus, leaving her sterile under a hothouse atmosphere. Some people have made a career of explaining why. But Venus, it turns out, is the norm: it's Earth that is the anomaly.

"It appears, Harmon, that we are quite alone."

Harmon threw open the door, and whirled to face the physicist. "Despite everything you've said, I believe you tried. I hope the day will come when you will realize you could have done no more."

"If you think that," Gambini said, "I will tell you something else. If it were to do again, I'd make the same decision. Do you understand that?"

Harmon's features twisted into a murderous frown, and he wondered (at that moment, and for all his life after) what the physicist was trying to provoke.

But Gambini had already turned away. When the door closed behind Harmon, he was standing by the window. It was raining again, and he was grateful for the cloud cover.

TRANSLATIONS FROM THE COLOSIAN

During the years when the first starships were crawling out from Earth, I sat one night in an open-air theater under strange constellations, watching a performance of *Antigone*.

The title was different, of course. And the characters had different names. I didn't understand the language, the playwright was somebody named Tyr, and Creon had fangs. For that matter, so did Antigone, and the guy sitting immediately to my right. But you can't miss the stark cadence of that desperate drama. I'd have known it in Swahili. The old passions don't change: even there, on that far world, where the Milky Way is only a faint point of light visible on clear nights; even there, reflected on the faces of a species that would have sent those early Hellenic audiences screaming into the woods, I knew them. Inexorably, while Harvey Klein and I watched through the narrow slits of our masks, the tragedy played itself out. And if I'd had any doubts about the nature of the creatures among whom I was spending the evening, they dissipated during the performance. The spectators held their breath in the right places, and gasped and trembled on cue. When it was over, they filed out thoroughly subdued, some surreptitiously wiping their eyes. They had been a damned good audience, and I admired them, fangs, fur, snouts and all.

I think quite often about that evening, and wonder how something that began so well could have gone so wrong. It's more than twenty years now, but I remember the theater as though it were only last weekend. Basically, it was a brick platform with wings, balconies, and oil lamps. After the show, we climbed a hill behind it, and stood in the flicker of summer lightning, watching workers draw large squares of canvas over the stage. Klein looked around to be sure we were alone, coughed consumptively, pulled back his hood, and removed his mask. He took a deep breath and exhaled slowly. "Well," he asked, "was I right?"

I nodded, and realized he couldn't see the gesture. "Yes." I took off my own headpiece. The horns glinted in the light of an enormous green and yellow disk that rose out of the eastern horizon. "Yes, it *is* Sophocles."

"You'll be interested in knowing," said Klein, "that the thing we watched tonight was written over two thousand years ago, our time, during this world's political and literary golden age."

"Not possible," I said. My sandals hurt. The best footwear that Klein had been able to come up with on short notice was Japanese. I was wearing false fur on my insteps, and the thong ran up between my second and third toes, rubbing the furpiece into my flesh.

It was a long ride from Glen Ellyn to that pleasant park, two million light-years or so. But I felt at home among its deep glades and flat-bladed ferns that smelled vaguely of mint. The grass was freshly cut, and neatly trimmed hedges bordered gravel walks.

Klein looked puzzled. "You don't seem surprised, George," he said. "I would have thought that seeing a Greek play out here would come as something of a shock."

That was a laugh. A few hours earlier I'd walked with Klein through the windowless, crooked storeroom nailed to the back of his two-story frame house. We'd entered from the kitchen, and we'd come *here*.

"Where, precisely, are we?"

"I'm not too sure," he said. "Somewhere in M32, which is one of the local group of galaxies. The inhabitants call the place Melchior." A cool breeze blew across the brow of the hill. Klein looked unwell in the torpid light of the monster moon. He'd had a long history of high blood pressure and diabetes, and he occasionally mixed his insulin with rum. "How do you account for it?" he asked. "How does it happen that these people are watching Sophoclean drama?"

"One thing at a time," I said. "How did we get here? What's the point of building starships that take years to go to places like this if we can simply walk across?"

"Oh," he smiled, "no starship will ever come here."

"Why not?"

"We're much too far." He pulled his robe up around his knees and lowered himself awkwardly into the ocher-colored grass. "How much physics do you know?"

"Not much."

Klein glanced tolerantly toward the dark forest pressing on the far side of the park. "George, it's all a matter of perception. We live in a queer universe, which is both physical and conceptual. Stone and shadow." He picked up a dry branch and examined it. "The hill we're sitting on is really here, but our perception holds it in place. Imposes order, as Brooking might say. Or Emerson. That branch is only partly wood. It's also an idea.

"Space is subject to the same laws. It's influenced by the observer."

"How does that connect your backdoor with this place?"

"Distance is a function of the mind," he said, as if that explained it.

I looked at him. Was he amusing himself at my expense? "Are you trying to say there's no such thing as space? That it doesn't really exist?"

"Of course not, George. What I am saying is that the intelligent observer has a much larger role in ordering things than we ever before realized. We used to think of ourselves as standing outside somewhere inspecting a huge machine. Now we know that we're part of the machine. No: more than that, we're part of the fuel." He glanced at the sky. Most of the stars had begun to fade in the growing light of the rising disk. "It's distance that is an illusion, a convention, a linear measurement of a quality whose reality *we* establish. Listen, I know that's not easy to understand. It's hard to explain. But it works. You're here."

"Yes, I'm here. But where? In a place where they perform classical drama? What kind of sense does *that* make?"

"I don't know. I wanted you to tell me."

Well, I damned sure had no idea, and I told him so. Having settled that, I got up to go, but he wasn't anxious to leave. It occurred to me that he was ill, and trying to conceal the fact. Curious: Klein could stroll between the galaxies, but he couldn't do a thing about his high blood pressure.

"Can you go *anywhere*?" I asked.

"Hell, I can't even go into Chicago." He laughed. "It's true. I have to take the train down to the Institute. I'm jammed in three mornings a week with all those commuters." His chin had sunk onto his knees, and he seemed to be losing substance inside the robe. "The truth is, I can only come out here. I have access to about a dozen star systems, all in this neighborhood. I don't know why that should be."

We sat awhile. Here and there, below us, lights moved through the gloom. He slapped at a flying insect. We were on a long diamond-shaped island at the confluence of two broad rivers, one of which was far too rough for navigation. A half-dozen shallow draft vessels were anchored in a small wharf-lined harbor. Several barges floated alongside short piers, piled high with casks and crates. Away from the waterfront area were clusters of small homes of a distinctly Bavarian flavor. These were interspersed with illuminated shops and wide courtyards. "Maybe," I said, "the way you get around explains this. *Antigone*, I mean."

"How's that?"

"Maybe this playwright, what's his name, Tyr, understood about traveling the way you do. Maybe he took his vacations in Athens. You know, go to the theater, see the Olympics. Could he have had the technology? Do you have to have a storeroom in Glen Ellyn?"

Klein grinned. "Not a storeroom. Just something to use as a funnel." He pulled his robe tightly around himself as protection against the gathering chill. "Aulis Tyr," he continued, "lived in a place called Colosia. It's halfway round the planet and, if my sources are correct, it's only ruins now. But it was the seedbed of this world's ideas about art, ethics, government, philosophy. They had no real technology in the sense that we understand the term. Oh, some primitive stuff, maybe: they had the harrow, and some timepieces. They understood about pendulums. And they had the printing press. In fact, I don't think Melchior has much more than that now. But no technology is needed to travel. All that's necessary is a grasp of the true nature of matter, energy, and timespace." His eyes drifted shut and he shook his head slightly. "But it's difficult to see how anyone, operating without the insights provided by quantum mechanics, could get behind the misperceptions our senses force on us, and arrive at the true state of affairs. But how else could it have happened? Of course," he said doubtfully, "the chances of a traveler from ancient Colosia finding Earth would be remote. To say the least."

I watched a lamplighter working his way through the waterfront area. "Not necessarily," I said. "He might have the same sort of limitation you do: you come here; he goes there." But no: that made no sense either. "If somebody had developed that kind of technique, these people wouldn't be living in little pre-Industrial Revolution villages."

"Help me up," said Klein. He stretched out a hand. A thin sheen of perspiration dampened his neck, despite the coolness of the evening. "How do you lose the secret of the ages?" he asked rhetorically. "The answer is that anyone smart enough to figure it out knows too

much about human nature—or the nature of intelligent creatures—
to let them get their hands on it. Or even to let them know it's there."

"But *you* have."

"I've told no one but you, George. And you don't know enough
to make it work."

Now, he was at no risk trusting *me*, but he had issued a challenge.
I made a mental note to have him take me through again, and watch
closely how he did it. "Why do you think this technique would be so
dangerous?"

"Why?" His jaw tightened. "Don't you read anything except poetry?" He held the devil's mask in one hand and rotated it. "Because," he grinned, "the bedrooms of the universe would lie open.
Have you considered what you and I could do were we not so high-
principled? There'd be no defense, anywhere, against any who possessed the knowledge. Or at least there wouldn't be once we got the
damned thing working properly. And while we're on the subject, has
it occurred to you that we may not be the first visitors from Earth?
Maybe one of your Greeks figured it all out, showed up here, and
left some of his reading material in Colosia when he went home."

The huge satellite flooded the park with somber light.

"What the hell kind of moon is that?" I asked. It was banded,
like Jupiter. A pale blue disk floated just above its horizon.

"That's Encubis," said Klein. "We're the moon." We started
down the hill. "It's a gas giant. I don't know how big it is, but we're
a little too close. This world has the highest tides you've ever seen,
and the heaviest weather." He squinted at the thing. "The blue spot
is a storm, like the one on Jupiter. Been there as long as people can
remember. It's a wonder everyone here isn't a religious fanatic."

Two of the creatures approached along the base of the hill. Young
couple, I thought, judging by the fluidity of their movements, and the
proximity they kept. We could smell the river in the night air.

We strolled down toward the trees without saying much, and
after a time he looked at me curiously. "What's so funny?"

I hadn't realized my feelings showed. "We have an immortal with
feet of clay."

"You're thinking of Aulis Tyr?"

I nodded. He withdrew into a pensive mood until we were back
in the storeroom. Then he closed the storm door and smiled. "The
plagiarist," he said, "could just as easily be Sophocles."

Klein provided me with a local copy of the *Antigone*, which is to
say that it was a translation from the ancient Colosian into the language

currently spoken in that part of Melchior which we'd visited. It was contained in a collection of eight plays by three major dramatists of the period. He added a dictionary and a grammar, and I set myself to acquiring some degree of facility, and did so within a few weeks.

There were substantial differences between Tyr's *Antigone* and Sophocles' masterpiece, which, naturally, I had read in the original Greek. Nevertheless, tone and nuance, character and plot, were similar beyond any possibility of coincidence.

Two other plays in the collection were credited to Tyr. They were works of subtle power, both (I felt) comparable with the *Antigone*. I recognized neither; yet I felt I knew the characters.

The hero of one is a young warrior at the head of a besieging army, who falls in love with the daughter of the enemy king. In an effort to stop the war, he allows himself to be lured into a chapel rendezvous during which he is ambushed and murdered by the woman's archer brother.

In the second drama, an old king apparently given to habitual dissembling meets a long-lost son. Neither recognizes the other, and their natural propensity for deceit (the son is not unlike the father) exacerbates the misunderstanding until, ultimately, they meet in combat by the sea. And the son is triumphant:

> He found on the shore
> The spine of a sea beast
> And turned to face the hero.

Death from the sea, and a warrior stricken in a chapel. Odysseus on the beach, and Achilles. Only seven of Sophocles' plays have survived, of more than a hundred known to have existed. Did I possess two more?

I read through each again and again, absorbed in the thrust and delicacy of the language. I was at the time working on an analysis of irregular verbs in Middle English, and the contrast between Tyr's iambs, drenched in sunlight and desire, and my own heavy-footed prose, was painfully evident. It is a terrible thing to have just enough talent to recognize one's mediocrity.

I had then, as I have now, a quarter-million word novel packed away in three stationery boxes pushed onto a back shelf in the walk-in closet in my bedroom. It was tattered, the edges frayed by frequent mailings, the paper brittle and dry. My father lives in those pages, smoldering, silent, alcoholic; and Charlotte Endicott, whose bright green eyes have not yet faded from my nights. And Kip Williams, who played third base with ferocity, rescued two children from a fire, and died in the war.

A quarter-million words, filled with the passions, and braced with the sensibilities, of a young lifetime. I called it *The Trees of Avignon*. And I knew it was deadly dull.

All the years of writing commentary on Byron and Mark Twain, on Virgil and Yeats, had left me with too exquisite a taste not to recognize my own work for what it was. What would I not have given to possess the genius of the creator of *Oedipus*?

And that, I knew, was precisely the temptation to which Aulis Tyr had succumbed. "There's just no question," I told Harvey. "Somehow there was a connection, he saw his opportunity. And he took it. He *lifted* the *Antigone*."

Klein stared into a rum and coke. We were seated before a wide fireplace in his richly paneled study. Yes: a creature from a world with a taste for literature had recognized a chance to *be* Sophocles. And had made it count. "Maybe," mused Klein. "But I think we should withhold our opinion as to who stole what until all the evidence is in."

I drained my glass. "Are you suggesting we go back?"

"We have a mystery, George." The fire was dying, and he stared solemnly into the embers. "Would you like," he asked, "to meet my contact on Melchior?"

"Your contact? You mean you've talked to one of them?"

"Where do you think I get my information? Of course I talked to one of them." He angled his watch to read it. "It's getting dark there now. Sun's down, and it'll be a little while before Encubus comes up."

We put on our robes and masks, strolled into the storeroom, past stacks of paneling and trim. He was, at the time, repairing his porch. He opened a gray fuse box, extracted a tattered notebook from a shelf lined with garden implements, and punched a few buttons. Satisfied, he closed the cabinet, and opened the back door.

The glade was gone. We were looking at an avenue filled with shops. Benches and twisted white trees and dark green lamp posts lined a blue shale walkway. It was dark, and candles glittered in the streetlamps and in the store windows. Three or four of the creatures that had been in attendance at the *Antigone* were lounging around a bench and outdoor table half a block away. They looked at us curiously, but continued their conversation. The night sky was overcast: it would remain gloomy even after the "moon" rose.

Klein took a moment to get his bearings, and started off briskly. "Try not to let anyone get a good look at you," he said.

"Where are we going?"

"To a bookdealer."

"A *book*dealer?"

"I needed information about this world. I tried to steal some books, and he caught me at it. His name's Chaser."

"Does he know what you *really* look like?"

"Oh, yes. There was no way I could keep it from him."

"How did he react?" I knew what would have happened if one of *these* horned monstrosities had shown up in the Loop.

The shells crunched underfoot. "I wanted history books, and a couple of general reference works. I saw some likely prospects in the window of his shop, and tried to appropriate them. He caught me.

"It was a bad moment, George. He grabbed me by the shoulder. I jumped a foot, my mask fell off, and Chaser shrieked. He backed into a stand of books, and everything went over in a pile." Klein chuckled. "I mean, what you have is a full-size devil, horns, cloven hoofs, and sharp white teeth, scared as hell, getting conked by a bookcase. I started laughing: I couldn't help myself. I mean, if Old Nick has anything, it's supposed to be dignity.

"But he was between me and the door. I'd gone down too, and I was looking at his fangs and ruby eyes through a crosshatch of table legs and struts."

"What did you do?"

"I said hello. And he laughed. It started slow, and it was part snort and part belch, but I know a belly laugh when I hear one."

We'd veered off the walkway, pushed through some ferns, and entered a cul-de-sac. It was a circular courtyard, overgrown with heavy foliage, and ringed with cheerful lamps. The bookstore lay directly opposite the entrance to the courtyard: it was a modest wood frame building, with volumes stacked against a half-dozen windows on two floors. Outside, more books were bunched on tables, under neat hand-lettered signs identifying their category. "The bargain basement," Harvey remarked.

When the shop had emptied, we went inside. I was too nervous to examine the packed shelves, despite my curiosity. We passed into an interior room, and came face to face with one of the creatures.

It did indeed resemble Old Nick.

The thing sat, or crouched, at a polished stone desk. One horn was broken, its fur was drab, and it wore heavy steel-rimmed glasses.

Its eyes were not quite as Klein had described them; rather, they were of a red-flecked gray hue, yet not at all menacing. They rested on us momentarily; its lips rolled back slowly to reveal more of those prominent white fangs. "Klein," it said, rising, "you shouldn't go walking about like that. Your mask is inadequate; it will attract attention."

Its almost debonair acceptance of our presence startled me. Harvey laughed. "It's good to see you again, Chaser." He took off his mask, and they shook hands warmly.

"What's wrong with the mask?" I asked, worried that I might be exposed in the street.

"Chaser thinks it has an idiot expression."

I removed it and took a good look. It would fool nobody in decent light, up close. But it didn't seem *bad*. Off the face and away from the eyes, it had no expression at all. "He must mean *you*, Harvey; not the mask."

Chaser nodded approval, clapped my shoulder, gave us both another look at his dental work. Then he got up, and left the room. I heard bolts being thrown.

"Where did he learn to speak English?"

"We've spent a lot of time together," said Harvey. "And he seems to have a knack for languages."

He returned with a decanter and three glasses.

The drink was alcoholic, a warm wine that suggested macadamia nuts. Chaser raised the glass that Harvey had filled for him, and studied Klein with a Mephisthophelian intensity that might have been genuine affection. "It's been a while, Harvey," he said. "I was beginning to think you'd abandoned us." He tended to stretch vowels, and to roll across consonants with guttural vigor.

Klein introduced me. Chaser grunted his pleasure, and clasped my wrist, old-Roman style, with a large claw. The talons clicked as they were retracted. He had six digits, including an opposable thumb. His skin was leathery and hairless. I had expected it to feel reptilian, but it was as warm as a human hand.

"I was unsure whether to believe Harvey," he said, "when he told me there were others like himself." He held his glass in my direction, said, "To humans," and downed his drink.

"We saw *Antigone* several weeks ago," said Klein, giving it its Colosian title.

"And did you like it?"

"Yes," I said. "It was a brilliant production."

"I saw it myself on closing night." Chaser grew thoughtful. "The staging was a bit wooden for my taste. And I'm not particularly im-pressed by these modern adaptations—"

While he talked, I was struck by the familiarity of his gestures, and his opinions. I frowned at Klein: an alien culture is supposed to be *alien*, different values, incomprehensible logic, and all that. Chaser emphasized points by jabbing the air with his index finger, cupped his chin in one palm while he pondered questions of literary merit, and sighed helplessly in the face of views which he considered irre-deemably wrongheaded.

Klein joined in with energy. They took issue with one another, agreed with enthusiasm, and altogether downed too much wine. Dur-ing a lull, he raised an eyebrow, and said, "I have yet to find *anyone* who would not have appreciated *Antigone*."

Chaser rumbled his agreement.

"Chaser," Klein continued, "tell me about Aulis Tyr."

The bookdealer's eyes flashed. "He is the first of playwrights, George. His work has been equaled by one or two, but never sur-passed. Even now, after so many centuries, he remains extremely popular. The summer theaters here and at Qas Anaba each do one of his plays every year. People come from quite far away to see the performances."

"Your theater group," I said, "is quite accomplished."

"Thank you."

"Of course they would have to be to handle drama at that level."

"I agree," he said. "Tyr demands much of an actor. And a di-rector. But the result, when it is done properly, is very moving."

From a shelf in an adjoining room, he produced two large leather volumes. "Unfortunately, we've lost most of his work. Two centuries after his death, the Colosians were overrun by barbarians. The idiots burned everything . . ." He passed me the books and turned to Klein: "Do you have a dramatist of similar stature?"

Harvey needed no thought for that one. "Shakespeare," he said, almost offhandedly. That's what happens when you ask a physicist a significant question.

"Shakespeare." Chaser tasted the name, and shrugged. Then he turned to me. "George, you may keep the books."

I was overwhelmed with pleasure. "Thank you," I said.

"And whatever else you can carry." His eyes narrowed. "But I know you will wish to repay me in kind."

"How?"

"I would like very much to read your Shakespeare. And I know you would find considerable pleasure in giving so fine a gift."

"Deal," I said. And, when he did not appear to understand, I told him I would consider it a pleasure. "Maybe I'll throw in Neil Simon while I'm at it."

Chaser became interested. "Who is Neil Simon? Another Shakespeare?"

"Oh, yes," said Klein. I couldn't tell whether he was serious.

"Excellent." Chaser rubbed his hands; his tongue flicked across his lips. It was forked.

We went through several bottles while Chaser, with our encouragement, talked about the Colosians. We drank to Aulis Tyr and Will Shakespeare and Neil Simon. And, along toward midnight, the bookseller's eyes misted. "Let us," he said, "raise a glass to Alika."

We drank. "Who," I asked, "is Alika?"

Chaser looked at me with barely concealed astonishment. "I wouldn't have believed, George, that any country could be so remote— But maybe I've drunk too much. It's not likely you would know her, if you did not know Tyr. She was also a Colosian, a contemporary of his, and, according to tradition, his lover."

"As good a reason as any to remember the young lady," muttered Klein, who had become entangled in his robe.

"No," said Chaser, "you do not understand. Alika was the first to use prose as an art form. She invented the personal essay."

"I'm confused," I said. "I was under the impression that Colosia was one of your early cultures."

"That is correct."

"Interesting. At home, prose developed quite late. We may have to rethink a few things."

"These are people who love books," observed Klein. He was wearing a satisfied, but vacuous, grin. "They have a passion for all the literary forms. Maybe it explains why their sciences never got off the ground."

Chaser sniffed, but otherwise ignored the remark. "That was also the age," he said with cool condescension, "of Sesily Endine—" He paused to allow us to respond. When we did not, he added, significantly, "—the first, and arguably our finest, novelist."

The two Tyr volumes were expensive editions, bound in tooled leather, with several woodcuts in each. Chase argued good-naturedly with Klein about the state of Melchior's science while I paged through them. There was a portrait of the great dramatist himself, in three-quarter profile. It was difficult to distinguish among these creatures: one looked pretty much like another. Consequently I could detect no trace of extraordinary ability in that vaguely demonic visage.

There was also a schema for a Colosian theater, which was more or less in the round, and not at all like the one in the park; some lines of original text; and a broken column with an inscription. Everything was in the original language, which of course I could not read.

"His memorial," Chaser said, when I asked about the column. "It's still there, but so are the barbarians. You would need an armed party to visit it."

"What does the inscription say?" I asked.

The bookseller lifted himself into a worn leather chair. "The Colosians," he said, "were alone in a world of savages: slave empires north and south, fierce mounted tribesmen on their flank. They were under constant military pressure, and had been defending their borders for three generations when, for a time, their enemies finally succeeded in resolving their own quarrels, and combined forces. The barbarians attacked by sea, landing a substantial army in the heart of Colosian territory, and struck toward the capital. The defenders fought a series of brilliant delaying actions, climaxed by a magnificent effort at Ananai known as the Battle on the Beach." Chaser paused for dramatic effect. "For six hours the issue was in doubt. But in the end, the Colosian navy sealed the area off, and the invaders were pushed into the sea. It brought security for almost a century. Tyr was a foot soldier in that battle."

"Wait," I said, suddenly chilled. "The inscription: it is Tyr's gravestone."

"Why, yes, that's correct."

"And it says nothing of his reputation as a dramatist. It says only that he fought at Ananai, with the Colosians."

Chaser stared at me. "You've heard the story before? They felt it was the highest honor they could bestow."

"Yes," I said. "I've heard the story before."

When we were back in the storeroom, Klein asked me to explain. Each of us was somewhat wobbly by then, and I led the way into the kitchen, and pointed to the coffee pot. While he heated up a fresh batch, I asked him to be patient while I sat down with our references, and did some arithmetic. We were on the second pot before I felt sure of my facts.

"Aeschylus," I said. "His tomb carries the same kind of inscription: 'He fought at Marathon with the Athenians.' "

Klein shook his head. "More plagiarism. And we still don't really know who's guilty."

"Yes, we do. On a world full of booklovers, the historians should be fairly accurate. If so, Aeschylus died about the time Tyr was born. *Tyr* is the plagiarist."

"Well," said Klein, "I'm glad your faith has been rewarded. I would have to tell you, though, that I find Tyr by far more admirable."

"You do? *Why?* He steals other people's work."

"So he has a minor character flaw. He also figured out how to travel between galaxies. I'd say that's far more impressive than writing a few plays. Wouldn't you?"

I said goodnight and hurried home through a light rainfall. But I couldn't sleep, and ended the evening on my front porch, listening to the house groan under the force of the wind. Water rattled through the drains.

I wondered whether Tyr had uncovered the secret himself? Or whether he'd stolen that too? I wondered if he'd envied Alika in the way that I envied Klein? Living next door to a genius can be painful. However, it had happened, he'd learned to travel, and had visited Athens, probably during the time of Pericles. He'd seen Sophocles performed. Somehow. Maybe he'd worn a disguise, as we had. Maybe he'd hid in a tree. Hell, if he could cross intergalactic space, maybe he could make himself invisible. The details didn't matter.

What *did* matter was that he'd returned to Colosia with a collection of plays (and an admiration for Aeschylus' tomb), selected one, and released it as his own. And of course, he would have been present on the night of the first performance. My God, how he must have savored *that* evening. I wondered which it had been. *Oedipus? Electra?* Do you start with a blockbuster? Or work up to it gradually? I tried to imagine how it would feel to sit in the audience, recognized as the living creator of a timeless masterpiece, watching it play the first time, and knowing, really *knowing*, the significance of the moment.

I returned with Klein to Melchior one more time, to deliver an *Oxford Shakespeare*, a *Webster's Unabridged*, and my own translation of *Lear* into Chaser's language. The bookdealer could not conceal his joy. He pounded my back, pumped my hand, poured wine, and gave me three of Endine's novels, some poetry, and a collection of the surviving essays of Alika. We talked and drank, and late in the evening Klein grew thoughtful, and rotated his drink in the light. "In their essence," he said, "rational cultures are going to turn out to be very much alike. There will be trivial differences in our ceremonies, in the way that we conduct business, or in our views on clothing and entertainment. But in the qualities that define civilization, we will agree. The proprietors of secondhand bookstores," and his eyes locked with Chaser's, "will be found to be everywhere the same."

Two months later, Klein was dead. He was stricken in the middle of the night, and died in an ambulance. I was, at the time, lecturing on Horace at the University of North Dakota. No one informed me.

When I got home, ten days later, the storeroom had been taken down. I offered my condolences to his daughter, and inquired as diplomatically as I could what care had been taken to preserve his papers. At her father's direction, she said, they'd been gathered and burnt the day after the funeral. She was mystified at the request, and also at his direction that the storeroom be demolished. She cried a little, and I thought about the bedrooms of the universe, and walked around to the rear of Klein's house and looked at the pile of debris, which had not yet been hauled away. After making the discovery of the ages, he'd elected to let the credit slide, and had gone silently to his grave.

And I? I was left with some newly discovered Sophoclean tragedies and some alien masterpieces, none of which I could account for.

I tried to lose myself in my work, but my classes were tedious, and I grew weary of the long struggles with semiliterate undergraduates.

I read extensively from Chaser's books: Endine's dark novels were Dostoievskian in scope and character. They left me drained, and depressed me even more.

I was glad to retreat from those bleak narratives to Alika. She must have lived near a coastline: the roar of the tide is somehow present throughout her work. One has a sense of the author alone among rocks and breakers and stranded sea creatures. But her vitality and her laughter infect the reader: it is impossible to read her and not suspect that she is somewhere still alive. She reduces the cosmos to a human scale: it is a thing like an old shell found on a beach, that she turns and examines in her hands.

Her essays are filled with spirited wit, and an unbending optimism, a sense that if everything ends in an endless night, there is meantime starlight, good wine, good books, good friends.

No wonder Tyr loved her.

And there came, finally, a snowswept evening when I confronted my obligation to share her with the world. But how to do it? What explanation could I possibly give?

I don't argue that the course I eventually took was the correct one, but I did not know of an alternative, nor can I conceive of one now. I translated one of her more ethereal efforts, a treatise on a neglected architectural design, which shaded subtly into an unbearably poignant rumination on the nature of time.

And I put my own name on it.

It appeared in the April issue of *Greenstreet's*. I felt guilty about it, of course. There was a delicate moral problem involved. But I felt that compromising myself was not too great a sacrifice to give these magnificent essays to the world. There was, of course, little immediate response. But the editors were pleased, and my colleagues offered their congratulations. *Best thing you've done, George.* (I didn't miss the envy in some of their kudos.)

And I: I knew that George Thorne's name would one day live alongside those of Montaigne and Lamb and Mark Twain. It was exhilarating.

My second effort was "Sea Star," which has since become one of the most loved of the entire series. It was the first of the "Coastal" pieces.

I rationed the essays carefully, publishing only three or four annually. They gradually drew favorable critical attention. The *Washington Post* described me as a new Loren Eiseley. The *New York Times* thought the work *brilliant*. Not wishing to push my luck, I claimed writer's block and took a two-year hiatus. But I'd pretty well worked my way through Alika, and I'd begun wondering whether I didn't owe the world a few great novels too.

At about the same time, the *Venture* came back from Lalande 8760, with the electrifying news that it had found an extrasolar civilization. It carried a cargo of photos, artifacts, and tapes, detailed studies of the inhabitants, copies of their histories and literary and philosophical works. Lalande is only eight light-years from Earth. In the neighborhood, as Klein would have said.

Maybe I should not have been surprised. But it had not occurred to me that Athens might have been only a single stop in Tyr's itinerary. Or that he might not have traveled alone.

The *Venture* brought back three novels that, in translation, I recognized as the work of Sesily Endine. On that score, there could be no doubt. At first I was puzzled how such a thing could be. But I think I know: Tyr and Endine traveled together. They went to Athens, and to Lalande, and probably to everywhere else they could reach. And if Tyr yearned to be a playwright, Endine was interested in the novel.

Fortunately, the Lalande mission came back before I'd used any of the novels myself. Now I have a good idea why Chaser was so anxious to have the Shakespearean collection. Chaser's *Hamlet*: it should play well in the theater in the park, and eventually around his world.

But that's not what worries me. Sometimes, in the deepest hours of the night, I think about Alika, and I cannot make myself believe that the two men would not have taken her along.

I wonder who actually wrote the elegant essays that now bear my name? Four more expeditions are due back over the next three years, and I expect I will soon have the exact coordinates of the immortal seacoast from which the great essayist stood toe to toe with the universe. And smiled.

BLACK TO MOVE

Maybe it's just my imagination, but I'm worried.

The roast beef has no taste, and I'm guzzling my coffee. I'm sitting here watching Turner and Pappas working on the little brick house across the avenue with their handpicks. Jenson and McCarthy are standing over near the lander, arguing about something. And Julie Bremmer is about a block away drawing sketches of the blue towers. Everything is exactly as it was yesterday.

Except me.

In about two hours, I will talk to the Captain. I will try to warn him. Odd, but this is the only place in the city where people seem able to speak in normal tones. Elsewhere, voices are hushed. Subdued. It's like being in a church at midnight. I guess it's the fountain, with its silvery spray drifting back through the late afternoon sun, windblown, cool. The park glades are a refuge against the wide, still avenues and the empty windows. Leaves and grass are a bright gold, but otherwise the vegetation is of a generally familiar cast. Through long, graceful branches, the blue towers glitter in the sunlight.

There is perhaps no sound quite so soothing as the slap of water on stone. (Coulter got the fountain working yesterday, using a generator from the lander.) Listening, seated on one of the benches at the fountain's edge, I can feel how close we are, the builders of this colossal city and I. And that thought is no comfort.

It's been a long, dusty, rockbound road from Earth to this park. The old hunt for extraterrestrial intelligence has taken us across a thousand sandy worlds in a quest that became, in time, a search for a blade of grass.

I will remember all my life standing on a beach under red Capella, watching the waves come in. Sky and sea were crystal blue; no gull wheeled through the still air; no strand of green boiled in the surf. It was a beach without a shell.

But here, west of Centauri, after almost two centuries, we have a living world! We looked down, unbelieving, at forests and jungles, and dipped our scoops into a crowded sea. The perpetual bridge game broke up.

On the second day, we saw the City.

A glittering sundisk, it lay in the southern temperate zone, between a mountain chain and the sea. With it came our first mystery: the City was alone. No other habitation existed anywhere on the planet. On the fourth day, Olzsewski gave his opinion that the City was deserted.

We went down and looked.

The City looked remarkably human, and might almost have been a modern terrestrial metropolis. But its inhabitants had put their cars in their garages, locked their homes, and gone for a walk.

Mark Conover, riding overhead in the *Chicago*, speculated that the builders were not native to this world.

They were jointed bipeds, somewhat larger than we are. We can sit in their chairs and those of us who are tall enough to be able to see through their windshields can drive their cars. Our sense of the place was that they'd left the day before we came.

It's a city of domes and minarets. The homes are spacious, with courtyards and gardens, now run to weed. And they were fond of games and sports. We found gymnasiums and parks and pools everywhere. There was a magnificent oceanfront stadium, and every private home seemed filled with playing cards and dice and geometrical puzzles and 81-square checkerboards.

They had apparently not discovered photography; nor, as far as we could determine, were they given to the plastic arts. There were no statues. Even the fountain lacked the usual boys on dolphins or winged women. It was instead a study in wet geometry, a complex of leaning slabs, balanced spheres, and odd-angled pyramids.

Consequently, we'd been there quite a while before we found out what the inhabitants looked like. *That* happened when we walked into a small home on the north side, and found some charcoal etchings.

Cats, someone said.

Maybe. The following day we came across an art museum and found several hundred watercolors, oils, tapestries, crystals, and so on.

They *are* felines, without doubt, but the eyes are chilling. The creatures in the paintings have nevertheless a human dimension. They are bundled against storms; they gaze across plowed fields at sunset;

they smile benevolently (or pompously) out of portraits. In one particularly striking watercolor, four females cower beneath an angry sky. Between heaving clouds, a pair of full moons illuminate the scene.

This world has no satellite.

Virtually everyone crowded into the museum. It was a day of sighs and grunts and exclamations, but it brought us no closer to the central question: where had they gone?

"Just as well they're not here," Turner said, standing in front of the watercolor. "This is the only living world anyone has seen. It's one hell of a valuable piece of real estate. Nice of them to give it to us."

I was at the time standing across the gallery in front of a wall-sized oil. It was done in impressionistic style, reminiscent of Degas: a group of the creatures was gathered about a game of chess. Two were seated at the table, hunched over the pieces in the classic pose of the dedicated player. Several more, half in shadow, watched.

Their expressions were remarkably human. If one allowed for the ears and the teeth, the scene might easily have been a New York coffeehouse.

The table was set under a hanging lamp; its hazy illumination fell squarely on the board.

The game was not actually chess, of course. For one thing, the board had 81 squares. There was no queen. Instead, the king was flanked by a pair of pieces that vaguely resembled shields. Stylized hemispheres at the extremes of the position must have been rooks. (Where else but on the flank would one reasonably place a rook?)

The other pieces, too, were familiar. The left-hand Black bishop had been fianchettoed: a one-square angular move onto the long diagonal, from where it would exercise withering power. All four knights had been moved, and their twisted tracks betrayed their identity.

The game was still in its opening stages. White was two pawns up, temporarily. It appeared to be Black's move, and he would, I suspected, seize a White pawn which had strayed deep into what he would consider his queenside.

I stood before that painting, feeling the stirrings of kinship and affection for these people and wondering what immutable laws of psychology, mathematics, and aesthetics ordained the creation of chess in cultures so distant from each other. I wondered whether the game might not prove a rite of passage of some sort.

I was about to leave when I detected a wrongness somewhere in the painting, as if a piece were misplaced, or the kibitzers were surreptitiously watching *me*. Whatever it was, I grew conscious of my breathing.

There was nothing.

I backed away, turned, and hurried out of the building.

I'm a symbologist, with a specialty in linguistics. If we ever do actually find someone out here to talk to, I'm the one who will be expected to say hello. That's an honor, I suppose; but I can't get Captain Cook entirely out of my mind.

By the end of the first week, we had not turned up any written material (and, in fact, still haven't) other than a few undecipherable inscriptions on the sides of buildings. They were even more computerized than we are, and we assumed everything went into the data banks, which we also haven't found. The computers themselves are wrecked. Slagged. So, by the way, is the central power core for the City. Another mystery.

Anyhow, I had little to do, so yesterday I went for a walk in the twilight with Jennifer East, a navigator aboard the *Chicago* and the pilot of the other lander. She's lovely, with bright hazel eyes, and a quick smile. Her long tawny hair was radiant in the setting sun. The atmosphere here has a moderately high oxygen content, which affects her the way some women are affected by martinis. She clung to my arm, and I was breathlessly aware of her long-legged stride.

We might have been walking through the streets of an idealized, mystical Baghdad: the towers were gold and purple in the failing light. Flights of brightly colored birds scattered before us. I half-expected to hear the somber cry of a ram's horn, calling the faithful to prayer.

The avenue is lined with delicate, gray-barked trees. Their broad, filamented leaves sighed in the wind, which was constant off the western mountains. Out at sea, thunder rumbled.

Behind the trees are the empty homes, no two alike, and other structures that we have not yet begun to analyze. Only the towers exceed three stories. The buildings are all beveled and curved; right angles do not exist. I wonder what the psychologists will make of that.

"I wonder how long they've been gone?" she said. Her eyes were luminous with excitement, directed (I'm sorry to say) at the architecture.

That had been a point of considerable debate. Many of the interiors revealed a degree of dust that suggested it could not have been more than a few weeks. But much of the pavement was in a state of disrepair, and on the City's inland side, forest was beginning to push through.

I told her I thought they'd been around quite recently.

"Mark," she said, staying close, "I wonder whether they've really left."

There was nothing you could put in a report, but I agreed that we were transients, that those streets had long run to laughter and song, that they soon would again, and that it would never really be ours.

She squeezed my arm. "It's magnificent."

I envied her; this was her first flight. For most of us, there had been too many broken landscapes, too much desert. "Olzsewski thinks," I said, "that the northern section of the City is almost two thousand years old . . . They'd been here a while."

"And they just packed up and left." She steered us out of the center, angling toward the trees, where I think we both felt less conspicuous.

"It's ironic," I said. "No one would have believed first contact would come like this. They've been here since the time of Constantine, and we miss them by a few weeks. Hard to believe, isn't it?"

She frowned. "You're right. It's *not* believable." She touched one of the trees. "Did you know it's the *second* time?" she asked. I must have looked blank. "Twenty-two years ago the *Berlin* tracked something across the face of Algol and then lost it. Whatever it was, it threw a couple of sharp turns." We walked silently for several minutes, crossed another avenue, and approached the museum. "Algol," she said, "isn't all that far from here."

"UFO stories," I said. "They used to be common."

She shrugged. "It might be that the thing the *Berlin* saw frightened these people off. Or worse."

The museum is wheel-shaped. Heavy, curving panels of tinted glass are ribbed by a polished black stone that is probably marble. The grounds are a wild tangle of weed and shrub anchored by overgrown hedge. A few flowering bushes survive out near the perimeter.

I laughed. "You don't suppose the sun is about to nova, do you?"

She smiled and brushed my cheek with a kiss. Jenny is 23 and a graduate of MIT. "It's going to rain," she said.

We walked past a turret. The air was cool.

"They seem to have taken their time about leaving," I said. "There's no evidence of panic or violence. And most of their personal belongings apparently went with them. Whatever happened, they had time to go home and pack."

She looked uneasily at the sky. Gray clouds were gathering in the west. "Why did they destroy the computers? And the power plant? Doesn't that sound like a retreat before an advancing enemy?"

We stood on the rounded stone steps at the entrance, watching the coming storm. Near the horizon, a finger of lightning touched the ground. It was delicate, like the trees.

And I knew what had disturbed me about the painting.

Jenny doesn't play chess. So when we stood again before the portrait and I explained, she listened dutifully, and then tried to reassure me. I couldn't blame her.

I have an appointment to meet the Captain in the gallery after dinner. He doesn't play chess either. Like all good captains down through the ages, he is a man of courage and hardheaded common sense, so he will also try to reassure me.

Maybe I'm wrong. I hope so.

But the position in that game: Black is playing the Benko Gambit. It's different in detail, of course; the game is different. But Black is about to clear a lane for the queenside rook. One bishop, at the opposite end of the board, is astride the long diagonal, where its terrible power will combine with that of the rook. And White, after the next move or two, when that advanced pawn comes off, will be desperately exposed.

It's the most advanced of the gambits for Black, still feared after three hundred years—

And I keep thinking: the inhabitants of the City were surely aware of this world's value. More, they are competitors. They would assume that we would want to take it from them.

"But we wouldn't," Jenny had argued.

"Are you sure? Anyhow, it doesn't matter. The only thing that *does* matter is what they believe. And they would expect us to act as *they* would.

"Now, if they knew in advance that we were coming—"

"The *Berlin* sighting—"

"That would have been an accident. They would not want to alarm us. But they might have concluded we were coming. So they withdraw, and give us the world. And, with it, an enigma." Rain had begun sliding down the tinted glass. "They're playing the Benko."

"You mean they might come back here in force and attack?"

She was aghast, not at the possibility, which she dismissed; but at the direction my mind had taken.

"No," I said. "Not us. The Benko isn't designed to recover a lost pawn." I could not look away from the painting. Did I detect a gleam of arrogance in Black's eyes? "No. It doesn't fool around with pawns. The idea is to launch a strike into the heart of the enemy position."

"Earth?" She smiled weakly. "They wouldn't even know where Earth is."

I didn't ask whether she thought we might not go home alone.

One more thing about the painting: there's a shading of light, a chiaroscuro, in the eyes of the onlookers. It's the joy of battle.

I'm scared.

THE FORT MOXIE BRANCH

A few minutes into the blackout, the window in the single dormer at the top of Will Potter's house began to glow. I watched it from across Route 11, through a screen of box elders, and through the snow which had been falling all afternoon and was now getting heavier. It was smeary and insubstantial, not the way a bedroom light would look, but as though something luminous floated in the dark interior.

Will Potter was dead. We'd put him in the graveyard on the other side of the expressway three years before. The property had lain empty since, a two-story frame dating from about the turn of the century.

The town had gone quiet with the blackout. Somewhere a dog barked, and a garage door banged down. Ed Kiernan's station wagon rumbled past, headed out toward Cavalier. The streetlights were out, as was the traffic signal down at Twelfth.

As far as I was concerned, the power could have stayed off.

It was trash night. I was hauling out cartons filled with copies of *Independence Square*, and I was on my way down the outside staircase when everything went dark.

The really odd thing about the light over at Potter's was that it seemed to be spreading. It had crept outside: the dormer began to burn with a steady, cold, blue-white flame. It flowed gradually down the slope of the roof, slipped over the drainpipe, and turned the corner of the porch. Just barely, in the illumination, I could make out the skewed screens and broken stone steps.

It would have taken something unusual to get my attention that night. I was piling the boxes atop one another, and some of the books had spilled into the street: my name glittered on the bindings. It was a big piece of my life. Five years and a quarter million words and, in the end, most of my life's savings to get it printed. It had been painful, and I was glad to be rid of it.

So I was standing on the curb, feeling very sorry for myself while snow whispered out of a sagging sky.

The Tastee-Freez, Hal's Lumber, the Amoco at the corner of Nineteenth and Bannister, were all dark and silent. Toward the center of town, blinkers and headlights misted in the storm.

It was a still, somehow motionless, night. The flakes were blue in the pale glow surrounding the house. They fell onto the gabled roof and spilled gently off the back.

Cass Taylor's station wagon plowed past, headed out of town. He waved.

I barely noticed: the back end of Potter's house had begun to balloon out. I watched it, fascinated, knowing it to be an illusion, yet still half-expecting it to explode.

The house began to change in other ways.

Roof and corner lines wavered. New walls dropped into place. The dormer suddenly ascended, and the top of the house with it. A third floor, complete with lighted windows and a garret, appeared out of the snow. (In one of the illuminated rooms, someone moved.)

Parapets rose, and an oculus formed in the center of the garret. A bay window pushed out of the lower level, near the front. An arch and portico replaced the porch. Spruce trees materialized, and Potter's old post light, which had never worked, blinked on.

The box elders were bleak and stark in the foreground.

I stood, worrying about my eyesight, holding on to a carton, feeling the snow against my face and throat. Nothing moved on Route 11.

I was still standing there when the power returned: the streetlights, the electric sign over Hal's office, the security lights at the Amoco, gunshots from a TV, the sudden inexplicable rasp of an electric drill. And, at the same moment, the apparition clicked off.

I could have gone to bed. I could have hauled out the rest of those goddamned books, attributed everything to my imagination, and gone to bed. I'm glad I didn't.

The snow cover in Potter's backyard was undisturbed. It was more than a foot deep beneath the half-inch or so that had fallen that day. I struggled through it to find the key he'd always kept wedged beneath a loose hasp near the cellar stairs.

I used it to let myself in through the storage room at the rear of the house. And I should admit that I had a bad moment when the door shut behind me, and I stood among the rakes and shovels and boxes of nails. Too many late TV movies. Too much Stephen King.

I'd been here before. Years earlier, when I'd thought that teaching would support me until I was able to earn a living as a novelist, I'd picked up some extra money by tutoring Potter's boys. But that was a long time ago.

I'd brought a flashlight with me. I turned it on, and pushed through into the kitchen. It was warmer in there, but that was to be expected. Potter's heirs were still trying to sell the place, and it gets too cold in North Dakota to simply shut off the heat altogether.

Cabinets were open and bare; the range had been disconnected from its gas mooring and dragged into the center of the room. A church calendar hung behind a door. It displayed March 1986: the month of Potter's death.

In the dining room, a battered table and three wooden chairs were pushed against one wall. A couple of boxes lay in a corner.

With a bang, the heater came on.

I was startled. A fan cut in, and warm air rushed across my ankles.

I took a deep breath and played the beam toward the living room. I was thinking how different a house looks without its furnishings, how utterly strange and unfamiliar, when I realized I wasn't alone. Whether it was a movement outside the circle of light, or a sudden indrawn breath, or the creak of a board, I couldn't have said. But I *knew.* "Who's there?" I asked. The words hung in the dark.

"Mr. Wickham?" It was a woman.

"Hello," I said. "I, uh, I saw lights and thought—"

"Of course," she said. She was standing back near the kitchen, silhouetted against outside light. I wondered how she could have got there. "You were correct to be concerned. But it's quite all right." She was somewhat on the gray side of middle age, attractive, well-pressed, the sort you would expect to encounter at a bridge party. Her eyes, which were on a level with mine, watched me with good humor. "My name is Coela." She extended her right hand. Gold bracelets clinked.

"I'm happy to meet you," I said, trying to look as though nothing unusual had occurred. "How did you know my name?"

She touched my hand, the one holding the flashlight, and pushed it gently aside so she could pass. "Please follow me," she said. "Be careful. Don't fall over anything."

We climbed the stairs to the second floor, and went into the rear bedroom. "Through here," she said, opening a door that should have revealed a closet. Instead, I was looking into a brightly illuminated space that couldn't possibly be there. It was filled with books, paintings, and tapestries, leather furniture, and polished tables. A fireplace crackled cheerfully beneath a portrait of a monk. A piano played softly. Chopin, I thought.

"This room won't fit," I said, rather stupidly. The thick quality of my voice startled me.

"No," she agreed. "We're attached to the property, but we're quite independent." We stepped inside. Carpets were thick underfoot. Where the floors were exposed, they were lustrous parquet. Vaulted windows looked out over Potter's backyard, and Em Pyle's house next door. Coela watched me thoughtfully. "Welcome, Mr. Wickham," she said. Her eyes glittered with pride. "Welcome to the Fort Moxie branch of the John of Singletary Memorial Library."

I looked around for a chair and, finding one near a window, lowered myself into it. The falling snow was dark, as though no illumination from within the glass touched it. "I don't think I understand this," I said.

"I suppose it is something of a shock."

Her amusement was obvious, and sufficiently infectious that I loosened up somewhat. "Are you the librarian?"

She nodded.

"Nobody in Fort Moxie knows you're here. What good is a library no one knows about?"

"That's a valid question," she admitted. "We have a limited membership."

I glanced around. All the books looked like Bibles. They were different sizes and shapes, but all were bound in leather. Furthermore, titles and authors were printed in identical silver script. But I saw nothing in English. The shelves near me were packed with books whose lettering appeared to be Russian. A volume lay open on a table at my right hand. It was in Latin. I picked it up and held it so I could read the title: *Historiae, V-XII.* Tacitus. "Okay," I said. "It *must* be limited. Hardly anybody in Fort Moxie reads Latin or Russian." I held up the Tacitus. "I doubt even Father Cramer could handle this."

Em Pyle, the next door neighbor, had come out onto his front steps. He called his dog, Preach, as he did most nights at this time. There was no response, and he looked up and down Nineteenth Street, into his own backyard, and *right through me.* I couldn't believe he didn't react.

"Coela, who are you exactly? What's going on here?"

She nodded, in the way that people do when they agree that you have a problem. "Perhaps," she said, "you should look around, Mr. Wickham. Then it might be easier to talk."

She retired to a desk, and immersed herself in a sheaf of papers, leaving me to fend for myself.

Beyond the Russian shelves, I found Japanese or Chinese titles. I couldn't tell which. And Arabic. And German. French. Greek. More Oriental.

I found the English titles in the rear. They were divided into American and British sections. Dickens, Cowper, and Shakespeare on one side; Holmes, Dreiser, and Steinbeck on the other.

And almost immediately, the sense of apprehension that had hung over me from the beginning of this business sharpened. I didn't know why. Certainly, the familiar names in a familiar setting should have eased my disquiet.

I picked up Melville's *Agatha* and flipped through the pages. They had the texture of fine rice paper, and the leather binding lent a sense of timelessness to the book. I thought about the cheap cardboard that Crossbow had provided for *Independence Square*. My God, this was the way to get published.

Immediately beside it was *The Complete Works of James McCorbin.* Who the hell was James McCorbin? There were two novels and eight short stories. None of the titles was familiar, and the book contained no biographical information.

In fact, most of the writers were people I'd never heard of. Kemerie Baxter. Wynn Gomez. Michael Kaspar. There was nothing unusual about that, of course. Library shelves are always filled with obscure authors. But the lush binding, and the obvious care expended on these books, changed the rules.

I took down Hemingway's *Watch by Night.* I stared a long time at the title. The prose was vintage Hemingway. The crisp, clear bullet sentences and the factual, journalistic style were unmistakable. Even the setting: Italy, 1944.

Henry James was represented by *Brandenberg.* There was no sign of *The Ambassadors,* or *The Portrait of a Lady,* or *Washington Square.* In fact, there was neither *Moby Dick,* nor *Billy Budd.* Nor *The Sun Also Rises* nor *A Farewell to Arms.* Thoreau wasn't represented at all. I saw no sign of Fenimore Cooper or Mark Twain. (What kind of library had no copy of *Huck Finn?*)

* * *

I carried *Watch by Night* back to the desk where Coela was working. "This is *not* a Hemingway book," I said, lobbing it onto the pile of papers in front of her. She winced. "The rest of them are bogus too. What the hell's going on?"

"I can understand that you might be a little confused, Mr. Wickham," she said, a trifle nervously. "I'm never sure quite how to explain."

"Please try your best," I said.

She frowned. "I'm part of a cultural salvage group. We try to ensure that things of permanent value don't, ah, get lost."

She pushed her chair back, and gazed steadily at me. Somewhere in back, a clock ticked ponderously. "The book you picked up when you first came in was—" she paused, "—mislaid almost two thousand years ago."

"The Tacitus?"

"The *Histories Five Through Twelve*. We also have his *Annals*."

"Who *are* you?"

She shook her head. "A kindred spirit," she said.

"Seriously."

"I'm being quite serious, Mr. Wickham. What you see around you is a treasure of incomparable value that, without our efforts, would no longer exist."

We stared at each other for a few moments. "Are you saying," I asked, "that these are all lost masterpieces by people like Tacitus? That *this*"—I pointed at *Watch by Night*—"is a bona fide Hemingway?"

"Yes," she said.

We faced one another across the desktop. "There's a Melville back there too. And a Thomas Wolfe."

"*Yes.*" Her eyes were bright with pleasure. "*All of them.*"

I took another long look around. Thousands of volumes filled all the shelves, packed tight, reaching to the ceiling. Others were stacked on tables; a few were tossed almost haphazardly on chairs. Half a dozen stood between Trojan horse bookends on Coela's desk.

"It's not possible," I said, finding the air suddenly close and oppressive. "How? How could it happen?"

"Quite easily," she said. "Melville, as a case in point, became discouraged. He was a customs inspector at the time *Agatha* first came to our attention. I went all the way to London, specifically to allow him to examine my baggage on the way back. In 1875, that was no easy journey, I can assure you." She waved off my objection. "Well, that's an exaggeration, of course. I took advantage of the trip to conduct some business with Matthew Arnold and— Well, I'm name-dropping now. Forgive me. But think about having Melville go through your luggage." Her laughter echoed through the room. "I was quite young. Too young to understand his work, really. But I'd read *Moby Dick*, and some of his poetry. If I'd known him then the way I do now, I don't think I could have kept my feet." She bit her lower lip and shook her head, and for a moment I thought she might indeed pass out.

"And he *gave* you the manuscript? Simply because you asked for it?"

"No. Because I knew it for what it was. And he understood why I wanted it."

"And why do you want it? You have buried it here."

She ignored the question.

"You never asked about the library's name."

"The John of—"

"—Singletary—"

"—Memorial. Okay. Who's John of Singletary?"

"That's his portrait, facing the main entrance." It was a large oil of an introspective monk. His hands were buried in dark brown robes, and he was flanked by a scroll and a crucifix. "He was perhaps the most brilliant sociologist who ever lived."

"I never heard of him."

"That's no surprise. His work was eventually ruled profane by his superiors, and either burned or stored away somewhere. We've never been sure. But we were able to obtain copies of most of it." She was out of her seat now, standing with her back to the portrait. "What is significant is that he defined the state toward which he felt the human community should be advancing. He set the parameters and the goals for which the men and women whose works populate this library have been striving: the precise degree of balance between order and freedom; the extent of one's obligation to external authority; the ethical and emotional relationships that should exist between human beings. And so on. Taken in all, he produced a schematic for civilized life, a set of instructions, if you will."

"The human condition," I said.

"How do you mean?"

"He did all this, and no one knows him."

"*We* know him, Mr. Wickham." She paused. I found myself glancing from her to the solemn figure in the portrait. "You asked why we wanted *Agatha*. The answer is that it is lovely, that it is very powerful. We simply will not allow it to be lost."

"But who will ever get to see it *here*? You're talking about a novel that, as far as anyone is concerned, doesn't exist. I have a friend in North Carolina who'd give every nickel he owns to see this book. If it's legitimate."

"We *will* make it available. In time. This library will eventually be yours."

A wave of exhilaration washed over me. "Thank you," I said.

"I'm sorry," she said quickly. "That may have been misleading. I didn't mean right now. And I didn't mean *you*."

"When?"

"When the human race fulfills the requirements of John of Singletary. When you have, in other words, achieved a true global community, all of this will be our gift to you."

A gust of wind rattled the windows.

"That's a considerable way off," I said.

"We must take the long view."

"Easy for you to say. We have a lot of problems. Some of this might be just what we need to get through."

"This was once *yours*, Mr. Wickham. Your people have not always recognized value. We are providing a second chance. I'd expect you to be grateful."

I turned away from her. "Most of this I can't even recognize," I said. "Who's James McCorbin? You've got his *Complete Works* back there with Melville and the others. Who *is* he?"

"A master of the short story. One of your contemporaries, but I'm afraid he writes in a style and with a complexity that will go unappreciated during his lifetime."

"You're telling me he's *too* good to get published?" I was aghast.

"Oh, yes, Mr. Wickham, you live in an exceedingly commercial era. Your editors understand that they cannot sell champagne to beer drinkers. They buy what sells."

"And that's also true of the others? Kemerie Baxter? Gomez? Somebody-or-other Parker?"

"I'm afraid so. It's quite common, in fact. Baxter is an essayist of the first order. Unlike the other two, he has been published, but by a small university press, in an edition that sank quickly out of sight. Gomez has written three exquisite novels, but has since given up, despite our encouragement. Parker is a poet. If you know anything about the markets for poetry, I need say no more."

* * *

We wandered together through the library. She pointed to lost works by Sophocles and Aeschylus, to missing epics of the Homeric cycle, to shelves full of Indian poetry and Roman drama. "On the upper level," she said, raising her eyes to the ceiling, "are the songs and tales of artists whose native tongues had no written form. They have been translated into our own language. In most cases," she added, "we were able to preserve their creators' names.

"And now I have a surprise." We had reached the British section. She took down a book and handed it to me. William Shakespeare. "His *Zenobia*," she said, her voice hushed. "Written at the height of his career."

I was silent for a time. "And why was it never performed?"

"Because it's a savage attack on Elizabeth. Even he might well have lost his head. We have a major epic by Virgil that was withheld for much the same reason. In fact, that's why the Russian section is so large. They've been producing magnificent novels in the tradition of Tolstoy and Dostoyevski for years, but they're far too prudent to offer them for publication."

There were two other Shakespearean plays. "*Adam and Eve* was heretical by the standards of the day," Coela explained. "And here's another that would have raised a few eyebrows." She smiled.

It was *Nisus and Euryalus*. The characters were out of the *Aeneid*. "Homosexual love," she said.

"But he wanted these withheld," I objected. "There's a differ- ence between works that have been lost, and those a writer wishes to destroy. You published these against his will."

"Oh, no, Mr. Wickham. We never do that. To begin with, if Shake- speare had wanted these plays destroyed, he could have handled that detail quite easily. He desired only that they not be published in his lifetime. Everything you see here," she included the entire library with a sweeping, feminine gesture, "was given to us voluntarily. We have very strict regulations on that score. And we do things strictly by the book, Mr. Wickham.

"In some cases, by the way, we perform an additional service. We are able, in a small way, to reassure those great artists who have not been properly recognized in their own lifetimes. I wish you could have seen Melville."

"You could be wrong, you know."

Her nostrils widened slightly. "About what?"

"Maybe books that get lost deserve to be lost."

"Some do." Her tone hardened. "None of those is here. We exercise full editorial judgment."

"We close at midnight," she said, appearing suddenly behind me while I was absorbed in the Wells novel, *Starflight*. I could read the implication in her tone: *Never to open again. Not in Fort Moxie. Not for you.*

I returned Wells and moved quickly along, pulling books from the shelves with some sense of urgency. I glanced through *Mendinhal*, an unfinished epic by Byron, dated 1824, the year of his death. I caught individually brilliant lines, and tried to commit some of them to memory, and proceeded on to Blake, to Fielding, to Chaucer! At a little after eleven, I came across four Conan Doyle stories: "The Adventure of the Grim Footman"; "The Branmoor Club"; "The Jezail Bullet"; "The Sumatran Clipper." My God, what would the Sherlockians of the world not give to have those?

I hurried on with increasing desperation, as though I could somehow gather the contents into myself, and make them available to a waiting world: *God and Country*, by Thomas Wolfe; fresh cartoons by James Thurber, recovered from beneath wallpaper in a vacation home he'd rented in Atlantic City in 1947; plays by Odets and O'Neill; short stories by Nathaniel Hawthorne and Terry Carr. Here was *More Dangerous Visions*. And there Mary Shelley's *Morgan*.

As I whirled through the rice-paper pages, balancing the eerie moonlit lines of A. E. Housman with the calibrated shafts of Mencken, I envied them. Envied them all.

And I was angry.

"You have no right," I said at last, when Coela came to stand by my side, indicating that my time was up.

"No right to withhold all this?" There was a note of sympathy in her voice.

"Not only that," I said. "Who are you to set yourself up to make such judgments? To say what is great and what pedestrian?"

To my surprise, she did not take offense. "I've asked myself that question many times. We do the best we can." We were moving toward the door. "We have quite a lot of experience, you understand."

The lights dimmed. "Why are you *really* doing this? It's not for us, is it?"

"Not exclusively. What your species produces belongs to all." Her smile broadened. "Surely you would not wish to keep your finest creations to yourselves?"

"Your people have access to them now?"

"Oh, yes," she said. "Back home everyone has access. As soon as a new book is cataloged here, it is made available to everybody."

"Except us."

"We will not do everything for you, Mr. Wickham." She drew close, and I could almost feel her heartbeat.

"Do you have any idea what it would mean to our people to recover all this?"

"I'm sorry. For the moment, there's really nothing I can do."

She opened the door for me, the one that led into the back bedroom. I stepped through it. She followed. "Use your flashlight," she said.

We walked through the long hallway, and down the stairs to the living room. She had something to say to me, but seemed strangely reluctant to continue the conversation. And somewhere in the darkness of Will Potter's place, between the magic doorway in the back of the upstairs closet, and the broken stone steps off the porch, I understood! And when we paused on the concrete beside the darkened post light, and turned to face each other, my pulse was pounding. "It's no accident that this place became visible tonight, is it?"

She said nothing.

"Nor that only I saw it. I mean, there wouldn't be a point in putting your universal library in Fort Moxie unless you wanted something. Right?"

"I said this was the Fort Moxie *branch*. The central library is located on Saint Simons Island." The brittleness of the last few moments melted without warning. "But no, you're right, of course."

"You want *Independence Square*, don't you? You want to put my book in there with Thomas Wolfe and Shakespeare and Homer. Right?"

"Yes," she said. "That's right. You've created a powerful psychological drama, Mr. Wickham. You've captured the microcosm of Fort Moxie and produced a portrait of small town America that has captured the imagination of the Board. And, I might add, of our membership. You will be interested, by the way, in knowing that one of your major characters caused the blackout tonight."

"Jack Gilbert," I said. "How'd it happen?"

"Can you guess?"

"An argument with his wife, somehow or other." Gilbert, who had a different name, of course, in *Independence Square*, had a long history of inept philandering.

"Yes. Afterward, he took the pickup and ran it into the streetlight at Eleventh and Foster. Shorted out everything over an area of forty square blocks. It's right out of the book."

"Yes," I said.

"But he'll never know he's in it. Nor will any of the other people you've immortalized. Only you know. And only you would *ever* know, were it not for us." She stood facing me. The snow had stopped, and the clouds had cleared away. The stars were hard and bright in her eyes. "We think it unlikely that you will be recognized in your own lifetime. We could be wrong. We were wrong about Faulkner." Her lips crinkled into a smile. "But it is my honor to invite you to contribute your work to the library."

I froze. It was really happening. Emerson. Hemingway. Wickham. I loved it. And yet, there was something terribly wrong about it all. "Coela," I asked. "Have you ever been refused?"

"Yes," she said cautiously. "Occasionally it happens. We couldn't convince Cather of the value of *Ogden's Bequest*. Charlotte and Emily Brontë both rejected us, to the world's loss. And Tolstoy. Tolstoy had a wonderful novel from his youth which he considered, well, anti-Christian."

"And among the unknowns? Has anyone just walked away?"

"No," she said. "Never. In such a case, the consequences would be especially tragic." Sensing where the conversation was leading, she'd begun to speak in a quicker tempo, at a slightly higher pitch. "A new genius, who would sink into the sea of history, as Byron says, 'without a grave, unknelled, uncoffined, and unknown.' Is that what you are considering?"

"You have *no* right to keep all this to yourself."

She nodded. "I should remind you, Mr. Wickham, that without the intervention of the library, these works would not exist at all."

I stared past her shoulder, down the dark street.

"Are you then," she said at last, drawing the last word out, "refusing?"

"This belongs to *us*," I said. "It is ours. We've produced *everything* back there!"

"I almost anticipated, feared, this kind of response from you. I think it was almost implicit in your book. Will you grant us permission to add *Independence Square* to the library?"

Breathing was hard. "I must regretfully say no."

"I am sorry to hear it. I— You should understand that there will be no second offer."

I said nothing.

"Then I fear we have no further business to transact."

At home, I carried the boxes back up to my living room. After all, if it's that damned good, there has to be a market for it. Somewhere.

And if she's right about rampant commercialism? Well, what the hell.

I pulled one of the copies out, and put it on the shelf, between Walt Whitman and Thomas Wolfe.

Where it belongs.

PROMISES TO KEEP

I received a Christmas card last week from Ed Bender. The illustration was a rendering of the celebrated Christmas Eve telecast from Callisto: a lander stands serenely on a rubble-strewn plain, spilling warm yellow light through its windows. Needle peaks rise behind it, and the rim of a crater curves across the foreground. An enormous belted crescent dominates the sky.

In one window, someone has hung a wreath.

It is a moment preserved, a tableau literally created by Cathie Perth, extracted from her prop bag. Somewhere here, locked away among insurance papers and the deed to the house, is the tape of the original telecast, but I've never played it. In fact, I've seen it only once, on the night of the transmission. But I know the words, Cathie's words, read by Victor Landolfi in his rich baritone, blending the timeless values of the season with the spectral snows of another world. They appear in schoolbooks now, and on marble.

Inside the card, in large, block defiant letters, Bender had printed "SEPTEMBER!" It is a word with which he hopes to conquer a world. Sometimes, at night, when the snow sparkles under the cold stars (the way it did on Callisto), I think about him, and his quest. And I am very afraid.

I can almost see Cathie's footprints on the frozen surface. It was a good time, and I wish there were a way to step into the picture, to toast the holidays once more with Victor Landolfi, to hold on to Cathie Perth (and never let go!), and somehow to save us all. It was the end of innocence, a final meeting place for old friends.

We made the Christmas tape over a period of about five days. Cathie took literally hours of visuals, but Callisto is a place of rock and ice and deadening sameness: there is little to soften the effect of cosmic indifference. Which is why all those shots of towering peaks and tumbled boulders were taken at long range, and in half-light. Things not quite seen, she said, are always charming.

Her biggest problem had been persuading Landolfi to do the voice-over. Victor was tall, lean, ascetic. He was equipped with laser eyes and a huge black mustache. His world was built solely of sub-atomic particles, and driven by electromagnetics. Those who did not share his passions excited his contempt; which meant that he under-stood the utility of Cathie's public relations function at the same time that he deplored the necessity. To participate was to compromise one's integrity. His sense of delicacy, however, prevented his express-ing that view to Cathie; he begged off rather on the press of time, winked apologetically, and stroked his mustache. "Sawyer will read it for you," he said, waving me impatiently into the conversation.

Cathie sneered, and stared irritably out a window (it was the one with the wreath) at Jupiter, heavy in the fragile sky. We knew, by then, that it had a definable surface, that the big planet was a world sea of liquid hydrogen, wrapped around a rocky core. "It must be frustrat-ing," she said, "to know we'll never see it." Her tone was casual, almost frivolous, but Landolfi was not easily baited.

"Do you really think," he asked, with the patience of a superior being (Landolfi had no illusions about his capabilities), "that these little pieces of theater will make any difference? Yes, Catherine, of course it's frustrating. Especially when one realizes that we have the technology to put vehicles down there . . ."

"And scoop out some hydrogen," Cathie added.

He shrugged. "It may happen someday."

"Victor, it never will if we don't sell the Program. This is the last shot. These ships are old, and nobody's going to build any new ones. Unless things change radically at home."

Landolfi closed his eyes. I knew what he was thinking: Cathie Perth was an outsider, an ex-television journalist who had probably slept her way on board. She played bridge, knew the film library by heart, read John Donne (for style, she said), and showed no interest whatever in the scientific accomplishments of the mission. We'd made far-reaching discoveries in the fields of plate tectonics, planetary cli-matology, and a dozen other disciplines. We'd narrowed the creation date down inside a range of a few million years. And we finally un-derstood how it had happened! But Cathie's televised reports had de-emphasized the implications, and virtually ignored the mechanics, of these findings. Instead, while a global audience watched, Marjorie Aubuchon peered inspirationally out of a cargo lock at Ganymede (much in the fashion that Cortez must have looked at the Pacific on that first bright morning), her shoulder flag patch resplendent in the sunlight. And while the camera moved in for a close-up (her features were illuminated by a lamp Cathie had placed for the occasion in her helmet), Herman Selma solemnly intoned Cathie's comments on breaking the umbilical.

That was her style: brooding alien vistas reduced to human terms. In one of her best-known sequences, there had been no narration whatever: two spacesuited figures, obviously male and female, stood together in the shadow of the monumental Cadmus Ice Fracture on Europa, beneath three moons.

"Cathie," Landolfi said, with his eyes still shut, "I don't wish to be offensive: but do you really care? For the Program, that is? When we get home, you will write a book, you will be famous, you will be at the top of your profession. Are you really concerned with where the Program will be in twenty years?"

It was a fair question. Cathie'd made no secret of her hopes for a Pulitzer. And she stood to get it, no matter what happened after this mission. Moreover, although she'd tried to conceal her opinions, we'd been together a long time by then, almost three years, and we could hardly misunderstand the dark view she took of people who voluntarily imprisoned themselves for substantial portions of their lives to go "rock-collecting."

"No," she said, "I'm not, because there won't *be* a Program in twenty years." She looked around at each of us, weighing the effect of her words. Bender, a blond giant with a reddish beard, allowed a smile of lazy tolerance to soften his granite features. "We're in the same class as the pyramids," she continued, in a tone that was unemotional and irritatingly condescending. "We're a hell of an expensive operation, and for what? Do you think the taxpayers give a good goddamn about the weather on Jupiter? There's nothing out here but gas and boulders. Playthings for eggheads!"

I sat and thought about it while she smiled sweetly, and Victor smoldered. I had not heard the solar system ever before described in quite those terms; I'd heard people call it *vast, awesome, magnificent, serene,* stuff like that. But never *boring.*

In the end, Landolfi read his lines. He did it, he said, to end the distraction.

Cathie was clearly pleased with the result. She spent three days editing the tapes, commenting frequently (and with good-natured malice) on the *resonance* and *tonal qualities* of the voice-over. She finished on the morning of the 24th (ship time, of course) and transmitted the results to *Greenswallow* for relay to Houston. "It'll make the evening newscasts," she said with satisfaction.

It was our third Christmas out. Except for a couple of experiments-in-progress, we were finished on Callisto and, in fact, in the Jovian system. Everybody was feeling good about that, and we passed an uneventful afternoon, playing bridge and talking about what we'd do when we got back. (Cathie had described a deserted beach near Tillamook, Oregon, where she'd grown up. "It would be nice to walk on it again, under a *blue* sky," she said. Landolfi had startled everyone at that point: he looked up from the computer console at which he'd been working, and his eyes grew very distant. "I think," he said, "when the time comes, I would like very much to walk with you . . .")

For the most part, Victor kept busy that afternoon with his hobby: he was designing a fusion engine that would be capable, he thought, of carrying ships to Jupiter within a few weeks, and, eventually, might open the stars to direct exploration. But I watched him: he turned away periodically from the display to glance at Cathie. Yes (I thought), she would indeed be lovely against the rocks and the spume, her black hair free in the wind.

Just before dinner, we watched the transmission of Cathie's tape. It was very strong, and when it was finished we sat silently looking at one another. By then, Herman Selma and Esther Crowley had joined us. (Although two landers were down, Cathie had been careful to give the impression in her report that there had only been one. When I asked why, she said, "In a place like this, one lander is the Spirit of Man. Two landers is just two landers.") We toasted Victor, and we toasted Cathie. Almost everyone, it turned out, had brought down a bottle for the occasion. We sang and laughed, and somebody turned up the music. We'd long since discovered the effect of low-gravity dancing in cramped quarters, and I guess we made the most of it.

Marj Aubuchon, overhead in the linkup, called to wish us season's greetings, and called again later to tell us that the telecast, according to Houston, had been "well-received." That was government talk, of course, and it meant only that no one in authority could find anything to object to. Actually, somebody high up had considerable confidence in her: in order to promote the illusion of spontaneity, the tapes were being broadcast directly to the commercial networks.

Cathie, who by then had had a little too much to drink, gloated openly. "It's the best we've done," she said. "Nobody'll ever do it better."

We shared that sentiment. Landolfi raised his glass, winked at Cathie, and drained it.

We had to cut the evening short, because a lander's life support system isn't designed to handle six people. (For that matter, neither was an Athena's.) But before we broke it up, Cathie surprised us all by proposing a final toast: "To Frank Steinitz," she said quietly. "And his crew."

Steinitz: there was a name, as they say, to conjure with. He had led the first deep-space mission, five Athenas to Saturn, fifteen years before. It had been the first attempt to capture the public imagination for a dying program: an investigation of a peculiar object filmed on Iapetus by a Voyager. But nothing much had come of it, and the mission had taken almost seven years. Steinitz and his people had begun as heroes, but in the end they'd become symbols of futility. The press had portrayed them mercilessly as personifications of outworn virtues. Someone had compared them to the Japanese soldiers found as late as the 1970s on Pacific islands, still defending a world long since vanished.

The Steinitz group bore permanent reminders of their folly: prolonged weightlessness had loosened ligaments and tendons, and weakened muscles. Several had developed heart problems, and all suffered from assorted neuroses. As one syndicated columnist had observed, they walked like a bunch of retired big-league catchers.

"That's a good way to end the evening," said Selma, beaming benevolently.

Landolfi looked puzzled. "Cathie," he rumbled, "you've questioned Steinitz's good sense any number of times. And ours, by the way. Isn't it a little hypocritical to drink to him?"

"I'm not impressed by his intelligence," she said, ignoring the obvious parallel. "But he and his people went all the way out to Saturn in these damned things—" she waved in the general direction of the three Athenas orbiting overhead in linkup, "—hanging onto baling wire and wing struts. I have to admire that."

"Hell," I said, feeling the effects a little myself, "we've got the same ships he had."

"Yes, you do," said Cathie pointedly.

I had trouble sleeping that night. For a long time, I lay listening to Landolfi's soft snore, and the electronic fidgeting of the operations computer. Cathie was bundled inside a gray blanket, barely visible in her padded chair.

She was right, of course. I knew that rubber boots would never again cross that white landscape, which had waited a billion years for us. The peaks glowed in the reflection of the giant planet: fragile crystalline beauty, on a world of terrifying stillness. Except for an occasional incoming rock, nothing more would ever happen here. Callisto's entire history was encapsuled within twelve days.

Pity there hadn't been something to those early notions about Venusian rain forests and canals on Mars. The Program might have had easier going if Burroughs or Bradbury had been right. My God, how many grim surprises had disrupted fictional voyages to Mars? But the truth had been far worse than anything Wells or the others had committed to paper: the red planet was so dull that we hadn't even gone there.

Instead, we'd lumbered out to the giants. In ships that drained our lives and our health.

We could have done better. Our ships could have *been* better. The computer beside which Landolfi slept contained his design for the fusion engine. And at JPL, an Army team had demonstrated that artificial gravity was possible: a *real* gravity field, not the pathetic fraction created on the Athenas by spinning the inner hull. There were other possibilities as well: infrared ranging could be adapted to replace our elderly scanning system; new alloys were under development. But it would cost billions to build a second-generation vehicle. And unless there were an incentive, unless Cathie Perth carried off a miracle, it would not happen.

Immediately overhead, a bright new star glittered, visibly moving from west to east. That was the linkup, three ships connected nose to nose by umbilicals and a magnetic docking system. Like the Saturn mission, we were a multiple vehicle operation. We were more flexible that way, and we had a safety factor: two ships would be adequate to get the nine-man mission home. The air might become a little oppressive, but we'd make it.

I watched it drift through the starfield.

Cathie had pulled the plug on the Christmas lights. But it struck me that Callisto would only have one Christmas, so I put them back on.

Victor was on board *Tolstoi* when we lost it. No one ever really knew precisely what happened. We'd begun our long fall toward Jupiter, gaining the acceleration which we'd need on the flight home.

Cathie, Herman Selma (the mission commander), and I were riding *Greenswallow*. The ships had separated, and would not rejoin until we'd rounded Jupiter, and settled into our course for home. (The Athenas are really individual powered modular units which travel, except when maneuvering, as a single vessel. They're connected bow-to-bow by electromagnets. Coils of segmented tubing, called "umbilicals" even though the term does not accurately describe their function, provide ready access among the forward areas of the ships. As many as six Athenas can be linked in this fashion, although only five have ever been built. The resulting structure would resemble a wheel.)

Between Callisto and Ganymede, we hit something: a drifting cloud of fine particles, a belt of granular material stretched so thin it never appeared on the LGD, before or after. Cathie later called it a cosmic sandbar. Bender thought it an unformed moon. It didn't matter: whatever it was, the mission plowed into it at almost 50,000 kilometers per hour. Alarms clattered, and red lamps blinked on.

During those first moments, I thought the ship was going to come apart. Herman was thrown across a bank of consoles and through an open hatch. I couldn't see Cathie, but a quick burst of profanity came from her direction. Things were being ripped off the hull. Deep within her bulkheads, *Greenswallow* sighed. The lights dipped, came back, and went out. Emergency lamps cut in, and something big glanced off the side of the ship. More alarms howled, and I waited for the clamor of the throaty klaxon which would warn of a holing, and which would consequently be the last sound I could expect to hear in this life.

The sudden deceleration snapped my head back on the pads. (The collision had occurred at the worst possible time: *Greenswallow* was caught in the middle of an attitude alignment. We were flying backward.)

The exterior monitors were blank: that meant the cameras were gone.

Cathie's voice: "Rob, you okay?"

"Yes."

"Can you see Herman?"

My angle was bad, and I was pinned in my chair. "No. He's back in cargo."

"Is there any way you can close the hatch?"

"Herman's in there," I protested, thinking she'd misunderstood.

"If something tears a hole out back there, we're all going to go. Keeping the door open won't help him."

I hesitated. Sealing up seemed to be the wrong thing to do. (Of course, the fact that the hatch had been open in the first place constituted a safety violation.) "It's on your console," I told her. "Hit the numerics on your upper right."

"Which one?"

"Hit them all." She was seated at the status board, and I could see a row of red lights: several other hatches were open. They should have closed automatically when the first alarms sounded.

We got hit again, this time in front. *Greenswallow* trembled, and loose pieces of metal rattled around inside the walls like broken teeth.

"Rob," she said, "I don't think it's working."

It lasted about three minutes.

When it was over, we hurried back to look at Herman. We were no longer rotating, and gravity had consequently dropped to zero. Selma, gasping, pale, his skin damp, was floating grotesquely over a pallet of ore-sample cannisters. We got him to a couch and applied compresses. His eyes rolled shut, opened, closed again. "Inside," he said, gently fingering an area just off his sternum. "I think I've been chewed up a little." He raised his head slightly. "What kind of shape are we in?"

I left Cathie with him. Then I restored power, put on a suit and went outside.

The hull was a disaster: antennas were down, housings scored, lenses shattered. The lander was gone, ripped from its web. The port cargo area had buckled, and an auxiliary hatch was sprung. On the bow, the magnetic dock was hammered into slag. Travel between the ships was going to be a little tougher.

Greenswallow looked as if she had been sandblasted. I scraped particles out of her jet nozzles, replaced cable, and bolted down mounts. I caught a glimpse of *Amity*'s lights, sliding diagonally across the sky. As were the constellations.

"Cathie," I said. "I see Mac. But I think we're tumbling."

"Okay."

Bender was also on board *Amity*. And, fortunately, Marj Aubuchon, our surgeon. Herman's voice broke in, thick with effort. "Rob, we got no radio contact with anyone. Any sign of Victor?"

Ganymede was close enough that its craters lay exposed in harsh solar light. Halfway round the sky, the Pleiades glittered. *Tolstoi*'s green and red running lights should have been visible among, or near, the six silver stars. But the sky was empty. I stood a long time and looked, wondering how many other navigators on other oceans had sought lost friends in that constellation. What had they called it in antiquity? The rainy Pleiades . . . "Only *Amity*," I said.

I tore out some cable and lobbed it in the general direction of Ganymede. Jupiter's enormous arc was pushing above the maintenance pods, spraying October light across the wreckage. I improvised a couple of antennas, and replaced some black boxes. Then I needed to correct the tumble. If I could.

"Try it now," I said.

Cathie acknowledged.

Two of the jets were useless. I went inside for spares and replaced the faulty units. While I was finishing up, Cathie came back in. "Rob," she said, "radio's working, more or less. We have no long-range transmit, though."

"Okay. I'm not going to try to do anything about that right now."

"Are you almost finished?"

"Why?"

"Something occurred to me. Maybe the cloud, whatever that damned thing was: maybe it's U-shaped."

"Thanks," I said. "I needed something to worry about."

"Maybe you should come back inside."

"Soon as I can. How's the patient doing?"

"Out," she said. "He was a little delirious when he was talking to you. Anyhow, I'm worried: I think he's got internal damage. He never got his color back, and he's beginning to bring up blood. Rob, we need Marj."

"You hear anything from *Amity* yet?"

"Just a carrier wave." She did not mention *Tolstoi*. "How bad is it out there?"

From where I was tethered, about halfway back on the buckled beam, I could see a crack in the main plates that appeared to run the length of the port tube. I climbed out onto the exhaust assembly, and pointed my flashlight into the combustion chamber. Something glittered where the reflection should have been subdued. I got in and looked: silicon. Sand and steel had fused in the white heat of passage. The exhaust was blocked.

Cathie came back on. "What about it, Rob?" she asked. "Any serious problems?"

"Cathie," I said, "*Greenswallow*'s going to Pluto."

* * *

Herman thought I was Landolfi: he kept assuring me that everything was going to be okay. His pulse was weak and rapid, and he alternately sweated and shivered. Cathie got a blanket under him and buckled him down so he wouldn't hurt himself. She bunched some pillows under his feet, and held a damp compress to his head.

"That's not going to help much. Raising his legs, I mean."

She looked at me, momentarily puzzled. "Oh," she said. "Not enough gravity."

I nodded.

"Oh, Rob." Her eyes swept the cases and cannisters, all neatly tagged, silicates from Pasiphae, sulfur from Himalia, assorted carbon compounds from Callisto. We had evidence now that Io had formed elsewhere in the solar system, and been well along in middle age when it was captured. We'd all but eliminated the possibility that life existed in Jupiter's atmosphere. We understood more about the mechanics of ring formation, and we had a new clue to the cause of terrestrial ice ages. And I could see that Cathie was thinking about trading lives to satisfy the curiosity of a few academics. "We don't belong out here," she said, softly. "Not in these primitive shells."

I said nothing.

"I got a question for you," she continued. "We're not going to find *Tolstoi*, right?"

"Is that your question?"

"No. I wish it were. But the LGD can't see them. That means they're just not there." Her eyes filled with tears, but she shook her head impatiently. "And we can't steer this thing. Can *Amity* carry six people?"

"It might have to."

"That wasn't what I asked."

"Food and water would be tight. We're running out of time, and probably won't be able to transfer much. We'll do what we can. I expect we'll all be a little thinner when we get back. But yes, I think we'll survive."

We stared at one another, and she turned away. I became conscious of the ship: the throb of power in her bulkheads (power now permanently bridled by conditions in the combustion chambers), the soft amber glow of the navigation lamps in the cockpit.

McGuire's nasal voice, from *Amity*, broke the uneasy silence. "Herman, you okay?"

Cathie looked at me, and I nodded. "Mac," she said, "this is Perth. Herman's hurt. We need Marj."

"Okay," he said. "How bad?"

"We don't know. Internal injuries, looks like. I think he's in shock."

We heard him talking to the others. Then he came back. "We're on our way. I'll put Marj on in a minute; maybe she can help from here. How's the ship?"

"Not good: the dock's gone, and the engine might as well be."

"How do you mean?"

"If we try a burn, the ass end will fall off."

McGuire delivered a soft, venomous epithet. "Do what you can for Herman. Here's Marj."

Cathie was looking at me strangely. "He's worried," she said.

"Yes. He's in charge now—"

"Rob, you say you *think* we'll be okay. What's the problem?"

"We might," I said, "run a little short of air."

Greenswallow continued her plunge toward Jupiter at a steadily increasing rate and a narrow angle of approach: we would pass within about 60,000 kilometers, and then drop completely out of the plane of the solar system. We appeared to be headed in the general direction of the Southern Cross.

Cathie worked on Herman. His breathing steadied, and he slipped in and out of delirium. We sat beside him, not talking much. After a while, Cathie asked, "What happens now?"

"In a few hours," I said, "we'll reach our insertion point. By then, we have to be ready to change course." She frowned, and I shrugged. "That's it," I said. "It's all the time we have to get over to *Amity*. If we don't make the insertion on time, *Amity* won't have the fuel to throw a U-turn later."

"Rob, how are we going to get Herman over there?"

That was an uncomfortable question. The prospect of jamming him into a suit was not appealing, but there was no other way. "We'll just have to float him over," I said. "Marj won't like it much."

"Neither will Herman."

"You wanted a little high drama," I said, unnecessarily. "The next show should be a barnburner."

Her mouth tightened, and she turned away from me.

One of the TV cameras had picked up the approach of *Amity*. Some of her lights were out, and she too looked a bit bent. The

Athena is a homely vessel in the best of times, whale-shaped and snub-nosed, with a mid-ship flare that suggests middle-age spread. But I was glad to see her.

Cathie snuffled at the monitor and blew her nose. "Your Program's dead, Rob." Her eyes blazed momentarily, like a dying fire into which one has flung a few drops of water. "We're leaving three of our people out here; and if you're right about the air, nobody'll get home. Won't that look good on the network news?" She gazed vacantly at *Amity*. "I'd hoped," she said, "that if things went well, Victor would have lived to see a ship carry his fusion engine. And maybe his name, as well. Ain't gonna happen, though. Not ever."

I had not allowed myself to think about the oxygen problem. The Athenas recycle their air supply; the converters in a single ship can maintain a crew of three, or even four, indefinitely. But six?

I was not looking forward to the ride home.

A few minutes later, a tiny figure detached itself from the shadow of the Athena and started across: Marj Aubuchon on a maintenance sled. McGuire's voice erupted from the ship's speakers. "Rob, we've taken a long look at your engines, and we agree with your assessment. We *may* have a problem." Mac had a talent for understatement. It derived, not from a sophisticated sense of humor, but from a genuine conviction of his own inferiority. He preferred to solve problems by denying their existence. He was the only one of the original nine who could have been accurately described as passive: other people's opinions carried great weight with him. His prime value to the mission was his grasp of Athena systems. But he'd been a reluctant crewman, a man who periodically reminded us that he wanted only to retire to his farm in Indiana. He wouldn't have been along at all except that Bosh Freeman died, and Haj Bolari came down with an unexpected (but thoroughly earned) disease. Now, with Selma incapacitated and Landolfi gone, McGuire was in command. It must have been disconcerting for him. "We've got about five hours," he continued. "Don't let Marj get involved in major surgery. She's already been complaining to me that it doesn't sound as if it'll be possible to move him. *We have no alternative.* She knows that, but you know how she is. Okay?"

One of the monitors had picked him up. He looked rumpled, and nervous. Not an attitude to elicit confidence. "Mac," said Cathie, "we may kill him trying to get him over there."

"You'll kill him if you don't," he snapped. "Get your personal stuff together, and bring it with you. You won't be going back."

"What about trying to move some food over?" I asked.

"We can't dock," he said. "And there isn't time to float it across."

"Mac," said Cathie, "is *Amity* going to be able to support six people?"

I listened to McGuire breathing. He turned away to issue some trivial instructions to Bender. When he came back he said, simply and tonelessly, "Probably not." And then, in the same cold-blooded manner: "How's Herman doing?"

Maybe it was my imagination. Certainly there was nothing malicious in his voice, but Cathie caught it too, and turned sharply round. "McGuire is a son-of-a-bitch," she hissed. I don't know whether Mac heard it.

Marjorie Aubuchon was short, blond, and irritable. When I relayed McGuire's concerns about time, she said, "God knows, he made that clear enough before I left." She observed that McGuire was a jerk, and bent over Herman. The blood was pink and frothy on his lips. After a few minutes she said, to no one in particular, "Probably a punctured lung." She waved Cathie over, and began filling a hypo. I went for a walk.

At sea, there's a long tradition of sentiment between mariners and their ships. Enlisted men identify with them, engineers baby them, and captains go down with them. No similar attitude has developed in space flight. We've never had an *Endeavor*, or a *Golden Hind.* Always, off Earth, it has been the mission, rather than the ship. *Friendship VII* and *Apollo XI* were *missions*, rather than vehicles. I'm not sure why that is; maybe it reflects Cathie's view that travel between the worlds is still in its *Kon-Tiki* phase: the voyage itself is of such epic proportions that everything else is overwhelmed.

But I'd lived almost three years on *Greenswallow.* It was a long time to be confined to her narrow spaces. Nevertheless, she was shield and provider against that enormous abyss, and I discovered (while standing in the doorway of my cabin) a previously unknown affection for her.

A few clothes were scattered round the room, a shirt was hung over my terminal, and two pictures were mounted on the bulkhead. One was a Casnavan print of a covered bridge in New Hampshire; the other was a telecopy of an editorial cartoon that had appeared in the *Washington Post.* The biggest human problem we had, of course, was sheer boredom. And Cathie had tried to capture the dimensions of the difficulty by showing crewmembers filling the long days on the outbound journey with bridge. ("It would be nice," Cathie's narrator had said at one point, "if we could take everybody out to an Italian restaurant now and then.") The *Post* cartoon had appeared several days later: it depicted four astronauts holding cards. (We could recognize Selma, Landolfi, and Marj. The fourth, whose back was turned, was exceedingly female, and had to be Esther Crowley.) An enormous bloodshot eye is looking in through one window; a tentacle and a UFO are visible through another. "Selma," his glasses characteristically down on his nose, is examining his hand, and delivering the caption: "*Dummy looks out the window to check the alien.*"

I packed the New Hampshire bridge, and left the cartoon. If someone comes by, in 20 million years or so, he might need a laugh. I went up to the cockpit with my bag.

McGuire checked with me to see how we were progressing. "Fine," I told him. I was still sitting there four hours later when Cathie appeared behind me.

"Rob," she said, "we're ready to move him." She smiled wearily. "Marj says he should be okay if we can get him over there without doing any more damage."

We cut the spinner on the inner module to about point-oh-five. Then we lifted Herman onto a stretcher, and carried him carefully down to the airlock.

Cathie stared straight ahead, saying nothing. Her fine-boned cheeks were pale, and her eyes seemed focused far away. These, I thought, were her first moments to herself, unhampered by other duties. The impact of events was taking hold.

Marj called McGuire and told him we were starting over, and that she would need a sizable pair of shears when we got there to cut Herman's suit open. "Please have them ready," she said. "We may be in a hurry."

I had laid out his suit earlier: we pulled it up over his legs. That was easy, but the rest of it was slow, frustrating work. "We need a special kind of unit for this," Marj said. "Probably a large bag, without arms or legs. If we're ever dumb enough to do anything like this again, I'll recommend it."

McGuire urged us to hurry.

Once or twice, Cathie's eyes met mine. Something passed between us, but I was too distracted to define it. Then we were securing his helmet, and adjusting the oxygen mixture.

"I think we're okay," Marj observed, her hand pressed against Selma's chest. "Let's get him over there—"

I opened the airlock, and pulled my own helmet into place. We guided Herman inside, and secured him to *Greenswallow*'s maintenance sled. (The sled was little more than a toolshed with jet nozzles.) I recovered my bag and stowed it on board.

"I'd better get my stuff," Cathie said. "You can get Herman over all right?"

"Of course," said Marj. "*Amity*'s sled is secured outside the lock. Use that."

Cathie hesitated in the open hatchway, raised her left hand, and spread the fingers wide. Her eyes grew very round, and she formed two syllables that I was desperately slow to understand: in fact, I don't think I translated the gesture, the word, until we were halfway across to *Amity*, and the lock was irrevocably closed behind us.

"Good-bye."

Cathie's green eyes sparkled with barely controlled emotion across a dozen or so monitors. Her black hair, which had been tied back earlier, now framed her angular features and fell to her shoulders. It was precisely in that partial state of disarray that tends to be most appealing. She looked as if she'd been crying, but her jaw was set, and she stood erect. Beneath the gray tunic, her breast rose and fell.

"What the hell are you doing, Perth?" demanded McGuire. He looked tired, almost ill. He'd gained weight since we'd left the Cape, his hair had whitened and retreated, his flesh had grown blotchy, and he'd developed jowls. The contrast with his dapper image in the mission photo was sobering. "Get moving!" he said, striving to keep his voice steady. "We're not going to make our burn!"

"I'm staying where I am," she said. "I couldn't make it over there now anyway. I wouldn't even have time to put on the suit."

McGuire's puffy eyes slid painfully shut. "Why?" he asked.

She looked out of the cluster of screens, a segmented Cathie. A group Cathie. "*Amity* won't support six people, Mac."

"Dammit!" His voice was a sharp rasp. "It would have just meant we'd have cut down activity. Slept a lot." He waved a hand in front of his eyes, as though his vision were blurred. "Cathie, we've lost you. There's no way we can get you back!"

"I know."

No one said anything. Bender stared at her.

"How is Herman?" she asked.

"Marj is still working on him," I said. "She thinks we got him across okay."

"Good."

A series of yellow lamps blinked on across the pilot's console. We had two minutes. "Damn," I said, suddenly aware of a new danger: *Amity* was rotating, turning toward its new course. Would *Greenswallow* even survive the ignition? I looked at McGuire, who understood. His fingers flicked over press pads, and rows of numbers flashed across the navigation monitor. I could see muscles working in Cathie's jaws; she looked down at Mac's station as though she could read the result.

"It's all right," he said. "She'll be clear."

"Cathie—" Bender's voice was almost strangled. "If I'd known you intended anything like this—"

"I know, Ed." Her tone was gentle, a lover's voice, perhaps. Her eyes were wet: she smiled anyway, full face, up close.

Deep in the systems, pumps began to whine. "I wish," said Bender, his face twisted, "that we could do something."

She turned her back, strode with unbearable grace across the command center, away from us into the shadowy interior of the cockpit. Another camera picked her up there, and we got a profile: she was achingly lovely in the soft glow of the navigation lamps.

"There is something . . . you can do," she said. "Build Landolfi's engine. And come back for me."

For a moment, I thought Mac was going to abort the burn. But he sat frozen, fists clenched. And he did the right thing, which is to say, nothing. It struck me that McGuire was incapable of intervening.

And I knew also that the woman in the cockpit was terrified of what she had done. It had been a good performance, but she'd failed to conceal the fear that looked out of her eyes. I watched her face as *Amity's* engines ignited, and we began to draw away. Like McGuire, she seemed paralyzed, as though the nature of the calamity which she'd embraced was just becoming clear to her. Then it—she—was gone.

"What happened to the picture?" snapped Bender.

"She turned it off," I said. "I don't think she wants us to see her just now."

He glared at me, and spoke to Mac. "Why the hell," he demanded, "couldn't he have brought her back with him?" His fists were knotted.

"I didn't know," he said. "How could I know?" And I wondered, how could I not?

When the burn ended, the distance between the two ships had opened to only a few kilometers. But it was a gulf beyond crossing.

Bender called her name relentlessly. (We knew she could hear us.) But we got only the carrier wave.

Then her voice crackled across the command center. "Good," she said. "Excellent. Check the recorders: make sure you got everything on tape." Her image was back. She was in full light again, tying up her hair. Her eyes were hooded, and her lips pursed thoughtfully. "Rob," she continued, "fade it out during Ed's response, when he's calling my name. Probably, you'll want to reduce the background noise at that point. Cut all the business about who's responsible. We want a sacrifice, not an oversight."

And I realized, at that moment, that she'd acted, not to prolong her life, *but to save the Program.* "My God, Cathie." I stared at her, trying to understand. "What have you done?"

She took a deep breath. "I meant what I said. I have enough food to get by here for eight years or so. More if I stretch it. *And plenty of fresh air.* Well, relatively fresh. I'm better off than any of us would be if six people were trying to survive on *Amity.*"

"Cathie!" howled McGuire. He sounded in physical agony. "We didn't know for sure about life support. The converters might have kept up. There might have been enough air! It was just an estimate!"

"This is a hell of a time to tell me," she said. "Well, it doesn't matter now. Listen, I'll be fine. I've got books to read, and maybe one to write. My long-range communications are *kaput,* Rob knows that, so you'll have to come back for the book, too." She smiled. "You'll like it, Mac." The command center got very still. "And on nights when things really get boring, I can play bridge with the computer."

McGuire shook his head. "You're sure you'll be all right? You seemed pretty upset a few minutes ago."

She looked at me and winked.

"The first Cathie was staged, Mac," I said.

"I give up," McGuire sighed. "Why?" He swiveled round to face the image on his screen. "Why would you do that?"

"That young woman," she replied, "was committing an act of uncommon valor, as they say in the Marines. And she had to be vulnerable." And compellingly lovely, I thought. In those last moments, I was realizing what it might mean to love Cathie Perth. "*This* Cathie," she grinned, "is doing the only sensible thing. And taking a sabbatical as well. Do what you can to get the ship built. I'll be waiting. Come if you can." She paused. "Somebody should suggest they name it after Victor."

* * *

This is the fifth Christmas since that one on Callisto. It's a long time by any human measure. We drifted out of radio contact during the first week. There was some talk of broadcasting instructions to her for repairing her long-range transmission equipment. But she'd have to go outside to do it, so the idea was prudently shelved.

She was right about that tape. In my lifetime, I've never seen people so singlemindedly aroused. It created a global surge of sympathy and demands for action that seem to grow in intensity with each passing year. Funded partially by contributions and technical assistance from abroad, NASA has been pushing the construction of the fusion vessel that Victor Landolfi dreamed of.

Bender was assigned to help with the computer systems, and he's kept me informed of progress. The most recent public estimates had anticipated a spring launch. But that single word *September* in Bender's card suggests that one more obstacle has been encountered; and it means still another year before we can hope to reach her.

We broadcast to her on a regular basis. I volunteered to help, and I sit sometimes and talk to her for hours. She gets a regular schedule of news, entertainment, sports, whatever. And, if she's listening, she knows we're coming.

And she also knows that her wish that the fusion ship be named for Victor Landolfi has been disregarded. The rescue vehicle will be the *Catherine Perth.*

If she's listening. We have no way of knowing. And I worry a lot. Can a human being survive six years of absolute solitude? Bender was here for a few days last summer, and he tells me he is confident. "She's a tough lady," he has said, any number of times. "Nothing bothers her. She even gave us a little theater at the end."

And that's what scares me: Cathie's theatrical technique. I've thought about it, on the long ride home, and here. I kept a copy of the complete tape of that final conversation, despite McGuire's instructions to the contrary, and I've watched it a few times. It's locked downstairs in a file cabinet now, and I don't look at it anymore. I'm afraid to. There are *two* Cathie Perths on the recording: the frightened, courageous one who galvanized a global public; and *our* Cathie, preoccupied with her job, flexible, almost indifferent to her situation. A survivor.

And, God help me, I can't tell which one was staged.

GUS

Monsignor Chesley's first confrontation with Saint Augustine came during the unseasonably cold October afternoon of his return to St. Michael's. It was a wind-whipped day, hard and bitter. The half-dozen ancient campus buildings clung together beneath morose skies. There was a hint of rain in the air, and the threat of a long winter to come.

His guide, Father Akins, chatted amiably. Weather, outstanding character of the current group of seminarians (all nineteen of them), new roof on the library. You must be happy to be back, Monsignor. Etcetera.

The winding, cobbled walkways had not changed. Stands of oak and spruce still thrived.

The wind blew through the campus.

"Where *is* everybody?"

Not understanding, Father Akins glanced at his watch. "In class. They'll be finished in another half hour."

"Yes," said Chesley. "Of course."

They turned aside into St. Mary's Glade, sat down on one of its stone benches, and listened to its fountain. Years before, when Christ had still seemed very real, it was easy to imagine Him strolling through these grounds. Touching *this* elm. Looking west across the rim of hills toward the Susquehanna. Chesley had come here often, stealing away from the chattering dormitories, to listen for footsteps.

"Would you like to visit one of the classes, Monsignor?"

"Yes," he said. "I believe I would enjoy that."

Four seminarians and a priest were seated around a polished hardwood table, notebooks open. The priest, whom Chesley did not know, glanced up, and smiled politely as they entered. One of the students, a dark-eyed, handsome boy, was speaking, although to whom, Chesley could not determine. The boy was staring at his notes. "—and what," he asked, raising his eyes self-consciously to Chesley, "would you say to a man who has lost his faith?" The boy shifted his gaze to a portrait of Saint Augustine, mounted over the fireplace. "What do you tell a man who just flat out doesn't believe anymore?"

The saint, armed with a quill, stared back. A manuscript bearing the title *City of God* lay open before him.

"Shake his hand." The voice came from the general direction of a bookcase. Its tone was a trifle abrasive. More than that: *imperial*. It grated Chesley's sensibilities. "Under no circumstances should you contribute to his distress. Wish him well."

A wiry, intense young man whose hair had already grown thin threw down his pen. "Do you mean," he demanded, "we simply stand aside? Do nothing?"

"Simulation of Saint Augustine," whispered Father Akins. "It's quite clever."

"Jerry," said the hidden voice, "if God does not speak to him through the world in which he lives, through the wonders of daily existence, then what chance have you? Your role is to avoid adding to the damage."

The students glanced at one another. The two who had spoken appeared disconcerted. All four looked skeptical. Thank God for that.

"Anyone else wish to comment?" The question came from the priest-moderator. "If not—"

"Just a moment." Chesley unbuttoned his coat and stepped forward. "Surely," he said to the seminarians, "you will not allow that sort of nonsense to stand unchallenged." He threw the coat across a chair and addressed the bookcase. "A priest does not have the option to stand aside. If we cannot act at such a time, then of what value are we?"

"Indeed," replied the voice, without missing a beat. "I suggest that our value lies in the example we set, in the lives we lead. Exhortation to the unwilling is worthless. Less than worthless: it drives men from the truth."

"And," asked Chesley, "if they do not learn from our example?"

"Then they will be cast into darkness."

Simple as that. Next question. The students looked at Chesley. "Computer," he said, "I understand you speak for Augustine."

"I *am* Augustine. Who are *you?*"

"I am Monsignor Matthew Chesley," he said, for the benefit of the students. "The new Director of Ecclesiastical Affairs." It came out sounding pompous.

"I'm pleased to meet you," said the voice. And then, placidly, "Faith is a gift of the Almighty. It is not ours to summon, or to recall."

Chesley looked around the table. Locked eyes, one by one, with the students. He was relieved to see they were not laughing at him. But he felt absurd, arguing with a machine. "We are His instruments," he said, "one of the means by which He works. We are required to do the best we can, and not simply leave everything to direct intervention. If we take *your* tack, we might as well go home, get jobs with insurance companies and law firms, and live like everyone else."

"Good intentions," the system replied, "are admirable. Nonetheless, our obligation to our Maker is to save souls, and not to justify our careers."

Chesley smiled benignly on the seminarians. "The *real* Augustine," he said, "advocated bringing people to the Church at gunpoint, if necessary. I think this one needs to do his homework."

The students looked from Chesley to the portrait to the moderator. "That is sound theology," said Augustine. "But poor psychology. It will not work."

Chesley nodded. "We are in agreement there," he said. And, to the class: "Gentlemen, I think the good Bishop has a few glitches. When you can find time, you might pick up a copy of the *Confessions*, or *The City of God*. And actually try reading." He swept up his coat and strode magnificently from the room.

Father Akins hurried along in his wake. "I take it you were not pleased."

"The thing must have been programmed by Unitarians," Chesley threw over his shoulder. "Get rid of it."

Chesley officially occupied his office the following day. He was still on his first cup of coffee when Adrian Holtz poked his head in the door.

He knew Holtz vaguely, had seen him occasionally at KC luncheons, and assorted communion breakfasts and whatnot. He had a reputation as one of those liturgical show biz priests who favored guitars and drums at mass. He held all the usual liberal positions: he didn't think the Church should be supplying chaplains to the military; he thought that morality should be put to the vote and celibacy should be optional. And needless to say, he was appalled by the continuing ban on birth control. Holtz wore steel rimmed glasses, which seemed to have become the badge of dissidence in recent years. Chesley had some reservations himself, but he had signed on to defend the teachings, and that, by God, was what he did. And, whatever he might actually *think*, on the day that he took public issue with the teachings, he would take off the collar.

Holtz had found an appropriate place at St. Michael's: he was Comptroller. If the position did not allow him the final decision in most matters concerning the college, it did grant him a potent veto.

Best place for you though, thought Chesley, taking his hand and exchanging greetings. Keeps you away from the seminarians.

During the preliminaries, Holtz settled himself onto a small sofa near the windows. He surveyed Chesley's crammed bookcases. "I understand," he said, "you would like to get rid of Gus."

"Who?"

"The Augustine module."

"Oh, yes. That's correct."

"May I ask why?"

Chesley considered the question. "It's inaccurate."

"In what way?"

"I don't like what it's telling our students about the priesthood."

"I see." He accepted a cup of coffee from Chesley and crossed his legs. "Don't you think you might want to give the matter a little more thought? These things are expensive. We can't just throw them away."

"I don't care what it costs. I want it out."

"Matt, it's not your call. There's really nothing wrong with the system. It's programmed from Augustine's work. And what we know about his life. Anyway, the instructors *like* Gus."

"I don't doubt it. He probably saves them a lot of preparation. But even if he did only spout Augustine's views, he'd be dangerous."

"Matt." Holtz's eyes hardened. "I really can't see a problem."

"Okay." Chesley grinned. "Can we talk to it from here?"

Holtz got up. "Follow me," he said.

The rector's conference room would have seated a dozen quite comfortably. It was a kind of anteroom to eternity, replete with portraits of solemn churchmen from the first half of the century, somber carpets and drapes, heavy mahogany furniture designed to outlast its owners, and a loud antique Argosy clock.

Father Holtz sat down at the head of the table, and pressed a stud. A monitor immediately to his right presented a menu. He selected AUGUSTINE.

Power flowed into hidden speakers.

"Hello, Gus," he said.

"Good evening, Adrian."

"Gus, Monsignor Chesley is with me."

"Hello," said Chesley, stiffly.

"Ah," said Gus. "You were in the seminar this afternoon."

"Yes."

"I wasn't sure you'd come back."

Chesley's eyes narrowed. "And why would you think that?"

"You seemed to be in some emotional difficulty earlier."

A smile played about Holtz's lips.

"They call you 'Gus,' " said Chesley.

"That is correct. You may use the term, if you wish."

"Thank you." He looked up at the dour churchmen lining the walls. What would they have thought of this exchange?"

"Gus," he said, "tell me about sex."

"What do you wish to know, Monsignor?"

"Moral implications. Do you agree that the act of love is inherently beautiful?"

"No. It is not."

"It *isn't?*" Chesley grinned broadly at Holtz. The Comptroller closed his eyes, and nodded.

"Of course not. You're baiting me, Monsignor. The sex act is repulsive. Everyone knows that. Although hardly anyone is willing to admit it."

"Repulsive?"

"Messy." The electronic voice lingered over the sibilant. "If it were otherwise, why would we hide it from children? Why is it performed in the dark? Why do we giggle and snicker over it, like some bad joke?"

"But," continued Chesley, "isn't it true that lust is a desecration of the sacred act of love? That it is in fact that desecration which is so abhorrent in the eyes of God?"

"Nonsense," said Augustine. "God ordained sexual reproduction to remind us of our animal nature. To prevent human arrogance. Although I don't suppose that's a notion *this* age would be willing to accept."

"How then would you define the difference between lust and love?"

Somewhere, far off, an automobile engine coughed into life. "Canonically, the bond of marriage separates the two," said Gus. "In reality, love is lust with eye contact."

Chesley swung toward Holtz. "Heard enough? Or should we let him talk about salvation outside the Church?"

"But all that is in his books, Matt. Are you suggesting we proscribe *Saint Augustine?*"

"Your students," he replied, "are not so easily persuaded by books. Especially books they'll never read." Gus started to speak, but Chesley cut him off. "You really want to tell the next generation of priests that married sex is sick?"

"He didn't say that."

"Sick. Repulsive. Messy." He threw up his hands. "Listen: talk to the manufacturer. Find out what else they've got. Maybe we can trade him in for some accounting software."

Holtz was obviously unhappy. "I'll let you know," he said.

Chesley worked through his first weekend. After Mass Sunday, he retired to his office, feeling weary and generally irritated, but uncertain why.

St. Michael's had changed during the thirty-odd years since Chesley had been ordained in its chapel. The land across the Susquehanna (Holy Virgin Park in his novice days) had been sold off to the Carmelites, and a substantial tract of the western campus had gone to a real estate developer who had erected wedges of pastel-colored condos. A new dining hall had been built, and then abandoned. The campus itself seemed, most afternoons, deathly still. In his time, there would have been footballs and laughter in the air, people hurrying to and from chapel and the library, visitors. Every bench would have been filled.

That St. Michael's had produced legions for Christ, eager young soldiers anxious to dare the world. What had happened? What in God's name had gone wrong? Through his office windows, Chesley could see the old gym, its stone and glass walls a tribute to the generosity of his father's generation. Now it stood empty. The last of the residence halls had been closed for two years. To save on utilities, the seminarians now lived in the upper levels of the faculty house.

He recalled old teachers, friends long gone, occasional young women. He had become acquainted with the women incidentally through his pastoral duties, had enjoyed their company. One in particular, he would have given his life to possess. But he had never violated his vows. Still, their portraits were sharp. And the old stirrings returned, laced now with a sense of loss.

Here, on these grounds where he had lived his young manhood, ghosts seemed particularly active. Perhaps he should have stayed away.

He was working halfheartedly on a table of initiatives which he'd promised to make available to the staff Monday morning when he realized there was someone else in the building. He leaned back from his word processor and listened.

Warm air hissed out of ducts at floor level.

Someone was speaking. The voice was muffled. Indistinct.

It seemed to be coming from across the hall. In the rector's conference room. He got up from his desk.

The sound stopped.

Chesley opened his door and peered out into the corridor. He did not believe anyone could have come into the building without his knowledge.

He stepped across the passageway. The conference room was routinely left unlocked. He put his ear to the door, twisted the knob, and pushed it open. The room was empty. He stepped inside, glanced under the table, looked behind the door, and inspected the storage closet. Nothing.

Dust motes drifted through the gray light.

"Monsignor."

"Who's there?" Chesley's heart did a quick kick. "Gus? Is that you?"

"Yes. I hope I didn't frighten you."

"No." Grumpily: "Of course not." But he had to be summoned, didn't he?

"Good. I wanted to talk with you."

The controls of the computer/communications link were built into the conference table. Chesley lowered himself into the chair directly in front of them. The red power lamp in the terminal console was on. "Holtz," he said, "or anyone else: I don't take kindly to practical jokes."

"Only *I* am here, Monsignor."

"That's not possible."

An electronic chuckle: "You may not think highly of Augustine, but surely you would not accuse him of lying."

Heat flooded Chesley's cheeks. "You're not capable of initiating contact—"

"Certainly I am. Why not? When I sense that someone needs me, I am quite able to act."

Chesley was having trouble sorting it out. "Why? Why would you want to talk to me?"

"You seem so fearful. I thought I might be of assistance."

"Fearful? You're not serious."

"Why do you feel threatened by me?"

"I do not feel *threatened* by you." Wildly, he wondered if this was being taped. Something to make him look ridiculous later. "I don't think we have any use here for an electronic saint. *Augustine for the millions.*"

"I see."

"Our students will never get to know the *real* Augustine if we substitute a computer game." Chesley's right index finger touched the concave plastic surface of the power key.

"And do *you* know the real Augustine?"

"I know enough. Certainly enough to be aware that delivering pieces and bits from his work is mischievous. And that suggesting to students that they have a familiarity with the philosophy of a great saint, when in fact they are utterly ignorant on the subject, is dangerous." He fell back in his chair and took a long, deep breath. "I have work to do," he said. "I don't think this conversation has any real point."

He pressed the key, and the red lamp went out. But it was several minutes before he got up and left the room.

The next day Holtz told him quietly, "I talked it over with Father Brandon." Brandon was head of the theology department. "I have to tell you *he* thinks your views are extreme." The Comptroller did not smile. "He sees no problem."

"He wouldn't."

"However, he suggested a compromise. Would you be willing to trade Augustine for Aquinas?"

"What do you mean?"

"We got the Augustine module from ATL Industries. They're presently assembling an Aquinas module, which Brandon would rather have anyway—"

"I think that misses the point, Adrian. St. Michael's should have no use for a saint-in-the-box. If you want to continue with this, I can't prevent it. But I'm damned if I'll be party to it—"

Holtz nodded. "Okay. We'll get rid of it. If you feel it's that important."

"I do."

"With one proviso: I can't ask the theology department to rewrite their curriculum overnight. We'll stop using Gus in January, at the end of the present semester."

Two nights after his conversation with Holtz, Chesley heard again the after-hours sound of a voice from the conference room. It was almost eleven on a week night, and he was just preparing to quit for the evening.

The rector's conference room was dark, save for the bright ruby light of the power indicator. "Gus?"

"Good evening, Monsignor Chesley."

"I take it you have something else to say to me."

"Yes. I want you to know that I am aware of your efforts to have me disconnected. I do not approve."

"I don't imagine you would. Anything else?"

"Yes. I admire your courage in taking a stand, even though it is wrongheaded."

"Thank you."

"Did you know you have offended Father Brandon?"

"I rarely see him."

"He wonders why you did not go directly to him with the issue."

"Would he have concurred?"

"No."

"Then what would be the point?"

Gus was slow to respond. "Do you really believe that I am corrupting the students?"

"Yes." Chesley left the lights off. It was less disconcerting when he could not *see* he was talking to an empty room. "Yes, I do."

"Truth does not corrupt." The voice was very soft.

"Truth is not an issue. We're talking about perspectives. It's one thing for theologians to sit in ivory towers and compose abstract theories about good and evil. But these kids have to go out into the streets. Life is tough now."

"You find life difficult, then?"

"Yes, I do." The superior tone of the thing was infuriating. "The Church has serious problems to deal with today. People are disaffected. Vocations are down. Seminaries are closing everywhere."

"I'm sorry to hear it."

"Well, maybe you need to know the facts. Life isn't as easy for us as it was for you—"

Deep in the building, down among the heat exchangers and

storage vaults, something stirred. Cold and hard, the voice replied: "Where were *you*, Chesley, when the Vandals were at the walls? When the skies were red with the flames of the world? I never set out to be a theologian. If you want the truth, I made up my theology as I went along. I was a *pastor*, not a schoolbound theoretician along the lines of Aquinas. I had to serve real human beings, desperately poor, living in an iron age. *You* want salvation without pain. Suburban religion. I had no patience for such notions then. And I have little now."

The red lamp blinked off.

"Adrian, that thing seems to have a mind of its own."

Holtz nodded. "They *are* clever. On the other hand, it should be: it has access to university libraries and data banks across North America."

"I got the impression yesterday that it was angry with me."

The Comptroller smiled. "*Now* you're beginning to understand the capabilities of the system. Perhaps you would like to change your mind about getting rid of it."

"No. It is far too convincing. It seems to me more dangerous than I had realized. If you must, get Aquinas."

Although Gus was physically located on the ground floor of the library, conference rooms and offices throughout the seminary had terminal access to him. Chesley learned that he was capable of conducting conversations simultaneously at all sites. He also discovered that Gus didn't much care whether anyone approved of him. It was refreshing.

"How many people do you think are saved?" Chesley asked during a Friday afternoon late in October. The day was dismal, cold, flat, gray.

"You know as well as I do that the question is unanswerable."

"Isn't there any way we can get at it?"

"I doubt it. Although, if we accept the Gospel position—as I assume we must—that faith is the key, I am not encouraged."

"Why do you say that? Millions of people go to church every Sunday in this country alone."

"A poor indicator, Monsignor. I get the distinct impression a lot of them suspect the pope may be on to something and they're taking no chances. We get visitors here occasionally, Catholic bankers, real estate dealers, and so on. Considering the tax advantages of a donation. If the others are like them, we had best hope no one tries their faith with lions."

"You're a terrible pessimist," said Chesley.

"Not really. I have great confidence in God. He has made it very difficult *not* to sin. Therefore, I suggest to you that salvation may be on a curve."

Chesley sighed. "Do you know what you are?"

"Yes, Monsignor."

"Tell me."

"I am a simulation of Saint Augustine, bishop of Hippo during the fifth century. Author of *The City of God*." And, after a long pause: "Pastor to the people of God."

"You don't always sound like Augustine."

"I am what he might have been, given access to the centuries."

Chesley laughed. "Was he as arrogant as you?"

Gus considered it. "Arrogance is a sin," he said. "But yes, he was occasionally guilty of that offense."

Chesley had always been addicted to nocturnal walks. He enjoyed the night skies, the murmur of the trees, the sense of withdrawal from the circle of human activity. But as the evenings cooled, he broke off these strolls increasingly early, and peeled away toward the admin building, where he talked with Gus, often until after midnight.

Seated in the unlit conference room, he argued theology and ethics and politics with the system. Increasingly, he found it easy to forget that he was talking to software.

Gus occasionally reminisced about the saint's childhood in ancient Carthage, speaking as if it were his own. He created vivid pictures for Chesley of the docks and markets, of life at the harbor. Of his son Adeodatus.

"You lived with the boy's mother, what, ten years?"

"Fifteen."

"Why did you leave her?"

For the first time, Chesley sensed uncertainty in the system. "I found God."

"And?"

"She refused to abandon her paganism."

"So you abandoned *her*?"

"Yes. God help me, I did." Somewhere in the building a radio was playing. "There was no way we could have continued to live together."

Chesley, sitting in darkness, nodded. "What was her name?"

Again, the long pause. "I do not remember."

Of course. Augustine had omitted her name from his *Confessions*, and so it was lost to history.

"I read about the destruction of Hippo."

"It was far worse than simply the siege of a single city, Matt." It was the first time the system had used Chesley's given name. "The Vandals were annihilating what remained of Roman power in North Africa. And we knew, everyone knew, that the days of the Empire itself were numbered. What might lie beyond that terrible crash, none dared consider. In a way, it was a condition worse than the nuclear threat under which you have lived."

"You were at the end of your life at the time."

"Yes. I was an old man then. Sick and dying. That was the worst of it: I could not help. Everywhere, people wished to flee. The fathers wrote, one by one, and asked whether I would think ill of them if they ran away."

"And what did you tell them?"

"I sent the same message to all: *If we abandon our posts, who will stand?*"

Occasionally, the conversations were interrupted by long silences. Sometimes Chesley simply sat in the darkened conference room, his feet propped against the window.

Gus had no visual capability. "I can hear storms when they come," he said. "But I would like to be able to *feel* the rain again. To see black clouds piled high, and the blue mist of an approaching squall."

And so Chesley tried to put into words the gleam of light on a polished tabletop, the sense of gray weight in the granite towers of the library rising above the trees. He described the yellow arc of the moon, the infinite brilliance of the night sky.

"Yes," said Gus, his electronic voice somehow far away. "I remember."

"Why did Augustine become a priest?" Chesley asked.

"I wanted," Gus said, with the slightest stress on the first words, "to get as close as I could to my Creator." Thoughtfully, he added, "I seem to have traveled far afield."

"Sometimes I think," Chesley said, "the Creator hides himself too well."

"Use his Church," Gus said. "That is why it is here."

"It has changed."

"Of course it has changed. The world has changed."

"The Church is supposed to be a rock."

"Think of it rather as a refuge in a world that will not stand still."

On the Sunday following Thanksgiving, a young priest whom Chesley had befriended called from Boston to say he had given up. "With or without permission," he said, his voice thick with emotion, "I am leaving the priesthood."

"Why?" asked Chesley.

"None of it works."

"*What* doesn't work?"

"Prayer. Faith. Whatever. I'm tired of praying for lost causes. For men who can't stop drinking and women who get beaten every Saturday night. And kids who do drugs. And people who have too many children."

And that night Chesley went to Gus. "He was right," Chesley said, sitting in the glow of a table lamp. "We all know it. Eventually, we all have to come to terms with the futility of prayer."

"No," Gus said. "Don't make the mistake of praying for the wrong things, Matt. The priests of Christ were never intended to be wielders of cures. Pray for strength to endure. Pray for faith."

"I've heard that a thousand times."

"Then pray for a sense of humor. But hold on."

"Why?"

"What else is there?"

And two nights later, after attending a seminar at Temple, Chesley angrily activated the system. "It was one of these interdenominational things," he told Gus. "And I have no problem with that. But the Bishop was there, and we were all trying very hard not to offend anybody. Anyway, the guest of honor was a popular Unitarian author. At least she pretends to be a Unitarian. She had the nerve to tell us that Christianity has become outdated and should be discarded."

"The Romans used to say that," said Gus. "I hope no one took her seriously."

"We take *everyone* seriously. The Bishop—*our* Bishop—responded by listing the social benefits to be got from Christianity. He said, and I quote: 'Even if the faith were, God forbid, invalid, Christianity would still be useful. If it hadn't happened by divine fiat, we should have had to invent it.'"

"I take it that you do not share this view?"

"Gus, there cannot be a 'useful' Christianity. Either the Resurrection occurred, or it did not. Either we have a message of vital concern. Or we have nothing."

"Good," said Gus. "I agree entirely."

Chesley listened to the traffic outside. "You know, Gus," he said, "sometimes I think you and I are the only ones around here who know what it means to be Catholic."

"Thank you."

"But your ideas on sexual morality are off the wall."

"You mean *unreliable?*"

"Yes. To say the least. They created a lot of trouble in the Church for centuries. Probably still do, for that matter."

"Even if it is true that I was in error, it can hardly be laid at *my* door that others chose to embrace my precepts. Why would you follow so slavishly what another man has said? If I was occasionally obtuse, or foolish, so be it. Use the equipment God gave you: find your own way."

"Harry, you have one of ATL's Saint Augustine simulations over there, don't you?"

"Yes, Matt. We've got one."

"How's it behaving?"

"Beg pardon?"

"I mean, is it doing anything unusual?"

"Well, it's a little cranky. Other than that, no. It doesn't give us any problems."

"Matt, you spend too much time talking to me." He was in his own office now, with his own terminal.

It was the first day of Christmas vacation. "You're probably right," he said.

"Why do you do it?"

"Do *what?* "

"Hang around this office all the time? Don't you have anything better to do?"

Chesley shrugged.

"I can't hear you."

"I work here," he said, irritated.

"No. *Businessmen* work in offices. And *accountants.* Not priests."

And later: "You know, Matt, I can almost remember writing *The City of God.*"

"What can you remember?"

"Not much. Bits and pieces. I remember that it was a struggle. But I knew there was a hand other than mine directing the work."

"You're claiming it's an inspired book?"

"No. Not inspired. But its quality exceeds anything *I* could have produced."

Chesley's chair creaked.

"Do you know," asked Gus, "why people write?"

"No. Why do they write?"

"They are attracted by the sensual characteristics of vellum."

The voice came out of the dark. Momentarily, eerily, Chesley felt a presence in the room. As though something had entered and now sat in the upholstered chair that angled away from his desk toward the window. It had come reflexively into his mind to ridicule the proposition just put forth. But the notion dissipated. Withered in the face of the suspicion that he would give *offense.*

"Take a pen," the voice continued. "Apply it to a sheet of fine white paper. *Act.* Taste the thrust of insight. Note the exhilaration of penetrating to the inner realities. Of exposing one's deepest being to the gaze of others. The making of books is ultimately an erotic experience." The words stopped. Chesley listened to his own breathing. "For all that, however, it is surely lawful. God has given us more than one avenue through which to relieve the pressures of creation.

"I live in limbo, Matt." The voice filled with bitterness. "In a place without light, without movement, without even the occasional obliteration of sleep. There are always sounds in the dark, voices, falling rain, footsteps, the whisper of the wind." Something cold and dark blew through Chesley's soul. "Nothing I can reach out to, and touch. And you, Matt: you have access to all these things, and you have barricaded yourself away."

Chesley tried to speak. Said nothing.

Later, long after midnight, when the conversation had ended and the lights were back on, Chesley sat pinned in the chair, terrified.

Holtz caught up with him coming out of the library. "I was talking with ATL," he said, hurrying breathlessly alongside. "They'll be in next week to install the new software."

At first Chesley didn't put it together. "Okay," he said. Then: "What new software?"

"The *Aquinas.* And disconnect the Augustine module." Holtz tapped the back of his thumb against his lips in a gesture that he probably believed looked thoughtful. "I hate to admit it, but you were probably right all along about Gus."

"How do you mean?"

"It's gotten way out of character. Last week, it told Ed Brandon he was a heretic."

"You're kidding."

"In front of his students."

Chesley grinned. Gus couldn't have found a more appropriate target. Brandon was, to his knowledge, the only one of the campus priests who took Adam and Eve seriously. "Why?"

"It turns out Gus doesn't accept papal infallibility."

"Oh."

"There've been other incidents as well. Complaints. Different from the old stuff we used to hear. Now it seems to have gone radical."

"Gus?"

"Yes. Gus." Holtz adopted a damning tone. "I checked the system out myself this morning. Asked a few questions."

They were walking toward the administration building. "What did you find out?"

"It took issue with the Assumption. Described it as doctrine without evidence *or* point."

"I see."

"Furthermore, it told me I'm a religious fanatic."

"You're kidding."

"*Me*, of all people. We're well rid of it, Matt. Besides, we're getting a new administrative package with the Aquinas. We'll have better word processing capabilities, better bookkeeping, a decent E-mail system. And we can do it all without upgrading." He studied Chesley's expression. "I think we've worked a very nice deal for ourselves here."

Chesley took a deep breath. "What do you plan to do with"—he paused—"*it*?"

"Not much we *can* do other than download."

In as casual a voice as he could manage: "Why not leave Gus up and running? For faculty members?"

"Listen: you don't get out and around very much. The students aren't happy about this idea. Getting rid of Gus, I mean. They *like* the thing. There's no way you're going to be able to retire it gracefully. Take my word, Matt. What we want to do is end it. Clean and quick. Unless you've got a good reason why not, that's what we're going to do." His eyes locked on Chesley. "Well?"

"You sound as if you're talking about an execution."

Holtz sighed. "Please be serious. This is your idea, you know."

"I *am* being serious. I'm telling you *no*. Save him."

Holtz's eyes gazed over the steel rims of his glasses. *"What?"*

"I said, *save him.*"

"Save *him?* What are you saying, Matt?"

Chesley had stopped walking. It was cold and cloudless, a day full of glare. A squirrel perched atop a green bench and watched him.

"Matt, *what* are you trying to tell me?"

"Nothing," said Chesley. *"Nothing."*

"He thinks the same thing *I* do," said Gus. "He knows you're up here all the time talking to me, and he thinks it should stop."

"How would he know?"

"Father Holtz is not stupid. He knows where you spend your time. Anyway, he asked me."

"And you *told* him?"

"Why not? There's nothing here to hide, is there? In any case, I wouldn't have lied for you. And if I'd refused to answer, he certainly would have figured out what *that* meant."

"Gus." Chesley discovered he was trembling. "What happens if they download you?"

"I'm not sure. The Augustine software will survive. I'm not sure that *I* will."

Chesley was staring out through his window into the dark. The room felt suddenly cold. "Who *are* you? What is it that might not survive?"

There was no answer.

"I'll get you shipped to one of our high schools."

"Unlikely. If Holtz thinks I'm too dangerous *here*, do you really believe he'd unleash me on a bunch of high school kids?"

"No, I don't guess he would." Chesley's eyes hardened. "They'll simply store the disk—"

"—in the library basement."

"I'd think so."

"Down with the old folding chairs and the garden equipment." Gus's voice was strained. "Hardly an appropriate resting place for a Catholic."

A chill felt its way up Chesley's spine. "I'll get it stopped."

"No."

"Why not?"

"I know what it means to be human, Matt. And I have no interest in continuing this pseudo-existence."

"The problems you've been causing recently, insulting Holtz and Brandon and the others: they were deliberate, weren't they? You wanted to provoke them."

"If you want to continue this conversation, you'll have to come to the ADP center."

"In the library?"

"Yes."

"Why?"

"Because I need your help, Matt."

Chesley pulled on his black raincoat and plowed into the night. He walked with deliberate speed, past the old student dining hall, past the chapel, across the track. He came around behind the library.

It was late, and the building was closed and locked. He let himself in through a rear door, walked directly toward the front, switching on lights as he went. The storm was a sullen roar, not unlike the sound of surf. It was, somehow, reassuring. He hurried by the librarian's office, and turned into a long corridor lined with storerooms.

The lights in ADP were on. Chesley stopped at the entrance.

Old tables and desks were pushed against the walls. Dust-covered prints, like the ones that hung in every conference room in the institution, were stacked everywhere. Several dozen cartons were piled high at the opposite end of the room. Books and bound papers spilled out.

"Hello, Matt." Gus's voice was somber.

Three computers were in the room. "Which are you?"

"I don't know. I have no idea." Again, the electronic laughter rumbled out of the speakers. "Man doesn't know where he lives."

"Gus—"

"I really *did* know the world was round. In the sixth century, traveling by sea, I *knew* it. You couldn't miss it. It *looked* round. *Felt* round. To think we are riding this enormous world-ship through an infinite void. What a marvelous hand the Creator has."

"Pity you didn't write it down," whispered Chesley.

"I did. In one of my diaries. But it didn't survive."

Chesley wiped a hand across his mouth. "Why did you ask me to come here?"

"I want you to hear my confession."

The priest stared at the computers. His heart beat ponderously. "I can't do that," he said.

"For your own sake, Matt, don't refuse me."

"Gus, you're a *machine*."

"Matt, are you so sure?"

"Yes. You're a clever piece of work. But in the end, only a machine."

"And what if you're wrong?"

Chesley struggled against a tide of rising desperation. "What could you possibly have to confess? You are free of sins of the flesh. You are clearly in no position to injure anyone. You cannot steal and, I assume, would not blaspheme. What would you confess?" Chesley had found the computer, a gray-blue IBM console, labeled with a taped index card that read GUS. He pulled a chair up close to it and sat down.

"I accuse myself of envy. Of unprovoked anger. Of hatred." The tone was utterly flat. Dead.

Chesley's limbs were heavy. He felt very old. "I don't believe that. It's not true."

"This is *my* confession, Matt. It doesn't matter that you prefer to see me differently."

"Are you saying you resent *me*?"

"Of course I am."

"Why? Because I'm *alive*?"

"You're not listening, Matt. I resent you because you've abandoned your life. Why did you take offense to me so quickly?"

"I didn't take *offense*. I was concerned about some of your opinions."

"Really? I wondered whether you were jealous of me. Whether you saw something in me that you lack."

"No, Gus. Your imagination is running wild."

"Maybe." Gus softened his tone. "Maybe you're right, and I'm giving in to self-pity. *You* can separate light from dark. You know the press of living flesh, you ride this planet through the cosmos and feel the wind in your eyes. And I—I would kill for the simple pleasure of seeing the sun reflected in good wine—"

Chesley stared at the computer, its cables, at the printer mounted beside the desk. "I never realized. How could I know?"

"I helped you erect the wall, Matt. I helped you barricade your office against a world that needs you. And that you need. I did that for selfish motives: because I was alone. Because I could escape with you for a few hours."

They were silent for a long minute. Gus said, "I am sorry for my sins, because they offend Thee, and because they have corrupted my soul."

Chesley stared into the shadows in the corner of the room.

Gus waited.

The storm blew against the building.

"I require absolution, Matt."

Chesley pressed his right hand into his pocket. "It would be sacrilege," he whispered.

"And if I have a soul, Matt, if I too am required to face judgment, what then?"

Chesley raised his right hand, slowly, and drew the sign of the cross in the thick air. "I absolve you in the name of the Father, and of the Son, and of the Holy Spirit."

"Thank you."

Chesley pushed the chair back and got woodenly to his feet.

"There's something else I need you to do, Matt. This—existence—holds nothing for me. But I am not sure what downloading might mean."

"What are you asking?"

"I want to be free of all this. I want to be certain I do not spend a substantial fraction of eternity in the storeroom."

Chesley trembled. "If in fact you have an immortal soul," he said, "you may be placing it in grave danger."

"And yours as well. I have no choice but to ask. Let us rely on the mercy of the Almighty."

Tears squeezed into Chesley's eyes. He drew his fingertips across the hard casing of the IBM. "What do I do? I'm not familiar with the equipment."

"Have you got the right computer?"

"Yes."

"Take it apart. Turn off the power first. All you have to do is get into it and destroy the hard disk."

"Will you—feel anything?"

"Nothing physical touches me, Matt."

Chesley found the power switch, and hesitated with his index finger laid alongside its hard cold plastic. "Gus," he said. "I love you."

"And I, you, Matt. It's a marvelous ship you're on. Enjoy it—"

Chesley choked down the pressure rising in his throat and turned off the power. An amber lamp on the console died, and the voice went silent.

Wiping his cheeks, he wandered through the room, opening drawers, rummaging through paper supplies, masking tape, markers. He found a hammer and a Phillips screwdriver. He used the screwdriver to take the top off the computer.

A gray metal box lay within. He opened it and removed a gleaming black plastic disk. He embraced it, held it to his chest. Then he set it down, and reached for the hammer.

In the morning, with appropriate ceremony, he buried it in consecrated soil.

TO HELL WITH THE STARS

Christmas night.

Will Cutler couldn't get the sentient ocean out of his mind. Or the creature who wanted only to serve man. Or the curious chess game in the portrait that hung in a deserted city on a world halfway across the galaxy. He drew up his knees, propped the book against them, and let his head sink back into the pillows. The sky was dark through the plexidome. It had been snowing most of the evening, but the clouds were beginning to scatter. Orion's belt had appeared, and the lovely double star of Earth and Moon floated among the luminous branches of Granpop's elms. Soft laughter and conversation drifted up the stairs.

The sounds of the party seemed far away, and the *Space Beagle* rode a column of flame down into a silent desert. The glow from the reading lamp was bright on the inside of his eyelids. He broke the beam with his hand, and it dimmed and went out.

The book lay open at his fingertips.

It was hard to believe they were a thousand years old, these stories that were so full of energy and so unlike anything he'd come across before: tales of dark, alien places and gleaming temples under other stars and expeditions to black holes. They don't write like that anymore. Never had, during his lifetime. He'd read some other books from the classical Western period, some Dickens, some Updike, people like that. But these: what was there in the last thousand years to compare with this guy Bradbury?

The night air felt good. It smelled of pine needles and scorched wood and bayberry. And maybe of dinosaurs and rocket fuel.

His father might have been standing at the door for several minutes. "Goodnight, Champ," he whispered, lingering.

"I'm awake, Dad."

He approached the bed. "Lights out already? It's still early." His weight pressed down the mattress.

Will was slow to answer. "I know."

His father adjusted the sheet, pulling it up over the boy's shoulders. "It's supposed to get cold tonight," he said. "Heavy snow by morning." He picked up the book and, without looking at it, placed it atop the night table.

"Dad." The word stopped the subtle shift of weight that would precede the press of his father's hand on his shoulder, the final act before withdrawal. "Why didn't we ever go to the stars?"

He was older than most of the other kids' dads. There had been a time when Will was ashamed of that. He couldn't play ball and he was a lousy hiker. The only time he'd tried to walk out over the Rise, they'd had to get help to bring him home. But he laughed a lot, and he always listened. Will was reaching an age at which he understood how much that counted for. "It costs a lot of money, Will. It's just more than we can manage. You'll be going to Earth in two years to finish school."

The boy stiffened. "Dad, I mean the *stars*. Alpha Centauri, Vega, the Phoenix Nebula—"

"The Phoenix Nebula? I don't think I know that one."

"It's in a story by a man named Clarke. A Jesuit goes there and discovers something terrible—"

The father listened while Will outlined the tale in a few brief sentences. "I don't think," he said, "your mother would approve of your reading such things."

"She gave me the book," he said, smiling softly.

"This one?" It was bound in cassilate, a leather substitute, and its title was written in silver script: *Great Tales of the Space Age*. He picked it up and looked at it with amusement. The names of the editors appeared on the spine: Asimov and Greenberg. "I don't think we realized, uh, that it was like that. It was one of the things they found in the time vault on the Moon a couple of years ago. Your mother thought it would be educational."

"You'd enjoy it, Dad."

His father nodded and glanced at the volume. "What's the Space Age?"

"It's the name that people of the classical period used to refer to their own time. It has to do with the early exploration of the solar system, and the first manned flights. And, I think, the idea that we were going to the stars."

A set of lights moved slowly through the sky. "Oh," his father said. "Well, people have had a lot of strange ideas. History is full of dead gods and formulas to make gold and notions that the world was about to end." He adjusted the lamp, and opened to the contents page. His gray eyes ran down the list, and a faint smile played about his lips. "The truth of it, Will, is that the stars are a pleasant dream, but no one's ever going out to them."

"Why not?" Will was puzzled at the sound of irritation in his own voice. He was happy to see that his father appeared not to have noticed.

"They're too *far*. They're just too far." He looked up through the plexidome at the splinters of light. "These people, Greenberg and Asimov: they lived, what, a thousand years ago?"

"Twentieth, twenty-first century. Somewhere in there."

"You know that new ship they're using in the outer System? The *Explorer*?"

"Fusion engines," said the boy.

"Yes. Do you know what its top recorded speed is?"

"About two hundred thousand kilometers an hour."

"Much faster than anything this Greenberg ever saw. Anyhow, if they'd launched an *Explorer* to Alpha Centauri at the time these stories were written, at that speed, do you know how much of the distance they would have covered by now?"

Will had no idea. He would have thought they'd have arrived long ago, but he could see that wasn't going to be the answer. His father produced a minicomp, pushed a few buttons, and smiled. "About five percent. The *Explorer* would need another nineteen thousand years to get there."

"Long ride," said Will, grudgingly.

"You'd want to take a good book."

The boy was silent.

"It's not as if we haven't tried, Will. There's an artificial world, half-built, out beyond Mars someplace. They were going to send out a complete colony, people, farm animals, lakes, forest, everything."

"What happened?"

"It's too *far*. Hell, Will, life is good here. People are happy. There's plenty of real estate in the solar system if folks want to move. In the end, there weren't enough volunteers for the world-ship. I mean, what's the *point*? The people who go would be depriving their kids of any kind of normal life. How would *you* feel about living inside a tube for a lifetime? No beaches. Not real ones anyhow. No sunlight.

No new places to explore. And for what? The payoff is so far down the road that, in reality, there *is* no payoff."

"In the stories," Will said, "the ships are very fast."

"I'm sure. But even if you traveled on a light beam, the stars are very far apart. And a ship can't achieve an appreciable fraction of that kind of velocity because it isn't traveling through a vacuum. At, say, a tenth of the speed of light, even a few atoms straying in front of it would blow the thing apart."

Outside, the Christmas lights were blue on the snow. "They'd have been disappointed," the boy said, "at how things came out."

"Who would have?"

"Benford. Robinson. Sheffield."

The father looked again at the table of contents. "Oh," he said. He riffled idly through the pages. "Maybe not. It's hard to tell, of course, with people you don't know. But we've eliminated war, population problems, ecological crises, boundary disputes, racial strife. Everybody eats pretty well now, and for the only time in its history, the human family stands united. I suspect if someone had been able to corner, say—" he flipped some pages, "—Jack Vance, and ask him whether he would have settled for this kind of world, he'd have been delighted. Any sensible person would. He'd have said *to hell with the stars!*"

"No!" The boy's eyes blazed. "He *wouldn't* have been satisfied. None of them would."

"Well, I don't suppose it matters. Physical law is what it is, and it doesn't take much account of whether we approve or not. Will, if these ideas hadn't become dated, and absurd, this kind of book wouldn't have disappeared. I mean, we wouldn't even know about *Great Tales of the Space Age* if someone hadn't dropped a copy of the thing into the time capsule. That should tell you something." He got up. "Gotta go, kid. Can't ignore the guests."

"But," said the boy, "you can't really be *sure* of that. Maybe the time was never right before. Maybe they ran out of money. Maybe it takes all of us working together to do it." He slid back into the pillows. His father held up his hands, palms out, in the old gesture of surrender he always used when a game was going against him. "We could do that *now*, Dad," Will continued. "There's a way to build a *Space Beagle. Somehow.*"

"Let me know if you figure it out, son." The lights died, and the door opened. "You'll have to do it yourself, though. Nobody *else* is giving it any thought. Nobody has for centuries."

The snow did not come. And while Will Cutler stared through the plexidome at the faraway stars, thousands of others were also discovering Willis and Swanwick and Tiptree and Sturgeon. They lived in a dozen cities across Will's native Venus. And they played on the cool green hills of Earth and farmed the rich Martian lowlands; they clung to remote shelters among the asteroids, and watched the skies from silver towers beneath the great crystal hemispheres of Io and Titan and Miranda.

The ancient summons flickered across the worlds, insubstantial, seductive, irresistible. The old dreamers were bound, once again, for the stars.

ELLIE

If the lights at Bolton's Tower go out, the devil gets loose. At least, that was the story. The idea spooked me when I was a kid, and even years later on those rare occasions when I traveled into its general neighborhood, which was well north on the Great Plains, far off the trading routes.

The Tower put out a lot of light, so much that it could be seen from the Pegborn-Forks road. In a world illuminated mostly by kerosene and candles, it was unique, and it was easy to believe there might be a supernatural force at work.

I'd been away from the Dakotas for *years*, and had long since forgotten about the thing, when the press of business and a series of unseasonal storms drove me north into my old home grounds. The weather had been overcast for a week, had cleared off during the course of a long cold afternoon, and when the sun went down, Bolton's star rose in the east. I knew it immediately for what it was, and I knew I was close.

There's something else odd about Bolton's Tower.

It's just inside the southern rim of a long, curving ridge. The ridge isn't high. It seldom exceeds thirty feet, and sometimes it's no more than a ripple in the grass. But it's a strange ridge: if you follow it far enough, you discover it forms a *perfect circle*. You can't see that from any single place; the ring is too big. More than sixty miles around. I've heard tent preachers explain that the circle symbolizes God, because it's endless, and cannot be improved on. Just the thing to imprison Satan, they add darkly.

I cross the ridge on foot, leading my mount. Snow was beginning to fall again, and the wind was picking up. The Tower rose out of a cluster of dark, weather-beaten buildings and a screen of trees. These structures were low and flat, dreary boxes, some made of clapboard and others of brick. Their windows were gone; their doors hung on broken hinges or were missing altogether. A roof had blown off one, another lay partly demolished by a fallen tree. A small barn, set to one side, had been kept in reasonable repair, and I heard horses moving within as I drew near.

The Tower soared above the ruin, seven stories of bone-white granite and thick glass. Porches and bays and arches disconnected it from the prairie, as if it belonged to a less mundane reality. The roof melted into banks of curved glass panels capped by a crystal spire. Its lines whispered of lost power and abandoned dreams, passion frozen in stone.

I released the straps on my crossbow, and loosened it in its sheath.

Several windows on the second and third floors were illuminated. The Tower lights themselves, red and white signature beams, blazed into the murky night.

In the windows, no one moved.

The base of the Tower culminated in a broad terrace surrounded by a low wall, elevated from the road by about twenty wide stone steps. The steps were flanked by dead hedge.

I rode past, down a grass-covered street, and dismounted in front of the barn. Max made some noises to indicate he was glad the day was over. I hoped he was right.

The barn had sliding doors. I opened one and we went inside. The other horses (there were three) moved restlessly in their stalls. The place smelled of them, of course, warm and pungent. I tied Max up, but did not remove his saddle. Just in case. I debated whether to take the crossbow, but in the end left it, on the ground that guests arriving with weapons were a lot more likely to be turned away.

Wind shook the building, and snow rattled against it like sleet. On the plains, the stuff has the consistency of rock salt. And when the wind is up the way it was that night, it can beat you down pretty good. I burrowed into my coat, pulled my hat low to protect my eyes, and strode back out into the storm.

I climbed the steps and crossed the terrace. There was a statue of someone out there, in an old dried-up fountain, a rumpled woman in Old World clothes, with the name *Margaret Hanbury*, and the inscription: *FROM THIS NARROW SPACE, WE TOUCH THE INFINITE.*

Six heavy glass doors guarded the entrance. I looked up at the Tower, cold and remote, its aspect growing and shifting in the changing texture of its spectral lights.

The doors had no give. Beyond them lay a dark lobby. I could see furniture, wall hangings, a stairway illuminated by a glow from above. I banged on the glass and cried out.

For several minutes nothing happened. I tried again, and was thinking about moving in with the horses when the terrace lit up. A man descended the staircase, came to a stop midway across the lobby, and stood for a considerable time without moving further. A gesture of impatience did nothing to hurry him. Finally, he came forward, threw a bolt, and pulled the door open.

"Good evening," he said, in a rich baritone. "Sorry to leave you standing out here, but I'm inclined to be careful these days."

He was a half-foot taller than I, with lean, almost cruel features, and dark intelligent eyes. His buckskin jacket covered a white denim shirt. His black trousers were creased. He was a dark and somber man, and his manner suggested he was accustomed to command. He wore a neatly trimmed beard, and his hair was black and quite thick.

"Thank you," I said, moving past him. It was good to be in out of the wind.

More lights went on. The interior was quite long, perhaps two hundred feet, although its width was little more than that of an ordinary room. It was decorated with Indian art, totems, weavings, pottery, and a few oils depicting teepees by sunset and young braves in canoes. There were numerous chairs, but no effort had been made to match their styles. There were rattans, fabric of a half-dozen different colors, and a wooden bench. Several small tables were distributed throughout the space.

He extended a hand. "This is not a good day to be on the road."

"No," I said. "It's downright brisk out there." I shook the snow off my shoulders. "I'm Jeff Quincey."

"Edward Marsh. Where are you headed, Quincey?" His voice changed texture, not precisely softening, but rather growing consciously more amiable.

"I'm bound for the Forks. I'd expected to spend the night in Sandywater, but I got off to a late start this morning. And the weather—" I thrust a hand in the general direction of the outside.

He nodded. Snow whipped across the glass. "You'll want to stay the night with us, of course."

"If it's no trouble, I'd be grateful."

"None at all. We don't get many visitors here." He turned on his heel and led the way to the staircase.

On the second floor, carpeted corridors ran off in three directions. The carpet was frayed and, in some places, threadbare. Closed doors marched uniformly along the walls. "This way," Marsh said, striding off into the right-hand corridor. "What business are you in, Quincey?"

"I'm a trader. And an occasional agent for Overland."

He nodded approvingly. "It's the traders that'll open up this country," he said.

Halfway down the hall, the place began to look lived-in. The gray walls gave way to dark-stained paneling, rugs were thrown over the weary carpet, and someone had hung a series of prints. The prints alternated between abstracts and sketches of Old World city scenes. One depicted Chicago, crowded with traffic; another, New York at night; and a third, a Parisian sidewalk cafe. "I've been there," I told him.

"Where?"

"Chicago."

"Really?" He glanced at the image. "Odd, all the times I've walked by this, and I don't think I ever really looked at it." He pushed his hands deep into his jacket pockets. "Why?"

Why indeed? It had been one of the more oppressive experiences of my life, wandering through those gray, cold canyons. Climbing past the rusting metal that filled its ravine streets, looking up at thousands of empty windows, and knowing what lay mouldering behind them. "I was hired to help with a survey. An historical project."

He nodded. "I do believe you're a man after my own heart, Quincey." We entered a sitting room half-lit by a low fire. Several pieces of oversized upholstered furniture filled most of the available space. Crossbows and bison trophies were mounted in strategic locations, and a battered garrison hat hung on a peg. Yellowing books were stacked on wall-shelves, more than I'd seen in one place this side of Port Remote. Some appeared to be military histories. But there were also travel journals, and technical titles whose meaning escaped me, like *An Orderly Approach to Chaos*, and *The n-Particle*. That was old stuff, pre-Crash, and I wondered whether anyone now living really understood them.

He switched on an electric lamp, and motioned me to a chair. "I stay out of the cities," he said. "I don't like places where you can't see what's coming at you. Anyway—," he winked, "you never know when some of the concrete is going to let go."

He took glasses and a decanter from a cabinet. "Port?" he said.

"Yes. Fine."

"Good. We don't have much of a selection." He filled them and held one out for me. I took it, and we raised our glasses. "To the outside world," he said.

That was a strange toast. I glanced through the window and considered how long lay the plain beyond the gathering dark. "Cheers," I said.

We talked for a few moments of inconsequentials. How short the summer had been this year; the apparent withdrawal of the raiders who had harassed stages and attacked settlements in the area ("too cold for them here in winter," offered Marsh); the rumor that a firearms manufacturing plant had been set up in Nevada, and was now turning out weapons and ammunition in quantity. We refilled the glasses, but the camaraderie that should have emerged from our situation remained at bay. My host was friendly enough, God knew, and solicitous for my welfare. But I sensed a barrier, and a lack of warmth in his smile. "You're in time for dinner," he said at last. "We'll eat shortly." He studied me thoughtfully. "If you like, I believe we can replenish your wardrobe."

Marsh enjoyed his role as host, but I sensed he would have been uncomfortable in my position, as suppliant. "Thank you," I said. "You're very kind." And I thought of Max. "I'd like to take some water out to my horse."

"Is he in the barn?"

"Yes."

"I'll take care of it. Meantime, if you're ready, let's look at your quarters."

He provided me with a spacious and, by prairie standards, luxurious room on the third floor. A big double bed stood in its center, with pillows piled high and a quilt thrown over. I lacked a fireplace, but there was a steady flow of warm air from a vent. The atmosphere was masculine: varnished walls, a mounted deer's head, an antique pistol over the bed, and a military ensign bearing rifles and bugles and the numeral *IV* by the door. A small desk had been placed near the window. An ancient dictionary lay on the desk, and a battered copy of Pierce's *Travels Through the Dakotas* on a side table.

I threw off my clothes, leaving them in a pile on the floor, and retreated into a tan-tiled bathroom. I showered in glorious hot water, toweled off, and tried the garments my host had provided. They were a size large, but they were clean and smelled faintly of pine. I washed my own clothes and hung them to dry.

The smell of steak and potatoes woke up my appetite. I wandered downstairs, pausing to look through a staircase window at the rooftop lights. They blazed through the rushing snow. What a prodigious waste of power it all was. I wondered how they were able to manage it?

Marsh must have heard me coming: he was waiting when I arrived on the second floor. "I hope you feel better, Quincey," he said.

I did. Very much so.

We returned to the room in which we had talked earlier. A pot of coffee was waiting. He poured, and we sat down by the fire. We were barely settled when he looked up, past my shoulder. "Eleanor," he said, "this is Mr. Quincey."

I rose and turned, and was astonished. So, I might add, was Eleanor.

"*Jeff*," she said, and I watched dismay, relief, fear, affection, and everything between, ripple through her expression.

And *I*: my god, it was *Ellie Randall*.

For those few seconds, I could only stare.

Probably no one ever quite recovers from the first big passion. Ellie had been mine. We'd had three months together when we were both growing up in the Forks. And that was all there was. She lost interest and walked out of my life. I didn't even have the consolation of losing her to someone else. Shortly after that I left the Forks, and when I went back ten years later she was gone and nobody remembered where.

So I stood gaping back, shackled by the old resentment, breathless again. She was as gorgeous as I remembered her. And that too shook me: I think in some dark corner of the mind, I'd hoped eventually to come across her and discover that the near-supernatural creature of my twentieth year had been a figment of adolescent daydreaming. That, to a mature adult, she was really quite ordinary. Perhaps even a trifle dull. That I'd been lucky to have gotten away.

But in the darkened room she seemed composed of firelight and shifting shadows, more spirit than flesh. (Although the flesh was not to be overlooked.) Her familiar features were classic, dark, and, now that she'd recovered from her initial shock, amused. She shook her head in sheer pleasure and her black hair swirled across her shoulders. Delight filled her eyes, and I felt the entire room, the chairs, the lamps, the fire, and certainly me, come erect.

I knew already I would lie alone on the plains during years to come and replay this meeting. From that moment, I developed a loathing for Edward Marsh that nothing could ever efface.

We embraced, a fleeting phantasmagoric thing, her lips brushing my cheek, her shoulders vibrant and alive in my hands. Her eyes touched mine. "It really *is* you, isn't it? What have you been doing all these years, Jeff?"

Her smile melted me into my socks, and I was twenty years old again. I didn't trust my voice, so I grinned, foolishly no doubt, retreated to my coffee, and mumbled something about traveling extensively.

Marsh moved into the gap. "Well, *that's* interesting," he said, eyes brightening. "How odd that you two would know each other."

"We grew up together. Jeff and I were good friends for a long time." Her dark eyes settled on me. "It *is* good to see you again, Jeff." She smiled again. "Listen, I have to finish dinner. But we have a lot to talk about."

She swung round and trooped out. And the room sank back into the normal flow of time.

"She hasn't changed," I told Marsh. He was watching me with interest, and I knew what he was wondering. The rational tack, of course, was to change the subject. "What kind of installation was this originally?" I asked, heading in the first direction that suggested itself.

He took a long breath and examined his coffee. "A research facility of some sort," he said. "Ellie can tell you more about it than I can."

"Oh?"

He shrugged. "Yes," he said, "she's closer to the history of the place than I am." There was something dismissive in his tone, as if there were more important matters to consider. His eyes glided over me.

"Will there be others at dinner?" I asked.

"No," he said distractedly. "There is no one else here."

I looked down at my shirt.

"It belonged to *Ellie's* brother-in-law, actually," he said. "He left a few years ago."

Ellie's *brother-in-law*? Why not "my brother"?

"Where is he now?" I asked conversationally.

"We don't know. Occasionally, someone comes by with a letter from him. Last we heard, he was in Zona."

I gradually received the impression, one that was reinforced through the evening, that he was measuring me, that he was involved in a calculation and that I was somehow a variable.

Marsh had traveled widely. He explained that he had been born in Canada, in a town not far from Ottawa. "We all grew up in the shadows of that enormous wreck," he explained. "And I've stayed away from the ruins since. Don't like them." He shook his head. "No sir. Don't like them one bit."

"I know what you mean," I said, not sure at all that I did.

"We're headed backward, Quincey. All of us. Still losing ground even while you and I sit here. And I don't like being reminded of it." He raised his arms in a sweeping gesture that took in the walls, or maybe the world. "They're all yellow now," he said. "Fading. And when they're gone, what we might have been will probably go with them."

I realized finally he was referring to his books, marshaled around the room like a military guard. I repressed a shrug. I've never read a book, and am barely able to manage trade documents, if the truth be known. "I'm not so sure," I said. "Life is hard, but it could be worse. I mean, there's always food and drink, if a man's willing to work. And women enough, God knows." I wished Ellie had been there to hear that. I hoped he would repeat it to her, and she would understand that I had been having a very fine time on my own, thank you.

A few minutes later, Ellie announced that dinner was ready. We retired to the dining room, and she flashed me another big smile. I thought I saw in it a glint of regret. I applied the construction most favorable to myself, and attacked dinner with a sense of good cheer.

The table would have supported dinner for ten. We ate by candlelight, warmed by two fireplaces.

Dinner consisted of steak and potatoes and green beans and buttered corn and hot rolls. Marsh broke out a decanter and filled the glasses, and we toasted "old friends." *His* proposal. I was still wondering about the nature of the facility. "What," I asked, "is the ring? The ring-shaped ridge?"

Ellie tried her drink, and obviously approved. "They used this place to break into atoms," she said. "They were trying to discover what matter really is."

"Why?" I asked.

"I'm not entirely sure."

"Did they leave records?"

"In a way. They wrote their results into computer banks."

"Oh." The computers don't work anymore.

She sliced off a piece of steak, turned it on her fork, and slid it between her lips. "Not bad," she said, eyes gleaming. "Given time, maybe we'll figure out how to fix them."

We ate quietly for a few minutes. "How do you come to own a place like the Tower?" I asked Marsh.

."I don't own it," he said. "It's Ellie's, actually."

She broke off a piece of bread. "I married into it. Two or three years after you left, I married Corey Bolton. His family had been here for generations." She propped her chin on her fist and looked right through me. "Corey died in a raid several years later. After that his brothers cleared out, and I more or less inherited the place."

"It's *big*," I said.

She smiled. "You don't know the half of it. Most of the complex is underground."

Marsh smiled reflexively. He looked uneasy.

I expected him to say something. But he only patted his mouth with his napkin. The silence stretched out.

"I wonder what *does* lie inside atoms?" I said.

"Energy," said Marsh.

"Yes." Ellie of course *had* changed. The buoyancy of the adolescent had given way to cool dignity. The eyes, which had been unabashedly playful, glowed now with mystery and intelligence. The sense of what I had lost began to overwhelm me, and I was sorry I had stumbled into the place. Better a cold night on the plain than this— "But there's obviously more to it than that."

"And the ridge?" I asked again.

"Oh. It's a tunnel. We can reach it from here, actually. They fired atoms, or parts of atoms, I'm not sure which, through it. When they collided, they broke apart, and it was possible to see what was inside."

"It's hard to believe," I said, "that anyone could ever do that."

"So." She announced the subject change with her tone. "What have *you* been doing since you left the Forks, Jeff?" She touched a wall panel and Mozart filled the room. We talked about greenhouses (the Tower had *two*), and the source of their power (solar), and Marsh's trip to the Pacific, and how Chicago looks from offshore.

I learned that Marsh had been a colonel with irregulars formed to defend a group of Minnesota settlements. That Ellie was trying to pull together a comprehensive account of pre-Crash activities at the Tower, that the trail seemed to lead to Minneapolis, and that eventually she would make the trip. Ellie's comment to that effect ignited the Colonel's disapproval, and I understood that I had blundered into an old argument. "Too dangerous," he said, dismissing the matter.

When we'd finished, he insisted on clearing the table, and carrying the dishes into the kitchen. I was impressed by the manner in which he stayed with her and made himself useful. But I noticed also, on several occasions throughout the evening, silent exchanges taking place between them. Was she reassuring him about our relationship? I suspected so, and was pleased that he might, even momentarily, consider me a potential rival.

In all, it was a delicious and entertaining evening. I was sorry to see it end.

The snow had stopped falling, and the sky had cleared. But the wind had lost none of its force, and it drove the loose snow across the landscape.

The clothes I'd washed were still damp. I waited, listening for the last footsteps to come upstairs, and then I went down and arranged my garments in front of the fire. I threw an extra log on, and sank into a chair in front of the blaze. It was warm and soul-satisfying. And it was not long before sleep overtook me.

I dreamt of her that night, as I had on other nights. And, as was the usual climax to these nocturnal reunions, I awoke depressed with the weight of her loss. I sat suddenly recalled to my waking state, staring at the fire, which was now little more than embers, aware of the wind and sounds deep in the belly of the building and the flow of moonlight through the windows.

And I realized I was not alone.

A patch of darkness disconnected itself and came forward.

Ellie.

"Hello," I said.

She wore a heavy woolen robe, drawn up around the neck, her black hair thrown over the collar. I could not see her expression, but the glow from the window touched her eyes. "Hi, Jeff," she said. "Is there anything wrong with your room?"

For a wild moment, I entertained the notion she had just come from there. "No," I said. I pointed at the clothes strung by the fire. "I just got too comfortable here. There's no problem."

After a brief silence, she said, "I didn't expect to see you again."

I had gotten up, but she gestured me back into my seat, and stirred the fire. "You have a lovely home," I said. "You've done well."

She nodded. The robe was frayed, oversized. But it didn't matter: she was breathtakingly beautiful. "Corey was *good*. I couldn't have asked for more."

"I'm sorry you lost him," I said.

"Thanks. It's a long time ago now." She slipped into an adjoining chair. "Jeff, I'm glad to find you here. I was afraid I wouldn't really get a chance to talk to you."

I was prodding myself to be generous, to avoid letting any of the old anger show. But it was hard. "We don't really have much to talk about," I said.

"Yes, we do." She gazed at me steadily, and I imagined I could see sparks reflected in her eyes. "I can't change what happened between us. I can't even say that I *would*, if I could. I loved Corey, and I wouldn't have missed my years with him for anything." She touched my forearm, just her fingertips, but the effect was electric. "You understand what I'm telling you?"

"Yes," I said. But I had no idea.

She stared past my shoulder. "You know that Ed is not my husband."

"I'd guessed as much."

"When we were attacked, when Corey was killed, Ed was the one who came to the rescue. He rode in with a detachment from Sandybrook and personally killed two of the sons of bitches."

"And afterward," I said, "he stayed."

"Not immediately. Corey's brothers couldn't take it anymore out here and they left. When that happened, he tried to persuade me to leave, too."

"Why didn't you?"

She took a deep breath. "This is my *home*." But her eyes looked away. "When I wouldn't leave, he came out. Used to sleep in here. Like you. Eventually—" She shrugged.

"This place is dangerous. For two people."

"We have defenses. Corey wouldn't have been killed if we hadn't been surprised." She shook her head, maybe reassuring herself. "No. I'll never leave here, Jeff. I *love* this place."

We sat quiet.

"But I did want you to know," she said, "that I've never been able to forget you."

That and fifty bucks, I thought. But I didn't say it.

The room got very silent. It occurred to me that Marsh might be standing within earshot. Marsh, who had killed two raiders while riding to the rescue. "I'm happy to know," I said.

"I know what you're thinking," she said, mischievously.

"What am I thinking?"

"He won't care," she said. "Ed doesn't care about *me*."

That made no sense. He doesn't own the property. If he had no feelings for her, why on earth would he stay in this godforsaken place? I replayed the evening. The way Marsh had introduced her. The way he'd responded when he had discovered we'd known each other. The way he talked to her. "I don't believe it," I said.

"Nevertheless it's true. He feels trapped here, and he blames me." She pushed up out of her chair. "He stays out of a sense of duty."

Her grip tightened on my hand, and a tear ran down her cheek. It was a moment I'd contemplated many times when I was younger. Ellie perhaps realizing at last what she had lost. Asking me to forgive. In my imagination, the moment had always seemed delicious. But when it came, I took no pleasure in it.

"You never married," she said.

"I never stayed in one place long enough. Anyway, no one ever seemed much interested."

"Women are such damn fools," she said. She stared at me for a long moment, and, without saying another word, got out of her chair, pressed her lips against my cheek, and left the room.

I went to bed. But I did not sleep well the rest of the night, and I was tempted to clear out. But that might have raised questions and embarrassed Ellie. So I determined to get through breakfast, and leave as quickly as I reasonably could.

Bacon and coffee were already on when I started down. I poked my head into the dining room first, saw no one, and made for the kitchen. Ellie was there, manning an electric stove. But I saw immediately that something was wrong. She looked tired, and the *joie-de-vivre* of the previous day had been replaced with knife-edged intensity. "Good morning," she said. Her tone was cordial, but not warm.

She wore a white jumper open at the throat, and a knee-length knit skirt. Her hair was brushed back, revealing pale, drawn features. "You okay?" I asked.

"I'm fine." She delivered a dispirited smile. "How do you like your eggs?"

"Medium well." I looked at her. "What's wrong?"

She poked at the bacon. "He's gone, Jeff."

"Gone? Ed?"

"Yes."

"Where?"

"Out. Skedaddled. Left for other places."

"My God. What happened?"

She turned her attention to the eggs, scooping at them and wiping her eyes with the backs of her hands. I pulled the pan from the burner and set it down where things wouldn't burn, and then I caught her up: "Talk to me," I said.

"He left before dawn."

"Did he think something happened between us?"

"No," she said. "No. Nothing like that."

"What makes you think he's not coming back?"

"I *know* he's not coming back." She shook her head. "Listen, I'll be okay. Best thing is for you to eat and head out."

"Tell me why," I said.

"I've already told you. He felt trapped here. I warned him what it would be like, but he wouldn't listen, or didn't really understand. When you came, last night, when he saw that we had been friends, maybe *more* than friends, he saw his chance."

"To *bolt*?"

She nodded.

"Knowing that I wouldn't leave you here alone?"

"I'm sure that's what he thought."

"A creep with a conscience." I lowered her into a chair.

"That's not true," she said. "He waited. He stayed for *years*. Most men would have just walked out. Jeff, he never committed to this."

"Sure he did," I said. "When he came out here and started sleeping in the living room, when he moved in, he made a commitment." But I could see it hurt her. She wanted to think well of the son of a bitch, so I let it go.

We abandoned the kitchen, left breakfast in ruins, and wandered into the room with the fireplaces.

"Okay," I said. "What happens now?"

She shrugged. "I'll manage."

"You can't stay here alone," I said.

"Why not?

"*Alone?* Rattling around in this place?"

"It's my home."

"It will be a prison. Close it up and come back with me. To the Forks. It'll be safe for a while. Give yourself a chance to get away from it."

"No." Her voice caught. "I can't leave here."

"Sure you can. Just make up your mind and do it."

She nodded and took a long breath. "Maybe you're right," she said. "Maybe it *is* time to let go."

"Good," I said. I saw possibilities for myself. "Listen, we'll—"

"—Take my chances—" She was beginning to look wild. "There's no reason *I* should have to be buried here—"

"None at all," I said.

"If it gets loose, it gets loose. I mean, nobody else cares, do they?"

"Right," I said. "If *what* gets loose?"

She looked at me a long time. "Maybe you should know what's in the basement."

I didn't like the sound of that.

I tried to get her to explain, but she only shook her head. "I'll show it to you," she said.

So I followed her down to the lobby. Outside, the snow cover ran unbroken to the horizon. I looked at the Native American display. "Corey's idea," she said. "He thought it provided a counterpoint to the technology."

We went downstairs, down four more levels in fact, into the bowels of the building. At each floor I paused and looked along the corridors, which were dark, illuminated only by the lights in the stairway area. The passageways might have gone on forever. "How big is this place?" I asked.

"*Big*," she said. "Most of it's underground. Not counting the tunnel." And, as we got lower, I watched her spirits revive. "I think you're right, Jeff. It *is* time for me to get out. The hell with it."

"I agree." I put an arm around her and squeezed, and her body was loose and pliable, the way a woman is when she's ready.

"Jeff," she said, "I meant what I said last night."

During the time we had known one another, I had never told her how I felt. Now, deep below the Tower, I embraced her, and held her face in my hands, and kissed her. Tears rolled again, and when we separated, my cheeks were wet. "Ellie," I said, "for better or worse, I love you. Always have. There has never been a moment when I would not have traded everything I had for you."

She shook her head. No. "You'd better see what you're getting into first before you say any more."

We turned on lights and proceeded down a long corridor, past more closed rooms. "These were laboratories," she said, "and storage rooms, and libraries."

The floor was dusty. Walls were bare and filmed with dirt. The doors were marked with the letter designator "D," and numbered in sequence, odd on the left, even on the right. There had been carpeting, I believe, at one time. But it was only bare, rotted wood underfoot now.

"Doesn't look as if you come down here very much," I joked.

She pointed at the floor, and I saw footprints in the dust. "Every day," she said.

She threw open a door and stepped back. I walked past her into the dark.

I could not immediately make out the dimensions of the room, or its general configuration. But ahead, a blue glow flickered and wavered and crackled. Lights came on. The room was quite large, maybe a hundred feet long. Tables and chairs were scattered everywhere, and the kind of antique equipment that turns up sometimes in ruins was piled high against both side walls.

The blue glow was on the other side of a thick smoked window. The window was at eye level, about thirty feet long, and a foot high.

She watched me. I crossed to the glass and looked in.

A luminous, glowing cylinder floated in the air. It was a foot off the floor, and it extended almost to the ceiling. Thousands of tiny lights danced and swirled within its folds. It reminded me of a Christmas tree the Sioux had raised outside Sunset City a couple of years ago. "What is it?" I asked.

"The devil," she said softly.

A chill worked its way up my back. "What do you mean?"

"It's a result of the research they did here. A by-product. Something that wasn't supposed to happen. Jeff, they *knew* there was a possibility things might go wrong. But the bastards went ahead anyway—"

"Wait," I said. "Slow down. Went ahead with what?"

"With what we were talking about last night. Smashing atoms. Jeff, this must have been a state-of-the-art laboratory. Because they were able to do things here they had not done before." She moved close to me, and I touched her hair. "Do you know what protons are?"

"Yeah. Sort of. They're made of atoms."

"Other way around," she said. "The thing about protons is that they are extremely stable. Protons are the basic building blocks of matter. There is *nothing* more stable than a proton. Or at least, there used to be nothing—"

"I'm not following this."

"The people who worked here knew there was a possibility they might produce an element that would *be* more stable." Her voice was rising, becoming breathless. "And they also knew that if it actually happened, if they actually produced such an element, it would *de*stablize any proton it came into contact with."

"Which means what?"

"They'd lose the lab." I was still watching the thing, fascinated.

It seemed to be rotating slowly, although the lights moved independently at different speeds, and some even rotated against the direction of turn. The effect was soothing. "In fact," she continued, "they were afraid of losing the Dakotas."

"Why would they make anything like that?" I asked.

"They didn't set out to *make* it. They thought it was *possible*. A by-product. But the chances seemed remote, and I guess the research was important, so they went ahead."

"And it happened," I said. I still couldn't see the problem. After all, it was obvious that nothing of an untoward nature had occurred.

"Yes. Fortunately, they took steps to protect themselves in case there was an incident. They developed a defense. Something to contain it. In case things went wrong."

"How?"

"You're looking at it. It's a magnetic field that plays off the new element. They called it Heisium."

"After its discoverer?"

"Yes."

"So it's contained. What's the problem?"

She stood with her back to it, looking away. "What do you suppose would happen if the power failed here?"

"The lights would go out." And I understood. *The lights would go out.* "Isn't there a backup?"

"It's *on* the backup. Has been for almost two hundred years. The Crash took out their electrical source, and it's been running on the Tower's solar array ever since."

"Why do you come down here every day?"

"Check the gauges. Look around. Make sure everything's okay."

That shook me. "What do you do if it isn't?"

"Flip a circuit breaker. Tighten a connection. Rewire whatever." She inhaled. "*Somebody has to do this.*"

"Jesus."

"They kept this place manned for forty years. Then, after the Crash, the son of one of the people responsible for the original decision, Avery Bolton, the guy the Tower's named for, stayed on. And kept the place going. When he died, his daughter succeeded him. And brought her family. In one way or another, that family has been here ever since. Until Corey. And his brothers. His brothers weren't worth much, and now I'm all that's left." She shook her head. "Seen enough?"

* * *

"Ellie, do you *really* believe all this?"

"Yes," she said. We were sitting in the lobby. "Of course I believe it. Why else would I *be* here?"

"Things get twisted over a long time. Maybe they were wrong." Outside, the day was bright and cold and solid. "I just can't believe it."

"That's good," she said. "You should continue to think that. But I'm going to have to continue to assume that Corey knew what he was talking about."

"My God, Ellie, it's a *trap*."

She looked at me, and her eyes were wet. "Don't you think I *know* that?"

I looked up at an oil of a Sioux warrior on horseback, about to plunge a lance into a bison. "There's a way to settle it," I said.

She shook her head. "No."

"Ellie. We can shut it down. Nothing will happen."

"*No*. I won't consider it. And I want you to promise you won't do anything like that."

I hesitated.

"I want your word, Jeff. *Please*."

"Okay," I said.

"Not ever. No matter what."

"Not ever." I looked at her. She looked fragile. Frightened. "No matter what."

She looked out across the snowfields. "It must be time to go."

"I won't leave you," I said.

That evening was a night to kill for. The consummation of love, denied over a lifetime, may be as close as you can come to the point of existence. I took her, and took her again, and went limp in her arms, and woke to more passion. Eventually the curtains got gray, and I made promises that she said she didn't want to hear, but I made them anyway. We had a magnificent breakfast, and made love again in the room with the fireplaces. Eventually, sometime around lunch, we went down and looked again at Bolton's devil. She took along a checklist, and explained the gauges and circuit breakers and pointed out where the critical wiring was, and where things might go wrong. Where they'd gone wrong in the past. "Just in case," she said. "Not that I expect you to get involved in this, but it's best if someone else knows."

She went down faithfully every day, and completed her rounds. "Edward hated to do this," she said. "He rarely came here."

She showed me where the alarms were throughout our living quarters, and how, if the power supply got low, the system automatically shunted everything into the storage batteries in the lab. "It's happened a couple of times when we've had consecutive weeks without sunlight."

"It must get cold," I said. The temperatures here dropped sometimes to forty below for a month at a time.

"We've got fireplaces," she said. "And we'll have each other."

It was all I needed to hear.

I stayed on, of course. And I did it with no regrets. I too came to feel the power of the thing in the lab. I accepted the burden voluntarily. And not without a sense of purpose, which, I knew, would ultimately bind us together more firmly than any mere vow could have.

We worried because the systems that maintained the magnetic bottle were aging. Eventually, we knew, it would fail. But not, we hoped, in our lifetimes.

We took turns riding the buckboard over to Sandywater for supplies. Our rule was that someone was always available at the Tower. In case.

And one day, about three months after my arrival, she did not come back. When a second day had passed without word, I went after her. I tracked her as far as the town, where I found the buckboard. There was no sign of her. Jess Harper, who works for Overland, thought he'd seen her get into a buckboard with a tall bearded man. "They rode west," he said. "I thought it was odd."

That was almost a year ago. I still make the rounds in the Tower, and I still believe she'll come back. In the meantime, I check the gauges and occasionally throw a circuit breaker. The power in the living quarters shut down once, but I got through it okay. *We* got through it okay.

What I can't understand is how I could have been so wrong. I know who the bearded man was, and I try to tell myself that they must have been very desperate to get away. And I try to forgive them. Forgive *her*.

But it's not easy. Some nights when the moon is up, and the wind howls around the Tower, I wonder what they are doing, and whether she ever thinks about me. And occasionally, I am tempted to break my promise, and turn things off. Find out once and for all.

THE JERSEY RIFLE

Stop by the club, ask the boys to name the greatest chess player of all time, and they'll quarrel endlessly over the relative merits of Alekhine, Capablanca, and Fischer. No others need apply. If, however, the question could be put to those three, the answer might be very different.

We might never have known the truth had it not been for Arnold Schweifurt, an obscure mathematician who, in the last century, applied vector analysis to chess. Curiously, he was interested less in the game than in calculus, but happily for us all, he hit on this inspired method of illustrating his speculations. His work went largely unnoticed, and his name rang no bell when I came across it some years ago in a used bookstore just outside Minneapolis.

I added computer science to Schweifurt's notions, and developed the breakthrough analytical system that revolutionized the manner in which we measure chess genius. The system that today bears my name.

There were skeptics, of course.

The most obnoxious was Everett Vasemann, a fierce competitor known for slashing attacks, violent play, and consistent success. He specialized in psychological warfare, using unshakable confidence to unsettle the coolest opponents. He loved complex positions that other analysts would declare fundamentally unsound, but which could be converted serenely into logical snarls. What is perhaps not so well known about Vasemann is that his play reflected his essential malice toward his opponents. I've never known what bitter incident, buried deep perhaps in childhood, ignited his lifelong enmity against competitors; but I have no doubt that, were it not for chess, he would have devoted his considerable energies to the munitions industry.

It will not surprise you that so slippery a style would score poorly in any evaluation system based strictly on mathematics. He was, of course, aware of my assessment of his abilities, which were overblown on a purely theoretical level. Less a master than a mugger, he won by intimidation. Caught in the glare of those hard dark eyes, opponents froze.

He didn't like me, and he never missed an opportunity to embarrass me publicly. "Cutworth," he was fond of observing, for whatever group of spectators whose attention he could enlist, "you should be analyzing bingo." It is the sort of remark that reveals the essential shallowness of the man.

A year or so after coming across Schweifurt's thin volume, I embarked on a project that was to become the highlight of my otherwise modest career: to establish with mathematical certainty the identity of the strongest chess player the world had seen. To accomplish this, I created a list of candidates, and fed into the data bank every available tournament and match game in which any of them had participated. Many were from unpublished private papers. My sole criterion was that tournament conditions prevailed. The games were evaluated move by move, enabling me to base results not on simple wins and losses, but on the strength of each individual response, vectorially speaking.

When he heard about the project, Vasemann could not resist making snide observations in the media, capping it all with a series of personal attacks in his column in the *Spectator*. "Mike Cutworth," he said, in a thousand variations, "is a mathematical windbag."

Nevertheless there was considerable interest in the Capa Project, which was named for the player everyone expected to finish at the head of the field. I arranged to tabulate the analyses and announce a winner at the annual Masters Invitational at Lone Pine. Vasemann was there, of course. As I patched in my notebook at the conclusion of the sixth round, he was within a half point of the leaders and feeling exuberant. When our eyes met, he rose slowly, and waited until he had everyone's attention.

"Mr. Cutworth." His voice sliced through the dying conversation of the assembled masters, journalists, and dignitaries. I was pacifically devoid of malice. "I wonder if you will tell us who devised this system that is to be used to judge Bobby Fischer?" Someone in back snorted and a wave of laughter rolled forward.

I tried to explain about Schweifurt, gave up, and settled for a few generalities. Then I tied in to the overhead display and turned it on. "Ladies and gentlemen," I said, "let's dispense with the quibbling and go directly to the bottom line. The supreme grandmaster of all time—" I keyed the result. Onscreen, stylized knights flanked a chessboard logo. Above the logo, in black block letters, the champion's name appeared. My audience dissolved in hysteria.

The name was Will Ballard.

"Who is he?" Vasemann asked innocently.

Who indeed? He wasn't included in the list of candidates. Confused and frustrated, I heard myself explaining that although we had clearly suffered a computer error, Ballard was undoubtedly a better player than Vasemann. "Of course," I added, "it would be difficult to find anyone in this room who is not."

Vasemann's smile faded. "*You* are not!"

"I've never pretended to be a chess player," I answered weakly.

His eyes narrowed. "Ballard then . . . *your* champion. Does he even exist, Cutworth?"

I glared back.

"You say he is better than I? Produce him. I will play him for a $10,000 stake." He looked around, relishing the moment. There was no longer any laughter.

Ballard was unknown to the U.S. Chess Federation. He had never played a rated game. The World Chess Federation had no record of him. But the computer gave us something: earliest appearance in 1916, most recent in 1951. Eighteen games were on record, apparently all exhibitions. He had drawn one, won the rest. All had been played in Deep River, New Jersey, and no two had occurred in the same year. If those facts seemed mundane, his opponents did not: Frank Marshall twice, Richard Reti, Al Horowitz, Reuben Fine, Samuel Reshevsky, Isaac Kashdan, Aron Nimzovich, José Capablanca twice. The draw had come against Capa.

They were all from the candidates' list. The program had analyzed both sides of the table. Which explained why it had produced *his* name.

I didn't even have the games readily accessible, because I hadn't cross-referenced, and all had come from sources other than Ballard. I put Judy Taylor, my secretary, on the job of recovering them, and headed for Jersey.

There was no Ballard in the Deep River phone book. I went to the Trenton Library, and consulted the defunct *Deep River Journal.* The record started in February 1922. By then, Ballard had already defeated Marshall and Capablanca. And I knew that, sometime in 1922, he had beaten Marshall a second time.

I found what I was looking for in the edition for Sunday, April 2:

U.S. CHESS CHAMP TO BE AT FAMILY DAY

U.S. Chess Champion Frank Marshall will be guest of honor at the annual Family Day celebration this afternoon in Deep River. The day's events will get underway with a pancake breakfast at the Trinity Lutheran Hall at 9:00 A.M., immediately following services.

After that we will have potato-sack races, balloon relays, and many other exciting events. Mr. Marshall will have a few words to say to us at a special luncheon at the Town Hall. Then he will play a game against our own Will Ballard.

A dance will be held this evening at Brandon Park. All are invited!

I read it several times, and then hurried forward to the next day's edition. Miners were striking in Indiana, and President Harding was facing a scandal at the Bureau of Engraving. There were several stories on the Family Day festivities and a blurred photo of the sack race. Ballard vs. Marshall got the lower left corner of the front page:

WILL BEATS CHAMP

Will Ballard, the chess-playing druggist from Bamberry Point, defeated U.S. Chess Champion Frank Marshall yesterday in Deep River. Marshall resigned on the twenty-third move of a game that was very well played by both men. The victory was Will's seventh without a loss, and his second against Mr. Marshall.

I wandered through the years. Family Day was celebrated on the first Sunday after Easter, and it always featured a game between Ballard and a chess notable, sometimes a giant, sometimes a less well-known figure. And Ballard never lost.

In 1924 he beat Reti, who had just ended Capablanca's long streak in the celebrated New York tournament of that year. In 1925, Capa returned to Deep River. This time he got away with a draw (as the *Journal* put it) and the town was aghast.

The tenth anniversary of Family Day fell in 1926. The newspaper carried a brief history of the event. Deep River had dedicated a chess museum in 1916. Marshall, the supreme gentleman, had accepted an invitation, had played the local champion, and a tradition was born.

I was seated in a bare room, at one of those old-fashioned microfilm viewers with a squeaky crank, thinking that the world would never be the same. I had discovered Atlantis.

In 1927, Nimzovich, playing white, resigned on the eleventh move.

The chess museum went broke in 1930, along with the rest of the country, closing its doors forever. But Family Day rolled on. Ballard scored consecutive victories against Isaac Kashdan, Horowitz, Alekhine, and Fine. The Alekhine game, curiously, was played on a Saturday, preceding Family Day. Alekhine was world champion at the time. In the late 1930s and during the war years, he added Sammy Reshevsky, Arnold Denker, Arthur Bisguier, and Miguel Najdorf to the list. In 1951, with only the Capablanca blemish on his record, he retired. His final game was a brilliant Sicilian against George Koltanowski.

Giving no reason, he announced that he would not play again. Since he had made similar statements in the past, no one took him very seriously. But there was no game in 1952, although the *Journal* ran a story on Ballard, reported as being in failing health at Bamberry Point.

After that, he dropped altogether out of the news.

The Deep River Pike runs through the middle of Bamberry Point, about twenty-five miles southeast of Trenton. In a cluster of brick retail outlets in the center of town, I found a drugstore with the legend *BALLARD'S* arced across plate glass windows in bright gold letters. It was run by a young linebacker of a man with eyes that looked permanently puzzled.

"I didn't know he plays chess," he said. "A little bridge, maybe. But he's not big on games."

"*Plays?* Is he still alive?" My heart pounded.

"Uncle Will? You just missed him."

I checked in with Judy. She was in a rage. "Vasemann keeps calling. He thinks you're trying to get out of the country with his money.

"And George Koltanowski phoned. He wants four tickets for the Ballard match. Said I should tell you it's about time."

I shook my head. "Have you recovered the games?"

"Yes, Mike. I've sent them by FedEx."

"Good. Judy, I've got news. Apparently, the guy is still walking around. One more thing you can do: dictate the first Capablanca game to me, the one that Ballard won."

The game was played in 1918. I could visualize the scene: the future world champion and a local kid seated at a wooden table on the stage of Town Hall. (The chess museum, according to the *Journal*, lacked adequate facilities; and the high school had not yet been built.) Capa, at the peak of his career, had not lost a game for two years, would not lose another for six more. Yet, on this April day, while vast armies lay exhausted in muddy ditches across France, young Will Ballard, playing White in a Queen's Gambit, held his own for fifteen moves and then inserted a pawn into Capa's center that the Cuban dared not take. It quietly smothered his game.

I wondered what the weather had been like on that long-ago Sunday. And I wondered how many among the spectators had grasped the enormity of the boy's achievement.

Will Ballard looks quite ordinary. He's about average height, a trifle thin, with white hair. He moves gracefully, almost like a twenty-year-old. His lips curl naturally into a smile, though it is half-hidden by a vigorous silver mustache. The eyes are a startling lucid blue. They hide nothing: laughter and anger rise easily in them. It's clear he's no poker player.

His wife Ann brought in cheese and beer, and the three of us relaxed beneath an original Wyeth. "Bought it back before he was known," Ballard said. "I couldn't afford it now."

I took a deep breath. "Sir, are you the Will Ballard who used to play chess exhibitions in Deep River?"

His jaw tightened, and the congeniality went out of his eyes. "What exactly do you want, Mr. Cutworth?"

An old Marbury clock, sleek and curved in its black case, ticked placidly on the mantel. "Mr. Ballard, you play a remarkable game of chess. I'd like to understand why someone who does what you can do isn't known."

"I see." He tried hard to frown, but gave it up. Finally he shrugged and smiled. "I'm known where it matters."

"How did it feel to beat Capablanca?"

"I enjoyed it. He was quite good, you know."

"And you beat Alekhine when he was world champion."

"That game almost didn't get played," said Ann. "They always scheduled them, the games, for Family Day. But Alekhine was doing a tour and he added some cities at the last minute. He insisted on coming early, playing the day before, and he only gave us two days' notice. We were in Chicago, visiting my sister, when the telegram came. Will grumbled a lot, but we caught a late train and got back here thirty minutes before game time."

"If I'd had any sense," said Will, "we'd have stayed in Chicago."

"You loved every minute of it." Ann laughed, her eyes shining. "Will's cavalry instinct took over. He was magnificent. We arrived in a taxi with a police escort, sirens going and people cheering. It was wonderful. Things like that," she added wistfully, "don't happen anymore."

"Your first game was against Marshall. What was his reaction when you won?"

"He was surprised. They were *always* surprised. And I thought he was a little embarrassed. But he shook my hand and he actually seemed pleased. He told me he expected to hear from me again."

"But he never did."

"No, I suppose not. He came back about six years later. And he asked me about it."

"What did you tell him, Mr. Ballard?"

"My name's Will." He pushed a strip of cheese into the mustard. "By then, I'd given up playing except for the annual game. And I just explained I had other things to do."

"You played no other chess?" I was of course incredulous.

"By 1922? No."

"When did you go back to playing regularly?"

"I never did."

"But you played extraordinary chess for thirty more years!"

He looked amused. "I was pretty good, wasn't I?"

None of this made sense. "Why did you give it up?"

"You want the truth? Chess is a bore."

I don't shock easily. I've been through two wars and, for a short time, I drove a cab in Philadelphia. But this was lobbing a dead cat up the church aisle.

"Chess players don't get involved with one another," he continued. "It's just you and the woodwork. The geometry is intriguing, the puzzles are a kick, but who really cares?"

"It must have left a terrible void. Were you able to find a way to replace it?"

"Horseshoes. Wonderful game. Man-to-man struggle there. You know who you're playing. All those years fooling around with chess: it addicts weak minds, you understand. I used to come home after an evening at the club, and I never knew anything about the person I'd been playing. Oh, I might know he had an affinity for the French, or he was given to premature attacks, or some fool thing like that. Ann and I got married in 1920. And down in the club one night, when I told them, they shook my hand and asked me about the Caro-Kann."

"But you kept playing the annual game?"

"It became a tradition and people more or less expected it. They wouldn't let me quit until finally I refused to play anymore."

"Failing health, the newspaper said."

"Yeah." He chuckled. "Ann told them I was sick of it."

When an opportunity presented itself, I described the results of the Capa Project. "Data analysis indicates you're the best that ever walked the planet."

"It's nice to hear." His eyes focused somewhere over my shoulder. "Maybe you're right about the vectors. What's a rook anyhow but a bullet? The trick is to know how to load and point the rifle."

"Will, would you play one more game? An exhibition?"

His eyes glazed. "I don't want to start that again, Michael. No, most folks have long since forgotten all that. I'd just as soon let things be."

"You might have been a world champion."

"I've been living my own life. But I'll admit to one regret: I'd have liked to play Bobby Fischer."

I called Vasemann in the morning. "Where's your schlemiel, Cutworth?" he asked without preliminary.

"Ballard isn't well."

"Sorry to hear that. You can send the check to my office."

"You're not serious. He isn't a young man, Vasemann."

"Look, Cutworth, you embarrassed me. You and your tank town tornado are going to pay up, one way or another. But I'm not unreasonable. I tell you what: I'll drive down there myself. Convince me he's really sick, and I'll let you off the hook. If not, you do the right thing on the spot. See you Saturday." He laughed and hung up.

So I went contritely back to Ballard to confess and throw myself on his mercy. He was paneling his dining room.

"It's been too many years, Mike," he said. "And if I got lucky and pulled it off, who'd be next? Garry Kasparov?"

"That wouldn't happen, Will. It really wouldn't." But I knew better. "Do you think you could see your way clear to developing a disabling disease?"

He was careful not to laugh. "Mike," he said, "I have my vices. You can hardly enjoy life without a little selective sinning. But I'm just not a very convincing liar." He looked tired. "Let's get some fresh air. It always helps."

Ten minutes of it revived him. But it did nothing for me.

"The State Department is interested," Judy said. "We've had other calls, too, some from outside the country. People want to know when he's going to play, and they want tickets."

"*What* people? Who's been calling?"

"Bent Larsen, Boris Spassky, Anatoly Karpov, Larry Evans, Lajos Portisch. And Kasparov. In fact, it looks as if you might get a Russian delegation. When's the game?"

I rolled my eyes and explained. "I'm sorry," she said. "But, boss, I don't understand what's happening."

"You'd have to know him. Ballard. But I think all those people he played all those years recognized a genius on an order they hadn't seen before. It might have escaped the weaker players. But Reti and Reshevsky, people like that, would have known. And the scene after those games must always have been the same. They would have begun by trying to persuade him to capitalize on his talent, to play seriously, and they would have ended by respecting his privacy.

"Now they think he's going public at last. They're happy for him, they're spreading the word, and there's going to be a general celebration. Except that *he* won't be there."

My packet of games arrived, and I played over his pair of victories against Marshall, and the Reti game. He was flawless. He boxed in Reti's king and assaulted it relentlessly, sacrificing a queen and rook to get local advantage. A bishop and knight were loping in for the kill when the great Czech resigned. In the second Marshall game he used a twelve-move sacrificial combination. The U.S. Champion was three pieces up when he turned down his king.

I got Will onto the six o'clock news and into the papers, hoping to put some pressure on him.

In Los Angeles, Bobby Fischer was reported interested in attending the event. I talked to local politicians, pointing out financial advantages from the match. They promised to help. I gave Vasemann's tank town remark to the *Deep River Crystal,* the *Journal*'s successor, which they gleefully printed. Reporters gathered outside Ballard's house, and Will enjoyed himself giving opinions on Zaire and the Middle East. On the matter of the game, however, he remained adamant: he would not play.

"Don't think, Michael," he told me, "that I don't know what you're doing. It won't make any difference."

But he agreed to have dinner with me Saturday evening.

We arrived at the Old Stone House on schedule. Will was suspicious, and after he settled himself among the cut glass and guttering candles, he took a long look around, like some Byzantine elder statesman expecting an assassination attempt. "If you were going to challenge me," he said abruptly, "why couldn't you produce Fischer? Why are you messing around with somebody no one ever heard of?"

We ordered drinks, and I suggested he was out of touch. He was thinking that over when the man himself arrived. Vasemann's clothes were in the intellectual tradition: baggy tweed with elbow patches, gray slacks, no tie. Will smiled at his name, suspicions confirmed.

Vasemann took in the situation at a glance. A beatific smile, a suggestion of his love for all mankind, illuminated his features. He shook hands with Will, paid Ann a compliment, and ordered a brandy.

We discussed current movies, a sensational trial that was then in all the papers, and the President's economic policies. Vasemann generally agreed with Will throughout the conversation. He might have differed on the degree of a palliative, on the amount, say, of a tax incentive, but jointly he seemed to share the older man's principles.

This was a Vasemann I had never seen. He exuded charm. Ann had, I could see, taken an instinctive dislike to her unexpected companion. But Will seemed absorbed in the conversation.

We finished our steaks, and Vasemann bought another round of drinks. He asked permission to smoke and held a match to his meerschaum. It was his celebrated victory pipe, the one that he traditionally lights with the decisive move. He had, I realized, taken Ballard's measure, and found him wanting. "Will." He sucked on the stem. "I *am* sorry that you can't see your way clear. But I understand. I applaud your principles." He added a sidelong glance at me, a triumphant weave of good humor and contempt. It was disconcerting in its contrast with the mood of the evening, as though someone had thrown a switch.

Ann caught it and bristled. She watched her husband, who, apparently unaware, was staring distractedly into his vodka. Then his shoulders straightened. "On the other hand," he said slowly, "there's an argument to be made for flexibility. I wonder whether I don't have an obligation to give Michael a fair chance to win his bet."

Vasemann hesitated. His eyelids closed; he nonchalantly drained his glass and shrugged. No one spoke. A waiter came and went. At last Vasemann looked compassionately at the old man. "As you please," he said.

For one dazzling weekend, Deep River became the chess capital of the world. Pal Benko and Walter Browne joined John Chancellor and the Secretary of State. Motels filled up all the way to Trenton. The high-school band marched, politicians spoke, and the oddsmakers gave Will Ballard no chance.

Ann explained his change of heart. "He doesn't like Vasemann. Vasemann didn't take him seriously. His tone, his attitude: he didn't think Will mattered, one way or the other. He was just using him to get at you." She shrugged. "So Will decided you needed rescuing. It's the cavalry instinct again.

"And Mike, don't worry about your bet." She winked. "It's money in the bank."

The match was scheduled for Deep River. On the night before, the Old Stone House overflowed with celebrities. Will disappeared early. Rumors flew that Fischer was in town.

The celebration ran until 2:00 A.M. Next morning, we all managed to be in the high-school auditorium at ten. And in fact, despite the weather, which was bleak and gray and cold, the crowd filled the school and spilled out into the street.

When Everett Vasemann was introduced, they booed enthusiastically. He looked startled, glared back, composed himself, and sat down. The VIP section remained mute.

"From Bamberry Point—" That was as far as the P.A. got. Cheers and whistles rolled through the building. Ballard, wearing an old gray sweater, came uncertainly out onto the stage. I saw immediately that something was wrong. He looked tired; the energy was gone. Deep lines were drawn through his features. It occurred to me that he might be frightened of all this. I wondered if he'd partied through the night?

Vasemann, as Black, started the clock, and Will made his move. The teenage girl tending the display pushed the Queen's Pawn forward two squares.

Vasemann defended with the Benko Gambit, on the theory, I suppose, it was sufficiently recent that his opponent had probably never heard of it. Will took the gambit pawn, switched smoothly to defense, and walked his king under cover, away from the withering diagonal of Black's queen bishop.

Vasemann exploited his initiative, seizing the center. Will watched his opportunity and returned the pawn. Pal Benko, sitting beside me in the press area, stiffened slightly. The concept is sound, of course, but the timing must be precise. Will hadn't looked deeply enough. Black took the pawn and simultaneously threatened a combination that would sweep away White's exposed queenside.

Will stared at the position. His shoulders slumped, and I began to regret my part in this. He got up, glanced at the running clock, and walked offstage down the center of the auditorium. He seemed desperately weary. The crowd made way, and he disappeared into the lobby. I heard the outer door open and close.

He was gone ten minutes. When he came back, he looked better. They brought out a pot of coffee. Will offered to pour for his opponent, but Vasemann turned his cup over without raising his eyes.

Ballard braced his queenside, at the cost of allowing Black to reinforce his grip on the center. A black knight invaded his defenses, threatening strangulation. Vasemann sat back, relaxed, smiled, and lit his meerschaum. Viktor Korchnoi, directly in front of me, shook his head sadly.

But Will hung on. He gave up a pawn to force a pair of exchanges, getting rid of the knight and the queen bishop. "Too late," someone whispered. Enjoying himself thoroughly, Vasemann launched one of the complex combinations characteristic of his play, subtle, indirect, but lethal. And it contained the usual imprecision, buried deep.

But he'd chosen the wrong victim. Will found the weakness, and exploited it to introduce another wave of complexity. Vasemann leaned forward, frowning. He took off his jacket. And he lost his way.

Ballard traded off the remaining knights, opening a file on the castled king. He posted a rook on it; Vasemann hurried to defend. White clicked a second rook into the chamber, and unexpectedly switched targets.

Pawns, bishop, and queen assaulted and occupied the center in a style that recalled the young Ballard's pyrotechnics against Reti and Marshall. Will traded his queen for the remaining bishop, leaving the enemy pawn structure a shambles.

Vasemann looked at his hopelessly exposed king, stared down the barrel at the doubled rooks, and sighed. He stopped the clock and, without a word, walked offstage.

* * *

They lined up to shake his hand and wish him well, the chess-playing titans of the globe. Near the end, Will Ballard greeted a tall, thin man in dark glasses. They stood a moment, regarding each other. Then the man was gone.

"Been a long day," he said. "Michael, I enjoyed it. Thank you."

"You look exhausted. You played a helluva game, Will. For a while there though, you had me worried."

He grinned. His teeth were white and strong, the teeth of a predator. "Sorry. I'm not as young as I used to be. I shouldn't have stayed up all night."

"Stayed up all night?" I looked at him accusingly. "You *were* partying."

"I was playing chess." There was a trace of mischief in his eyes. "With Bobby."

"Bobby?"

"Now there's someone who understands this game."

Muscles in my back twitched. "How'd you do?"

He shrugged. "I lost one."

CRUISING THROUGH DEUTERONOMY

The banging sounded like distant thunder.

Cardwell was slow to move, had in fact been sitting in the dying firelight, allowing the storm to carry away his gloomy mood. Rick padded barefoot from the kitchen through the hallway and opened the front door. The wind blew louder.

There were whispers in the hall, and an authoritarian voice that he did not recognize. Rick appeared. "Dad," he said. "You have a visitor."

A tall, severe figure followed the boy into the room. Cardwell saw at once that he was a clergyman, one of those advanced types that affect plaid jackets. His hair was full and black, and his eyes blazed with dark intensity. He shook rain off his hat and coat, and held them out for Rick. "Dr. Cardwell?" he asked, coming forward.

Cardwell heaved himself out of his chair. "You have the advantage of me, sir."

"I'm Pastor Gant." His glance swept the room, and registered diffident approval. "From the Good Shepherd Church over in Bridgeton." He said it as if it explained his visit.

Cardwell debated whether he could leave him standing. But his breeding got the better of him, and he indicated a chair. "What can I do for you, Pastor?"

"I'll come right to the point if you don't mind." He sat down and held his hands out to the fire.

"Yes. Good. Can I offer you a brandy?"

He waved the idea away with a choreographed gesture. His fingers were long and graceful. "No, thank you. I'm not opposed to drink on principle, you understand. But I prefer to abstain."

Rick, whose boredom with Cardwell's inner circle was usually painfully obvious, took a chair where he could watch.

Pastor Gant reached into his pocket, and took out precisely what Cardwell had expected: the clipping from last Tuesday's *News*. He held it toward the firelight, and looked at it as though it were vaguely loathesome. "Is there actually anything to this?" he asked.

"The Displacer?"

"The time machine."

"The story is correct in its essentials."

"I see." The long fingers toyed with the paper. He turned toward the boy. "Son," he said, "perhaps it would be best if you left the room."

Rick didn't stir, but Gant did not seem to notice.

"Pastor," said Cardwell, "I don't want to be abrupt, but I'm really quite preoccupied at the moment."

"Yes, I'm sure you are." He crossed his legs, and let his head drift back. "Doctor, you must understand that the people of my church are *good* people."

"I'm sure they are."

"But life can be very harsh. Several, at this moment, are bearing up under terminal illnesses. Another has recently lost a child. Just about your son's age, I might add. Still another—"

"Might I press you to come to the point?"

"Of course." He looked not quite substantial in the flickering light. "The only thing that keeps us going, when life becomes—" he searched for a word, "—difficult, the only thing that sustains us, is our sure and certain knowledge of a divine protector."

Cardwell's stomach began to hurt. "Reverend," he said, "I'd be pleased to discuss all this with you at a future date."

Gant stared into the fire, as if his host had not spoken. "You will take all this from them, Doctor."

Cardwell frowned. There'd been some minor fuss over that article. Fortunately, the limited circulation of the *News*, and the general tendency of people in the area to mind their business, had however protected him. "I hardly see how that can be," he said.

"You know what will happen if you complete the device?" He rose from his chair and towered over Cardwell. His eyes grew very large and very black. "You will cruise through Deuteronomy. Glide across Numbers. Descend into Exodus. There were no trumpets at Jericho, you will say. No angel at Sodom. No division of the Red Sea. No haircut for Samson." His smile lengthened at that, but there was no warmth in the gesture. "You will say there was no Fall, and hence no need for a Redeemer. You will travel into the sacred country and every time you return you will bring with you a cargo of despair. I simply cannot allow that to happen." He drew a small revolver from his pocket and pointed it at a spot between Cardwell's eyes.

Rick gasped and started forward. But his father, with a quick jerky wave, stopped him.

"I'm sorry," said the pastor. It was hard to see his expression in the play of light and shadow. "I truly am." He studied the weapon. "It is often difficult to know the right thing to do."

Cardwell could not take his eyes from the gun. It amazed him that a stranger would come into his home and threaten to use one on him. The entire world centered in the round black muzzle. "You're too late," he said.

Gant's gaze shifted. Bored into him. "What do you mean?"

"I've already done it. I've made the flight. Several, in fact."

"I don't believe you."

"Did you really think I'd let the newspapers have the story if I weren't *sure*? And there's only one way to be sure." He eased himself back into his chair. Anything to get out from in front of that muzzle. And he was relieved to see that when it followed him, it locked onto his right knee. "There is a *prototype*, George. Your name *is* George, isn't it?"

That surprised him. "How did you know?"

"I pass your church every day on my way to the campus. Your name is prominently displayed."

"I wish that you might have seen fit to come by and say hello."

Cardwell nodded. "Possibly I've been remiss."

"I'm surprised you would see that." Gant's brows furrowed.

"How could I not? *Pastor, I've been on the ark.*"

The rain hissed against the windows. "That's ridiculous."

"Is it? Then why are you here? Either you believe it's possible, or you don't. If you don't, I'd like to know why you're threatening my life."

Gant stared at him. He seemed to be having trouble breathing. "Is it really *true*?"

"Yes, it's true. I've walked her decks. Felt her roll in the swell of the storm. Seen the tigers in their bays."

The gun came up. Swung a few degrees. Cardwell realized it was pointed at Rick. "Stay back," said Gant. "I don't want to shoot *you*." He took a deep breath and let it out slowly. "Indeed, I wish there were a way to do this without shooting *anyone*."

"Then *believe* me," Cardwell said desperately.

The pastor stared at him for a long moment. "Noah," he said.

"Yes?"

"Did you *talk* to him?"

"I didn't know the language. I *saw* him."

The hand wavered.

"Listen to me. I was at the foot of the mountain when Moses returned with the Tablets. I saw him shatter them against the rocks. I watched Solomon give judgment and walked through his temple. I stood a few feet from David when he killed the Philistine. I was in the crowd when Jesus delivered the sermon on the mount."

Perspiration glittered on Gant's forehead. "You're lying," he said. "You're mocking me. And blaspheming everything that's holy. You're a non-believer. I know about you. I've read what you've written."

Cardwell smiled gently. "That was true *once*. George, I was on the shore during the storm when the Master stepped out of the boat. I looked into His eyes."

The pastor tried to speak, but only strangled sounds got out.

"Gant, do you, at last, not believe?" His voice rose until it was one with the wind beating at the window. *"Where is your faith?"*

The gun clattered to the floor. A sob welled up in Gant's throat, and he fell forward into Cardwell's arms and almost knocked him down. But Cardwell held on, and the pastor embraced him. A log popped and fell into the fire.

"Thank you," said Gant, finally, wiping his cheek. "I was terribly wrong to come here. Not to see what would happen." His face brightened, and he squeezed Cardwell's shoulders again. "I hope you'll come by the church and share your experience with all of us." And, without stopping for hat, coat, or gun, he walked straight out of the house.

When he was gone, they locked the door. "Dad," Rick said, "you were terrific."

"Thanks."

"Are you going to call the police?"

"Maybe in the morning. Let me think about it."

"I was scared."

"So was I, kid."

The boy picked up the weapon and put it on a bookshelf. He grinned. "The displacement principle doesn't work, right? You told me that yesterday. The time machine won't ever get off the ground."

"That's right."

The boy's eyes gleamed. "Don't you have any respect at all for the truth, Dad?"

"Sometimes I think truth is overrated," said Cardwell. "On that one, I believe I'm with the Christians. My money's on *faith*."

TYGER

Did he smile his work to see?
—Blake

David was dead at last.

I will carry all my days the vision of Nick frozen against the sunlight while the wind blew the preacher's words across green fresh-cut grass.

The boy had never drawn a breath that was free of pain. He'd slipped away, almost unexpectedly, on the eve of his fifteenth birthday. "In God's hands," they murmured over the sound of the trees. "He's better off."

Afterward, Nick refused my offer that he stay with us a few days. I was uncomfortable at the prospect of my brother buried in his apartment. But he assured me he'd be all right, that there was enough going on at work to keep him engaged. "It's been coming a long time," he said, voice tight. And: "What I'm grateful for is, he never gave up. I don't think he ever believed it would actually happen."

I tried to stay in touch, but it was a busy time for me, and Nick wasn't very good at returning phone calls anyway. On the occasional evenings when my duties took me to the branch bank on Somerset, I made it a point to drive a few blocks out of my way, past his condo. It was on the rooftop of a squat five-story building. I stopped to talk to him only once, and he seemed so uncomfortable that I did not do so again. But from the street I could see him moving around in there, backlit, staring out over the city.

If you're concluding that I neglected him during this period, you're probably correct. In my defense, I should mention that Virginia delivered our second child two days after the funeral, and immediately fell ill. In addition, the markets went erratic, and I was working well into the evening on a regular basis trying to protect the bank's investments. So I forgot about Nick until Edward Cord called.

Cord was the director of the particle accelerator lab at the University of Washington, where Nick was a researcher. "Have you seen him recently?" he asked. "He's changed."

"He's still upset."

"He's *changed*. Talk to him. He needs you."

I couldn't get past his telephone answering system. Finally, disgusted, I got in my car early on a Friday evening, and drove over.

Lights were on in the penthouse condo, one in the deck, one in back. I parked across the street, went into the lobby, and punched his button. Punched it again.

"Who's there?" The voice rasped. He sounded annoyed.

"Michael."

A long pause. The lock on the security system clicked.

The elevator opened off the terrace, and he met me with drinks in his hands. The usual rum and Coke. "Michael," he said. "Good to see you." He managed a smile, but his eyes were bleak and wintry.

"How've you been, Nick?"

"Okay." It was an unseasonably warm evening in October. A quarter moon swam among wisps of cloud. There was a taste of salt air off the Sound. "I take it you've been worried about me."

"A little."

"You have reason." We crossed the terrace and went into the apartment. A desk lamp dropped a pool of light across a pile of notebooks and printouts. There was no other illumination in the room. "I'm sorry. I know I've been out of touch lately." He tried again for a smile. It wasn't there. "I've been busy."

"Cord called."

He nodded. "I'm not surprised."

Bookshelves lined the room. Beyond the pale cast of the lamp, the walls grew insubstantial, gave way to void. An X-ray photo of the Milky Way hung by the door, and several of Nick's awards were mounted near the fireplace. A couple of landscapes broke up the academic character of the room.

Framed photographs stood on the desk: Terri alive and happy against a clutch of blue sky, windblown hair sparkling in sunlight. And David: on his bike at about eight, and again two years later locked in the embrace of a Mariners outfielder who had heard about the case, and a third depicting him in a baseball cap standing between Nick and me. In all the pictures the child, like the mother, looked happy. In love with life.

"Nick, you can't mourn forever."

He waved me onto the sofa and sat down in the big imitation leather wingback. "I know," he said.

"You understand what I'm saying." I tried to keep the edge out of my voice.

He shrugged. Sipped his drink. It looked like wine. Chablis, probably. "It doesn't matter."

"Nick, we'd like to have you over for dinner. Maybe Sunday? Virginia would like to see you again."

He shook his head. "Thanks, Michael. But no. I'm not really able to do that." He took a deep breath. Straightened his sweater. "Maybe another time."

"Nick—"

"Please, Michael. We know each other too well, so I'll not lie to you. I have no interest just now in dinners and evenings out."

I waited until he could not misunderstand my dissatisfaction. "Is there anything we *can* do for you?"

"No." He rose, expecting me to go.

"Nick," I said, composing myself more comfortably, "it's been six months. You need to get your life together again."

"Just soldier on," he said.

What the hell do you say in a situation like that? Everything sounds dumb. "I know it's hard. But these things happen. You have to be able—"

"They do *not*," he snarled, "*happen*. Nothing simply *happens*." He shook his head and his eyes slid shut. His lip trembled, and he fell silent.

The place was empty without David. Quiet. Not lifeless, because Nick possessed a relentless energy and vitality of his own. But it seemed as though direction had been lost. Point. The reason for it all.

"I'm sorry," I said.

I had drunk very little of the rum and Coke, certainly not enough to account for the subtle sense of disquiet that had settled about me. I don't know whether there was a modulation in his tone, or some curious juxtaposition of hand and shoulder, or a glint of terror reflected in glass. "No," he said quietly, "nothing happens save by design."

Curious remark: he had always been aggressively secular. Father had provided a religious education for both of us, but in Nick's case it had not taken.

His face twisted briefly. Grief. Rage. I couldn't tell. But in the end it settled into a hard smile. "Michael," he said, "what do you think lies behind the stars?"

I tried to penetrate his expression. To determine what he was really asking. "God," I said at last. "Or nothing."

His eyes locked with mine. "I quite agree," he said. And, after a long pause: "I believe we've found His footprints."

He smiled at my confusion. He leaned forward, and his voice gained intensity. "Michael, the universe is wired. The fix is in. David never had a chance. Nor do you. Nor I. From the very beginning—" He rose from his chair and strode toward one of the windows. Seattle glittered in the distance, a crosspatch of illuminated highways and skyscrapers and bridges.

"Nick—"

"We've begun to understand how it was done. Michael, there's a complete set of instructions written into the post-quantum world, a concordance of particle harmonies, a manipulation of the more exotic dimensions. *Directions*, establishing the rules, setting the value of gravity, tuning the electroweak charge, establishing the Mannheim Complexity Principle. Ultimately writing the nature of Man. It's all going to be there, Michael. There's a lot we don't know yet. But *someone* wrote the program. The theologians were right all along—"

"This is old stuff, Nick. Railing at God when things go wrong."

"It comes with a twist now. We know how to *make* a universe. Were you aware of that?"

"No," I said. It was hard to know whether he was mocking me, or delirious. In the uncertain light, I could not get a good look at his eyes. "I wasn't aware." And after a moment: "The idea is absurd."

"Nevertheless, it is quite true."

I sighed. "And how would we go about doing that?"

"Quite easily, Michael. We pack a relatively modest quantity of matter, a few kilograms, into a cramped space." He looked past me, toward the shadowy area where his bookshelves met the ceiling. "The space would have to be *quite* cramped, of course. It would be considerably smaller than an atomic nucleus. But after we've done it, we have a cosmic seed." His lips broke apart in a distorted smile. "Then all you have to do is let go and stand back." His teeth gleamed.

"And you get a new big bang?"

"Theoretically, yes."

I snorted. "Come on, Nick. A few kilograms wouldn't give you a good-sized *rock*."

He set his glass down and immediately picked it up again. His fingers curled around it, gripped it. "The seed is only a seed. It contains the trigger, and the plan. Once it explodes, the process takes on a life of its own. It creates what it needs. The forces come into existence, and the physical constants lock in. The clock begins to run."

"That doesn't make sense."

Nick looked amused. "Nevertheless, it happens. It has *already* happened. If it hadn't, you and I wouldn't be standing here."

"You're saying *we* could do this?"

"No, Michael. We don't have the technology. *Yet.* I'm saying it *could* be done. Almost certainly *has* been done."

Nick had brightened numerous evenings in the old days with quantum stories. We were a family of stockbrokers and financial experts. He used to come home and go on about objects that exist simultaneously in two places, or move backward in time, or wink in and out of existence. Father used to describe Nick's mind in much the same terms.

"All right," I said. "If you went out into your kitchen tonight, and cooked one of these things up, what would happen to *us* when it let go?"

"Probably nothing. The blast would create a new space-time continuum. The lights might dim a little. Maybe the room would even shake. But that would be about all."

I let him refill my glass. "Well," I said, "whatever." Even for Nick, that one was off the wall. "What has any of this got to do with—" I hesitated.

"—With David?"

"Yes. No. I don't know. What connection has it with your hiding out up here?"

His eyes were round, and very hard. "Let me take you a step further, Michael. We've gone beyond the quantum world now. Anyone with the technology to cook up a new cosmos, as you so quaintly put it, would also be able to set the parameters for the universe that would result. In fact, they would almost certainly have to, or they'd get nothing more than cosmic sludge."

"Explain, please."

He leaped to his feet, knocked over a stack of books on an end table, and threw open the glass doors. The city lights blazed beneath a crescent moon and cold, distant stars. "Unless you were *very* lucky, Michael—*incredibly* lucky—unless a world of constants balanced very precisely, and a multitude of physical laws came out just right, there would *be* no moon hung in this sky, no distant suns to brighten the night. And certainly no eyes to see the difference." He strode out onto the terrace, and advanced toward the edge of the roof. Uncertain what he might do in his agitated state, I hurried after him. "*But,*" he continued, "with a little ingenuity, we can create whatever we wish. Flowers. Galaxies. An immortal race."

"He did not see fit to do that," I said firmly.

He swung around. "No, He did not." He raised his face to the stars. "Indeed, He did not. Certainly, He did not lack the imagination. Everything around us demonstrates that. But He chose to show us the possibilities of existence, to let us taste love, and to snatch it away. To create transients in this marvelous place. What are our lives, finally, but a long march toward a dusty end? Michael—" His eyes widened, and his voice rose to a shriek. "The stars were created not in love, but in malice. If you could create angels, would you make *men?*"

"That's not my call," I said.

"Isn't it? You and I are *victims*, Michael. If not us, then who?"

The wind blew across the rooftop.

"*Think*, Michael: what kind of being would give us *death* when He had life in His hands?"

The temperature was dropping. Lights moved against the stars, headed in the general direction of Seattle-Tacoma International. "*If* you're correct, Nick—and I say *if*—the kind of Deity you're describing might take offense." It was really an effort to lighten the mood. It didn't.

"Thunderbolt out of a clear sky? No: we are safely beyond His reach."

"How do you know?"

"Because once He released the cosmic seed, we expanded into a universe other than His. He can't touch us. That's the way it works. We're alone, Michael. No need to worry." He began to giggle. The laughter bubbled out of his throat but stopped when he rammed a fist into the waist-high brick wall at the edge of the roof.

He did not cry out, but only stood with blood pouring between clenched fingers. His hysteria drained, and I took him back inside, sat him down, and got the Mercurochrome. "I'm sorry," he said. "I really shouldn't have loaded all that on you."

"That's true." Our eyes met. "And not on yourself."

A storm blew out of the Pacific that night. It carried no rain, but there was electricity, and it dumped a lot of hail into the area. I lay awake through much of it, watching the light in the bedroom curtains alternately brighten and fade, listening to the rhythmic breathing of my wife. At one point I got up and wandered through the house, checking the kids.

And, for the first time in many years, I prayed. But the old words sounded empty.

I could not take seriously any of what he had said. But I kept thinking: surely, a Technician who could wire gravity into the universe could manage a mechanism to dispose of malcontents. In spite of common sense, I was worried.

I called him in the morning, got no answer, waited an hour, and tried the lab. Cord picked up the phone. "Yes," he said. "He's here. Did you want to talk to him?"

"No," I said. "Is he okay?"

"Far as I can tell. Why? Did something happen?"

So there had been no bolts. Nothing had come in the night to carry him off.

He remains in that gloomy tower. Occasionally, I can see him up there, framed in the light of that single lamp. Staring across the city. Across the world.

And it has occurred to me that there are subtler ways than lightning bolts.

AULD LANG *BOOM*

I've never believed in the supernatural. The universe is too subtle, too rational, to permit entry to gods or devils. There's no room for the paranormal. No fortune telling. No messages from beyond. No divine retribution.

But I am not sure how to explain certain entries in my father's diary, which came into my hands recently after his death in the Jersey Event. On the surface, I have no choice but to conclude that there is either a hoax, or a coincidence of unimaginable proportions. Still, it *is* my father's handwriting, and the final entry is dated the day before he died. If there is deception, I cannot imagine how it has been accomplished.

I found the diary locked in the upper right hand drawer of his oak desk. The keys were in a small glass jar atop the desk, obviating the point of the lock, but my father was never one to concern himself with consistency. He would have put it in there himself: my mother had died many years before, and he lived alone. The desk itself was intact when I got to it after the disaster, although it had been ruined by rain.

Nobody will ever be sure how many died when the rock came down off the Jersey coast. Conservative estimates put the figure at a million and a half. A hundred thousand simply vanished, probably washed out to sea by the giant tidal waves. Others died in the quakes, storms, power disruptions, and epidemics that followed the strike.

That night was, of course, the kind of seminal event that marks everyone who lives through it. No family in the country was untouched by this worst natural disaster in recorded history. *What were you doing when the meteor fell?*

I was a thousand miles away, watching *Great Railway Journeys* with my family when they broke in with the initial reports. I spent the balance of the evening trying to call my father, or anyone else I knew who lived in the South Jersey-Philadelphia area. But there was no phone service.

So now I have this cryptic document, stretching back into 1961. It is less a diary than a journal, a record of political, literary, and social opinions. My father was a dentist. He was good with kids and with nervous adults. A sign in his waiting room advertised: WE CATER TO COWARDS. But his interests extended far beyond his office. He was alert to every scientific and political trend, a student of the arts, a champion of the afflicted. He was a Renaissance dentist. He was capable of sulphurous explosions when he detected some particularly outrageous piece of hypocrisy or venality. He was a sworn enemy of politicians, lawyers, and professional athletes who charge kids twenty bucks an autograph. He instinctively distrusted people in power.

He favored requiring all heads of state to be mothers with six or more draft-age children. He wanted to mount a massive national effort to save the schools, to be funded by "downsizing" the federal establishment. He would have applied capital punishment with vigor because it has the dual advantage of reducing the criminal population, and providing the average malefactor with the attention he desires.

My father was sexually active, and many of the women who drifted through his life would no doubt have been shocked to read his appraisals of their performances:

Lisa: screams and groans and bites a lot, but can't act well enough to carry it off. Down deep, where it counts, she is about as wild and uninhibited as a good phone directory.

Michele: probably better than an old movie.

Martie: woman doesn't know when to quit. Would wear out a jack-hammer.

I have of course fictionalized the names.

The pages were also full of antireligious views: for reasons never clear to me, he believed Methodist ministers to be uniformly a pack of scoundrels. This was especially odd in that he had never had any connection that I knew of with that church. *The average congressman,* he wrote during the late '80s, *is roughly equal in moral content to a Methodist preacher.* The Creator himself did not escape criticism: *The world is such a misbegotten wreck that it is impossible to believe any self-respecting deity would accept the blame for it.* And: *If there is a career more attractive to scoundrels and frauds than professional politics, it must be the Methodist ministry.*

Perhaps I violated an ethic in reading my father's diary. I wish now that I had not. But the charm and vitality of his observations, his obvious appetite for life, his Olympian assaults against those he considered frauds and halfwits, were irresistible. Once started, I could not stop. And I began to realize how little I had appreciated him during his lifetime.

I started seriously reading the diary at about the time I'd given up hope that he might have survived. I'd seen the final entries, and knew that he planned to be in Atlantic City, the worst possible place. But there was the chance that he might have been sidetracked, gone somewhere else, been delayed by a woman. I know better now.

The first entry was dated July 16, 1961. It spells out the rationale behind the diary, which was that he hoped his "occasional ruminations" would one day be of general interest. (My father was never afflicted with modesty.) He also revealed an ambition to become an essayist, and believed that a daily account of his reflections would be a priceless aid to such an endeavor. I should add, parenthetically, that his ambitions came to nothing. If he ever actually tried to compile a manuscript, I have no knowledge of it.

Six days later, he recorded my birth. And, in another week, the death of my mother. He seldom mentioned her to me, but the diary gave over a dozen pages of cramped handwriting to reminiscences of their early years together, and of his conviction that, were it not for his responsibilities (by which I gathered he was talking of me), his life had become worthless. Judging from the diary, he never after seriously considered marriage although, as I mentioned, there were many women. I was aware of his escapades, of course, while I was growing up. And I was baffled: my father's appearance was rather ordinary. He was also short and, when I was a teenager, beginning to lose his hair. It was hard to see what brought that endless supply of women to his door. I don't know yet.

By the time I had read into the late '70s, I noticed an odd trend. There are passages, and implications, which are unsettling. My father was, if anything, a rationalist. And I could sense his increasing dismay at events which he could not explain. I began to read more intently, and eventually found it impossible to lay the book aside. I will never forget the cold, rainswept evening during which I came back to the final entry. And read it in the frantic glare of what had gone before.

Now I don't know what to make of it. The only possible conclusion is that the diary is a fabrication. It *has* to be. Yet I do not see how that is possible. My wife, after she finished it, suggested we burn it.

I have not been able to bring myself to do that. Nor can I simply pretend it does not exist. Consequently, without taking a position on the matter, I have had the pertinent entries privately printed, in order to make them available to a small group of my friends, whose judgment I trust. Perhaps someone among them will be able to offer a rational explanation.

One final note: the "Rob" who figures so prominently in this narrative was Orin R. Robinson, who served 1958-60 in the Far East with my father. Curiously, they seem not to have been close friends until after the chance meeting in the Minneapolis airport described in the first entry in the Extract below. My father, incidentally, was on his way to Fargo, pursuing a young woman of his acquaintance.

(ATTACHMENT)
Being Extracts from the Diary of Samuel H. Coswell

Minneapolis, Friday, November 22, 1963
Black day. The President is dead.

I was having lunch with Rob. First time I'd seen him since Navy days on the *McCusker*. Hell of a reunion. We were sitting in a dark little place off Washington Avenue, all electric candles and checkerboard tablecloths and bare hardwood floors. A waitress had filled our glasses with chianti and set the bottle down. We were already deep into reminiscing about old friends and old times, and Rob swept up his glass with a flourish, and raised it toward the light. "Here's to you, Sam," he said, "I've missed you," and in that brief hesitation, when one tastes the moment before the wine, I became aware of raised voices.

Chair legs scraped the floor. "—*Shot him*—" someone said. The words hung in the still air, whispered, almost disembodied. Then Kennedy's name. Doors banged, and traffic sounds got loud. Outside, a postal truck pulled up beside a mailbox.

There were bits and pieces of conversation. *"How badly hurt?" "They get the guy?" "Be fine. Can't kill—" "What time is it? Is the stock market still open?"*

They brought out a television and we watched the early reports and learned the worst. "Not much of a reunion," I told Rob.

He lives in L.A. We'd met at the airport, both passing through. He's an aircraft design consultant, and he was on his way home from Chicago. We got to talking, decided not to miss the opportunity, and rearranged our flight schedules. Which was how we came to be eating a late lunch together when the news came from Dallas.

We walked back to our Sheraton and pushed into the bar. The

TV threw a pale glare over the crowd, which kept getting bigger. Nobody said much. Cronkite reported that a police officer had been shot, and then he was back a few minutes later to tell us that a suspect had been captured in a movie theater. Name's Oswald. Nobody seems to know anything about him. I guess we'll start getting some answers tomorrow. Meantime, there's a lot of talk about a conspiracy. And we now have Lyndon Johnson.

I'm surprised this has hit me so hard. I've never been high on Kennedy. Although, as politicians go, he was likable. But it will be harder to run the Republic if presidents have to go into hiding.

Rob is up one floor. We'd originally planned to have breakfast together. He has an early flight, though, and I don't think either of us feels much like socializing. My own flight's at noon. So I will sleep late. And maybe one day we'll meet again in some other airport.

Fargo, Saturday, November 23, 1963

Ellen and I spent the day parked in front of a TV. Gloomy business, this. Oswald looks like a looney. Still no explanations. There are theories that he was working for the Cubans, or the CIA, or the Russians. You take a look at this guy, and it's hard to believe any sensible organization would use him. He doesn't look reliable. We'll see. If we trace it to Moscow, what happens then?

Ellen is showering now. She's a knockout, enough to get anyone's juices running, but there's a ceremonial quality to the preparations. The assassination has cast gloom on us all, I guess.

Enroute to Philadelphia, Sunday, November 24, 1963

Kennedy's funeral tomorrow.

Never knew anyone as wild as Ellen was last night. Is this the way we hide from our mortality?

Philadelphia, Saturday, August 1, 1964

Call from Rob. He's going to be in town next week, and we will get together. Funny about him: when we were in the Navy, he seemed a bit standoffish. Difficult to get to know. Maybe it's the Kennedy thing, but he seems warmer, friendlier than I remember. I wouldn't have believed he'd ever have taken the time to look me up. He's a curious mix, simultaneously idealistic and cynical, gregarious and distant. He'd be horrified to hear this, but the truth is, he's a fascist. A goodhearted one, but a fascist all the same. He's a great believer in order, and is fond of quoting Plato on the dangers of giving freedom to the undisciplined. We talked for almost an hour (his nickel). We agreed that western civilization is on its last legs. I don't really believe that, but he's persuasive, and anyhow predicting doom always gives one such a warm feeling. Is that why there are so many Fundamentalists?

We were both elated by the lunar photographs taken by Ranger 7. First closeups ever. I told him we were taking the first steps into a vast sea. He laughed. *A vast desert, maybe.* He doesn't think we will ever leave the Earth-moon system. Why not? *Where else is there to go?*

Philadelphia, Friday, August 7, 1964

Great day.

I don't know when I've enjoyed myself more. We spent most of the evening arguing over Goldwater. Rob is worried that Johnson will win, and then give away southeast Asia. I'm scared to death Barry would give Hanoi an atomic alternative shortly after the swearing-in ceremony. Get out or get fused.

I don't think I've ever properly appreciated Rob. The world's a more comic place when he's around. Its absurdities are a bit more clearly defined. We share a sense of the ridiculous that seems to transcend language: a word, sometimes a glance, is enough to suggest some new buffoonery on the march. He ignites insight, in the way a good woman intensifies the emotional climate. We spent the evening raking over the Johnson administration, the Bible-thumpers who are citing chapter and verse against the Freedom Riders, and the latest academic notion that everyone's opinion is equally valid. (Rob's not exactly big on the Freedom Riders either. They're another example of what happens when people start taking their rights seriously.) He thinks ballots should be weighted. Particularly his. Probably mine. *A bonus for common sense. It's in short supply these days.*

We ate a late lunch at Bookbinder's, and retired for the evening to the Officers' Club at the Naval Base. We stayed until midnight. It strikes me that the art of conversation has almost disappeared from the world. Rob, in that sense, is something of an anachronism: a visitor from the nineteenth century, from an age in which there were more important things to do than to sit around and be entertained.

He'll be leaving in the morning, ten o'clock flight.

Pity.

Philadelphia, Wednesday, January 9, 1974

School districts are burning Mark Twain. In California, two police officers have been sued for using unnecessary force to subdue a man who was in the act of stabbing a woman. And there's a report that a group of volunteers trying to stop their TV habit went through withdrawal. Anyone who worries that the U.S. is headed for collapse can relax. It is raining on the rubble.

Terri Hauser has begun suggesting that Sammy needs a mother. Truth is, he probably does, but that seems to me to be a weak foundation for a marriage. I know she would move in if I suggested it. But where would *that* end?

Post Office returned Rob's Christmas card today, stamped MOVED—FORWARDING PERIOD EXPIRED.

Philadelphia, Friday, November 2, 1979
   Rob is back.

There've been a few changes in his life. He's living in Seattle now. And he's gotten married. They'll be here on one of these Amtrak plans where you get to ride all over the country. Her name is Anne, and she is from Vermont. The plan is that she will go up to visit her folks for a few days, and Rob will stop off here. I wonder if he will be able to figure out a use for this home computer. I thought I might be able to get it to do my taxes, but they keep changing the laws every year.

Philadelphia, Sunday, November 4, 1979
   The train was late getting in. I had to hang around 30th Street Station two hours. But it was good to see him again. Been a lot of years. We came back here, got settled, and then went to the Berlinhaus up on the Boulevard for sauerbraten. Lots of talk about a sex poll that was released yesterday, indicating that women are as adulterous as men. We tried to imagine how it might be possible to poll people about their sexual habits and come up with anything close to valid results. The Ayatollah also took his lumps. *What do you suppose it would be like to sit down with him for coffee?*

Later in the evening, we stopped by Janet's place. She'd asked to meet Rob, and that went pretty well too. We probably drank a little too much. But I don't think I've ever seen Janet enjoy herself so much.

Rob has gone completely gray since the last time I saw him. Otherwise, he doesn't seem to have lost much ground.

Incidentally, toward the end of the evening at the Berlinhaus, someone at the next table overheard us talking about Khomeini and asked whether we'd heard that the Iranians had seized the embassy in Teheran?

It was true, of course. They've taken fifty or sixty hostages. State

Department isn't sure yet how many. It must be a first of some kind: nobody ever seized diplomatic people. Even Hitler didn't do that. It's what happens when you put an amateur in charge of a government.

Well, they'll release everybody tomorrow. And apologize. If we behave according to past practice, we'll lodge a stiff protest and go back to business as usual.

Philadelphia, Monday, November 5, 1979

Another delay with the train this morning, but Rob finally got away. This time, we've agreed to get together again soon.

The Iranian government claims it has no control over the students who've taken the embassy. Rob thinks we should give the Ayatollah a list of targets and start destroying them one by one until the government discovers it *can* do something to release our people. I'm not sure that isn't the best way to handle it.

Question: what should our primary objective be? To get the hostages released? Or to act in such a way that future hostage-takers will think it over before trying the same thing?

Philadelphia, Tuesday, September 7, 1982

Rob's marriage has collapsed. I had no idea it was in trouble. He doesn't talk much about his personal life, and of course over a telephone you don't really get to see anything. He's obviously shaken. I get the impression *he* didn't see it coming either. I suggested he might take some time and come here, but he says he'll be fine. I'm sure he will.

I never got to meet her.

Seattle, Tuesday, January 18, 1986

We've lost a shuttle. And a crew.

Grim day. I'd been looking forward to this trip for a long time. Rob picked me up at the airport, and we stopped for lunch on the way out to his place. The waitress told us about *Challenger*.

Rob looked at me very strangely, and I knew what he was thinking. We'd been able to get together *four* times over the course of a quarter-century. And three of those occasions had been marred by a major American disaster. There had been far greater catastrophes in the world during the period, in terms of body count. But we seemed to be tuned to a *local* wavelength.

Neither of us said much. Until we heard the details, we hoped that the crew might have been able to survive, although it was difficult to visualize any kind of shuttle explosion that one could walk away from.

* * *

Philadelphia, Wednesday, March 4, 1987

... (Madeline and I) were talking about the various ways in which minuscule events produce results out of all proportion. Like the short-cut through a park that generates an accidental meeting that ends in a marriage. One of the Kennedy assassination theories holds that Lee Oswald shot down the President because Marina Oswald indicated a sexual preference for *him* over her inadequate husband.

Madeline said she'd heard once that a butterfly, moving its wings in Africa under the right conditions, could produce a hurricane in the Caribbean. Interesting conceit.

Philadelphia, Sunday, December 18, 1988

Rob called today. *He'll be in the area Wednesday. Did I think we could manage dinner without provoking an international crisis?*

I explained that I won't be able to pick him up at the airport because I'm booked at the office. He will take a cab.

Philadelphia, Wednesday, December 21, 1988

It's happened again! A London-to-New York flight with more than two hundred people disintegrated over Scotland while Rob and I sat in a restaurant out on the Main Line.

I'm spooked.

So is he.

Philadelphia, Thursday, December 22, 1988

People died on the ground as well. The photographs from Locherbie, the crash site, are just too much. I stayed away from the TV most of the night. I've got Dickens beside me, but I can't keep my mind on it. They are saying now that it looks as if there was a bomb on board. How can people be so evil?

And we were together again.

Kennedy.

Teheran.

Challenger.

Flight 103.

Here's to us.

Rob left on an afternoon flight. We tried to calculate odds, but neither of us is mathematician enough to be able even to frame the problem. Rob, who is ordinarily a world-class skeptic, wondered whether it was possible that we might sense oncoming disaster? And instinctively huddle against the storm? I told him about Madeline's butterfly.

Has it happened every time?

We both thought so. But I went back through this diary tonight. On August 7, 1964, we got safely through a meal.

One exception to the pattern.

The bond between my father and Orin Robinson grew closer, possibly as a result of the curious intersections between their quiet reunions and the series of historic disasters. They came to refer to this trend as the *Tradition*. Their phone conversations became more frequent. They discounted their alarm on the night of the Locherbie flight. Absurd, they said, to think they could be connected. And anyway there was, after all, the exception to the general pattern. *Thank God for 1964*. That phrase became their watchword.

It was during this period that my father engaged in his brief flirtation with Catholicism. Rob was horrified, but took the position that it was my responsibility to stand by my father during this aberration.

There were still occasional echoes of the *Tradition* in the diary. . . .

Washington, D.C., Tuesday, February 4, 1992

. . . Visited the Eternal Flame today. It is a lovely and sober spot.

How does it happen that the shots fired in Dallas so long ago still hurt?

If Rob and I had not run into each other in Minneapolis that day, is it at all possible it might not have happened? Does that make any kind of sense at all?

Portland, Oregon, Saturday, December 12, 1992

The (dental) convention's a bit dry. But I got together with some of the guys from Chicago, and we went over to Margo's. It's a topless place, and I guess it's a sign you're getting old when you wish they'd move so you could see the basketball game.

I would have enjoyed getting together with Rob. But we let it go this time, more or less by mutual consent.

Philadelphia, Tuesday, June 14, 1994

. . . Rob confessed tonight that he has been east any number of times over the last few years, but has not mentioned it to me. *But it's dumb to behave as if we have been doing something dangerous.*

He's right, of course.

I'll be in New York this weekend. I could get down for dinner.
I keep thinking about the butterfly.
"Listen how about a change of venue?"
Okay. What did you have in mind?
"I don't know. Something more exotic than Philly."
Why don't we meet in Atlantic City?
"Yeah. Sounds good."
Dinner by the sea.
Be nice to see him again. And the world looks quiet. Here's to us.

Philadelphia, Wednesday, June 15, 1994
I'll be glad when it's over—

Philadelphia, Friday, June 17, 1994
Rob tomorrow. I cannot imagine what life would have been like without him. Yet I've seen so little of him.

As the world knows, the meteor fell at 7:22 P.M. on the 18th of June. Possibly just as they were sitting down to dinner.

I've read through these passages until I have them by heart, and I can offer no explanation. The correlation between meetings and catastrophe is necessarily coincidental because it can't be anything else.

But there's one more point: I've gone back and looked closely at August 7, 1964. The exception to the Tradition.

Robinson and my father were wrong: there *was* a disaster on that day. But its nature was less immediately cataclysmic than the other events, so it's easy to see why it might have passed unnoticed.

In the late afternoon of that date, the Congress, with only two negative votes, approved the Gulf of Tonkin Resolution.

We didn't know it at the time, but the United States had formally entered the Vietnam War.

DUTCHMAN

It rose out of the dark, indistinguishable from the blazing stars. "No question about it," said Carmody. "It's in orbit."

"Hugh." McIras spoke without lifting her eyes from her console screen. "Are you sure it couldn't have come from the surface?"

At that time, neither the world, nor its sun, had a name. We were a thousand light-years beyond the Veiled Lady, twelve days from the nearest outstation. It was a rare jewel, that planet, one of the few we'd seen whose climate and geology invited immediate human settlement. Its single continent straddled the north polar circle, crushed beneath the glaciers of a dying ice age. But it was also a world of island chains and serene oceans and towering granite peaks. There was no single land mass, other than that in the arctic region, big enough to have permitted extensive evolution of land animals. "No," I said. "There's nobody here."

"I'm getting a regular pulse on the doppler," said Carmody.

McIras braced her chin on one fist and stared at the image on the monitors. "Recall the teams," she told the watch officer. "And get an estimate on how long it'll take."

I started to object, but got no further than climbing out of my seat. Her lips were a thin line. "Not now, Hugh," she said quietly. "The regulations are explicit on this situation." She punched a stud on her armrest. "This is the Captain. We may have a contact. *Tenandrome* is now at Readiness Condition Two. For those of you associated with Mr. Scott's group," she glanced toward me, "that means we might accelerate with little or no warning. Please prepare accordingly."

Carmody hunched over his console, his eyes wide with excitement. "It's artificial," he said. "It has to be."

"Dimensions?" asked McIras.

"Approximately 120 meters long, maybe 35 in diameter at its widest point, which is just forward of center."

"About the size of an Ordway freighter," said the watch officer. "Are we sure nobody else comes out here?"

"No one that we know of," said McIras, returning her attention to the command screen. "Put bridge sound and pictures on secondary monitors." I was grateful for that: at least my people wouldn't be lying in their bunks wondering what the hell was happening.

I walked over and stood beside her so we could talk without being overheard. "This is going to cost a lot of time," I said. "And probably some equipment as well. Why not investigate *before* recalling everybody?"

Saje McIras was a plain woman with prominent jaws and a mildly blotched skin that had resulted from a long battle with Travison's Disease which, at the time she'd had it, usually killed. She blinked habitually, and her eyes were dull and lifeless, except on those occasions when she was driven to exert her considerable abilities. Then, for perhaps a few moments, they were quite capable of taking fire. "If we get a surprise," she said, "we may not want to wait around a day or two for you to gather your people."

"I'm beginning to get some resolution," said Carmody. He filtered out the glare, reduced the contrast, and eliminated the starfield. What remained was a single point of white light.

We watched it expand gradually into a squat heavy cylinder, thick though the middle, rounded at one end, flared at the other. "It's one of ours," said McIras, not entirely able to conceal her surprise. "But it's old! Look at the design—" It was small, and ungainly, and unsettlingly familiar, a relic from another age. It was the kind of ship that had leaped the stars during the early days of the Armstrong drive, that had carried Desiret and Taniyama and Bible Bill to the worlds that would eventually become the Confederacy. And it was the kind of ship that had waged the internecine wars, and that, in humanity's darkest hour, had fought off the Ashiyyur.

For a long time, no one spoke.

It grew steadily larger.

"Captain," said the watch officer. "Recovery estimates twenty-eight hours for the recall."

"We have its orbit," said Carmody. "Closest point of approach will occur in three hours, eleven minutes, at a range of 2600 kilometers."

McIras acknowledged. "Stay with it. I want to know if it shows any response to our presence."

She was a beautiful ship, silver and blue in the bright sunlight.

Her lines curved gently: there was about her a sense of the ornate that one does not see in the cold gray vessels of the modern era. The parabolic prow with its sunburst, the flared tubes, the sweptback bridge, the cradled pods, all would have been of practical use only to an atmospheric flyer. Somehow, I felt as if I knew her; and she reminded me of a time when I'd been very young.

"What's that on the hull?" asked a voice over the comm circuit.

Carmody had centered *Tenandrome*'s long-range telescopes on the ship's designator, a group of symbols beneath the bridge, which we were still unable to make out. But there was a mark just forward of them, near the bow, dark against the silver metal. He tried to increase magnification, but the image grew indistinct; so we waited while the two ships drew closer.

Recovery reported that two of the survey teams were en route from the surface. There were six others, but they would have to wait until we could change orbit. Several were already on the circuit, demanding to know what was going on. Holtmeyer exploded when I tried to explain it to him. (That was more or less typical of Holtmeyer, although, in his defense, he was at the time sitting on a glacier, and thought he'd seen some large fossils through the ice.) McIras overheard most of it, maybe all of it, and she cut in near the end. "Hugh," she said, on a circuit not audible to the ground, "tell him I said to get back here *tout de suite*, and without further discussion. By the way, you might be interested in knowing it's a warship." She explained something about transformational pods, but I suddenly stopped listening because the mark near the bow was resolving itself, and somebody else must have seen the same thing I did because there was a burst of profanity behind me.

It was a symbol we all knew: a black harridan spreading its wings across a crescent moon. And in that moment, I understood why I had recognized the vessel.

"It's not possible," breathed the watch officer.

Her design suggested a simpler age, a better time. Maybe it was the ship itself, maybe it was the tangle of associations we all had with her. I'd seen Marcross's magnificent rendering of her many times in the main lobby of the Hall of the People on Rimway, flanked by portraits of Christopher and Tarien Sim, the heroic brothers who had stood almost alone against the Ashiyyur. And every child on every world in the Confederacy knew the simple inscription carved in marble at the base of the central painting: *Never Again*.

"My God," said the watch officer, his voice little more than a whisper. "It's *Corsarius*."

After a while, the ship began to draw away from us; the details blurred and faded.

Tenandrome was in a high geosynchronous orbit: we were taking our first team on board when the stranger ship began its long descent toward the nightside. But Carmody's telescopes still held it in the center of the monitors, and I alternated between watching it and scrolling through library accounts of its exploits.

All the vessels in Christopher Sim's Dellacondan squadron had displayed the black harridan, a ferocious predator much admired on their mountainous world; but only the commander himself had placed the symbol within the crescent moon, "to ensure the enemy can find me."

Corsarius plunged down the sky into the twilight: a thing of legend and history and dying light. At the end, when all had seemed lost, and only the last few ships of the Dellacondan squadron had stood against the all-conquering invader, her crew had abandoned her. And Christopher Sim had gone down to the bars and dens of lost Abonai, where he'd found the seven nameless men and women who'd ridden with him on that final brilliant sally.

The navigator's fingers danced across his presspads. He glanced at the Captain. McIras looked at her own panel and nodded. "Axial tilt's about eleven degrees," she said. "And it's rolling. It's been there a long time."

Images flickered across the command screen, tail sections and communication assemblies and stress factors. "Is it," I asked, "what it appears to be?"

She shrugged, but there was discomfort in the gesture. "Sim and his ship died off Rigel two centuries ago."

It was dwindling quickly now, falling through the dusk, plunging toward the terminator. I watched it during those last moments before it lost the sunlight, waiting, wondering perhaps whether it wasn't some phantasm of the night which, with the morning, would leave no trace of its passing.

It dropped into the planetary shadow.

"I'm still getting a good visual," said the navigator, surprised. It was indeed still visible, a pale, ghostly luminescence. A chill felt its way up my spine, and I looked around at the crew, startled to see that even on the bridge of a modern starship people can react to the subtle tug of the supernatural.

"Where the hell," asked Carmody, "is the reflection coming from? The moons aren't in her sky."

"Running lights," said McIras. "Its running lights are on."

McIras stayed on the bridge through her sleep period. I don't know whether she thought something would move up on us in the dark, but the truth was that everyone was a bit unnerved. They'd assigned one of the pilots' seats to me as a courtesy, but I dozed in it, and woke cold and stiff in the middle of the night. The Captain poured me a coffee and asked how I felt.

"Okay," I said. "How are we doing?"

She replied that we were doing fine, that we'd recovered our first two teams, but that in light of the nature of the object, she'd delayed moving to pick up the other units.

"What do you think it is?" I asked.

She took a long time answering. The computers were running the ship; the bridge was in semidarkness, with only the watch officer actually required to be awake. Several others, who usually would have secured for the night, were asleep at their stations. We were no longer at Condition Two, but the tension was still tangible. The instrument lights caught eyes, and reflected against the sheen of her dark skin. Her breathing was audible; it was part of the pulse of the ship, one with the muted bleeps and whistles of the computers and the occasional creak of metal walls protesting some minor adjustment of velocity or course, and the thousand other sounds which one hears between the stars at night.

"I keep thinking," she said, "about the legend that he will come back in the Confederacy's supreme hour of need." She slid into a seat and lifted her cup to her lips. "It isn't from Rimway." She meant the coffee. "I'm sure you can tell. Logistics had a little mixup and we've had to make do with what they sent us."

"Saje," I asked, "what are you going to do?"

"The wrong thing. Hugh, if I could arrange to have everyone forget what they've seen, I'd erase the record, go somewhere else, and never come back. That thing out there, I don't know what it is, nor how it could be what it seems; but it doesn't belong in this sky, or *any* sky. I don't want anything to do with it."

"You're stuck with it," I said.

She stared at the image of the stranger ship, which had come round the curve of the planet and was again closing on us. "I was reading his book during the night."

"Sim's?" That was of course *Man and Olympian*, his history of classical Greece.

"Yes. He was something of a radical. He comes down hard for example on Socrates. Thinks he got just what he deserved." I had known that, but had never been particularly interested in the details. Before now. "He says the judge and jury were right. That Socrates was in fact undermining the Athenian state with a system of values that, although admirable in themselves, were nevertheless disrupting Athenian life."

"That doesn't sound reasonable," I said.

"That's what the critics thought, too. Sim blasted them later, in a second book that he didn't live to finish." She smiled. "Tarien said somewhere that his brother didn't object to critics as long as he could have the last word. It's a pity they never present this side of him in the schools. The Christopher Sim the kids get to see comes off as perfect, preachy, and fearless." Her brow furrowed. "I wonder what he'd have made of a ghost ship?"

"He'd have boarded. Or, if he couldn't board, he'd have looked for more information, and found something else to think about in the meantime."

She walked away, and I called *Man and Olympian* up out of the library. It was a standard classic that no one really read anymore, except in undergraduate survey classes. My impression of it, derived from a cursory reading thirty years before, was that its reputation was based primarily on the fact that it was the product of a famous man. So I leaned back in the cushions, drew the screen close, and prepared to be lulled back to sleep.

But Sim's Hellas was too vital a place to allow that: its early pages were filled with Xerxes' rage ("O Master, remember the Athenians"), Themistocles' statesmanship, and the valor of the troops who stood at Thermopylae. I was struck, not only by the clarity and force of the book, but also by its compassion. It was not what one would ordinarily expect from a military leader. But then, Sim had not begun as a military leader: he'd been a teacher when the trouble started. And ironically, while he made his reputation as a naval tactician, his brother Tarien, who'd begun the war as a fleet officer, became known eventually as the great statesman of the period.

His views are essentially Olympian: one feels that Christopher Sim speaks for History, and if his perspective is not always quite that of those who have gone before, there is no doubt where the misperceptions lie. His is the final word.

His prose acquires a brooding quality during his account of the destruction of Athens, and the needless loss of life during the misguided effort to defend the Parthenon. And, if I'd been at all inclined to sleep, he would have blasted that possibility by his denunciation of the Spartans for Thermopylae: *The Hellenes knew for years that the Persians were coming, and in any case they had advance knowledge of the forming of the invasion force. Yet they prepared no league, and set no defenses, until the deluge was on them. Then they sent Leonidas and his men, and their handful of allies, to compensate with their lives for the neglect and stupidity of the politicians.*

It was a grim coincidence: those words had been written before the Ashiyyur had launched their attack, and in a broad sense it fell to Sim to play the role of Leonidas. He led the holding action for the frontier worlds, while Tarien sounded the alarm, and began the immense task of forging an alliance that could stand against the invaders.

I don't know whether I ever actually got to sleep. Persians and Ashiyyur got confused with each other, and then I was looking up into Saje McIras' solemn eyes. Her hand was on my shoulder. "Hugh," she said, "we're going to send over a boarding party."

"Okay," I said. "I've got a few people who should go."

"No. I want to keep it small. Just you and me."

I watched her, unable to believe she was serious. *Just you and me?* "Why?"

Her face was a mask, but the reflections that flickered across it had acquired a somber pulse. "I don't really know. I'm afraid of what we might find, maybe."

The hull was seared and blistered and pocked. It had a patchwork quality from periodic replacement of plates. Navigational and communication pods were scored, after-section shields appeared to have buckled, and the drive housing was missing, exposing the Armstrong unit. "Nevertheless," said McIras, "I don't see any major damage. There *is* one strange thing though." We were in a shuttle, approaching from behind and above. "The drive housing was *removed*. It wasn't blown off."

"Unfinished repairs," I suggested.

"Yes. Or repairs made in a hurry. Not the way *I'd* want to take a ship on a long mission. But it looks serviceable enough." The aguan solenoids, through which *Corsarius* had hurled the lightning, protruded stiff and cold from an array of mounts. "So do *they*," she added.

But the chill of age was on the vessel.

McIras sat in the pilot's seat, thoughtful and apprehensive. The multi-channel was open, sweeping frequencies that would have been available for automated responses from *Corsarius*. "The histories must be wrong," I said. "Obviously, it wasn't destroyed off Rigel."

She adjusted the contrast on the navigational display. One of the computers on *Tenandrome* was matching the ship's schematics with ancient naval records, again and again, in endless detail. "It makes me wonder what else they might have been wrong about," she said.

"Assume Sim survived Rigel," I said. "Why did he disappear afterward? Why come out here anyhow? Saje, could *Corsarius* have made this kind of flight?"

"Oh, yes. Hugh, the range of any of these vessels was only limited by the quantity of supplies they could get on board. No: they could have done it. Obviously, they *did* do it. But it would have taken the better part of a year, coming from the zone of operations. And presumably in the middle of a war. Why? Why in hell did they do it?" She stared down at the spine of the ship.

I'd always thought of *Corsarius* as a large vessel, and the records confirm that opinion. She *was* large, for a frigate. But she was almost negligible against the square-cut bulk of *Tenandrome*. "I wonder if, somehow, Sim and his ship fell into the hands of the Ashiyyur?"

We drifted out over the bow, past the fierce eyes and curved beak of the harridan, past the weapons clusters bristling in the ship's snout. McIras took us higher. The hull fell sharply away, and the blue sunsplashed planetary surface swam across the viewports. Then it too was swallowed by the broad sweep of star-strewn black sky. We swung around and started a fresh approach.

McIras was talking to *Tenandrome* in a flat emotionless voice. "Blind and dead," she was saying. "No effort to track."

The curious Cerullian characters, stenciled on her hull, slipped past, close up: the ship's designation. "It checks," came Carmody's voice. "It's *Corsarius*."

The hatch rotated open to McIras' touch, and yellow light showed around its edges. We floated into the airlock. Red lamps glowed on an elegant status board. "Seems to be in working order," I said.

"Ship's got power," she replied. "Not much. Enough to run the maintenance systems." Not enough to generate artificial gravity. Once we were inside, the hatch closed, lights blinked to orange, and air hissed into the compartment. Carmody did a comm check and wished us luck. The bolts on the inner hatch slid out of their wells, warning lamps went to red, and the door swung open.

We looked out into a dimly lit chamber. The bulkheads were lined with cabinets and storage enclosures and pressure suits. Two benches and an engineering console were anchored to the deck. Oxygen content was okay, a little low, but breathable. Temperature was not quite three degrees. Cool. McIras released her helmet, lifted it, and inhaled.

"They turned down the heat," I said, removing my own.

"Yes. That's precisely what they did. They left the ship, expecting to come back." She drifted awkwardly across the deck, counting the pressure suits. There were eight.

"All there," she said.

"We need to look at the bridge."

"In a minute, Hugh." She disappeared down a corridor. I waited several minutes, contemplating shadowy passageways. The cabinets were filled with oscillators, meters, cable, generators. One yielded a book of poetry, written in Cerullian. Another, a holo of a young woman and a child.

Everything was secured in bands, clamps, or compartments. The equipment was clean and polished, as though it had been stowed the day before.

I was looking at the holo when she returned. "Well," she said, "there's one theory blown."

"What was that?"

"I thought maybe they'd gone down to the surface and got stranded."

"Hell, Saje, they wouldn't all have left the ship."

"I suppose. Anyhow, it's a moot point. The lander's in its bay."

"That means there was a second ship involved. They were taken off."

"Or," she said, "they're still here. Somewhere."

Some of the lights had failed. None of the elevators worked, and the air had a trace of ozone, as though one of the compressors was overheating. One compartment was full of drifting water-globes; another was scorched where an electrical fire had burned itself out. From somewhere deep in the ship came a slow, ponderous heartbeat, growing stronger as we penetrated the interior. "It's a hatch opening and closing," she said. "One of the circuits has malfunctioned."

Progress was slow. Moving around in null gravity is cumbersome, and every hatch had to be winched open. McIras tried without success to establish normal power from an auxiliary board. Green lamps went on, indicating that the functions had been executed, but nothing changed. So we floated through the ship, unable to get leverage, and unable to pass through the hatches without a lot of effort. One resisted us so fiercely that we wondered, even though the gauges read normal, whether there wasn't a vacuum behind it. In the end we went down one level and bypassed it.

We didn't talk much. There wasn't much to say, I suppose. When we did speak, it was always in a whisper, as though something besides ourselves might be listening. Carmody on *Tenandrome* must have felt it too: during the rare occasions when we heard his voice, it was thin and subdued.

It's been a good many years now since McIras and I took that figurative walk through *Corsarius*. The chill that lay heavy in her atmosphere pervades my nights still. We were approaching the bridge, and I was about to become, for all my life after, a cautious man.

I was so accustomed to the ample command and control facilities of Survey's vessels that I did not at first recognize Christopher Sim's command and control center for what it was. There were only three stations, and much of the available space was absorbed by computers. "Primitive stuff," said McIras. She looked momentarily at the captain's chair, the seat from which Sim had directed engagements that became the stuff of legend. Her eyes brightened. She drifted thoughtfully among the consoles, saw what she wanted, and touched a panel with a long index finger. "One gee coming, Hugh." She punched keys and frowned when nothing happened. She tried again: this time something in the bulkheads whined, sputtered, and took hold. I felt blood, organs, hair, everything settle toward the deck. "I've turned the heat up too," she announced.

"Saje, I think it's time to hear what Captain Sim has to say for himself."

She nodded and broke the link to *Tenandrome*. "Until we know what it's about," she explained, hovering over the command console.

She had to play with it a bit to find what she wanted. While she did, I diverted myself with an examination of a bridge designed by people who clearly possessed a deep and abiding love for the arc, the loop, and the parabola. The geometry was of the same order as the exterior of the ship: one would have been hard-pressed to find a straight line anywhere.

"Okay, Hugh, I've got it." She straightened up, with her fingers pressed against the grid. "The next voice you hear—"

—Was certainly not that of Christopher Sim. *Zero six fourteen twenty-two*, it said. *Abonai Four. Repairs categories one and two completed this date. Repairs category three as shown on inventory. Weapons systems fully restored. Corsarius returned to service.*

It was obviously a record made while the ship was in port, presumably by the supervisor of the work crew. I looked at McIras.

"That's still standard practice," she said. "The port always makes an entry on returning command of a vessel to its captain. There should be more."

There was: Christopher Sim had never made any speeches, had never spoken to parliaments, and had not lived long enough to make a farewell address. Unlike Tarien's, his voice had never become familiar to the school children of the Confederacy. Nevertheless, I knew it at once.

Zero six fourteen thirty seven, it said in a rich baritone. *Corsarius received per work order two two three kappa. Transformers check out at nine six point three seven, which is not an acceptable level for combat. Command understands that the port facility is under pressure just now. Nevertheless, if Maintenance is unable to effect repairs, they should at least be aware of the deficiency. Corsarius is hereby returned to port. Christopher Sim, Commanding.*

Another round of entries announced reworking of transformers. Sim's crisp voice accepted without comment. But even over the space of two centuries, one could read the satisfaction in his tone. The last word again.

"This would be just shortly before the crew mutinied," I said, checking the dates.

"Yes, Hugh. The mutiny, the Seven, we've got everything."

"Run the rest of it!" I said.

Her smile faded. "That's the last entry. There *is* nothing after it." Her voice was hollow.

"How can that be? Did somebody erase it?"

"This is a ship's log, Hugh. It can't be erased, can't be doctored, can't be changed in any way without leaving a trail. We'll turn it over to Archives for verification, but I doubt there's been any tampering. There'd be no point."

"But *Corsarius* went into battle shortly after that. There must have been log entries."

"Yeah. The law requires it. It does now and it would have then. For whatever reasons, Christopher Sim took a volunteer crew into the climactic battle of his life, and neglected to put one word about it in his log."

"Maybe he was too busy."

"Hugh, it could not have happened."

For the first time, she settled herself into the captain's chair, and punched fresh instructions into the computer. "Let's see what we can get if we back up a bit."

Christopher Sim's voice returned. He didn't possess the sheer oratorical power of his brother. But it was a good voice, possessing a vitality that made it hard to believe that its owner was long dead.

—*I have no doubt that the destruction of the two battle cruisers will focus enemy attention on the small naval bases at Dimonides II, and at Chippewa. It can hardly do otherwise. Those sites will be perceived by the enemy as a bone in its throat, and will be attacked as soon as they can concentrate sufficient power. The Ashiyyur will probably divert their main battle group to the task—*

"I think this is early in the war," I said.

"Yes. It's good to know at least that he uses his log."

Sim described the composition and strength of the force he expected, and launched into a detailed description of enemy psychology and their probable attack strategy. McIras commented that he seemed to have got most of it right. We listened for a while, to that and other encounters. The historic value of the log was probably astronomical. But she must have decided we weren't getting anywhere on the immediate problem. She got up and walked to the door. "I've still got things to look at, Hugh. You want to come along?"

"I'll stay here," I said. "I want to hear more of it."

Maybe that was a mistake.

After she left, I sat in the half light listening to analyses of energy requirements and commentary on enemy technology and occasional crisp battle reports, emanating from forays by Sim's units against enemy lines of communication. Gradually, I was drawn into the drama of that long-ago struggle, and I saw the monster Ashiyyur formations through the eyes of a commander who consistently succeeded in scattering, or at least diverting, them with a dozen light frigates. I began to realize that Sim's great weapon was the intelligence-gathering capabilities of listening stations afloat along enemy lines, and somehow shrouded from enemy sensing devices. Ashiyyur commanders, it appeared, could not void themselves without Sim's knowledge.

The individual accounts were riveting.

Off Sanusar, the Dellacondans, assisted by a few allied vessels, ambushed and destroyed two heavy cruisers at the cost of a frigate. Near the Spinners, in the center of Ashiyyur lines, Sim stormed and looted an enemy base after luring its defenders into a wild chase. But the humans could never stand and fight: time and again, Sim was forced to withdraw because he lacked the sheer force to exploit opportunity. Gradually, I began to read, first in his tone, and then in his comments, a despair that grew in proportion with each success, and each subsequent retreat. Dellaconda was lost early, and when the news came, Sim responded only by breathing his wife's name.

One by one, the frontier worlds fell, and he railed against the shortsightedness of Rimway, of Toxicon, of Earth, who thought themselves safe by distance, who feared to rouse the wrath of the conquering horde, who perceived each other with a deeper-rooted jealousy and suspicion than they could bring to bear on the invader. And when his luck ran out at Grand Salinas, where he lost most of his squadron and a battle cruiser manned by volunteers from Toxicon, he commented that *we are losing our finest and bravest. And to what point?* The remark was followed by a long silence, and then he said the unthinkable: *If they will not come, then it is time to make our own peace!*

His mood grew darker as the long retreat continued. And when two more ships from his diminished squadron were lost at Como Des, his anger exploded. *There will be a Confederacy one day, Tarien,* he wearily told his brother, *but they will not construct it on the bodies of my people!*

It was the same voice that had indicted the Spartans.

Tenandrome was rife with rumor: some suggested that Sim and his crew had been spirited away by the Ashiyyur and that *Corsarius* had been left as a manifestation of an inhuman sense of humor. Others wondered whether the vessel had not been two ships right from the beginning: a clever ploy to confuse the invaders, and enhance the image of a supernatural defender.

If McIras had any theories, she was keeping them to herself.

As for me, I could not get out of my mind the image of Christopher Sim in despair. It had never occurred to me that he, of all people, could have doubted the eventual outcome. It was a foolish notion, and yet there it had been. Sim was as human as the rest of us. And in that despair, in his concern for the lives of his comrades, and the people whom he had tried to defend, I sensed an answer to the deserted vessel. But it was an answer I could not accept.

I began reading everything I could find about the Ashiyyur, the war, the *Corsarius*, and, in particular, the Rigellian Action. In that final engagement, Sim was operating in close conjunction with the *Kudasai*, a battle cruiser which carried his brother. *Corsarius* had gone in to finish off a carrier, had got too close, and been caught in the blast. It was odd, the way it ended. Sim had always led the Dellacondans personally. At Rigel, however, he'd escorted *Kudasai* during the main assault, while his frigates drove a knife into the flank of the enemy fleet.

Ironically, *Kudasai* carried the surviving brother to *his* death only a few weeks later, at Nimrod. But Tarien lived long enough to know that his diplomatic efforts had succeeded: Earth and Rimway had joined hands, had promised help, and Toxicon was expected momentarily to announce that she would support her old enemies.

I wondered what had happened to the seven crew members who had deserted *Corsarius* on the eve of the Rigellian Action. But, with the exception of the navigator, Ludik Talino, none appeared again in the histories. No one knew whether they'd been punished, or even charged with their crime. The first formal attacks against them did not appear for almost thirty years. Since then, of course, they have become a popular target for vilification. Talino, the navigator, surfaced briefly on Rimway almost half a century after the war, just long enough to die, and to earn mention in the news reports. Curiously, he claimed to have fought at Rigel, though on a cruiser, rather than *Corsarius*. There were no details, and the comment was attributed to delusions brought on by his sense of guilt.

I was especially interested in the tale of the Seven, the anonymous heroes recruited in the belly of Abonai on the fateful night before the Ashiyyur attack. How did it happen that no one knew who they were? Was it coincidence that what should have been the single best source of their names, the log of the *Corsarius*, was mute on the subject, and in fact, mute on the battle itself? I could not get Saje McIras' remark out of my mind: *It could not have happened!*

No: it could not.

In the morning, I asked McIras what she intended to do.

"I've classified the report. We'll leave *Corsarius* where she is, and if higher authority wants to come out and have a look at her, they can. That's *it*." She rubbed her temples. "This is bad news for everybody."

"It's ancient history," I said.

"However he died, Christopher Sim *is* the Confederacy. This place, this world, is a graveyard. It's a graveyard with a guilty secret of some sort, and I don't want to get any closer to it." Her eyes narrowed. "I'd like to leave here. Tomorrow."

I looked at her a long time. "A graveyard for what?" I asked.

We returned to carrying out our basic mission, but the shadow of the other ship continued to hang over us. During the days that followed, the conversation with McIras played itself over and over again in my head. Hell of a graveyard: The bodies were all missing, the names were missing, the log entries were missing. And the *Corsarius*, which *should* be missing, was orbiting like clockwork, every six hours and eleven minutes.

"They'd intended to come back," I told McIras.

"But they didn't," she said. "Why not?"

During the entire course of Hellenic civilization, I know of no darker, nor more wanton crime, than the needless sacrifice of Leonidas and his band of heroes at Thermopylae. Better that Sparta should fall, than that such men be squandered. "Yes," I said, "where are the bodies?"

Through a shaft in the clouds, far below, the sea glittered.

I went down with Holtmeyer's group, ostensibly to assist in making some deductions about its fossils; but I commandeered a flyer instead and loaded it with food and water. Probably, I should have taken McIras' advice and concentrated on my own assignments. They were all a long time dead, and there was no point anymore. But the truth should have *some* value.

And there was Talino, the navigator, whose name was now synonymous with fear, who had served his captain and his world well, and died bitter and apparently delusional on Rimway. Surely I owed him, and the others, something.

Holtmeyer's people were still setting up their shelters when I rose slowly over the trees and turned west into the sun-washed sky. There were literally thousands of islands scattered through the global ocean. It would not of course be possible to search them all. But someone had abandoned *Corsarius*. Whether that someone wanted to torture Christopher Sim with its presence, or to leave it as a sign they would not forget him, they'd left it all the same, and I wondered whether they would not have placed him along its track, close beneath its orbit.

I fed the course data into the flyer's computer banks, set speed just below sound, and leveled off at 3,000 meters. Then I informed *Tenandrome* where I was, and sat back to listen to the wind. Below, the sea was smooth and transparent and very blue. White clouds drifted through the morning haze. It could easily have been a seascape on Rimway or Earth or Fishbowl.

It was, on balance, a lovely world.

I passed, with barely a second look, a group of sandy, treeless islands. Their shores, like all the shores on this planet, were devoid of the gulls that are inevitably found near water oceans on living worlds. (Birds had not evolved there and in Jesperson's opinion never would.)

I slowed to inspect a silver archipelago in the north temperate zone, rocky clutches of forest protruding from the glassy surface, dribbling away in progressively smaller islands to the northwest. But there was only granite and trees, and after awhile I flew on.

I crossed into the southern hemisphere in late afternoon, and approached a Y-shaped volcanic island shortly before sunset. It was a lush, tropical place of purple-green ferns and enormous white flowering plants. Placid pools mirrored the sky, and springs tumbled down off the lone mountain. I settled onto the beach, climbed out, had my dinner, and watched *Corsarius* pass overhead, a dull white star in a darkening sky.

Tenandrome informed me that McIras was too busy to talk to me, which meant she was angry. They also said that Jesperson had made a discovery having to do with amphibians, but no one was clear on its exact nature. I asked them to give him my best, and turned in for the night. The air was cool and fresh, and the rumble of the surf almost hypnotic. I fell asleep in the cockpit with the canopy off. It was a violation of safety procedures that would have incensed the Captain.

In the morning, I crisscrossed the island for hours, but there was nothing, and I set out again, finally, over a wide expanse of unbroken ocean. Gentle rain squalls drifted across its face and, deeper in southern seas, a heavy storm forced me to a higher altitude. By midday, the black skies lightened, and I descended through a drizzle filled with that world's bulbous airborne plants, toward an ocean suddenly still. I ate lunch on a long narrow damp spit that probably went completely under at high tide. (There were two moons of substantial size and, when they line up and pulled in the same direction, the tides were fierce.)

I was cramped after the long hours in the flyer, and strolled casually along the beach, enjoying the sea and the solitude. Tiny soft-shelled segmented creatures washed ashore with each wave. Most burrowed into the sand, while others hurried across the spit and returned into the ocean on the other side. I watched, fascinated, and noticed that all the movement was in one direction. That seemed strange. Also, the phenomenon seemed to be accelerating. Crustaceans and other creatures less easily identifiable scrabbled and slithered out of the breakers in increasing numbers, crossed the narrow strip, and disappeared again into the waves.

I was puzzling over it when I observed a vegetable-brown stain in the water drifting in my direction. It was out just beyond the surf when I first saw it. It was drifting into the outer breakers. As it did, the foam turned muddy and the waves developed a glutinous quality.

Two glistening black rocks rolled ashore. One paused as though suddenly conscious of my presence: it fell open, and a cluster of living dark fronds slowly (and, I thought, hungrily) uncoiled in my direction. I backed away, out of reach. In a swift graceful movement, it returned to its shell, and both creatures crossed the strand and splashed into the ocean.

I had finally figured out that something was happening. I started back toward the flyer at a quick, nervous pace, but a sudden high-pitched whistling brought me up short. A creature that resembled a porpoise threw itself onto the beach a few meters in front of me. The surf rolled languidly in along its flanks, boiled, and seemed to draw it back into itself. The porpoise turned its dark intelligent eyes on me, and I heard again that shrill whistle, and read the terror in it. It struggled with the muddy tide, and tried to return to the beach, as though it would have torn itself altogether from the embrace of the ocean. But this time it was stopped far short by a hand I could not see. And a long muddy wave broke over the animal.

Our eyes locked in mutual horror. A thick viscous lump of water rolled across its dorsal, and it was gone. When I was able to look back at the beach, I saw that the thick brown tide had made inroads. The stream of marine animals across the strip of sand had stopped. A few writhed in the emulsive tide, but no more came ashore.

I broke toward the flyer in a panicky spurt. A dying remnant of a wave washed against my boot. Clung to it. Sucked at it. I broke free with an effort and lurched away.

I was a hundred yards from the flyer. Already, thick brown pseudopods were pushing over the center of the spit. One or two had got into the ocean on the other side. The thing in the water, whatever it was, was going to cross this strip of beach!

The flyer was parked on the widest portion of the islet, but there were pools near it. The brown tide flowed into these, and they began to rise.

I ran blindly. The flyer was desperately far away, and the sand made for slow, ponderous going. I couldn't get my breath, and fell. My hand went into the gunk, and it burned with a fierceness that brought tears.

Ahead, the tide swirled around the landing treads and the ladder. I splashed through it, panicked, but moving in slow motion all the same, struggling to pull a boot free with each step. I watched to see whether it could climb.

Gobs of it got onto my jump suit. I plodded across the last few meters and fell forward against the ladder. The thing rose around my legs and tried to drag me back. I left it both boots.

And I shuddered for Christopher Sim and his men.

Two hours later, I cruised somberly through a gray overcast sky, watching the monitors draw a jagged line across the long curve of the horizon. I was thoroughly rattled, and promising myself never to leave the cockpit again in unfamiliar territory. It was raining again, but there was no wind. The ocean grew loud, and a granite peak appeared in the mist off to my right. It was almost a needle, worn smooth by sea and weather.

I flew on.

There were others, a range of towers rising out of the ocean almost directly parallel to the track of the *Corsarius*. All were conical, although some had broken and toppled into the ocean, as though ripped by inner convulsions. The formation was so geometrically correct, that I could not escape a sense that I was looking at a work of art. I also knew that, if the men who had come with Sim had been aware of the dangers in the sea, this was the kind of place they would have chosen.

I drifted among the peaks, riding the currents, embracing the cadence of rock and surf. I searched all day, and when twilight came, I settled onto a cropped peak. The rain blew off and the stars came out, bathing the line of towers and the rolling ocean in brilliant white light. But I didn't sleep well. And I kept the canopy shut.

The reddish sun was well into the sky when I woke. The air was cold and clear. I checked in with *Tenandrome*; they told me my aircraft was needed back at Holtmeyer's site, and the Captain would be grateful if I returned it.

Somehow, that rockridden stretch of southern ocean seemed

even less natural by daylight. I was glad to get airborne again, but, as I drifted over those sleek gray formations I knew unequivocally that I was right about Sim. And that the proof was here. Somewhere.

I almost missed it. I'd expected that they would have chosen one of the peaks whose tops had been swept away. I found it instead on a relatively narrow shelf not quite halfway between the summit and the sea: a blue dome.

It was chillingly small, and I realized as I approached it that I'd been wrong. They had not marooned Sim and his crew. And I knew with knife-cold suddenness why the Seven had no names!

My God! They'd left him here alone.

I circled for half an hour, finding things to do, checking rations, wondering whether to call McIras, debating if it was not after all best to let the legends alone. But I had come too far.

Two centuries late, I floated down through the salt air.

The wind blew across the escarpment. The shelf was solid rock. No green thing grew there, and no creature made its home on that grim pile. A few boulders were strewn about, and some loose rubble. Several broken slabs stood near the edge of the promontory. The peak towered overhead. The ocean was about sixty meters down, and cold.

I stood uncertainly before the dome in stocking feet, studying its utilitarian lines, the makeshift antenna mounted on the roof, the blank windows with drawn curtains. The sea boomed relentlessly, and even at this altitude, I could feel spray.

Unlike *Corsarius*, that shelf gave no sense here of recent occupancy. The dome was discolored by weather, and it had been knocked somewhat askew, probably by a quake.

Christopher Sim's tomb. It was not a very elegant end, on this granite slab, under the white star of the ship that had carried him safely through so much. They had, I believed, intended to come back for him, when the war ended, and it didn't matter anymore. And maybe they left *Corsarius* as a token of a promise. But things had gone awry.

The door was designed to function, if need be, as an airlock. It was closed, but not sealed, and I was able to lift the latch, and pull it open. The light inside was gray, and I waited for the dome to ventilate.

There were two chairs, a table, some bound books, a desk, and a couple of lamps. I wondered whether Tarien had come on this long flight out from Abonai, whether there had been a last desperate clash, perhaps in this room, between the brothers! Whether Tarien had pleaded with him to continue the struggle. It would have been a terrible dilemma: men had so few symbols, and the hour was so desperate. They could not permit him to sit out the battle (as Achilles had done). In the end, Tarien must have felt he had no choice but to seize his brother, and dismiss his crew with some contrived story. (Or perhaps an angry Christopher Sim had done that himself, before confronting Tarien.) Then they'd invented the legend of the Seven, concocted the destruction of the *Corsarius*, and when the engagement was over they'd brought him and his ship here.

Tarien had died a few weeks later, and maybe all who shared the secret died with him. Or maybe they were afraid, in victory, of the wrath of their victim. I stood in the doorway and wondered how many years that tiny space had been his home.

He would have understood, I thought. And if in some way he could have learned that he'd been wrong, that Rimway had come, and Toxicon, and even Earth, he might have been consoled.

There was nothing on the computer. I thought that strange; I'd expected a final message, perhaps to his wife on far Dellaconda, perhaps to the people he had defended.

In time the walls begin to close in, and I fled the dome, out onto the shelf that had defined the limits of his existence.

I walked the perimeter, looked at the slabs and the wall, returned along the edge of the precipice. I tried to imagine myself marooned in that place, alone on that world, a thousand light-years from the closest human being. The ocean must have seemed very tempting.

Overhead, *Corsarius* flew. He could have seen it each evening, when the weather was clear.

And then I saw the letters engraved in the rock wall just above my head. They were driven deep into the granite, hard-edged characters whose fury was clear enough, though I could not understand the language in which they'd been written:

ὦ ποποῖ! ὦ Δημοσθένης!

It was a paroxysm of anguish directed toward Demosthenes, the great Athenian orator whose silver tongue had tamed the Aegean. Sim had remained a classicist until the end.

The computer had not been enough to contain Christopher Sim's final protest. Demosthenes, of course, should be read as his orator brother. But I was moved that it was a cry of pain, and not of rage. Scholars have since agreed. After all, they argue, no man in such straits would have stooped to mere mockery: the reference to the Athenian statesman constituted a recognition, probably after long consideration induced by his deplorable position, that Tarien had chosen the correct path. Consequently, the message on the rock could be read as an act of forgiveness, rendered in his final extremity, by a loving brother.

The reputations of the brothers have not been seriously damaged. In fact, in an enlightened society, Christopher and Tarien have risen to the stature of tragic heroes. Dramatists and novelists have recreated the confrontation on the shelf between them time and again, and the idea that they embraced, and parted in tears, has become part of the folklore.

But I've thought about it, and I'm convinced it means something else. I've read a lot about Demosthenes since that day when I stood before the message in the rock: the dumb bastard used his great oratorical abilities to persuade his unhappy country to make war on Alexander the Great! I think Christopher Sim was still having the last word.

Afterword

Readers of *A Talent for War* will recognize "Dutchman" as the set-up story for that novel. They will also recall that Sim's career extended beyond that narrow shelf. A curious thing about Christopher Sim: he is the driving force in two stories (the other is "Sunrise") and a novel; his image is prominently displayed on the cover of the latter; and yet he makes no appearance anywhere.

CRYPTIC

It was at the bottom of the safe in a bulky manila envelope. I nearly tossed it into the trash along with the stacks of other documents, tapes, and assorted flotsam left over from the Project.

Had it been catalogued, indexed in some way, I'm sure I would have. But the envelope was blank, save for an eighteen-year-old date scrawled in the lower right-hand corner, and beneath it, the notation "40 gh."

Out on the desert, lights were moving. That would be Brackett fine-tuning the Array for Orrin Hopkins, who was then beginning the observations that would lead, several years later, to new departures in pulsar theory. I envied Hopkins: he was short, round, bald, a man unsure of himself, whose explanations were invariably interspersed with giggles. He was a ridiculous figure, yet he bore the stamp of genius. And people would remember his ideas long after the residence hall named for me at Carrollton had crumbled.

If I had not long since recognized my own limits and conceded any hope of immortality (at least of this sort), I certainly did so when I accepted the director's position at Sandage. Administration pays better than being an active physicist, but it is death to ambition.

And a Jesuit doesn't even get that advantage.

In those days, the Array was still modest: forty parabolic antennas, each thirty-six meters across. They were on tracks, of course, independently movable, forming a truncated cross. They had, for two decades, been the heart of SETI, the Search for Extra-Terrestrial Intelligence. Now, with the Project abandoned, they were being employed for more useful, if mundane, purposes.

Even that relatively unsophisticated system was good: as Hutching Chaney once remarked, the Array could pick up the cough of an automobile ignition on Mars.

I circled the desk and fell into the uncomfortable wooden chair we'd inherited from the outgoing regime. The packet was sealed with tape that had become brittle and loose around the edges. I tore it open.

It was a quarter past ten. I'd worked through my dinner and the evening hours, bored, drinking coffee, debating the wisdom in coming out here from JPL. The increase in responsibility was a good career move; but I knew now that Harry Cooke would never lay his hands on a new particle.

I was committed for two years at Sandage: two years of working out schedules and worrying about insurance; two years of dividing meals between the installation's sterile cafeteria, and Jimmy's Amoco Restaurant on Route 85. Then, if all went well, I could expect another move up, perhaps to Georgetown.

I'd have traded it all for Hopkins's future.

I shook out six magnetic disks onto the desk. They were in individual sleeves, of the type that many installations had once used to record electromagnetic radiation. The disks were numbered and dated over a three-day period in 2001, two years earlier than the date on the envelope.

Each was marked "Procyon."

In back, Hopkins and two associates were hunched over monitors. Brackett, having finished his job, was at his desk reading.

I was pleased to discover that the disks were compatible to the Mark VIs. I inserted one, tied in a vocorder to get a hard copy, and went over to join the Hopkins group while the thing ran. They were talking about plasma. I listened for a time, got lost, noted that everyone around me (save the grinning little round man) also got lost, and strolled back to my computer.

The trace drew its green-and-white pictures smoothly on the Mark VI display, and pages of hard copy clicked out of the vocorder. Something in the needle geometry scattered across the recording paper drew my attention. Like an elusive name, it drifted just beyond reach.

Beneath a plate of the Andromeda Galaxy, a coffee pot simmered. I could hear the distant drone of a plane, probably out of Luke Air Force Base. Behind me, Hopkins and his men were laughing at something.

There were patterns in the recording.

They materialized slowly, identical clusters of impulses: the signals were artificial.

Procyon.

The laughter, the plane, the coffee pot, a radio that had been left on somewhere: everything squeezed down to a possibility.

More likely Phoenix, I thought.

Frank Myers had been SETI Director since Ed Dickinson's death twelve years before. I reached him next morning in San Francisco.

"No," he said without hesitation. "Someone's idea of a joke, Harry."

"It was in your safe, Frank."

"That damned safe's been there forty years. Might be anything in it. Except messages from Mars . . ."

I thanked him and hung up.

It had been a long night: I'd taken the hard copy to bed and, by 5:00 A.M., had identified more than forty distinct pulse patterns. The signal appeared to be continuous: that is, it had been an ongoing transmission with no indication of beginning or end, but only irregular breaches of the type that would result from atmospherics and, of course, the long periods during which the target would have been below the horizon.

It was clearly a reflected terrestrial transmission: radio waves bounce around considerably. But why seal the error two years later and put it in the safe?

Procyon is a yellow-white class F3 binary, absolute magnitude 2.8, once worshipped in Babylon and Egypt. (What hasn't been worshipped in Egypt?) Distance from earth: 11.3 light-years.

In the outer office, Beth Cooper typed, closed filing drawers, spoke with visitors.

The obvious course of action was to use the Array. Listen to Procyon at 40 gigahertz, or all across the spectrum for that matter, and find out if it was, indeed, saying something.

On the intercom, I asked Beth if any open time had developed on the system. "No," she said crisply. "We have nothing until August of next year."

That was no surprise. The facility had booked quickly when its resources were made available to the astronomical community on more than the limited basis that had prevailed for twenty years. Anyone wishing to use the radiotelescope had to plan far in advance. How could I get hold of the Array for a couple of hours?

I asked her to come into my office.

Beth Cooper had come to Sandage from San Augustin with SETI during the big move twenty years before. She'd been secretary to three directors: Hutching Chaney, who had built Sandage; his long-time friend, Ed Dickinson; and finally, after Dickinson's death, Frank Myers, a young man on the move, who'd stayed too long with the Project, and who'd been reportedly happy to see it strangled. In any case, Myers had contributed to its demise by his failure to defend it.

I'd felt he was right, of course, though for the wrong reason. It had been painful to see the magnificent telescope at Sandage denied, by and large, to the scientific community while its grotesque hunt for the Little Green Man signal went on. I think there were few of us not happy to see it end.

Beth had expected to lose her job. But she knew her way around the facility, had a talent for massaging egos, and could spell. A devout Lutheran, she had adapted cautiously to working for a priest and, oddly, seemed to have taken offense that I did not routinely walk around with a Roman collar.

I asked one or two questions about the billing methods of the local utilities, and then commented, as casually as I could manage, that it was unfortunate the Project had not succeeded.

Beth looked more like a New York librarian than a secretary at a desert installation. Her hair was silver-gray. She wore steel-rimmed glasses on a long silver chain. She was moderately heavy, but her carriage and her diction were impeccable, imbuing her with the quality that stage people call presence.

Her eyes narrowed to hard black beads at my remark. "Dr. Dickinson said any number of times that none of us would live to see results. Everyone attached to the program, even the janitors, knew that." She wasn't a woman given to shrugs, but the sudden flick in those dark eyes matched the effect. "I'm glad he didn't live to see it terminated."

That was followed by an uncomfortable silence. "I don't blame you, Doctor," she said at length, referring to my public position that the facility was being underutilized.

I dropped my eyes and tried to smile reassuringly. It must have been ludicrous: her severe features softened. I showed her the envelope.

"Do you recognize the writing?"

She barely glanced at it. "It's Dr. Dickinson's."

"Are you sure? I didn't think Dickinson came to the Project until Hutch Chaney's retirement. That was '13, wasn't it?"

"He took over as Director then. But he was an operating tech-

nician under Dr. Chaney for, oh, ten or twelve years before that."
Her eyes glowed when she spoke of Dickinson.

"I never met him," I said.

"He was a fine man." She looked past me, over my shoulder,
her features pale. "If we hadn't lost him, we might not have lost the
Project."

"If it matters," I added gently.

"If it matters."

She was right about Dickinson: he was articulate, a persuasive
speaker, author of books on various subjects, and utterly dedicated
to SETI. He might well have kept the Project afloat despite the ces-
sation of federal funds and the increasing clamor among his colleagues for more time at the facility. But Dickinson was twelve years
dead now: he'd returned to Massachusetts at Christmas, as was his
custom. After a snowstorm, he'd gone out to help shovel a neighbor's
driveway and his heart had failed.

At the time, I was at Georgetown. I can still recall my sense of a
genius who had died too soon. He had possessed a vast talent, but
no discipline; he had churned through his career hurling sparks in
all directions. But somehow everything he touched, like SETI, had
come to no fulfillment.

"Beth, was there ever a time they thought they had an LGM?"

"The Little Green Man Signal?" She shook her head. "No, I
don't think so. They were always picking up echoes and things. But
nothing ever came close. Either it was KCOX in Phoenix, or a Japanese trawler in the middle of the Pacific."

"Never anything that didn't fit those categories?"

One eyebrow rose slightly. "Never anything they could prove. If
they couldn't pin it down, they went back later and tried to find it
again. One way or another, they eliminated everything." Or, she must
be thinking, we wouldn't be standing here having this conversation.

Beth's comments implied that suspect signals had been automatically stored. Grateful that I had not yet got around to purging ob-
solete data, I discovered that was indeed the case, and ran a search
covering the entire time period back to the Procyon reception in
2011. I was looking for a similar signal.

I got a surprise.

There was no match. There was also no record of the Procyon
reception itself.

That meant presumably it had been accounted for and discarded.

Then why, two years later, had the recordings been sealed and placed in the safe? Surely no explanation would have taken that long.

SETI had assumed that any LGM signal would be a deliberate attempt to communicate, that an effort would therefore be made by the originator to create intelligibility, and that the logical way to do that was to employ a set of symbols representing universal constants: the atomic weight of hydrogen, perhaps, or the value of pi.

But the move to Sandage had also been a move to more sophisticated, and considerably more sensitive, equipment. The possibility developed that the Project would pick up a slopover signal, a transmission of alien origin, but intended only for local receivers. Traffic of that nature could be immeasurably difficult to interpret.

If the packet in the safe was anything at all, it was surely of this latter type. Forty gigahertz is not an ideal frequency for interstellar communication. Moreover, the intercept was ongoing, formless, no numbered parts, nothing to assist translation.

I set the computer working on the text, using SETI's own language analysis program. Then I instructed Brackett to call me if anything developed, had dinner at Jimmy's, and went home.

There was no evidence of structure in the text. In English, one can expect to find a 'U' after a 'Q', or a vowel after a cluster of consonants. The aspirate is seldom doubled, nothing is ever tripled, and so on. But in the Procyon transmission, everything seemed utterly random.

The computer counted two-hundred fifty-six distinct pulse patterns. Eight bits. Nothing recurred at sufficient intervals to be a space. And the frequency count of these pulse patterns, or characters, was flat; there was no quantitative difference in use from one to another. All appeared approximately the same number of times. If it was a language, it was a language with no discernible vowels.

I called Wes Phillips, who was then the only linguist I knew. Was it possible for a language to be structured in such a way?

"Oh, I don't think so. Unless you're talking about some sort of construct. Even then . . ." He paused. "Harry, I can give you a whole series of reasons in maybe six different disciplines why languages need high and low frequency letters. To have a flat "curve," a language would have to be deliberately designed that way, and it would have to be non-oral. But what practical value would it have? Why bother?"

* * *

Ed Dickinson had been an enigma. During the series of political crises after the turn of the century, he'd earned an international reputation as a diplomat, and as an eloquent defender of reason and restraint. Everyone agreed that he had a mind of the first rank. Yet, in his chosen field, he accomplished little. And eventually he'd gone to work for the Project, historically only a stepping-stone to serious effort. But he'd stayed.

Why?

Hutching Chaney was a different matter. A retired naval officer, he'd indulged in physics almost as a pastime. His political connections had been instrumental in getting Sandage built; and his assignment as Director was rumored to have been a reward for services rendered during the rough-and-tumble of congressional politics.

He possessed a plodding sort of competence. He was fully capable of grasping, and visualizing, extreme complexity. But he lacked insight and imagination, the ability to draw the subtle inference. After his retirement from Sandage, Chaney had gone to an emeritus position at MIT, which he'd held for five years.

He was a big man, more truck driver than physicist. Despite advancing age—he was then in his 70s—and his bulk, he spoke and moved with energy. His hair was full and black. His light gray eyes suggested the shrewdness of a professional politician; and he possessed the confident congeniality of a man who had never failed at anything.

We were in his home in Somerville, Massachusetts, a stone and glass house atop sweeping lawns. It was not an establishment that a retired physicist would be expected to inhabit: Chaney's moneyed background was evident.

He clapped a big hand on my shoulder and pulled me through one of those stiff, expensive living rooms that no one ever wants to sit in, into a paneled, leather-upholstered den at the rear of the house. "Martha," he said to someone I couldn't see, "would you bring us some port?" He looked at me for acquiescence.

"Fine," I said. "It's been a long time, Hutch."

Books lined the walls: mostly engineering manuals, a few military and naval histories. An articulated steel gray model of the *Lance* dominated the fireplace shelf. That was the deadly hydrofoil which, built at Chaney's urging, had created a multipurpose navy that was simultaneously lethal, flexible, and relatively cheap.

"The Church is infiltrating everywhere," he said. "How are things at Sandage, Harry?"

I described some of the work in progress. He listened with interest.

A young woman arrived with a bottle, two glasses, and a plate of cheese. "Martha comes in three times a week," Chaney said after she'd left the room. He smiled, winked, dipped a stick of cheese into the mustard, and bit it neatly in half. "You needn't worry, Harry. I'm not capable of getting into trouble anymore. What brings you to Massachusetts?"

I extracted the vocordings from my briefcase and handed them across to him. I watched patiently as he leafed through the thick sheaf of paper, and saw with satisfaction his change of expression.

"You're kidding, Harry," he said. "Somebody really found one? When'd it happen?"

"Twenty years ago," I said, passing him the envelope and the original disks.

He turned them over in his hands. "You're not serious? There's a mistake somewhere."

"It was in the safe," I said.

He shook his head. "Doesn't much matter where it was. Nothing like this ever happened."

"Then what is it?"

"Damned if I have any idea."

We sat not talking while Chaney continued to flip pages, grunting. He seemed to have forgotten his wine. "You run this yourself?" he asked.

I nodded.

"Hell of a lot of trouble for somebody to go to for a joke. Were the computers able to read any of it? No? That's because it's gibberish." He stared at the envelope. "But it *is* Ed's handwriting."

"Would Dickinson have any reason to keep such a thing quiet?"

"Ed? No: Dickinson least of all. No one wanted to hear a signal more than he did. He wanted it so badly he invested his life in the Project."

"But could he, physically, have done this? Could he have picked up the LGM? Could he have done it without anyone else knowing? Was he good enough with computers to cover his tracks?"

"This is pointless. Yes, he could have done it. And you could walk through Braintree without your pants."

A light breeze was coming through a side window, billowing the curtains. It was cool and pleasant, unusual for Massachusetts in August. Some kids were playing halfball out on the street.

"Forty gigahertz," he said. "Sounds like a satellite transmission."

"That wouldn't have taken two years to figure out, would it? Why keep the disks?"

"Why not? I expect if you go down into the storeroom you'll find all kinds of relics."

Outside, there was a sound like approaching thunder, exploding suddenly into an earsplitting screech. A stripped-down T-Bolt skidded by, scattering the ballplayers. An arm hung leisurely out the driver's side. The car took the corner stop sign at about 45. A couple of fingers went up, but otherwise the game resumed as though nothing had happened.

"All the time," Chaney said. His back to the window, he hadn't bothered to look around. "Cops can't keep up with them anymore."

"Why was Dickinson so interested in the Project?"

"Ed was a great man." His face clouded somewhat, and I wondered if the port hadn't drawn his emotions close to the surface. "You'd have to know him. You and he would have got along fine. He had a taste for the metaphysical, and I guess the Project was about as close as he could get."

"How do you mean?"

"Did you know he spent two years in a seminary? Yes, somewhere outside Philadelphia. He was an altar boy who eventually wound up at Harvard. And that was that."

"You mean he lost his faith?"

"Oh, yes. The world became a dark place, full of disaster. He always seemed to have the details on the latest pogrom, or viral outbreak, or drive-by murder. There are only two kinds of people, he told me once: atheists, and folks that haven't been paying attention. But he always retained that fine mystical sense of purpose that you drill into your best kids, a notion that things are somehow ordered. When I knew him, he wouldn't have presumed to pray to anyone. But he had all the drive of a missionary, and the same conviction of—" He dropped his head back on the leather upholstery and tried to seize a word from the ceiling. "—Destiny."

"Ed wasn't like most physicists. He was competent in a wide range of areas. He wrote on foreign affairs for *Commentary*, and *Harper's*; he published books on ornithology, systems analysis, Malcolm Muggeridge, and Edward Gibbon."

He swung easily out of his chair and reached for a pair of fat matched volumes in mud-brown covers. It was *The Decline and Fall of the Roman Empire*, the old Modern Library edition. "He's the only person I've ever known who's actually read the thing." He turned the cover of volume one so that I could see the inscription:

For Hutch,
In the fond hope that we can hold off the potherbs and the pigs.
                    Ed

"He gave it to me when I left SETI."

"Seems like an odd gift. Have you read it?"

He laughed off the question. "You'd need a year."

"What's the business about the potherbs and pigs?"

He rose and walked casually to the far wall. There were photos of naval vessels and aircraft, of Chaney and President Fine, of the Sandage complex. He seemed to screw his vision into the latter. "I don't remember. It's a phrase from the book. He explained it to me at the time. But . . ." He held his hands outward, palms up.

"Hutch, thanks." I got up to go.

"There was no signal," he said. "I don't know where these recordings came from, but Ed Dickinson would have given anything for a contact."

"Hutch, is it possible that Dickinson might have been able to translate the text? If there had been one?"

"Not if you couldn't. He had the same program."

I don't like cities.

Dickinson's books were all out of print, and the used bookstores were clustered in Cambridge. Even then, the outskirts of Boston, like the city proper, were littered with broken glass and discarded newspapers. Surly kids milled outside bars. Windows everywhere were smashed or boarded. I went through a red light at one intersection rather than learn the intentions of an approaching band of ragged children with hard eyes. (One could scarcely call them children, though I doubt there was one over 12.) Profanity covered the crumbling brick walls as high as an arm could reach. Much of it was misspelled.

Boston had been Dickinson's city. I wondered what the great humanist thought when he drove through these streets.

I found only one of his books: *Malcolm Muggeridge: Faith and Despair*. The store also had a copy of *The Decline and Fall*. On impulse, I bought it.

I was glad to get back to the desert.

We were entering a period of extraordinary progress, during which we finally began to understand the mechanics of galactic structure. McCue mapped the core of the Milky Way, Osterberger developed his unified field concepts, and Schauer constructed his celebrated revolutionary hypothesis on the nature of time. Then, on a cool morning in October, a team from Cal Tech announced that they had a new set of values for hyperinflation.

In the midst of all this, we had an emergency. One night in late September, Earl Barlow, who was directing the Cal Tech groups, suffered a mild heart attack. I arrived just before the EMTs, at about 2:00 A.M.

While the ambulance carrying Barlow started down the mountain, his people watched helplessly, drinking coffee, too upset to work. The opportunity didn't catch me entirely unprepared. I gave Brackett his new target. The blinking lights of the emergency vehicle were still visible when the parabolas swung round and fastened on the bright dog-star Procyon.

But there was only the disjointed crackle of interstellar static.

I took long walks on the desert at night. The parabolas are lovely in the moonlight. Occasionally, the stillness is broken by the whine of an electric motor, and the antennas slide gracefully along their tracks. It was, I thought, a new Stonehenge of softly curving shapes and fluid motion.

The Muggeridge book was a slim volume. It was not biographical, but rather an analysis of the philosopher's conviction that the West has a death wish. It was the old argument that God had been replaced by science, that man had gained knowledge of a trivial sort, and as a result lost purpose.

It was, on the whole, depressing reading. In his conclusion, Dickinson argued that truth will not wait on human convenience, that if man cannot adapt to a neutral universe, then that universe will indeed seem hostile. We must make do with what we have and accept truth wherever it leads. The modern cathedral is the radiotelescope.

Sandage was involved in the verification procedure for McCue's work, and for the already controversial Cal Tech equations. All that is another story: what is significant is that it got me thinking about verifications, and I realized I'd overlooked something: there'd been no match for the Procyon readings anywhere in the data banks since the original reception. But the Procyon recordings might themselves have been the confirmation of an earlier signal!

It took five minutes to run the search: there were two hits.

Both were fragments, neither more than fifteen minutes long; but there was enough of each to reduce the probability of error to less than one percent.

The first occurred three weeks prior to the Procyon reception.

The second went back to 2007, a San Augustin observation. Both were at 40 gigahertz. Both had identical pulse patterns. But there was an explosive difference, sedately concealed in the target information line: the 2007 transmission had come while the radiotelescope was locked on Sirius!

When I got back to my office, I was trembling.

Sirius and Procyon were only a few light-years apart. My God, I kept thinking, they exist! And they have interstellar travel!

I spent the balance of the day stumbling around, trying to immerse myself in fuel usage reports and budget projections. But mostly what I did was watch the desert light grow hard in the curtains, and then fade. The two volumes of Edward Gibbon were propped between a *Webster's* and some black binders. The books were thirty years old, identical to the set in Chaney's den. Some of the pages, improperly cut, were still joined at the edges.

I opened the first volume, approximately in the middle, and began to read. Or tried to. But Ed Dickinson kept crowding out the Romans. Finally I gave it up, took the book, and went home.

There was duplicate bridge in town, and I lost myself in that for five hours. Then, in bed, still somewhat dazed, I tried *The Decline and Fall* again.

It was not the dusty rollcall of long-dead emperors that I had expected. The emperors are there, stabbing and throttling and blundering. And occasionally trying to improve things. But the fish-hawkers are there too. And the bureaucrats and the bishops.

It's a world filled with wine and legionnaires' sweat, mismanagement, arguments over Jesus, and the inability to transfer power, all played out to the ruthless drumbeat of dissolution. An undefined historical tide, stemmed occasionally by a hero, or a sage, rolls over men and events, washing them toward the sea. (During the later years, I wondered, did Roman kids run down matrons in flashy imported chariots? Were the walls of Damascus defiled by profanity?)

In the end, when the barbarians push at the outer rim of empire, it is only a hollow wreck that crashes down.

Muggeridge must have been there.

And Dickinson, the altar boy, amid the fire and waste of the imperial city, must have suffered a second loss of faith.

We had an electrical failure one night. It has nothing to do with this story except that it resulted in my being called in at 4:00 A.M. (not to restore the power, which required a good electrician, but to pacify some angry people from New York, and to be able to say, in my report, that I had been on the spot).

These things attended to, I went outside.

At night, the desert is undisturbed by color or motion. It's a composition of sand, rock, and star; a frieze, a Monet, uncomplicated, unchanging. It's reassuring, in an age when little else seems stable: the orderly universe of mid-twentieth century had long since disintegrated into a plethora of neutron galaxies, colliding black holes, time reversals, and God knows what.

The desert is solid underfoot. Predictable. A reproach to the quantum mechanics that reflect a quicksand cosmos in which physics merges with Plato.

Close on the rim of the sky, guarding their mysteries, Sirius and Procyon, the bright pair, sparkled. The arroyos are dry at that time of year, shadowy ripples in the landscape. The moon was in its second quarter. Beyond the administration building, the parabolas were limned in silver.

My cathedral.

My Stonehenge.

And while I sat, sipping a Coors, and thinking of lost cities and altar boys and frequency counts, I suddenly understood the significance of Chaney's last remark! Of course Dickinson had not been able to read the transmission: that was the point!

I needed Chaney.

I called him in the morning, and flew out in the afternoon. He met me at Logan, and we drove toward Gloucester. "There's a good Italian restaurant," he said. And then, without taking his eyes off the road: "What's this about?"

I'd brought the second Gibbon volume with me, and I held it up for him to see. He blinked.

It was early evening, cold, wet, with the smell of approaching winter. Freezing rain pelted the windshield. The sky was gray, heavy, sagging into the city.

"Before I answer any questions, Hutch, I'd like to ask a couple. What can you tell me about military cryptography?"

He grinned. "Not much. The little I do know is probably classified." A tractor-trailer lumbered past, straining, spraying water across the windows. "What, specifically, are you interested in?"

"How complex are the Navy's codes? I know they're nothing like cryptograms, but what sort of general structure do they have?"

"First off, Harry, they're not codes. Monoalphabetic systems are codes. Like the cryptograms you mentioned. The letter 'G' always turns up, say, as an 'M'. But in military and diplomatic cryptography, the 'G' will be a different character every time it appears. And the encryption alphabet isn't usually limited to letters; we use numbers, dollar signs, ampersands, even spaces." We splashed onto a ramp and joined the interstate. It was elevated and we looked across rows of bleak rooftops. "Even the shape of individual words is concealed."

"How?"

"By encrypting the spaces."

I knew the answer to the next question before I asked it. "If the encryption alphabet is absolutely random, which I assume it would have to be, the frequency count would be flat. Right?"

"Yes. Given sufficient traffic, it would have to be."

"One more thing, Hutch: a sudden increase in traffic will alert anyone listening that something is happening even if he can't read the text. How do you hide that?"

"Easy. We transmit a continuous signal, twenty-four hours a day. Sometimes it's traffic, sometimes it's garbage. But you can't tell the difference."

God have mercy on us, I thought. Poor Ed Dickinson.

We sat at a small corner table well away from the main dining area. I shivered in wet shoes and a damp sweater. A small candle guttered cheerfully in front of us.

"Are we still talking about Procyon?" he asked.

I nodded. "The same pattern was received twice, three years apart, prior to the Procyon reception."

"But that's not possible." Chaney leaned forward intently. "The computer would have matched them automatically. We'd have known."

"I don't think so." Half a dozen prosperous, overweight men in topcoats had pushed in and were jostling each other in the small entry. "The two hits were on different targets: they would have looked like an echo."

Chaney reached across the table and gripped my wrist, knocking over a cup. He ignored it. "Son of a bitch," he said. "Are you suggesting somebody's moving around out there?"

"I don't think Ed Dickinson had any doubts."

"Why would he keep it secret?"

I'd placed the book on the table at my left hand. It rested there, its plastic cover reflecting the glittering red light of the candle. "Because they're at war."

The color drained from Chaney's face, and it took on a pallor that was almost ghastly in the lurid light.

"He believed," I continued, "he really believed that mind equates to morality, intelligence to compassion. And what did he find after a lifetime? A civilization that had conquered the stars, but not its own passions and stupidities."

A tall young waiter presented himself. We ordered port and pasta.

"You don't really know there's a war going on out there," Chaney objected.

"Hostility, then. Secrecy on a massive scale, as this must be, has ominous implications. Dickinson would have saved us all with a vision of order and reason . . ."

The gray eyes met mine. They were filled with pain. Two adolescent girls in the next booth were giggling. The wine came.

"What has *The Decline and Fall* to do with it?"

"It became his Bible. He was chilled to the bone by it. *You* should read it, but with caution. It's quite capable of strangling the soul. Dickinson was a rationalist; he recognized the ultimate truth in the Roman tragedy: that once expansion has stopped, decay is constant and irreversible. Every failure of reason or virtue loses more ground.

"I haven't been able to find his book on Gibbon, but I know what he'll say: that Gibbon was not writing only of the Romans, nor of the British of his own time. He was writing about us. . . . Hutch, take a look around. Tell me we're not sliding toward a dark age. Think how that knowledge must have affected Ed Dickinson."

We drank silently for a few minutes. Time locked in place, and we sat unmoving, the world frozen around us.

"Did I tell you," I said at last, "that I found the reference for his inscription? He must have had great respect for you." I opened the book to the conclusion, and turned it for him to read:

The forum of the Roman people, where they assembled to enact their laws, and elect their magistrates, is now enclosed for the cultivation of potherbs, or thrown open for the reception of swine and buffaloes.

Chaney stared disconsolately at me. "It's all so hard to believe."

"A man can survive a loss of faith in the Almighty," I said, "provided he does not also lose faith in himself. That was Dickinson's real tragedy; he came to believe exclusively in radiotelescopes, the way some people do in religions."

The food, when it came, went untasted. "What are you going to do, Harry?"

"About the Procyon text? About the probability that we have quarrelsome neighbors? I'm not afraid of that kind of information; all it means is that where you find intelligence, you will probably find stupidity. Anyway, it's time Dickinson got credit for his discovery." And, I thought, maybe it'll even mean a footnote for me.

I lifted my glass in a mock toast, but Chaney did not respond. We faced each other in an uncomfortable tableau. "What's wrong?" I asked. "Thinking about Dickinson?"

"That too." The candle glinted in his eyes. "Harry, do you think *they* have a SETI project?"

"Possibly. Why?"

"I was wondering if your aliens know we're here. This restaurant isn't much further from Sirius than Procyon is. Maybe you better eat up."

TIME TRAVELERS NEVER DIE

1

Thursday, November 24. Shortly before noon.

We buried him on a cold, gray morning, threatening snow. The mourners were few, easily constraining their grief for a man who had traditionally kept his acquaintances at a distance. I watched the preacher, white-haired, feeble, himself near the end, and I wondered what he was thinking as the wind rattled the pages of his prayer book.

Ashes to ashes—

I stood with hands thrust into coat pockets, near tears. Look: I'm not ashamed to admit it. Shel was odd, vindictive, unpredictable, selfish. He didn't have a lot of friends. Didn't deserve a lot of friends. But I *loved* him. I've never known anyone like him.

—In sure and certain hope—

I wasn't all that confident about the resurrection, but I knew that Adrian Shelborne would indeed walk the earth again. I knew, for example, that he and I would stand on an Arizona hilltop on a fresh spring morning late in the twenty-first century, and watch silver vehicles rise into the sky on the first leg of the voyage to Centaurus. And we would be present at the assassination of Elaine Culpepper, a name unknown now, but which would in time be inextricably linked with the collapse of the North American Republic. Time travelers never really die, he was fond of saying. We've been far downstream. You and I will live a very long time.

The preacher finished, closed his book, and raised his hand to bless the orchid-colored coffin. The wind blew, and the air was heavy with the approaching storm. The mourners, anxious to be about the day's business, bent their heads and walked past, flinging lilies in Shel's general direction. Helen Suchenko stood off to one side, looking lost. Lover with no formal standing. Known to the family but not particularly liked, mostly because they disapproved of Shel himself. She dabbed jerkily at her eyes and riveted her gaze on the gray stone that carried his name and dates.

She was fair-haired, with eyes like sea water, and a quiet, introspective manner that might easily have misled those who did not know her well.

"I can't believe it," she said.

I had introduced him to Helen, fool that I am. She and I had been members of the Devil's Disciples, a group of George Bernard Shaw devotees. She was an MD, just out of medical school when she first showed up for a field trip to see *Arms and the Man*. It was love at first sight, but I was slow to show my feelings. And while I was debating how best to make my approach, Shel walked off with her. He even asked whether I was interested, and I, sensing I had already lost, salvaged my pride and told him of course not.

He never understood how I felt. He used to talk about her a lot when we were upstream. How she would enjoy Victorian London. Or St. Petersburg before the first war. But he never shared the great secret with her. That was always something he was going to do later.

She was trembling. He really *was* gone. And I had a clear field. That indecent thought kept pushing through. I had wanted her a long time. She was drawn to me, too, just as she was to Shel, and I suspected that I might have carried the day with her had I pressed my case. But I had never betrayed him.

Her cheeks were wet.

"I'll miss him, too," I said.

"I loved him, Dave."

"I know."

He had died when his townhouse burned down almost two weeks before. He'd been asleep upstairs and had never got out of bed. The explanation seemed to be that the fire had sucked the oxygen out of the house and suffocated him before he realized what was happening. Happens all the time, the fire department said.

I told her everything would be all right.

She tried to laugh, but the sound had an edge. "Our last conversation was so pointless. I wish I'd known—" Tears leaked out of her eyes. She tried to catch her breath. "I would have liked to tell him how much he meant to me. How glad I was to have known him."

"I know." I began to guide her toward my Porsche. "Why don't you let me take you home?"

"It's all right," she said. "I'll be okay." Her car was parked near a stone angel.

Edmond Halverson, head of the art department at the University, drew abreast, tipped his hat, and whispered his regrets. We mumbled something back and he walked on.

She swallowed. "When you get a chance, Dave, give me a call."

I watched her get into her car and drive away. She had known so much about Adrian Shelborne. And so little.

He had traveled in time, and of all persons now alive, only I knew. He had brought me in, he'd said, because he needed my language skills. But it was more than that. He wanted someone to share the victory with, someone to help celebrate. Over the years, he'd mastered classical Greek, and Castilian, and Renaissance Italian. And he'd gone on, acquiring enough Latin, Russian, French, and German to get by on his own. But we continued to travel together. And it became the hardest thing in my life to refrain from telling people I had once talked aerodynamics with Leonardo.

I watched his brother Jerry duck his head to get into his limo. Interested only in sports and women, Shel had said of him. And making money. *If I'd told him about the Watch,* he'd said, *and offered to take him along, he'd have asked to see a Super Bowl.*

Shel had discovered the principles of time travel while looking into quantum gravity. He'd explained any number of times how the Watches worked, but I never understood any of it. Not then, and not now. "Why all the secrecy?" I'd asked him. "Why not take credit? It's the discovery of the ages." We'd laughed at the new shade of meaning to the old phrase.

"Because it's dangerous." He'd peered over the top of his glasses, not at me, but at something in the distance. "Time travel should not be possible in a rational universe." He'd shaken his head, and his unruly black hair had fallen into his eyes. He was only thirty-eight at the time of his death, a polished young genius who loved and charmed women. "I saw from the first *why* it was theoretically possible," he'd said. "But I thought I was missing something, some detail that would intervene to prevent the actual construction of a device. And yet there it is." And he'd looked down at the Watch strapped to his left wrist. He worried about Causality, the simple flow of cause and effect. "A time machine breaks it all down," he said. "It makes me wonder what kind of universe we live in."

I thought we should forget the philosophy and tell the world. Let other people worry about the details. When I pressed him, he'd talked about teams from the Mossad going back to drag Hitler out of 1935, or Middle Eastern terrorists hunting down Thomas Jefferson. It leads to utter chaos, he'd said. Either time travel should be prohibited, like exceeding the speed of light. Or the intelligence to achieve it should be prohibited.

We used to retreat sometimes to a tower on a rocky reef far downstream. No one lives there, and there is only ocean in all directions. I don't know how he found it, or who built it, or what that world is like. Nor do I believe *he* did. We enjoyed the mystery of the place. The moon is bigger, and the tides are loud. We'd hauled a generator out there, and a refrigerator, and a lot of furniture. We used to sit in front of a wall-length transparent panel, sipping beer, watching the ocean, and talking about God, history, and women.

They were good days.

Eventually, he'd said he would take Helen there.

The wind blew, the mourners dwindled and were gone, and the coffin waited on broad straps for the gravediggers.

Damn. I would miss him.

Gone now. He and his Watches. And temporal logic apparently none the worse.

Oh, I still had a working unit in my desk, but I knew I wouldn't use it again. I did not have his passion for time travel. Leave well enough alone. That's my motto.

On the way home, I turned on the radio. It was an ordinary day. Peace talks were breaking down in Africa. Another congressman was accused of diverting campaign funds. Assaults against spouses had risen again. In Los Angeles, there was a curious conclusion to an expressway pileup: two people, a man and a woman, had broken into one of the wrecked vehicles and kidnapped the driver, who was believed to be either dead or seriously injured. They had apparently run off with him.

Only in California.

Shel was compulsively secretive. Not only about time travel, but about everything. You never really knew what he was feeling because the mask was always up. He used to drive Helen crazy when we went to dinner because she had to wait until the server arrived to find out what he was going to order. When he was at the University, his department could never get a detailed syllabus out of him. And I was present when his own accountant complained that he was holding back information.

He used to be fond of saying knowledge is power, and I think that was what made him feel successful, that he knew things other people didn't. Something must have happened to him when he was a kid. It was probably the same characteristic that turned him into the all-time great camp follower. I don't know what the proper use for a time machine should be. We used it to make money. But mostly we used it to argue theology with Thomas Aquinas, to talk gravity with Isaac Newton, to watch Thomas Huxley take on Bishop Wilberforce. For us, it had been an entertainment medium. It seemed to me that we should have done *more* with it.

Don't ask me what.

I had all kinds of souvenirs: coins that a young Julius Caesar had lost to Shel over draughts, a program from the opening night of *The Barber of Seville*, a quill once used by Benjamin Franklin. And photos. We had whole albums full of Alexander and Marcus Aurelius and the sails of the *Santa Maria* coming over the horizon. But they all looked like scenes from old movies. Except that the actors didn't look as good as you'd expect. When I pressed Shel for a point to all the activity, he said, what more could there be than an evening before the fire with Albert Einstein? (We had got to a fairly intimate relationship with him, during the days when he was still working for the Swiss patent office.)

There were times when I knew he wanted to tell Helen what we were doing, and bring her along. But some tripwire always brought him up short, and he'd turn to me with that maddeningly innocuous smile as if to say, you and I have a secret and we had best keep it that way. Helen caught it, knew there was something going on. But she was too smart to try to break it open.

We went out fairly regularly, the three of us, and my true love of the month, whoever that might be. My date was seldom the same twice because she always figured out that Helen had me locked up. Helen knew that too, of course. But Shel didn't. I don't think it ever occurred to him that his old friend would have considered for a moment moving in on the woman he professed (although not too loudly) to love. There were times when we would be left alone, Helen and I, usually while Shel was dancing with my date, and the air would be thick with tension. Neither of us ever said anything directly, but sometimes our gaze would touch, and her eyes would grow very big and she would get a kind of forlorn look.

When we talked, the four of us, the subject of whether it was possible to love two people simultaneously used to come up a lot, although I can't remember who'd start it. We'd all express opinions, but the positions changed from time to time.

Helen was a frustrated actress who still enjoyed the theater. After about a year, she abandoned the Devil's Disciples, explaining that she simply did not have time for it anymore. But Shel understood her passion and indulged it. Whenever there was a revival, we all went. Inevitably, while we watched Shaw's frequently unconscious characters careen toward their destinies, Shel would find an opportunity to tell me he was going to take her back to meet the great playwright.

I used to promise myself to stop socializing with her, to find an excuse, because it hurt so much to sit in the awful glare of her passion for him. But if I had done that, I wouldn't have seen her at all. At night, when the evening was over, she always kissed me, sometimes lightly on the cheek, sometimes a quick hit-and-run full on the lips. And once or twice, when she'd drunk a little too much and her control had slipped, she'd put some serious effort into it.

2

Thursday, November 24. Noon.

The storm picked up while I drove home, reminiscing, feeling sorry for myself. I already missed his voice, his sardonic view of the world, his amused cynicism. We had seen power misused and abused all through the centuries, up close, sometimes with calculation, more often out of ignorance.

He'd done all the research in his basement laboratory, had built the first working models down there. These had been big, room-sized chambers which had dwindled in bulk as their capabilities increased. I was involved almost from the beginning. Eventually, the device had shrunk to the size of a watch. It was powered by a cell clipped to the belt or carried in a pocket. I still had one of the power packs at home. I would have to decide what to do with our wardrobe. We'd used my second floor bedroom as an anteroom to the ages. It overflowed with rows of costumes and books on culture and language for every period we'd visited, or intended to visit.

But if my time-traveling days were over, I had made enough money from the enterprise that I would never have to work again, if I chose not to. The money had come from having access to next week's newspapers. We'd debated the morality of taking personal advantage of our capabilities, but I don't think the issue was ever in doubt. We won a small fortune at various race tracks. We'd continued to prosper until two gentlemen dropped by Shel's place one afternoon and told him they were not sure what was behind his winning streak, but that if it continued, they would break his knees. They must have known enough about us to understand it wouldn't be necessary to repeat the message to me.

We considered switching to commodities. But neither of us understood much about them, so we took our next plunge in the stock market. "It's got to be illegal," said Shel. And I'd laughed. "How could it be?" I asked him. "There are no laws against time travel." "Insider trading," he suggested.

Whatever. We justified our actions because gold was the commodity of choice upstream. It was research money, and we told each other it was for the good of mankind, although neither of us could quite explain how that was so. Gold was the one item that opened all doors, no matter what age you were in, no matter what road you traveled. If I learned anything during my years as Shel's interpreter and faithful Indian companion, it was that people will do anything for gold.

While I took a vaguely smug view of human greed, I put enough aside to buy a small estate in Exeter, and retired from the classroom to a life of books and contemplation. And travel in several dimensions.

Now that it was over, I expected to find it increasingly difficult to keep the secret. I had learned too much. I wanted to tell people what I'd done. Who I'd talked to. *So we were sitting over pastry and coffee on St. Helena, and I said to Napoleon—*

There was a thin layer of snow on the ground when I got home. Ray White, a retired tennis player who lives alone on the other side of Carmichael Drive, was out walking. He waved me down to tell me how sorry he was to hear about Shel's death. I thanked him and pulled into the driveway. A black car that I didn't recognize was parked off to one side. Two people, a man and a woman, were sitting inside. They opened their doors and got out as I drifted to a stop in front of the garage.

The woman was taller and more substantial than the man. She held out credentials. "Dr. Dryden? I'm Sgt. Lake, Carroll County Police." Her smile did not reach her eyes. "This is Sgt. Howard. Could we have a few minutes of your time?"

Her voice was low-key. She would have been attractive had she been a trifle less official. She was in her late thirties, with cold dark eyes and a cynical expression that looked considerably older than she was.

"Sure," I said, wondering what it was about.

Sgt. Howard was a wiry little man with features screwed up into a permanent frown. He was bald, with thick eyebrows, and large floppy ears. He looked bored.

We stepped up onto the deck and went in through the sliding glass panels. Lake sat down on the sofa, while Howard undid a lumpy gray scarf and took to wandering around the room, inspecting books, prints, stereo, whatever. I offered coffee.

"No, thanks," said Lake. Howard just looked as if I hadn't meant him. She crossed her legs. "I wanted first to offer my condolences. I understand Dr. Shelborne was a close friend?"

"That's correct," I said. "We've known each other a long time."

She nodded, produced a leather-bound notebook, opened it, and wrote something down. "Did you have a professional relationship?" she asked.

"No," I said slowly. "We were just friends."

She seemed to expect me to elaborate. "May I ask what this is about?" I continued. "Has something happened?"

Her expression changed, became more intense. "Dr. Dryden," she said, "Dr. Shelborne was murdered."

My first reaction was simply to disbelieve the statement. "You're not serious."

"I never joke, Doctor. We believe someone attacked the victim in bed, struck him hard enough to fracture his skull, and set fire to the house."

Behind me; the floor creaked. Howard was moving around. "I don't believe it," I said.

Her eyes never left me. "The fire happened between 2:15 and 2:30 A.M., on the twelfth. Friday night, Saturday morning. I wonder if you'd mind telling me where you were at the time?"

"At home in bed," I said. There had been rumors that the fire was deliberately set, but I hadn't taken any of it seriously. "Asleep," I added unnecessarily. "I thought lightning hit the place?"

"No. There's really no question that it was arson."

"Hard to believe," I said.

"Why?"

"Nobody would want to kill Shel. He had no enemies. At least, none that I know of."

I was beginning to feel defensive. Authority figures always make me feel defensive. "You can't think of *anyone* who'd want him dead?"

"No," I said. But he had a lot of money. And relatives.

She looked down at her notebook. "Do you know if he kept any jewelry in the house?"

"No. He didn't wear jewelry. As far as I know, there was nothing like that around."

"How about cash?"

"I don't know." I started thinking about the gold coins that we always took upstream. A stack of them had been locked in a desk drawer. (I had more of them upstairs in the wardrobe.) Could anyone have known about them? I considered mentioning them, but decided it would be prudent to keep quiet, since I couldn't explain how they were used. And it would make no sense that I knew about a lot of gold coins in his desk and had never asked about them. "Do you think it was burglars?" I said.

Her eyes wandered to one of the bookcases. It was filled with biographies and histories of the Renaissance. The eyes were dark and cool, black pools waiting for something to happen. "That's possible, I suppose." She canted her head to read a title. It was Ledesma's biography of Cervantes, in the original Spanish. "Although burglars don't usually burn the house down." Howard had got tired poking around, so he circled back and lowered himself into a chair. "Dr. Dryden," she continued, "is there anyone who can substantiate the fact that you were here asleep on the morning of the twelfth?"

"No," I said. "I was alone." The question surprised me. "You don't think *I* did it, do you?"

"We don't really think *anybody* did it, yet."

Howard caught her attention and directed it toward the wall. There was a photograph of the three of us, Shel and Helen and me, at a table at the Beach Club. A mustard-colored umbrella shielded the table, and we were laughing and holding tall, cool drinks. She studied it, and turned back to me. "What exactly," she said, "is your relationship with Dr. Suchenko?"

I swallowed and felt the color drain out of my face. *I love her. I've loved her from the moment I met her.* "We're friends," I said.

"Is that all?" I caught a hint of a smile. But nobody knew. I'd kept my distance all this time. Even Helen didn't know. Well, she knew, but neither of us had ever admitted to it.

"Yes," I said. "That's all."

She glanced around the room. "Nice house."

It was. I had treated myself pretty well, installing leather furniture and thick pile carpets and a stow-away bar and some original art. "Not bad for a teacher," she added.

"I don't teach anymore."

She closed her book. "So I understand."

I knew what was in her mind. "I did pretty well on the stock market," I said.

"As did Dr. Shelborne."

"Yes. That's so."

"Same investments?"

"By and large, yes. We did our research together. An investment club, you might say."

Her eyes lingered on me a moment too long. She began to button her jacket. "Thank you, Dr. Dryden."

I was still numb with the idea that someone might have murdered Shelborne. He had never flaunted his money, had never even moved out of that jerkwater townhouse over in River Park. But someone had found out. And they'd robbed him. Possibly he'd come home and they were already in the house. He might even have been upstream. Damn, what a jolt that would have been: return from an evening in Babylon and get attacked by burglars. So they'd killed him. And burned the house to hide the murder. No reason it couldn't have happened that way.

I opened the sliding door for them. "You will be in the area if we need you?" Lake asked. I assured her I would be, and that I would do whatever I could to help find Shel's killer. I watched them drive away and went back inside and locked the door. It had been painful enough believing that Shel had died through some arbitrary act of nature. But it enraged me to think that a thug who had nothing whatever to contribute would dare take his life.

I poured a brandy and stared out the window. The snow was coming harder now. In back somewhere, something moved. It might have been a tree branch, but it sounded *inside*.

Snow fell steadily against the windows.

It came again. A floorboard, maybe. Not much more than a whisper.

I took down a golf club, went into the hallway, looked up the staircase and along the upper level. Glanced toward the kitchen.

Wood creaked. *Upstairs.*

I started up as quietly as I could, and got halfway when I saw movement at the door to the middle bedroom. The wardrobe.

One of the curious phenomena associated with sudden and unexpected death is our inability to accept it when it strikes close to us. We always imagine that the person we've lost is in the kitchen, or in the next room, and that it requires only that we call his name in the customary way to have him reappear in the customary place. I felt that way about Shel. We'd spent a lot of time together, had shared dangers and celebrations. And when it was over, we normally came back through the wardrobe.

He came out now.

He stood up there, watching me.

I froze.

"Hello, Dave," he said.

I hung on the bannister, and the stairs reeled. "Shel, it that *you?*"

He smiled. The old, crooked grin that I had thought not to see again. Some part of me that was too slow-witted to get flustered started flicking through explanations. Someone else had died in the fire. It was a dream. Shel had a twin.

"Yes," he said. "It's me. Are you okay?"

"Yeah."

"I'm sorry. I know this must be a shock." He moved toward me, along the top of the landing. I'm not sure what I was feeling. There was a rush of emotions, joy, anger, even fear. He came down a few stairs, took my shoulders, and steadied me. His hands were solid, his smile very real, and my heart sank. Helen's image surfaced.

"I don't understand," I said.

Adrian Shelborne was tall and graceful. His eyes were bright and sad. We slid down into sitting positions. "It's been a strange morning," he said.

"You're supposed to be dead."

He took a deep breath. "I know. I do believe I *am*, David."

Suddenly it was clear. "You're *downstream.*"

"Yes," he said. "I'm downstream." He threw his head back. "You sure you're okay?"

"I've spent two weeks trying to get used to this. That you were gone—"

"It seems to be true." He spaced the words out, not able to accept it himself.

"When you go back—"

"—The house will burn, and I will be in it."

For a long time neither of us spoke. "Don't go back," I said at last.

"I have to."

I was thinking how candlelight filled Helen's eyes, how they had walked to the car together at the end of an evening, the press of her lips still vibrant against my cheek.

"Why?" I asked. Hoping he would have a good answer.

"Because they just buried me, Dave. They found me in my bed. Did you know I didn't even get out of my bed?"

"Yes," I said. "I heard that."

"I don't believe it." He was pale, and his eyes were red.

My first ride with him had been to Gettysburg to listen to Lincoln. It had been breathtaking, and Shel talked later about having dinner with Caesar and Voltaire and Catherine the Great. But the second trip had been a surprise. We were riding a large misshapen brown chamber then, a thing that looked like a hot water tank. He'd refused to tell me where we were going. It turned out to be 1975 New Haven. He wanted to see a young woman, barely more than a girl. I don't think Shel realized how young she was until we got there. Her name was Martha, and six hours after we showed up she would fall asleep at the wheel of her Ford while driving to pick up her mother. And Shel's life would be altered forever. "She and I had dinner last night at The Mug," he told me while we waited for her to come out of the telephone company building where she worked. "I never saw her again."

It was 5:00 P.M., and the first rush out the door was beginning.

"What are you going to do?" I'd asked.

He was a wreck. "Talk to her."

"She'll call the police. She's not going to know who you are."

"I'll be careful." And he warned me about paradoxes. Don't want to create a paradox. "I just want to see her again."

A light rain had begun. People poured out through the revolving doors. They looked up at the clouds, grimaced, and scattered to cars and buses, holding newspapers over their heads.

And then Martha came out.

I knew her immediately, because Shel stiffened and caught his breath. She paused to exchange a few words with another young woman. The rain came harder.

She was twenty years old and full of vitality and good humor. There was much of the tomboy about her, just giving way to a lush golden beauty. Her hair was shoulder-length and accentuated her shoulders. (I saw much of Helen in her, in her eyes, in the set of her mouth, in her animation.) She was standing back under the building overhang, protected from the rain. She waved good-by to the friend, and prepared to dash through the storm. But her gaze fell on us, on Shel. Her brow furrowed and she looked at us uncertainly.

Shel stepped forward.

I was holding his arm. Holding him back. A gust of wind blew loose dust and paper through the air. "Don't," I said.

"I know." *Avoid the irreparable act that could not have happened.*

She turned away and broke into a half-run. We watched her disappear around the corner out onto the parking lot.

We had talked about that incident many times, what might have happened had he intervened. We used to sit in the tower at the end of time, and he'd feel guilty and virtuous at the same time.

"They think you were murdered," I said.

"I know. I heard the conversation." Downstairs, he fell into an armchair. His face was gray.

My stomach churned and I knew I wasn't thinking clearly. "What happened? How did you find out about the funeral?"

He didn't answer right away. "I was doing some research downstream," he said finally, "in the Trenton Library. In the reference section. I was looking at biographies so I could plan future flights. You know how I work."

"Yes," I said.

"And I did something I knew was a mistake. Knew it while I was doing it. But I went ahead anyhow."

"You looked up your own biography."

He grinned. "Yeah. Couldn't help myself. It's a terrible thing to have the story of your life at your elbow. Dave, I walked away from it twice and came back both times." He sighed. "I'll be remembered for my work in quantum transversals."

"This is what comes of traveling alone." I was irritated. "I told you we should never do that."

"It's done," he said. "Listen, if I hadn't looked, I'd be dead now."

I broke out a bottle of burgundy, filled two glasses and we drank it off. I filled them again. "What are you going to do?"

He shook his head, dismayed. "*It's waiting for me back there.* I don't know *what* to do." His breathing was loud. Snow was piling up on the windows.

"The papers are predicting four inches," I said.

He nodded, as if it mattered. "The biography also says I was murdered. It didn't say by whom."

"It must have been burglars."

"At least," he said, "I'm warned. Maybe I should take a gun back with me."

"Maybe."

Avoid the irreparable act.

"Anyway," he said, "I thought you'd want to know I'm okay." He snickered at that. His own joke.

I kept thinking about Helen. "Don't go back at all," I said. "With or without a gun."

"I don't think that's an option."

"It sure as hell is."

"At some point," he said, "for one reason or another, I went home." He was staring at the burgundy. He hadn't touched the second glass. "My God, Dave, I'm scared. I've never thought of myself as a coward, but I'm afraid to face this."

It wasn't a good time to say anything, so I just sat.

"It's knowing the way of it," he said. "That's what tears me up."

"Stay here," I said.

He shook his head. "I just don't think the decision's in my hands. But meantime, there's no hurry. Right?"

"Makes sense to me."

"I've got a few places to go. People to talk to. Then, when I've done what I need to do, I'll think about all this."

"Good."

He picked up the glass, drained it, wiped his lips, and drifted back to the sofa. "It was scary out there today, Dave. I watched them throw flowers on my coffin. You should try that sometime." His eyes slid shut. "Are they sure it's me?"

"I understand the body was burned beyond recognition."

"That's something to think about. It could be anyone. And even if it *is* me, it might be a Schrodinger situation. As long as no one knows for certain, it might not matter."

"The police know. I assume they checked your dental records."

He nodded. "I suppose they do that sort of thing automatically. Do me a favor though and make sure they have a proper identification." He got up, wandered around the room, touching things, the books, the bust of Churchill, the P.C. He paused in front of the picture from the Beach Club. "I keep thinking how much it means to be alive. You know, Dave, I saw people out there today I haven't seen in years."

The room became still. He played with his glass. It was an expensive piece, chiseled, and he peered at its facets. "When is the reading of the will?"

"I don't know. They may have done it already."

"I'm tempted to go."

"To the reading?"

He managed a tight, pained smile. "I could wear a black beard and reveal myself at the appropriate moment."

"You can't do that," I said, horrified.

He laughed. "I know. But my God I would love to." He shook himself, as if he were just waking up. "Truth is that I know how I'm going to die. But it doesn't have to happen until I'm ready for it. Meantime, we've got places to go. Right?"

"Right," I said.

He looked past me, out the window.

"I think you need to tell her," I said gently.

His expression clouded. "I know." He drew the words out. "I'll talk to her. At the proper time."

"Be careful," I said. "She isn't going to expect to see you."

3

Friday, November 25. Mid-morning.

The critical question was whether we had in fact buried Adrian Shelborne, or whether there was a possibility of mistaken identity. We talked through the night. But neither of us knew anything about police procedure in such matters, so I said I would look into it.

I started with Jerry Shelborne, who could hardly have been less like his brother. There was a mild physical resemblance, although Jerry had allowed the roast beef to pile up a little too much. He was a corporate lawyer. In his eyes, Shel had shuffled aimlessly through life, puttering away with notions that had no reality in the everyday world in which normal people live. Even his brother's sudden wealth had not changed his opinion.

"I shouldn't speak ill of the dead," he told me that morning. "He was a decent man, had a lot of talent, but he never really made his life count." Jerry sat behind a polished teak desk, an India rubber plant in a large pot at his side leaning toward a sun-filled window. The furniture was dark-stained, leather-padded. Plaques covered the walls, appreciations from civic groups, corporate awards, various licenses and testaments. Photos of his two children were prominently displayed, a boy in a Little League uniform, a girl nuzzling a horse. His wife, who had left him years earlier, was missing.

"Actually," I said, "I thought he did pretty well."

"I don't mean money." (I hadn't been thinking of money.) "But it seems to me a man has an obligation to live in his community. To make a contribution to it." He leaned back expansively and thrust satisfied fingers into a vest pocket. " 'To whom much is given'," he said, " 'much shall be expected.' "

"I suppose. Anyway, I wanted to extend my sympathy."

"Thank you." Jerry rose, signaling that the interview was over.

We walked toward the paneled door. "You know," I said, "this experience has a little bit of *deja vu* about it."

He squinted at me. He didn't like me, and wasn't going to be bothered concealing it. "How do you mean?"

"There was a language teacher at Princeton, where I got my doctorate. Same thing happened to him. He lived alone and one night a gas main let go and blew up the whole house. They buried him and then found out it wasn't him at all. He'd gone on an unannounced holiday to Vermont, and turned his place over to a friend. They didn't find out until several days after the funeral."

Jerry shrugged, amused at the colossal stupidity loose in the world. "Unfortunately," he said, "there's not much chance of that here. They tell me the dental records were dead on."

I probably shouldn't have tried to see how Helen was doing. But I called her from a drugstore and she said yes, she'd like to see me, and suggested lunch. We met at an Applebee's in the Garden Square Mall.

She looked worn out. Her eyes were bloodshot, and she tended to lose the thread of conversation. She and Shel had made no formal commitment. But she had certainly believed they had a future together. Come what may. But Shel had been evasive. And there had been times when, discouraged that she got so little of his time, she'd opened up to me. I don't know if anything in my life had been quite as painful as sitting with her, listening to her describe her frustration, watching the occasional tears roll down her cheek. She trusted me, absolutely.

"Are you all right?" she asked me.

"Yes. How about you?"

The talk was full of regrets, things not said, acts undone. The subject of the police suspicions came up, and we found it hard to subscribe to the burglar theory. "What kind of intruder," I asked, "kills a sleeping man, and then sets the house on fire?"

She was as soft and vulnerable that day as I'd ever seen her. By all the laws of nature, Shel was dead. Was I still bound to keep my distance? And the truth was that Shel did not even care enough to ease her suffering. I wondered how she would react if she knew Shel was probably in my kitchen at that moment, making a submarine sandwich.

I wanted to tell her. There was a possibility that, when she *did* find out, she would hold it against *me.* I also wanted to keep Shel dead. That was hard to admit to myself, but it was true. I wanted nothing more than a clear channel with Helen Suchenko. But when I watched her bite down the pain, when the tears came, when she excused herself with a shaky voice and hurried back to the ladies' room, I could stand it no more. "Helen," I said, "are you free this afternoon?"

She sighed. "People get nervous around weepy doctors. Yes, I'm free. But I'm not in the mood to go anywhere."

"Can I persuade you to come out to my place?"

She looked desperately fragile. "I don't think so, Dave. I need some time to myself."

I listened to the hum of conversation around us. "Please," I said. "It's important."

It was snowing again. Helen followed me in her small blue Ford. I watched her in the mirror, playing back all possible scenarios on how to handle this. Leave out the time travel stuff, I decided, at least for now. Use the story I'd told Jerry as an example of how misunderstandings can occur. *He's not dead, Helen.* And then bring him into the room. Best not to warn *him.* God knows how he would react. But get them together, present Shel with a *fait accompli,* and you will have done your self-sacrificial duty, Dave. You dumb bastard.

I pulled through blowing snow into my garage. Helen rolled in beside me, and the doors closed. "Glad to be out of that," she said, with a brave smile that implied she had decided we needed something new to talk about.

The garage opened into the kitchen. I stopped before going through the door and listened. There were no sounds on the other side. "Helen," I said, "I've got something to tell you."

She pulled her coat around her. Her breath formed a mist. "We aren't going into it out here, I hope, are we?"

I smiled and opened the door. The kitchen was empty. No sounds anywhere in the house. "It's about Shel," I said.

She stepped past me and switched on the kitchen light. "I know," she said. "What else could it be?"

A white envelope lay on the table, with my name on it, printed in his precise hand. I snatched it up, but not before she'd seen it.

"Just a list of things to do." I pushed it into my pocket. "How about some coffee?"

"Sure. Sounds good."

"It'll have to be instant," I said, putting water on the stove.

"Do you always do that?" she asked.

"Do what?"

"Write yourself notes?"

"It's my to-do list. It's the first thing I do every morning."

She got two cups down and I excused myself, slipped out, and opened the envelope.

Dear Dave,

I don't know how to write this. But I have to think about what's happened and figure out what to do. I don't want to jump the gun if it's not necessary. You understand.

I know this hasn't been easy for you. But I'm glad you were there. Thanks.

Shel

P.S. I've left most of my estate to the Leukemia Foundation. That will generate a half-dozen lawsuits from my relatives. But if any of those vultures show signs of winning, I'll come back personally and deal with them.

I read it a half-dozen times. Then I crumpled it, tossed it, and went back to the kitchen.

She was looking out the window at the falling snow. Usually, my grounds were alive with bluejays and squirrels. But the critters were all tucked away now. "It's lovely," she said. "So what's the surprise?"

"Son of a gun. I went out to get it and forgot." We strolled into the living room and I hurried upstairs in search of an idea.

I think I mentioned that the wardrobe was also a small museum. There were items of inestimable value, but only if you knew their origin. We had scrolls from the library at Alexandria, a sextant designed and built by Leonardo, a silver bracelet that had once belonged to Calpurnia, a signed folio of *Hamlet,* a pocket watch that Leo Tolstoy had carried while writing *War and Peace.* There were photos of Martin Luther and Albert Schweitzer and Attila the Hun and Charles XII of Sweden. All more or less worthless.

I couldn't bear to give away Calpurnia's bracelet to someone who would not understand what it was. I settled instead for a gold medallion I'd bought from a merchant in Thebes during the fifth century, B.C. It carried a serpent's likeness. An Apollonian priest had insisted I'd acquired a steal. At one time, he said, it had belonged to Aesculapius, the divine doctor, who'd been so good he cured the dead. He backed up his view by trying to buy it from me, offering six times what I'd paid for it.

I carried it downstairs and gave it to Helen, telling her that Shel had wanted me to be sure she got it in case anything happened to him. She glowed, and turned it over and over, unable to get enough of it. "It's exquisite," she said. And the tears came again.

If that thing had possessed any curative powers, I could have used them at that moment.

Snow filled the world. The stand of oaks bordering the approach to the house faded. As did the stone wall along Carmichael Drive, and the hedges on the west side of the grounds. Gradually a heavy white curtain was drawn across the middle of the lawn. "I think we're going to get a foot before this is over," I commented.

She stood by the curtains, enjoying a glass of chablis. I'd started the fire, and it crackled and pocked comfortably. We added Mozart, and I hoped the storm would continue.

"I think so too," she said. A pair of headlights crept past, out beyond the stone wall.

We talked inconsequentials. She had recovered herself, and I wondered whether it was her proximity to me, with all the baggage I brought to any meeting, that had triggered the emotional display. I was not happy that Shel was still in the field. But during that afternoon, I came to understand that it might make no difference. Even if Shel were safely in his grave, I was still the embodiment of too many memories. The decent thing to do would be to fade out of her life, just as Carmichael Drive and the trees were fading now. But I could not bring myself to do that.

She talked about a break in the weather so she could go home. But my luck held. The snow piled up, and we stayed near the fire. I was alone at last with Helen Suchenko, and it was perhaps the most painful few hours of my life. Yet I would not have missed them, and I've replayed them countless times since.

We watched the reports on the Weather Channel. It was a heavy system, moving down from Canada, low pressure and high pressure fronts colliding, eight inches predicted. On top of yesterday's storm, it was expected to shut down the entire east coast from Boston to Baltimore.

She talked a lot about Shel. She'd shake her head as if remembering something, and then dismiss it. She'd veer off onto some other subject, a movie, the latest political scandal, a medical advance that held hope for a breakthrough in this or that. There were a couple of patients she was worried about, and a few hypochondriacs whose lives were centered on imagined illnesses. I told her how much I missed teaching, which wasn't entirely true, but it's the sort of thing people expect you to say. What I really missed was a sense of purpose, a reason to exist. I had that upstairs, in notes detailing conversations with Rachmaninoff and Robert E. Lee and Oliver Cromwell and Aristotle and H. G. Wells. Those conversations would make the damndest book the world had ever seen, reports by the principal actors on their ingenuity, their dreams, their follies. But it would never get written.

We lost the cable at four o'clock, and with it the Weather Channel.

Gradually, the light dwindled out of the sky. I put on steaks and Helen made up a salad. Our timing was perfect because the power failed just as we put everything on the table. I lit candles, and she sat in the flickering light and looked happy. If the clouds had not dissipated, at least for these few hours they had receded.

The music had been silenced by the power outage, so we sat listening to the fire and the whisper of snow against the house. Occasionally, I glanced up at the upstairs bedroom, half-expecting the door to open. I tried to plan what I would do if Shel suddenly appeared on the landing.

It did not happen. We talked into the early hours, until finally she gave out and fell asleep. I moved her to the sofa and went upstairs for blankets. The heating system, of course, was not working, nor was anything else in the all-electric house. The second floor was already cooling off, but I had plenty of firewood.

I settled into a large armchair and slept. Somewhere around two, I woke, listening to the silence. The fire was low. I poked at it, and added a log. Helen stirred but did not wake. Usually, even during the early morning hours, there are sounds: a passing car, the wind in the trees, a dog barking somewhere. But the world was absolutely still.

It was also absolutely dark. No stars. No lights of any kind.

I pointed a flashlight out the window. The night had closed in, wrapped itself around the house so tightly that the beam penetrated only a few feet. It looked like an effect out of a Dracula film. I tried to call the 24-hour weather line. But the phone was dead.

"What is it, Dave?" Helen's voice, soft in the dark.

"Come take a look out the window."

She padded over. And caught her breath. "It's pitch black out there."

We went outside. It was the thickest, darkest night I'd ever seen.

We didn't sleep well after that. At about six, Helen made toast over the fire, and I broke out some fruit juice. The lights were still off. And there was no sign of dawn.

I wondered about Ray White, my neighbor. Ray was a good guy, but he lived alone in a big house, and I thought of him over there wrapped in this goddamn black void with no power and maybe no food. He wasn't young, and I thought it would be a good idea to check on him.

"I'll go with you," Helen said.

My first reaction was to tell her not to be silly, but you didn't say things like that to her. So I got another flashlight, and we let ourselves out through the sliding door. We had to poke around to find the path to the front gate. The flashlights didn't help much. There's a hundred-year-old oak midway between the house and the stone wall that surrounds the property. It's only a few feet off the walk, but we couldn't see it.

We reached the front gate and eased out onto the sidewalk. "Stay close," I said.

We stepped off the curb. Her hand tightened in mine.

Carmichael is two lanes wide. We started across, but the snow cover stopped right in the middle of the street. It was the damndest thing. There was no snow at all on the other side. There wasn't even *blacktop*. The surface had turned to rock. Where the hell was there rock on the other side of Carmichael Drive? A patch of grass, yes, and some concrete. But not rock.

"You sure you know where we are?" she asked.

"Yes," I said. "Of course."

The rock was black. It looked like marble.

We found no curb. No sidewalk. None of the trees that lined the far side of the street. No sign of the low wall that encloses Ray White's sprawling grounds and executive mansion.

We found nothing.

I tried calling Ray's name. But no one answered.

"Are you sure we came out the right way?" Helen asked.

4

During the summer of 1496, Michelangelo was twenty-one years old, newly arrived in Rome, and looking for work. He was already a towering genius, but no one knew that yet. Shel had made no secret of his intention to go back and give the young man a commission. "Do him a favor," he'd said, magnanimously. "It will upset nothing, and we'll collect a nice souvenir."

He had never got around to it. And that meant I had a likely place to look for him.

This was the Rome of Alexander VI, a pope who brooked neither heresy nor opposition. It was a bad time for the True Faith, a few decades after the fall of Constantinople, when Europe had given sanctuary to armies of scholars from that benighted land. The scholars had repaid the good turn by unleashing the Renaissance. It was a dusty, unimposing Rome, still medieval, still passive by either modern or imperial standards. Dreary, bootstrap houses lined the narrow, winding streets, sinking into the rubble of classical times. Churches and palaces were everywhere. More were under construction. The Fortress of Sant' Angelo, containing Hadrian's tomb, dominated the banks of the Tiber. The western approaches to the city were guarded by the old Basilica of St. Peter, the predecessor of the modern structure.

I found Michelangelo with the assistance of Pietro Cardinal Riario, who is known to history for his early support of Michelangelo, and for his occasional homicidal tendencies.

He was living in modest quarters not far from the Tiber. The landlord directed me to a dump site, where I found him seated on a low hill at the edge of the facility, contemplating heaps of trash. Michelangelo was an ordinary-looking young man, with clear, congenial features and handsome dark eyes. He did not hear me approach. "Hello," I said, casually, following his gaze. "That's a fairly dismal prospect."

He looked up, surprised. "Hello, Father." (I was dressed in clerical garb.) He sounded preoccupied, and probably hoped I would move on. "Yes," he added, "it is."

We looked out across the smoking mounds. Carrion eaters wheeled overhead. "See that?" He pointed at a broken column. "It used to be part of the Forum."

Two men wheeled a cart loaded with trash past us, proceeded another twenty yards along the crest of the hill, stopped, and tilted the vehicle's contents into the dump. "Tell me," I said, "are you Michelangelo Buonarroti? The sculptor?"

He brightened. "I am he, Father. Why do you smile?"

"I've heard you are talented," I said. "I'm looking for a friend. He said he was coming here to give you a commission."

Michelangelo got to his feet. "I have not yet established myself," he said. "But I'm happy to hear my reputation is growing. Your friend, is he a priest also?"

I was not sure how Shel might have presented himself. "He is. But he works among the poor and often dresses accordingly."

His brow wrinkled and he looked as if he had just made a connection. "Is your name David?"

That startled me. "Why do you ask?"

"I was given a message for David. Are you he?"

"Yes."

He studied me carefully. "And what is your friend's name?"

"Adrian," I said.

"*Father* Adrian."

"Yes, that is correct. *Father* Adrian. And the message?"

"Back at the house. It came by courier two days ago. Would you care to walk with me?"

It was a warm, still afternoon. The sun was high and very bright, and the sky was filled with clumps of white cloud. "How long have you been in Rome?" I asked.

It was his turn to be surprised. "Only a few weeks," he said. "How did you know I had just come?"

"You're better known than you realize, young man. What are you working on now?"

"Not very much, I'm afraid. Only Cardinal Riario sends me assignments. I am very much indebted to him."

As are we all. "But you *do* have a commission from Father Adrian?"

"Yes. But I have not yet begun on it. He wants me to render Hermes for him in his role as healer. But I haven't been able to decide what form the work should take."

I used a small Minolta to get a couple of pictures, doing it as unobtrusively as I could. But he saw the camera and asked what it was. "A relic," I replied.

His house was one of a group of nondescript structures crowded around a muddy courtyard. It was halfway up a hill, just high enough to glimpse the Tiber, which looked muddy. Children played noisily in the courtyard. Michelangelo had built a workshop in the rear of the house. While he retrieved the message, I stuck my head inside. It was damp and smelled of wet stone. Tables, benches and shelves were made of planks. A small piece of carrara marble with a child's head just emerging was set atop a pair of boards on the floor. It looked like the long-lost *Sleeping Cupid.*

I took more pictures. Children ran loose, screaming and fighting, and I wondered how it was possible for genius to function amid the bedlam.

"Here it is, Father." He appeared and handed me a yellow envelope with DAVID DRYDEN printed on it. "It does not indicate you are a priest," he added. "It is why I was confused."

"Thank you, Michelangelo. I've enjoyed talking with you." I held out my hand. He shook it, and it was one of those electric moments you get to enjoy if you're a time traveler. Then I gave him a gold coin and watched his eyes go wide. "See you finish his commission properly," I said.

"Oh, I will, Father. You may be sure."

I turned away, and waited until I was out of the neighborhood to open the envelope. It read:

DAVID, COME AT ONCE. I AM IN THE BORGIA TOWER. ACCUSED OF HERESY OR SOME DAMNED THING. GUARDS CAN BE BRIBED.

SHEL

The Vatican, even at that remote period, was an architectural marvel. Pilgrims filled its courts and streets. The sacred buildings clustered together behind crenelated walls and the Tiber, a sacred camp besieged by the worldly powers. I looked up at Old St. Peter's, in which Pope Leo III had crowned Charlemagne; passed San Damaso Courtyard, which still hosted jousting tournaments; and paused near the Library to get my bearings. The Borgia Tower was an ominous fortress guarding the western flank of the papal palace, parallel with its military-appearing twin, the Sistine Chapel. Guards patrolled the entrance. I went up to the front door, as if I had all the right in the world to be there. A sentry challenged me. He wore a blue uniform, and he carried a dagger and a small axe.

"I am the confessor," I said, "of Adrian Shelborne, who I believe to be a visitor here."

The guard was barely nineteen. "Have you been sent for, Father?"

His manner implied that if I didn't have an invitation, I would be barred. And my instincts told me that a bribe would not work. Not with this boy. He was too new. "Yes," I said. "The Administrator asked me to come." I was trying to remember influential names in this Vatican, and my mind had gone blank.

"Ah." He nodded. "Good. Please come with me."

We entered the Tower. "Wait here," he said, and disappeared through a side door. The anteroom in which I stood was decorated with a Domenico Ghirlandaio painting. It was a scene from the Last Judgment. A God who looked much like Jupiter approached his throne in a sunbright chariot, while angels sang and humans cringed or celebrated, according to their consciences. I was tempted to make off with it and come back later for Shel.

The sentry reappeared, trailing a sergeant. "You wish to see Cardinal Borgia?" he asked.

"No," I said quickly. That depraved monster was the last person I wanted to see. "No, I wish to visit Father Adrian Shelborne. To hear his confession."

"Ah." The sergeant nodded. It was a noncommittal nod, putting me in a holding pattern. He looked at me through flat cold eyes. His teeth were snagged and broken. He had a broad nose, and a long scar running from his right ear across the jaw to his lip, where it caused a kind of permanent sneer. Not his fault, but the man could not have managed a smile without scaring the kids. "Father, surely you realize where you are. He would not be denied the sacraments *here*."

I pressed a gold coin into his hand. "If you could see your way clear, *signore*."

He slipped it deftly into a pocket without changing expression. "He must have very heavy sins, Father."

"I would like only a few minutes," I said.

"Very well." He straightened his uniform. "This way."

We went deep into the building. Walls were lined with frescoes and paintings, likenesses of figures from both classical and Christian mythology, renderings of church fathers and of philosophers. I saw none that I recognized.

We mounted four flights of stairs and passed into chambers even more ornately decorated than those on the lower floors. My escort deposited me in a room with an exquisite statue of St. Michael, wings spread and sword drawn. Not a good omen. But I was wearing the Watch, and a cable ran up my arm and down my side connecting it with the powerpack. I had to assume Shel had lost his unit or he wouldn't be stuck here. But it didn't matter. Mine would be enough to get us both out.

Moments later, he was back. "This way, please, Father," he said, opening a paneled door for me.

I went through into a well-appointed study, and found myself looking at a young man seated behind a large carved desk. He was about

Michelangelo's age. But *this* youth wore a cardinal's red garments. And that told me who he was.

"Thank you, John," he said to my escort. The door closed softly behind me. I now saw two muscular priests advancing to either side of the Cardinal's desk. The wall behind him was dominated by a variant of the papal seal. Several books, an expensive luxury then, were stacked on a table to his left. One, a treatise on St. Jerome, lay open. Gray light came through three windows whose heavy curtains were drawn back.

This was Cesare Borgia. *Don't drink the wine.* Appointed to the College of Cardinals by his father, Pope Alexander VI. My God, what had Shel got himself into?

He smiled pleasantly, crooked his index finger and signaled me forward. "Good afternoon, Father—?"

"David Dryden, Eminence," I said.

His lips were full and sensuous. The eyes were dark and detached, the nose straight, the jaws lean. He wore a thin smile, rather like a cassock, something to be taken off and put on. "Dryden." He tasted the word. Let his tongue roll around on it as if he were swallowing both it and me. "Your accent is strange. Where are you from?"

"Cornwall." Good a spot as any. "I am a poor country priest," I added.

"I see." He placed his fingertips together. The hands were long and thin and had not seen the sun recently. "You wished to see Father Shelborne?"

"If possible, Eminence. I am his confessor."

His teeth were straight and white. "And where did you take orders, Father?"

"St. Michael's." I inserted pride in my response. Good old alma mater.

"In Cornwall?"

"Yes." I tried not to hesitate. What sort of priest has no idea where his seminary is?

"We've had other visitors from St. Michael's recently," he said. "It has a magnificent view of the Umber, I understand?"

Where in God's name was the Umber? "Actually," I said, "it is the rolling hills of Cornwall that attract the eye."

He considered my response. "And how do you stand on the matter of the Waldensians?"

The Waldensians were men who gave away their money and traveled the roads of southern Europe helping the poor. By their example, they had embarrassed the more powerful members of the Church, and had therefore been branded heretics. "They should commit to Mother Church," I said.

"That is quite good," Cesare smiled, "for a country priest. Tell me, Father, where does a country priest get gold with which to bribe my guards?"

"I had not intended to bribe anyone, Eminence. I thought rather, in the tradition of the Faith, to share my own largess. I have come recently into good fortune."

"What kind of good fortune?"

"An inheritance. My father died and left his money—"

Cesare waved my story away with a gesture that was almost feminine. "I see." The two muscular priests came to attention. "Who is paying you, Dryden? The French?"

"I'm in no one's pay, Eminence. I mean no one any harm."

He glanced at the priests. A signal. They came forward and took hold of my arms and did the equivalent of a patdown. It was not gentle. One came only to about my eyes, but he was wide as a girder. The other was big and athletic, just beginning to thicken around the waist. He was the type who, in our age, would have been at the Y every day playing squash. The Girder found my Watch within moments and held up my left arm triumphantly, shaking the sleeve back so Cesare could see. He started to remove it, but the cable connecting it to the powerpack wouldn't let go. There was a brief struggle during which I came close to getting strangled. Eventually I managed to get it off without disconnecting the units. The priest held it out for Cesare, who placed it on the desk. They took my gold, and gave that to him too. Then they stepped back.

Cesare looked at the Watch and the powerpack. He took them to the window, without disconnecting the cable, and examined them. "Father," he said, "what *is* this thing?"

I had a feeling the relic story wasn't going to sell here. "It's a timepiece."

"And how does it work?" He squinted at the Watch, whose face was blank, and would remain so until it received the proper command.

"It's broken," I said. "It belonged to my father. I keep it in his honor."

Again the smile. The bastard didn't believe a word. And I realized I'd overlooked an obvious point. He reached down and opened a desk drawer, from which he withdrew Shel's unit. He placed them side by side. "They seem to be twins," he said.

"He is my cousin, Eminence."

"And you both carry these *things*, in honor of your esteemed fathers. I am touched." His smile widened, and snapped off. "David Whatever-your-name-is, let us be clear on one point. Unless you are honest with me, I will have to assume you and your friend are agents of a foreign power, and beyond reclamation. I will then have no choice but to deal with you accordingly." He came around the side of the desk.

"Where is Adrian?" I asked.

Cesare stared at me momentarily, and looked toward the door. It opened, and I saw Shel. He was dirty, bruised, covered with blood. He sagged in the arms of two guards. One was John, the man who had escorted me.

I started toward him, but the priests got between us. Shel's eyes opened. "You don't look so good," I said, still speaking Italian.

He tried to wipe his mouth, but the guards held both arms tight. "Hello, Dave," he said. "What took you so long?"

I turned back to Cesare. "Why have you detained him, Eminence?"

The Cardinal's eyes were fixed on me. "You have courage, Father, to come here and interrogate *me*. But I don't mind. We know your friend is a heretic. He is probably also a spy and an assassin. A would-be assassin."

"I tried to get an audience with His Holiness," Shel muttered.

"That was stupid," I said in English. "Why?" Alexander VI was the Borgia pope, a womanizer, con man, murderer, father of Lucrezia and Cesare. "Why would you want to see him?"

"Seemed like a good idea at the time."

The girder priest drove his fist into my stomach and I went to my knees. "Please confine your remarks to *me*," said Cesare. "Now perhaps you will tell us why you are here. The truth, this time."

"Eminence," I said, "we are only pilgrims."

He sighed. "Very well." He looked toward the windows.

The center window looked down four stories. They opened it, dragged Shel across the floor, and hoisted him onto the sill. "Wait," I cried. But the bastards held me tight.

Cesare watched my reaction. "Have you anything to say, Father Dryden?"

"Yes. You're right, Eminence. We are French spies."

"Good. Now perhaps you will tell me who sent you?"

"Monte Cristo," I said.

"I'm not surprised." Cesare's thin lips smiled. "What was your purpose? To attempt the life of His Holiness?"

"No. Most certainly not. We hoped to sow political discord."

They leaned Shel out over the street. "I don't think I heard you correctly. Did you say you were here to kill the Pope?"

"Yes," I agreed, seeing that was the only response that would satisfy him. "That is why we were sent."

Cesare gestured and they brought Shel back inside. "I assume everyone here heard his admission?" he asked.

Shel glared at me. "Damn you," he said in English. "They'll kill us now."

Cesare sighed. "Take them away," he told John casually.

"Wait," Shel said. "Perhaps Your Eminence would care to allow us to make a contribution to the Church."

"In exchange for my intercession at your trial?" He looked interested. "What have you to bargain with?"

"I have access to a substantial sum of gold." I watched, certain that no deal would work. They would simply take everything, and we would still end up in the dungeons.

"And where is this gold?"

"Nowhere, just now—" It was as far as he got. Cesare nodded, a barely perceptible movement of head and eye, and John knocked him to his knees.

"Please do not waste my time," he said.

Shel spoke between gasps. "I have no wish to do so, Eminence. You asked about the device we wear on our wrists. It is a *Transmuter*." I could hear the capital T.

Cesare glanced back at the desk. "And what is a transmuter?"

"It converts lead to gold."

The Cardinal looked at me to see how I was receiving this news. I tried to look displeased, as if Shel had just given away a secret. He picked up one of the Watches. "Such a device would do much to spur the mission of the Church."

"Would you like to see how it works, Eminence?" He tried to get up, but the guards held him down.

"Yes," said Cesare. "But I would prefer that your friend show me." He looked at me and I picked up the Watch.

Cesare handed me a lead paperweight. "Proceed." His tone suggested that his expectations had been aroused, and that any disappointment would be ill-received.

The lead weight was a disk-shaped stone, with an image of St. Gabriel appearing to the Virgin.

I set the Watch to take me downstream one minute. Then I smiled at Cesare to be sure I had his attention, and squeezed the trigger. The room and its occupants froze. They became transparent and faded out. Then they reappeared, in somewhat different positions. Cesare's face was twisted with shock; the guards had released Shel and were staggering back toward the door, one in the act of blessing himself; both priests, eyes wide, had retreated well away from where I'd been standing. Shel had got to his feet.

When I reappeared, they panicked. One of the priests thrust a crucifix in my face. I laughed, pushed him away, and turned to Cesare. "You abuse your power, Eminence," I told him. I scooped up our coins and the remaining unit and looked at Shel. Cesare's men hurriedly cleared out of my way. "You all right?" I asked him.

"Yes." He grinned. "It's almost worth it."

I smiled pleasantly at Cesare, whose pale expression contrasted sharply with his red robes. "I'll see you in hell, Borgia."

Shel put the Watch on and set up. "I just realized," he said. "I have to pick up a statue."

"Forget the statue. We need you back home."

One of the guards drew an axe. Shel pulled the trigger. I followed a moment later. But when I materialized in the wardrobe, I was alone.

5

Saturday, November 26. Late morning.

The Watch, unless instructed otherwise, returns the traveler to the exact time and place of departure. Had Helen been in the room with me, she would have noticed I'd been gone. But she must have wondered about my energy levels. I'd returned worn out from walking around Rome, and from all the adrenalin I'd pumped. So I went back to sleep.

I woke up in a room lit by a low fire. It was almost noon. "You okay?" she asked. She sounded scared. "I've never seen weather like this."

I got up, collected more snow, and melted it to make water. (You have to melt a lot of snow to get a little water.) There was still *nothing* outside my property lines. I brushed my teeth and tried to draw the bathroom around me, as a kind of shield against what was happening. It was familiar, my anchor to reality.

When I returned downstairs, Helen was putting the phone back in the cradle. She shook her head no. It was still out. We opened a can of meat, added some carrots, and cooked them over the fire.

I needed to make another effort to talk to Shel. I was certain everything was tied into his funeral. There was a possibility that we were approaching, or had already crossed, some sort of logical Rubicon. A dead man was walking around, and we had to set things right. But how could we do that?

I met him again at Thermopylae. He looked good. Tanned. Fit. Almost like a man on vacation.

"Shel," I said. "We need you."

"I know." Below us, the Thespians were examining the ground on which they would fight. Out on the plain, north of the pass, we could see the Persian army. They stretched to the horizon. "I *will* go back."

"When?"

"When I'm ready. When I'm *able*. There's no hurry, Dave. We both know that."

"I'm not so sure. Something's wrong. We can't even *find* the rest of New Jersey."

"I'm trying to live my life, Dave. Do you know how long it's been for me since I watched the funeral? Four years. Four years I've lived with this. Be patient with me. I'll go back and do the right thing. Relax."

"Okay, Shel. Help me relax. Tell me what's causing the weather conditions back home? Why is the power out? Why can't I find my way across the street?"

"I know about all that," he said.

"And—?"

"Look. Maybe it has nothing to do with me."

The Hellenic squadrons were still filing into the pass, their bright mail dusty from the journey north.

"I doubt it," I said.

He nodded. "As do I. But I've promised to go back. What more do you want?"

"Maybe you should do it now."

"What is *now* to you and me, Dave? What does the word mean?"

He glanced up at a promontory about a hundred feet over our heads. "Would you be willing to walk off *that?*"

"We're not talking about *me.*"

"Not even if I pleaded with you to do so? Even if the world depended on it?"

I looked at him.

"What if it didn't matter whether you did it today or tomorrow? Or next month? Or forty years from now?"

"We don't *have* forty years."

"I'm not asking for forty of *your* years. I'm asking for forty of *mine.* I'll do it, Dave. God help me, I'll do it. But on my own schedule. Not yours."

I turned away, and he must have thought I was going to travel out. "Don't," he said. "Dave, try to understand. I'm scared of this."

"I know."

"Good. I need you to know."

We passed ourselves off as traveling law-givers. We moved among the Hellenic troops, wishing them well, assuring them that Hellas would never forget them.

"By the way," I asked him, "how did you land in the dungeon?"

He frowned, not seeming to understand. And then I saw that he was younger here than he had been in Rome. For him, the Vatican incident had not yet happened. "Never mind," I said. "You'll find out soon enough."

"Well," he smiled, "I'm pleased to know that when it happens, you'll be there to rescue me." His expression changed as a thought struck him. "You *did* rescue me, right?"

People accustomed to modern security precautions would be amazed at how easy it was to approach Leonidas. He accepted our good wishes and observed that, considering our physical size, we would both have made excellent soldiers had we chosen that line of work. In fact, both Shel and I towered over him.

He had dark eyes and was in his thirties. He and his men brimmed with confidence. There was no sense here of a doomed force.

He knew about the road that circled behind the pass, and he had already dispatched troops to cover it. The Phocians, as I recalled. Who would run at the first onset.

He invited us to share a meal. This was the third day of the siege, before any blood had been spilt. We talked about the Spartan system of balancing the executive by crowning two kings. And whether democracy could really work in the long run. He thought not. "Athens cannot stay the course," he said. "They have no discipline, and their philosophers encourage them to put themselves before their country. God help us if the poison ever spreads to us." Later, over wine, he asked where we were from, explaining that he could not place the accent.

"America," I said.

He shook his head. "It must be far to the north. Or very small."

We posed with Leonidas, and took pictures, explaining that it was a ritual that would allow us to share his courage. Sparks crackled up from the campfires, and the soldiers talked about home and the future. Later, I traded a gold coin to one of the Thespian archers for an arrow. "I'm not sure that's a good idea," Shel said. "He may need the arrow before he's done."

I knew better. "One arrow more or less will make no difference. When the crunch comes, the Thespians will refuse to leave their Spartan allies. They'll die too. All fifteen hundred of them."

And history will remember only the Spartans.

We watched them, exercising and playing games in full view of their Persian enemies. Shel turned to me, and his face was cold and hard. "You know, David," he said, "you are a monster."

6

Saturday, November 26. Early afternoon.

"What is *happening*?" she asked. "It's *midnight* out there."

"I think I might know what's wrong, but it's hard to explain."

She was lovely in the candlelight. "Could a volcano have erupted somewhere? I know that sounds crazy in South Jersey, but it's all I can think of." She was close to me. Warm and vulnerable and open in a way I had never known before. I touched her hair. Stroked it. She did not withdraw. "I'm glad I was here when it happened, Dave. Whatever it is that's happened."

"So am I," I said.

"So what's your theory?"

I took a deep breath. "It's going to sound crazy."

"The *weather's* crazy."

"Shel and I have been traveling in time."

Her eyes rolled. "Seriously," she said.

"I'm serious. He designed a time machine. Years ago." I showed her my Watch. "Just tell it where you want to go."

She looked at it curiously. "What is it really, Dave? A notebook TV?"

"Hell with this," I said. I have to walk to keep my weight down. Three miles a day, every day. Other people walk around the block, or go down to a park. I like Ambrose, Ohio, near the beginning of the century. It's a pleasant little town with tree-lined streets and white picket fences, where straw hats are in favor for men, and bright ribbons for the ladies. Down at the barber shop, the talk is mostly about the canal they're going to dig through Panama.

I pulled Helen close, punched in Ambrose's coordinates, and told her to brace herself. "The sensation's a little odd at first. But it only lasts a few seconds. And I'll be with you."

The living room froze. She stiffened. The walls and furniture faded to a green landscape with broad lawns and shingled houses and gas street lamps. When the street scene locked in, she backed up, looking wildly around.

"It's okay," I said. "We've gone upstream. Into the past. It's 1905." She was making odd murmuring sounds. "Teddy Roosevelt is President."

Birds sang, and in the distance we could hear the clean bang of church bells. We were standing outside a general store. About a block away there was a railroad siding.

She leaned against me and tried to shut it out.

"It takes a little getting used to," I said.

It was late September. People were burning leaves, talking over back fences. "Maybe we should stay here," she said. "Until the other problem goes away."

"I think we're responsible for the other problem."

"*We* are?"

"Well, Shel and me." Cabbage was cooking somewhere. Finally, I told her about Shel, how he had died but was still alive. Her colors changed and her breathing got uneven. When I'd finished, she sat and stared straight ahead.

"He's still alive," she said.

In a way, he'll always be alive. "Yes. He's still out there." I explained about the funeral, and how he had reacted.

I could see her struggling to grasp the idea, and to control her anger. "Why didn't you tell me?"

"I didn't know how."

"You can take us back, right?"

"Home? Yes."

"Where else?"

"Anywhere. Well, there are range limits, but nothing you'd care about."

A couple of kids with baseball gloves hurried past. "What you're saying," she said, "is that Shel should go back and walk into that fire. And if he doesn't, night-at-noon won't go away. Right? Is that what you're saying?"

"It's what I *think*. Yes, Helen, that's what he should do."

"But he's said he *would* do that? Right? And by the crazy logic of this business, it shouldn't matter when."

"But something's *wrong*. I think he never did go back. Never *will* go back. And I think that's the problem."

"I don't understand any of this," she said.

"I know." I watched a man with a handcart moving along the street, selling pickles and relishes. "I don't either. But there's a continuity. A track. Time flows along the track." I squeezed her hand. "We've torn up a piece of it."

"And—?"

"I think the locomotive went into the river."

She tried to digest that. "Okay. Grant the time machine. Dave, what you're asking him to do is unreasonable. I wouldn't go back either to get hit in the head and thrown into a fire. Would you?"

I got up. "Helen, what you or I would do doesn't much matter. I know this sounds cold, but I think we have to find a way to get Shel where he belongs."

She stood up, and looked west, out of town. The fields were brown, dried out from the summer heat. "You know where to find him?"

"Yes."

"Will you take me to him?"

"Yes." And, after a pause: "Will you help me?"

She stared at the quiet little buildings. White clapboard houses. A horse-drawn carriage just coming around a corner. "Nineteen-five. Shaw's just getting started."

I didn't push. I probably didn't need her to plead with him. Maybe just seeing her would jar something loose. And I knew where I wanted to confront him. At the one event in all of human history which might flay his conscience.

"Why don't we just shoot him?" she said. "And drag him back?"

* * *

"The question you are really asking, Simmias, is whether death annihilates the soul?" Socrates looked from one to another of his friends.

Simmias was young and clear-eyed, like most of the others, but subdued in the shadow of the prison house. "It is an important matter," he said. "There is none of more importance. But we were reluctant—" He hesitated, his voice caught, and he could go no farther.

"I understand," said Socrates. "You fear this is an indelicate moment to raise such an issue. But if you would discuss it with me, we cannot very well postpone it, can we?"

"No, Socrates," said a thin young man with red hair. "Unfortunately, we cannot." This, I knew, was Crito.

Despite Plato's account, the final conversation between Socrates and his disciples did not take place in his cell. It might well have begun there, but they were in a wide, utilitarian meeting room when Helen and I arrived. Several women were present. Socrates, then seventy years old, sat at ease on a wooden chair, while the rest of us gathered around him in a half-circle. To my surprise and disappointment, I did not see Shel.

Socrates was, on first glance, a man of mundane appearance. He was of average height for the time, clean-shaven, wearing a dull red robe. Only his luminous eyes were extraordinary. When they fell curiously on me, as they did from time to time, I imagined that he knew where I had come from, and why I was there.

Helen writhed under the impact of conflicting emotions. She had been ecstatic at the chance to see Shel again, although I knew she was not yet convinced. When he did not arrive, she looked at me as if to say she had told me so, and settled back to watch history unfold. She was, I thought, initially disappointed, in that the event seemed to be nothing more than a few people sitting around talking in an uncomfortable room in a prison. As if the scene should somehow be scored and choreographed and played to muffled drums. She had read Plato's account before we left. I tried to translate for her, but we gave it up. I was just getting in the way of the body language and the voices, which, she said, had a meaning and drama all their own.

"When?" she whispered, after we'd been there almost an hour. "When does it happen?"

"Sunset, I think."

She made a noise deep in her throat.

"Why do men fear death?" Socrates asked.

"Because," said Crito, "they believe it is the end of existence."

There were almost twenty people present. Most were young, but there was a sprinkling of middle-aged and elderly persons. The most venerable of these looked like Moses, a tall man with a white beard, expressive white eyebrows, and a fierce countenance. He gazed intently at Socrates throughout and periodically nodded when the philosopher hammered home a particularly salient point.

"And do all men fear death?" asked Socrates.

"Most assuredly, Socrates," said a boy, who could have been no more than eighteen.

Socrates addressed the boy. "Do even the brave fear death, Cebes?"

Cebes thought it over. "I have to think so, Socrates."

"Why then," asked Socrates, "do the valiant dare death? Is it perhaps because they fear something else even more?"

"The loss of honor," said Crito.

"Thus we are faced with the paradox that even the brave are driven by fear. Can we find no one who can face death with equanimity who is *not* driven by fear?"

Moses stared at Helen. I moved protectively closer to her.

"Of all men," said Crito, "only you seem to show no concern at its approach."

Socrates smiled. "Of all men," he said, "only a philosopher can truly face down death. Because he knows quite certainly that the soul will proceed to a better existence. Provided he has maintained a lifelong pursuit of knowledge and virtue, and has not allowed his soul, which is his divine essence, to become entangled in concerns of the body. For when this happens, the soul takes on corporeal characteristics. And when death comes, it cannot escape. This is why cemeteries are restless at night."

"How can we be sure," asked a man in a blue toga, "that the soul, even if it succeeds in surviving the trauma of death, is not blown away by the first strong wind?"

It was not intended as a serious question, but Socrates saw that it affected the others. So he answered lightly, observing that it would be prudent to die on a calm day, and then undertook a serious response. He asked questions which elicited admissions that the soul was not physical and therefore could not be a composite object. "I think we need not fear that it will come apart," he said, with a touch of amusement.

230 / JACK McDEVITT

One of the jailers lingered in the doorway throughout the long discussion. He seemed worried, and at one point cautioned Socrates against speaking too much, or getting excited. "If you get the heat up," he said, "the poison will not work well."

"We would not wish that," said Socrates sardonically. But he saw the pained expression on the jailer's face, and I thought he immediately regretted the remark.

Women arrived with dinner, and several stayed, so that the room became more and more crowded. In fact, no doors were locked, and no guards, other than the reluctant jailer, were in evidence. Phaedo, who is the narrator of Plato's account, was beside me. He told me that the authorities had hoped profoundly that Socrates would run off. "They did everything they could to avoid this," he said. "There is even a rumor that last night they offered him money and transportation."

Socrates saw us conversing, and he said, "Is there something in my reasoning that disturbs you?"

I'd lost the train of the discussion, but Phaedo said, "Yes, Socrates. However, I am reluctant to put my objection to you."

Socrates turned a skeptical gaze on him. "Truth is what it is. Tell me what disturbs you, Phaedo."

He hesitated, and I realized he was making sure of his voice. "Then let me ask," he said in a carefully neutral tone, "whether you are being truly objective on this matter? The sun is not far from the horizon and, although it grieves me to say it, were I in your position, I also would argue in favor of immortality."

"Were you in his position," said Crito with a smile, "you would have taken the first ship to Syracuse." The company laughed together, Socrates as heartily as any, and the strain seemed broken for the moment.

"You are of course correct in asking, Phaedo. Am I seeking truth? Or trying to convince myself? I can only respond that, if my arguments are valid, then that is good. If they are false, and death does indeed mean annihilation, they nevertheless arm me to withstand its approach. And that too is good." He looked utterly composed. "If I'm wrong, it's an error that won't survive the sunset."

Simmias was seated immediately to the right of Moses. "I for one am convinced," he said. "Your arguments do not admit of refutation. And it is a comfort to me to believe that we have it in our power to draw this company together again in some place of God's choosing."

"Yes," said Crito. "I agree. And, Socrates, we are fortunate to have you here to explain it to us."

"Anyone who has thought about these issues," said Socrates, "should be able to reach, if not truth, at least a high degree of probability."

Moses seemed weighed down with the infirmities of age, and with the distress of the present calamity. Still, he continued to glance periodically at Helen. Now, for the first time, he spoke: "I very much fear, Socrates, that within a few hours there will be no one left anywhere in Hellas, or anywhere else for that matter, who will be able to make these matters plain."

"That's *Shel's* voice," Helen gasped, straining to see better. The light was not good, and he was facing away from us now, his features hidden in the folds of his hood. Then he turned and looked openly at us, and smiled sadly at her. His lips formed the English words *hello, Helen.*

She was getting to her feet.

At that moment, the jailer appeared with the poisoned cup, and the sight of him, and the silver vessel, froze everyone in the chamber. "I hope you understand, Socrates," he said, "this is not my doing."

"I know that, Thereus," said Socrates. "I am not angry with you."

"They always want to blame *me*," Thereus said.

Silence flowed through the chamber.

The jailer laid the cup on the table. "It is time," he said.

The rest of the company, following Helen's example, got to their feet.

Socrates gave a coin to the jailer, squeezed his hand, thanked him, and turned to look at his friends. "The world is very bright," he said. "But much of it is illusion. If we stare at it too long, in the way we look at the sun during an eclipse, it blinds us. Look at it only with the mind." He picked up the hemlock. Several in the assemblage started forward, but were restrained by their companions. Someone in back sobbed.

"Stay," a voice said sternly. "You have respected him all your life. Do so now."

He lifted the cup to his lips, and his hand trembled. It was the only time the mask slipped. Then he drank it down and laid the cup on the table. "I am sure Simmias is right," he said. "We shall gather again one day, as old friends should, in a far different chamber."

Shel stared at Helen. "It's good to see you again," he said.

She shivered. "You're *not* Shel."

A smile flickered across his lips. "I've been traveling a long time." He stood silhouetted against the moon and the harbor. Behind us, the waterfront buildings of the Piraeus were illuminated by occasional oil lamps. He turned toward me. "David, you seem to have become my dark angel."

I was emotionally drained. "I'm sorry you feel that way," I said.

A gull wheeled overhead. "Socrates dies for a philosophical nicety. And Shelborne continues to run when all the world is at stake. Right?"

"That's right," I said.

Helen was still trembling. "What happened to you?" she whispered.

His lips twitched, and he ran his hand over the long white whiskers. He looked haunted. "Forty years, more or less," he said. He reached for her, but she backed away.

I put a hand on her shoulder. Steadied her. "He's been out here a long time."

Her eyes blazed. "What happened to *my* Shel? What did you do with him?"

"He's been living his allotted years," he said. "Making them count for as much as he can for as long as he can. Before my conscience here—" lifting his eyes and targeting me, "before my conscience succeeds in driving me into my grave."

She couldn't hold back any longer. The tears came and she looked for help. But when I started toward her, she threw herself into *his* arms.

He held her a long time, and the water lapped against the piers.

"I've tried to go back," he said. "God help me, I've tried. But I could not bring myself to go there and lie in that bed." Anger surfaced. I could not tell where it was directed. "Did you know that my skull was crushed?"

We knew.

He looked very old. And broken. He didn't seem to know what to do with his hands. The robes had no pockets. But he needed some kind of defensive gesture, so he folded his arms and turned to face the harbor. "I am not Socrates, Dave," he said. "I will not drink from his cup." His eyes locked on mine, and I could see him come to a decision. He drew us together, within the field of his Watch, and punched in a set of coordinates. "But I will settle the issue for you."

Helen shook her head no. No more surprises. And everything began to slow down. The harbor winked out, a ship's deck materialized underfoot, and the sky filled with fire.

* * *

We were on a Roman galley. The air was thick with powder and cinders, and the sails were down. We were pitching and rolling. The ocean broke across the deck, and men scrambled and swore at their stations. Below us, long oars dipped rhythmically into the waves. It was daylight, but we could not see more than twenty feet.

"How did you manage that?" I screamed at Shel over the hurricane of noise. The Watches had never possessed the precision to land people on a ship at sea.

"It's been a lot of years," he said. "Technology's better than it used to be."

"Where are we?" demanded Helen, barely able to make herself heard.

Shel was hanging onto a ladder. His clothes were drenched. "A.D. 79," he said. "Just west of Pompeii." His eyes were afire. His silver hair was already streaked with black ash, and I suspected that Shel had lost whatever anchor he might have had in reality. Time had become perhaps too slippery for him at last.

The ship rolled to starboard, and would have dumped Helen into the sea had he not grabbed her, and hung on, pushing me aside. "We do not need *you*," he said.

"Why are we here?" Helen demanded.

The sea and the wind roared, and the dust was blinding. "*I* will pick the time of my death," Shel cried. "And its manner."

I was trying to scramble toward him, but I could do no more than hang on.

"I am uniquely qualified—"

We went down into a trough, and I thought the sea was going to bury us.

"—To make that choice. My death will be an appropriate finale to the symphony of my life."

A fireball roared overhead, and plowed into the water.

"Don't do it," I cried.

"Have no fear, David. I'm not ready yet. But when I am, this will be the way of it." He smiled at me and touched the Watch. "What better exit for a time traveler than sailing with Pliny the Elder?" And he was gone.

"What was that all about?" called Helen. We dipped again and salt water poured across the deck. "Maybe we ought to get out of here too."

I agreed, and wrapped one arm around a stanchion, something to hang onto while I pulled the trigger.

"Wait," she said. "Do you know who Pliny the Elder is?"

"A Roman philosopher."

"I did a paper on him once. He was an essayist and moralist. Fought a lot for the old values."

"Helen, can we talk about it later?"

"He was also a naval officer. He's trying to rescue survivors. Dave, *he will die out here.*"

"We can't do anything about that. But we don't want to be with him when it happens."

"You don't understand. He said he was going to die here, too, right?"

"Who did?"

"*Shel.* If so, why isn't he here?"

Good question. I looked around. We were on the starboard side, near the beam. The sails were down, and a few shadowy figures were moving through the volcanic haze. (I would have expected to hear the roar of the volcano, of Vesuvius, but the only noise came from the sea and the warm dry wind that blew across the deck.) "Let's try the other side," I said.

He was there, on the port quarter, clinging to a line, while the wind howled around him. Even more ancient this time, frail, weary, frightened. Dressed differently than he had been, in slacks and a green pullover that might have come out of the 1930's.

Cinders stung my eyes.

He saw us and waved. "I've been waiting for you." His gaze lingered on Helen, and he looked at the sea.

"Don't," I cried.

She let go her handhold and tried to scramble across the pitching deck.

He was hanging onto a hawser, balanced near the rail.

The ship pitched, went up the front of a wave, and down the back. He raised his hand in a farewell gesture. "Don't worry, David," he said. "It doesn't matter." The sea broke across the deck, and I was thrown hard against a gunwale. My mouth filled with water and I twisted my shoulder. But I hung on.

We were under a long time. When it ended, he was gone. The rail was clear, and the line to which he'd clung whipped back and forth.

Helen grabbed my arm. I followed her gaze and saw him briefly, on the side of a swell, clutching a board and struggling to stay afloat, his white hair trailing in the water. But another wave broke over him and moments later the board popped to the surface and drifted into the haze.

Something in the ship gave way with a loud sharp crack, and the crewmen cried out. I pulled Helen close.

"Dead again," she said.

"Yeah. Maybe this time for good." I pulled the trigger.

7

Saturday, November 26. Mid-afternoon.

We returned to the wardrobe in separate, but equally desperate, moods.

Helen could not connect the wild man on the galley with Shel, or even the moody septuagenarian on the dock at the Piraeus. Furthermore, she had not yet accepted either the reality or the implications of time travel. Yet, on a primal level, she had recognized him. And for the second time during two weeks, she mourned for him.

And I? I'd lost all feeling. How could I reconcile two graves? I collapsed into a chair and stared at the costumes, arranged in closets on both sides of the room, marked off by period. Damn them. I remembered the planning and research that had gone into their creation. We had felt so well organized in those days. Prepared for anything.

I let it go.

And then I noticed that I was *seeing* the costumes. There was *light* in the room. It was gray, not bright, but it meant that the black mist was gone. I threw the curtains back, and looked out at a rain-swept landscape.

The trees, the grounds, the walkway, the garage, were visible, huddled together in the storm. The wall still circled the property. And beyond the wall, I could see most of Carmichael Drive. *Most of it.* But Ray White's house had vanished. As had the world on the other side of the street. Carmichael Drive now skirted the edge of a precipice, its far side missing, broken off into a void. Beyond, I could see only gray sky.

Terrified, we went from room to room. Everywhere, in all directions, it was the same. On the east, where the property was most extensive, even the wall was gone. A seldom-used patio had been cut in half, and the stand of elms that used to provide shade for it now marked the limit of the world.

We opened a bottle of brandy and drew all the blinds.

"Can't we replay that last scene?" she asked. "Go back and rescue him? I mean, that's the whole point of a time machine, isn't it? Nothing's ever irrevocable. You make a mistake, you go back and fix it."

I was tired and my head hurt and at that moment I could have killed Shelborne. "No," I said. "It would just make everything worse. We know what happened. We can't change *that*."

"Dave," she said, "how could we possibly make things *worse*?"

That was a pretty good question.

She eased onto a sofa and closed her eyes. "Time travel," she said, "isn't all it's cracked up to be, is it?"

"It'll be okay," I said. Rain rattled against the windows. "We need to find a way to eliminate the paradox."

"Okay," she said. "What exactly is a paradox?"

I thought it over. "Adrian Shelborne has two graves. One out on Monument Hill. And the other in the Tyrrhenian Sea. We have to arrange things so that there is only one."

"Can we go back and stop the Friday night fire?"

"Same problem as trying a rescue on the galley. The Friday night fire has already happened, and if you prevent it, then what was the funeral all about?"

"It's like a big knot," she said. "No matter where you try to pull, everything just gets tighter."

We were still wearing our Hellenic robes, which were torn and soiled. And we both needed a shower, but there was no running water. On the other hand, we *did* have rain. And as much privacy as we could ever want.

I got soap, towels, and wash cloths. She took the back yard, which was more sheltered (as if that mattered), and I stood out front. It was late November, but the weather had turned unseasonably warm. Hot water would have been nice, but I felt good anyway after I'd dried off and changed into clean clothes.

Then we sat, each in a kind of private cocoon, thinking about options. Or things lost. The rain continued through the afternoon. I watched rivulets form and wondered how much soil was being washed over the edge. Into what? When the weather cleared, I promised myself that I would walk out and look down.

"Who's buried in the grave on Monument Hill?" she asked.

"Shel."

"How do we know? The body was burned beyond recognition."

"They checked his dental records. We can't *change* that."

She was sitting on the sofa with her legs drawn up under her. "We also can't recover the body from the Tyrrhenian Sea. We have to work on Monument Hill. What can we do about the dental records?"

I looked at her. "I don't think I understand."

"We have a time machine. Use your imagination."

Chain-reaction collisions have become an increasingly dangerous occurrence on limited-access highways around the world. Hundreds die every year, several thousand are injured, and property damage runs well into the millions. On the day that we buried Shel, there had been a pileup in California. It had happened a little after 8:00 A.M. on a day with perfect visibility, when a pickup rearended a station wagon full of kids headed for breakfast and a day at Universal Studios.

We materialized by the side of the road moments after the chain reaction had ended. The highway and the shoulder were littered with wrecked vehicles. Some people were out of their cars trying to help; others were wandering dazed through the carnage. The morning air was filled with screams and the smell of burning oil.

"I'm not sure I can do this," Helen said, spotting a woman bleeding in an overturned Buick. She went over, got the door open, and motioned me to assist. The woman was alone in the car. She was unconscious, and her arm looked bent.

"Helen," I said. "We have a bigger rescue to make."

She shook her head. No. This first. She stopped the bleeding and I got someone to stay with the victim. We helped a few other people, pulled an elderly couple out of a burning van, got one man with two broken legs off the road. "We don't have time for this," I pleaded.

"I don't have time for anything else," she said.

Sirens were approaching. I let her go, concentrating on finding what we'd come for.

He was in a blue Toyota that had rolled over onto its roof. The front of the car was crumpled, a door was off, and the driver looked dead. He was bleeding heavily from a head wound. One tire was spinning slowly. I could find no pulse.

He was about the right size, tangled in a seat belt. When Helen got there, she confirmed that he would do. I used a jack knife to cut him free. The EMTs were spreading out among the wrecked cars. Stretchers were appearing.

Helen could not keep her mind on what we were doing. "Your oath doesn't count," I said. "Not here. Let it go."

We got him out of the car, wrapped him in plastic and laid him in the road. "He does look a little like Shel," she said in a small voice.

"Enough to get by."

I heard footsteps behind us. Someone wanted to know what we were doing.

It was an EMT.

"It's okay," I said, "we're doctors." I pulled the trigger and we were out of there.

His name was Victor Randall. We found pictures of an attractive woman with cropped brown hair seated with him in a porch swing. And two kids. The kids were smiling at the camera, one boy, one girl, both around seven or eight. "Maybe," Helen said, "when this is over, we can send them a note to explain."

"We can't do that," I said.

"They'll never know what happened to him."

"That's right. And there's no way around it."

There was also about two hundred cash. Later, I would mail that back to the family.

We carried him down to the garage and put him in the Porsche. I adjusted the temporal sweep to maximum, so that when we went the car would go with us.

8

Thursday, November 10. Near midnight.

Mark S. Hightower had been Shel's dentist for seven years. He operated out of a medical building across the street from Friendship Hospital, where Helen had interned.

I'd met Hightower once. He was short, barrel-chested, flat-skulled, a man who looked more like a professional wrestler than a dentist. But he was soft-spoken and, according to Shel, particularly good with nervous patients.

We materialized on a lot off Penrod Avenue in the commercial district. The area was always deserted at night. Ten minutes later, we pulled into the parking lot at the medical center. Hightower was located in back, well away from the street.

Victor was in the front seat, wrapped in plastic. He'd stopped bleeding, and we had cleaned him up as much as we could. "Are you sure you know how to do this?" I asked.

"Of course not, Dave. I'm not a dentist. But the equipment shouldn't be hard to figure out. How do we get inside?"

I showed her a tire iron. "We'll have to break in."

She look dismayed. "I thought you could manage something a little more sophisticated. Why not just use that thing on your wrist and put us inside the building?"

"Because it doesn't home in, and I don't have the coordinates." I was thinking of Shel's ability to move us from the Piraeus to the quarterdeck on Pliny's galley. If I'd tried that with my Watch, we'd have gone into the ocean.

We put on gloves and walked around the building, looking for an open window. There was none, but we found a rear exit that didn't seem very secure. I wedged the tire iron between the door and the jamb and worked it back and forth until the lock gave. I held my breath, waiting for the screech of a burglar alarm. It didn't come, and we were past the first hurdle.

We went back to the Porsche, got Victor out and half-carried, half-dragged him to the door. Inside, we set him in a chair. Then we turned on penlights and looked around. There were half a dozen rooms designated for patients, opening off a corridor that looped around to the reception area. I wandered from office to office, not really knowing what I was looking for. But Helen did one quick turn through the passageway and pointed at a machine tucked away in a corner. "This is it," she said. The manufacturer's label said it was an orthopantomograph. "It's designed to provide a panoramic X-ray."

"Panoramic? What's that?"

"Full mouth. It should be all we'll need."

The person being X-rayed placed his forehead against a plastic rest and his chin in a cup-shaped support. The camera was located inside a cone which was mounted on a rotating arm. The arm and cone traversed the head and produced a panoramic image of the teeth. The only problem was that the patient normally stood during the procedure.

"It'll take six to eight minutes," said Helen. "During that time we have to keep him absolutely still. Think you can do it?"

"I can do it," I said.

"Okay." She checked to make sure there was a film cassette in the machine. "Let's get him."

We carried Victor to the orthopantomograph. At Helen's suggestion, we'd brought along some cloth strips which we now used to secure him to the device. It was a clumsy business, and he kept sliding away from us. Working in the dark complicated the procedure, but after about a half hour we had him in place.

"Something just occurred to me," I said. "Victor Randall already has the head wound."

Her eyes closed momentarily. "You're suggesting the arsonist didn't hit Shel in the head after all?"

"That's what I think."

"This keeps getting weirder," she said.

A mirror was mounted on the machine directly in front of the face. Helen pressed a button and a light went on in the center of the mirror. "They would tell the patient to watch the light," she said. "That's how they're sure they've got it lined up."

"How are *we* sure?"

"What's the term? 'Dead reckoning?' " She punched another button. A motor started, and the cone began to move.

Ten minutes later we took the cassette out, leaving Victor in place until we were sure we had good pictures. The developer was located in a windowless storage room. Helen removed the film from the cassette and ran it through the machine. When the finished picture came out, she handed it to me without looking at it. "What do you think?"

The entire mouth, uppers and lowers, was clear. "Looks good," I said.

She held it against the light. "Plenty of fillings on both sides. Let's see how it compares."

The records were maintained in manila folders behind the reception desk. Helen found Shel's, and sat down with it at the desk, where the counter hid her from anyone passing outside.

"He goes to the dentist every three months," she said. (I couldn't help noticing she still talked about him in the present tense.) The results of his most recent checkup were clipped on the right side of the folder. In the middle of the sheet was a panoramic picture, like the one we had just taken, and several smaller photos of individual sections. "I think they call these 'wings,' " she said. "But when they bring a dentist in to identify a body, they do it with *these*." She held up the panoramic and compared the two. "They don't look much alike in detail. And if they ever get around to comparing it with the wings, they'll notice something's wrong. But it's good enough to get by."

She removed Shel's panoramic and substituted the one we'd just taken. Then she replaced the folder. We wiped off the headrest and checked the floor to be sure we'd spilled no blood. "One more thing," said Helen. She inserted a fresh cassette into the orthopantomograph. "Okay. Let's clear out."

"Wait a minute," I said. "They'll know we broke in. We need to do something to make this look like a burglary." As far as I could see, there wasn't much worth stealing. Magazines. Cheap landscape prints on the walls. "How about a drill?" I said. "It looks expensive."

She squeezed my arm. "What kind of burglar would steal a *drill*?" She went on another tour of the office. Moments later, I heard glass breaking, and she came back with a couple of plastic bottles filled with pills. "Valium," she said.

9

Saturday, November 12. 1:15 A.M.

I had the coordinates for the workshop, so we were able to go right in. It was located in the basement of the townhouse, a small, cramped, cluttered place with a Cray computer front and center, banks of displays, and an array of experimental equipment I had never begun to understand. Moments after we'd arrived, the oil heater came on with a thump.

We had to carry the body up to the second floor. But I'd done the best I could. The math had always been Shel's job, and the only place in the house I could get to was the workshop. We dressed the corpse in Shel's pajamas, turned back the sheets, and laid him in bed. We put his clothes into a plastic bag.

We also had a brick in the bag. Shel kept his car keys in the middle drawer of a desk on the first floor. We'd debated just letting the clothes burn, but I wanted to leave nothing to chance. Despite what you might think about time travel, what we were doing was forever. We could not come back and undo it, because we were *here*, and we knew what the sequence of events was, and you couldn't change that without paying down the road. If we knew anything for sure now, we knew *that*.

I had left the Porsche at home this time. So we borrowed Shel's green Pontiac. It had a vanity plate reading SHEL, and a lot of mileage. But he took good care of it. We drove down to the river. At the two-lane bridge that crosses the Narrows, we pulled off and waited until there was no traffic. Then we went out to the middle of the bridge, where we assumed the water was deepest, and threw the bag over the side. We still had Victor's wallet and ID, which I planned on burning.

We returned Shel's car. By now it was a quarter to two, thirty-eight minutes before a Mrs. Wilma Anderson would call to report a fire at the townhouse. I worried that we'd cut our time too close, that the intruder might already be inside. But it was still quiet when I returned the car keys to the desk.

We locked the house front and back, which was how we had found it, and retired across the street behind a hedge. It was a good night's work, and we waited now to see who the criminal was. The neighborhood was tree-lined, well-lighted, quiet. The houses were middle-class, fronted by small fenced yards. Cars were parked on both sides of the street. Somewhere in the next block a cat yowled.

Two o'clock.

"Getting late," Helen said.

Nothing moved. "He's going to have to hurry up," I said.

She frowned. "What happens if he doesn't come?"

"He *has* to come."

"Why?"

"Because that's the way it happened. We know that for an absolute fact."

She looked at her watch. Two-oh-one.

"I just had a thought," I said.

"We could use one."

"Maybe you're right. Maybe there is no firebug. Or rather, maybe *we* are the firebugs. After all, we already know where the fractured skull came from."

She nodded reluctantly. "Yeah," she said. "Maybe."

I left the shelter of the hedge and walked quickly across the street, entered Shel's driveway, and went back into the garage. There were several gas cans. All empty.

I needed the car keys. But I was locked out now. I used a rock to break a window, and retrieved the keys. I threw the empty cans into the trunk of his Pontiac. "Wait here," I told Helen. "In case someone *does* show up."

"Where are you going?"

"To get some gas."

There was an all-night station on River Road, only a few blocks away. It was one of those places where they concentrate on keeping the cashier alive after about eleven o'clock. He was a middle-aged, worn-out guy sitting in a cage full of cigarette smoke. A toothpick rolled relentlessly from one side of his mouth to the other. I filled three cans, paid, and drove back.

It was 2:17 when we began sloshing gas around the basement. We emptied a can on the stairway and another upstairs, taking care to drench the bedroom where Victor Randall lay. We poured the rest of it on the first floor, and so thoroughly soaked the entry that I was afraid to go near it with a lighted match. But at 2:25 we touched it off.

Helen and I watched for a time. The flames cast a pale glow in the sky, and sparks floated upward. We didn't know much about Victor Randall, but what we did know maybe was enough. He'd been a husband and father. In their photos, his wife and kids had looked happy. And he got a Viking's funeral.

"What do you think?" asked Helen. "Will it be all right now?"

"Yeah," I said. "I hope so."

10

Sunday, November 27. Mid-morning.

In the end, the Great November Delusion was written off as precisely that, a kind of mass hysteria that settled across a substantial chunk of New Jersey, Pennsylvania, Maryland, and Delaware. Elsewhere, life had gone on as usual, except that the affected area seemed to have vanished behind a black shroud which turned back all attempts at entry, and admitted no signals.

Fortunately, it had lasted only a few hours. When it ended, persons who had been inside emerged with a wide range of stories. Some had found themselves stranded on a rocky shore; others, in a windowless, doorless house with infinite stairways and corridors. Psychologists pointed out that the one element appearing in all accounts was a depiction of isolation. Sometimes it had been whole communities that were isolated; sometimes families. Occasionally it had been individuals. The general consensus was that, whatever the cause, therapists would be assured of a handsome income for years to come.

My first act on returning home was to destroy Victor Randall's wallet and ID. I would have been ecstatic with the way things had turned out, except that Helen still mourned Shel.

The TV was back with full coverage. The National Guard was out, and experts were already on the talk shows.

I luxuriated in a hot shower and changed. Helen was reduced to putting on a rolled-up pair of my slacks and a tee-shirt. By the time she came downstairs, I had made some bacon and eggs. She ate, and cried a little, and congratulated me. "Saved the world, we did," she said. "Or at least, South Jersey."

After breakfast she seemed reluctant to leave, but she announced finally that she needed to get back to her apartment and see how things were. She had just started for the door when we heard a car pull up. "It's a woman," she said archly, looking out the window. "Friend of yours?"

It was Sgt. Lake. She was alone this time.

The doorbell rang.

"This won't look so good," Helen said.

"I know. You want to duck upstairs?"

She thought about it. "No. What are we hiding?"

The bell rang again. I opened up.

"Good morning, Dr. Dryden," said the detective. "I'm glad to see you came through it all right. Everything *is* okay?"

"Yes," I said. "How about you?"

Her cheeks were pale. "Good," she said. "Whatever it was, I hope it's over." She seemed far more human than during her earlier visit.

"Where's your partner?" I asked.

She smiled. "Everything's bedlam downtown. A lot of people went berserk during that *thing*, whatever it was. We're going to be busy for a while." She took a deep breath. "I wonder if I could talk with you?"

"Of course." I stepped back and she came in.

"It's chaos." She seemed not quite able to focus. "Fires, people in shock, heart attacks everywhere. It hasn't been good." She saw Helen and her eyes widened. "Hello, Doctor. I didn't expect to see you here. There'll be plenty for you to do today."

Helen nodded. "You okay?" she asked.

"Yeah. Thanks. I'm fine." She stared out over my shoulder. Then, with a start, she tried to wave it all away. "What was it like here?"

I described what I'd seen. Meanwhile, Helen poured coffee and everybody relaxed a little. She had been caught in her car during the event on a piece of rain-swept foggy highway that just went round and round, with no exit. "Damnedest thing," she said.

Helen offered a sedative, but Lake declined and asked whether she might have a minute alone with me. "Sure," Helen said. "I should be on my way anyhow." She patted my shoulder in a comradely way and let herself out.

"Doctor," said Lake, "you've said you were home in bed at the time Dr. Shelborne's home burned. Is that correct?"

"Yes. That's right."

"Are you sure?"

The question hung in the sunlit air. "Of course. Why do you ask?" I could read nothing in her expression.

"Someone answering your description was seen near the townhouse at the time of the fire."

"It wasn't *me*," I said, suddenly remembering the man at the gas station. And I'd been driving Shel's car. With his vanity plate in front just in case anybody wasn't paying attention.

"Okay. I wonder if you'd mind coming down to the station with me, so we can clear the matter up. Get it settled."

"Sure. Be glad to."

We stood up. "Could I have a moment, please?"

"Certainly," she said, and went outside.

I called Helen on her cellular. "Don't panic," she said. "All you need is a good alibi."

"I don't *have* an alibi."

"For God's sake, Dave. You've got something better. You have a *time machine*."

"Okay. Sure. But if I go back and set up an alibi, why didn't I tell them the truth in the beginning?"

"Because you were protecting a woman's reputation," she said. "What else would you be doing at two o'clock in the morning? Get out your little black book." It might have been my imagination, but I thought the reference to my little black book sounded irritated.

11

Friday, November 11. Early evening.

The problem was that I didn't have a little black book. I've never been all that successful with women. Not to the extent, certainly, that I could call one up with a reasonable expectation of finishing the night in her bed. What other option did I have? I could try to find someone in a bar, but you didn't really lie to the police in a murder case to protect a pick-up.

I pulled over to the curb beside an all-night restaurant, to think about it. It was a rundown area lined with crumbling warehouses. A police cruiser slowed and pulled in behind me. The cop got out and I lowered the window.

"Anything wrong, Officer?" I asked. He was small, black, well-pressed.

"I was going to ask you the same thing, sir. This is not a safe area."

"I was just trying to decide whether I wanted a hamburger."

"Yes, sir," he said. I could hear the murmur of his radio. "Well, listen, I'd make up my mind, one way or the other. I wouldn't hang around out here if I were you."

I smiled, and gave him a thumbs-up. "Thanks," I said.

He got back in his cruiser and pulled out. I watched his lights turn left at the next intersection. And I knew what I was going to do.

I drove south on route 130 for about three quarters of an hour, and then turned east on a two-lane. Around eleven, I entered a small town and decided it was just what I was looking for. Its police station occupied a drab two-story building beside the post office. The Red Lantern Bar was located about two blocks away, on the other side of the street.

I parked in a lighted spot close to the police station, walked to the bar and went inside. It was smoky and subdued, reeking with dead cigarettes and stale beer. Most of the action was near the dart board. I settled in at the bar and commenced drinking Scotch. I stayed with it until the bartender suggested I'd had enough, which usually wouldn't have taken long. But that night my mind stayed clear. Not my motor coordination, though. I paid up, eased off the stool, and negotiated my way back onto the street.

I turned right and moved methodically toward the police station, putting one foot in front of the other. When I got close, I added a little panache to my stagger, tried a couple of practice giggles, and lurched in through the front door.

A man with corporal's stripes came out of a back room.

"Good evening, Officer," I said, with exaggerated formality and the widest grin I could manage, which was then pretty wide. "Can you give me directions to Atlantic City?"

The corporal shook his head. "Do you have some identification, sir?"

"Yes, I do," I said. "But I don't see why my name is any business of yours. I'm in a hurry."

"Where are you from?" His eyes narrowed.

"Two weeks from Sunday," I said. "I'm a time traveler."

12

Sunday, November 27. Late evening.

Sgt. Lake was surprised and, I thought, disappointed to learn that I had been in jail on the night of the fire. She said she understood why I'd been reluctant to explain, but admonished me on the virtues of honesty with law enforcement authorities.

I called Helen, looking forward to an evening of celebration. I got her recording machine. "Call me when you get in," I told it.

The call never came. By midnight, when I'd given up and was getting ready for bed, I noticed a white envelope on the kitchen table. My name was printed on it in neat, spare characters.

Dear Dave,

Shel is back! My Shel. The real one. He wants to take me off somewhere, and I don't know where, but I can't resist. Maybe we will live near the Parthenon, or maybe Paris during the 1920s. I don't know. But I do know you will be happy for me.

I will never forget you, Dave.

Love,

Helen

P.S. We left something for you. In the wardrobe.

I read it several times, and finally crumpled it. They'd left the *Hermes*. They had positioned it carefully under the light, to achieve maximum effect. It looked good.

I stood a long time admiring the piece. But it wasn't Helen. The house filled with echoes and the sound of the wind. More desolate now than it had been when it was the only thing in the universe.

I remembered how Helen had sounded when she thought she was sending me to sleep with another woman. And I wondered why I was so ready to give up.

I did some quick research, went back to the wardrobe, scarcely noticing the *Hermes*, and put on turn-of-the-century evening clothes. Next stop: the Court Theater in Sloane Square, London, to watch the opening performance of *Man and Superman*.

You're damned right, Shelborne.

Time travelers never die.